PENGUIN CLASSICS

LADY MACBETH OF MTSENSK
AND OTHER STORIES

NIKOLAI SEMYONOVICH LESKOV was born in 1831 in Gorokhovo, Oryol Province. Orphaned early, he took his first job at
sixteen with the Civil Service. His next post entailed a great deal
of travelling around Russia and he became familiar with the lives,
customs and speech of all levels of Russian society. In 1860 he
took up journalism and moved to St Petersburg where he published
his first story. His novels *Nekuda* (1864) and *Na nozhakh* (1872)
were anti-nihilistic and thus isolated him from the literary circles
of his day. He wrote a number of folk legends and Christmas
tales; his later works are more satirical, particularly with regard
to the clergy and the bureaucracy. Leskov, now considered an
extremely original storyteller, died in St Petersburg in 1895.

DAVID McDUFF is a British translator of Russian and Nordic
literature. His translations of nineteenth- and twentieth-century
Russian prose classics (including works by Dostoyevsky, Tolstoy,
Bely and Babel) are published by Penguin. In 2013 he received
Finland's State Award for Foreign Translators.

NIKOLAI LESKOV

Lady Macbeth of Mtsensk and Other Stories

Translated and with an Introduction and Notes by
DAVID McDUFF

PENGUIN BOOKS

PENGUIN CLASSICS

UK I USA I Canada I Ireland I Australia
India I New Zealand I South Africa

Penguin Books is part of the Penguin Random House group of companies
whose addresses can be found at global.penguinrandomhouse.com.

This edition first published in Penguin Classics 1987
Reprinted in Penguin Classics 2015
001

Translation, Introduction and Notes copyright © David McDuff, 1987
All rights reserved

Set in 10.25/12.25 pt Adobe Sabon
Typeset by Jouve (UK), Milton Keynes
Printed in Great Britain by Clays Ltd, St Ives plc

ISBN: 978-0-141-39674-3

Contents

LADY MACBETH OF MTSENSK
AND OTHER STORIES

Introduction

The name of the great nineteenth-century Russian prose writer Nikolai Leskov is possibly less familiar to readers of English than those of his illustrious contemporaries, Turgenev, Tolstoy and Dostoevsky. The reasons for this being so are various: not the least of them is the fact that, unlike the other three writers mentioned, Leskov was, even to his fellow-Russians, an outsider – neither a radical nor a conservative, neither a member of the aristocracy nor a representative of the literary and cultural establishment. Yet his links with the English-speaking world were at least as strong as those of the 'Anglophile' Turgenev, if not stronger, and there is a true sense in which, as a sculptor of individual and idiosyncratic human characters who may be said to stand for an entire nation, it is possible to view him as an heir and disciple of Charles Dickens. He is also, after Gogol, the most quintessentially Russian of writers. His work is difficult to translate, but rewarding to the reader in search of an understanding of the Russian soul and character.

Nikolai Semyonovich Leskov was born in the village of Gorokhovo, in the district of the Russian provincial town of Oryol, some two hundred miles south of Moscow, on 4 February 1831.[i] He spent his earliest childhood in a little farm called Panino, in the district of Kromy, Oryol province, where his father, an impoverished former civil servant, was endeavouring to scrape together a living from 'a water-mill with a grindstone, an orchard, two households of peasants and about forty desyatinas of land', as Leskov described it in an autobiographical memoir. The family of father, mother and seven children, of whom Leskov was the eldest, had to live in a tiny farmhouse which was really little more than a one-roomed peasant *izba*. The strains of such a crowded and penurious existence must have been considerable; in the face of them, Leskov's father tended to take a more and more passive role in the household, withdrawing into his books, while his mother, Marya Petrovna, a woman of strong character and great will-power, increasingly took over responsibility for the running of both farm and house. She also had to rear her seven children, and the methods she used were far from gentle. Leskov recalls how she once smacked her favourite daughter Masha, made her stand in a corner and fenced her in with a heavy armchair, promising to return later and thrash her: 'Forgiveness was granted only in trivial cases, and then the child, sentenced by its father or mother to corporal punishment with the birch, would have to throw itself at their feet countless times, beg for mercy, and then sniff the birch and kiss it in the presence of everyone. Children of a very young age will usually refuse to kiss the birch, and only with years and education realize the necessity of placing their lips against the twigs that have been reserved for their bodies. Masha was still too young to know better; in her, feeling prevailed over calculation; she was thrashed, and long after midnight she was still whimpering pitifully in her sleep and, convulsively shuddering, pressing against the side of her bed.'

Leskov's parents had not the means to provide him at home with the kind of education his intelligence showed that he needed; to take him out of the crowded domestic environment and supply him with something more akin to a proper school training, he was sent to live in the household of his uncle, M. A. Strakhov, whose children were instructed by resident Russian, German and French tutors. This uncle – his Russian surname means 'Fear' – was a rich, powerful and demonic nobleman of fifty, a bachelor who had married a fifteen-year-old girl; to the young Leskov he was a larger-than-life figure, a demigod of whom he went in awe, at once admiring him and regarding him with trepidation and hatred. In Strakhov's home, the boy experienced much that left an indelible mark on him. Leskov wrote later: 'He was ill-bred, despotic and, I think, slightly insane: some forty years my aunt's senior, he slept with her, sometimes tying her by the leg to the foot of his double bed ... The sufferings of my aunt were the subject of universal commiseration, but neither my father nor anyone else dared to intercede on her behalf ... These were the first impressions of my childhood, and terrible ones they were – I consider that they began in me the development of that agonizing nervousness from which I have suffered all my life and which has made me do in it so many crass and stupid things.'

Later in life, Leskov was fond of claiming aristocratic descent for himself, particularly on his mother's side of the family. Although he did possess legal nobility on his father's side (the stories about his mother's 'aristocratic' origins were his own invention), his family was descended from a long line of priests in the Oryol village of Leski (the name means 'little forests'). What he really inherited was a religious sensibility, and a lifelong conflict between his mother's magical Orthodox ritualism and his father's essentially Protestant outlook on the world. Leskov tells us that although his mother was religious in a conventionally Orthodox, churchgoing way – she read *akathisti* (Orthodox hymns) at home and on the first day of each month held a prayer meeting, 'watching to see what effects this might have on the circumstances of her daily life' – his father, who in his youth had trained as a seminarist but had shocked his family by refusing thereafter to become a priest, had evolved his own, very personal form of Christian belief, going to church only seldom, and taking part in none of the ecclesiastical ceremonies apart from confession and Holy Communion, which he regarded as a purely commemorative religious observance: 'He had no time for any of the other rituals,' Leskov writes, 'and as he was dying he included as part of his will a stipulation that no requiem mass be sung over him.'

This religious dualism was further reinforced by the personalities of two relatives who were to play an important role in the young Leskov's development. The first of these was Leskov's uncle by marriage, Alexander Scott (or Aleksandr Yakovlevich Shkott, as he was known in the country of his adoption), the son of a Russified Scottish Nonconformist, who had established in Russia a private agricultural commercial company named 'Scott & Wilkins'. Scott's Protestantism, sexual puritanism and practical British temperament, which survived his almost total assimilation of the Russian language and Russian social manners, made a profound impression on his nephew during the many visits his family paid to the Scott residence in Penza. The second was Leskov's maternal grandmother, Akilina Vasilevna Alferyeva, a devout Orthodox believer who often took her grandson with her on her rounds of the local 'hermitages', or monasteries, which were a feature of the wooded Oryol countryside. The magic of these country travels is invoked particularly vividly by Leskov in his tale *Musk-Ox*, which is included in the present volume.

During his educational sojourn in the Strakhov household, Leskov began to sense that his presence was not an altogether welcome one; in particular, he felt that he had incurred the displeasure of his aunt by being more gifted than his cousins. A humiliating episode, in which he was made to receive a 'scroll of honour' which turned out to be a rolled-up advertisement for rheumatism ointment, brought his stay with the Strakhovs to an end. Thereafter he was sent to attend classes at the Oryol gymnasium (or 'grammar school'), but failed to complete the course there. From the age of fifteen onwards, what education he had was largely self-obtained. In the years to come, Leskov bitterly regretted his lack of application in his formal studies, even going so far as to claim that external events had been responsible for his lack of success. In *A Note About Myself*, published five years before his death, he ascribed his failure to complete the gymnasium to being 'left fatherless in my sixteenth year and entirely helpless. The insignificant amount of property my father left behind was destroyed in a fire. This was the time of the famous Oryol fires. This put an end to the proper continuation of my studies. After that I was an autodidact.' In fact, however, Leskov's father did not die until 1848, two years after his son had stopped attending the gymnasium, and the Great Fire of Oryol likewise happened in 1848; an additional fact is that the Leskov family possessed no property in Oryol – they had sold their house there before their move to Panino in 1839.

Leskov's American biographer, Hugh McLean, has offered the following instructive commentary on the nature of Leskov's education, and the effect it had on his writing:

Later Leskov more than made up for his lack of schooling, and few people suspected that he had no university degree. His general culture was broad, and his detailed knowledge of such recondite subjects as church history was such that he would have been qualified to teach them in a university. Like many autodidacts, however, he tended to educate himself in pockets, acquiring specialized information on a great variety of subjects, many of them out of the way from the point of view of his more conventional contemporaries – icons, Old Believers, Jewish rituals, Protestant theology and ethics, jewelry, clocks, rare editions, even spiritualism – in fact, the range of his competences is astonishing. And it is not even that he lacked general knowledge for these specialities to rest upon; what he missed was the confidence in dealing with cultural matters usually exhibited by people with university degrees.

This lack of confidence may help to account for some of Leskov's peculiarities as a writer. Feeling somewhat out of depth in the mainstream of nineteenth-century European literature, he tried to find some lesser streams, a bit shallower perhaps, where his feet could touch bottom. He knew that there were areas of Russian life with which he was better acquainted than Turgenev, Tolstoy and Dostoyevsky – for instance, the world of the Russian clergy; and after some unhappy early attempts, he learned to avoid their patented genre, the novel. Instead, he became a master of all sorts of other forms – short story, novella, reminiscence, 'chronicle', 'pot-pourri', 'story à propos', 'picture from nature' – and he developed a particular fondness for the spoken inner narrative, or *skaz*, in which he could exhibit and exploit his ultra-Russian Russian, a Russian no one could learn in a university. Perhaps part of the explanation for the *samobytnost*, the peculiar 'self-nature' that Tolstoy perceived in Leskov, stemmed from his fateful abandonment of the Oryol gymnasium at the age of fifteen.[ii]

Leskov was slow to begin his literary career. During his eight years of service as an assistant clerk in the Kiev army recruiting office, a position obtained for him by his Uncle Sergei, he read a great deal, developed emotionally and intellectually, and married

Olga Vasilevna Smirnova, a Kiev merchant's daughter. The marriage was not a happy one. In his biography of his father, Andrei Leskov writes that 'according to the unanimous consensus of the members of our family, [Olga Vasilevna] possessed neither brains, beauty, heart nor self-control . . . she represented an abundance of unredeemed "not's". Given the fact that Leskov's gifts did not include gentleness or an easy disposition, success could not have been expected. And it was not forthcoming . . .'[iii] In 1857, Leskov moved with his family to Penza, in north-eastern Russia, to work as a commercial agent for the firm of his uncle, Alexander Scott. During his term of employment, he travelled the length and breadth of European Russia – 'from the White Sea to the Black and from Brody to Krasny Yar', was how he put it later in a letter to a friend. The precise nature of the business Leskov did in the course of his three years 'on Scott's barges' remains unclear, though it is certain that at one point he was assigned to accompany a river transport of peasant serfs who were being taken from their homes in Oryol and Kursk to be resettled in south-eastern Russia. This 'barge' life gave him a deep insight into the psychology of the common people and an intimate acquaintance with the byways of the Russian countryside. At another period he worked as his uncle's general factotum, supervising the running of an estate in the Penza area on which the principal activities were the milling of grain and the distilling of vodka.

Eventually, however, Scott's firm ran into financial difficulties and, much to his chagrin, for he had enjoyed these years of travel very much, Leskov had to consider a return to government service. It was not until 1860, after he stopped working for Scott and before he briefly resumed his Kiev government office work, that Leskov tried his hand at writing for publication. He began as a journalist. His first attempts in the field were two articles – one in a specialist economics journal and the other in the St Petersburg News – complaining about the overpricing in a Kiev bookshop of the recently authorized Russian translation of the Gospels (previously only the Slavonic version had been allowed). These were followed by five articles for the journal Contemporary Medicine, covering such topics as the inferior design of hospitals and other public buildings in Russia, the poor quality of Russian physicians, and the prevalence of slum conditions in urban working-class districts. The articles are lively and well written; they display a Protestant humanitarianism of approach, and they fitted in well with the prevailing liberal mood among the St Petersburg intelligentsia. Spurred on by the favourable reception of his work, Leskov decided to escape from the intolerable burden of his married life – his wife's behaviour was becoming more and more difficult, and she was eventually, but not until much later, declared insane – and seek employment as a journalist in St Petersburg, where he was helped by the editor of the economics journal in which he had begun his career. During the next year he launched himself upon a whole series of articles in various journals, and was soon involved in the thick of St Petersburg politics.

One of the first things Leskov had to do once he began to take part in the literary political debates which raged in the Russian capital was to define his stance *vis-à-vis* the divide between liberals and radicals which existed in the early 1860s. In 1861, with the emancipation of the serfs an accomplished fact, dissension had arisen between those members of the intelligentsia who were by and large satisfied with the changed order of society, and those who regarded any reform of what they regarded as a corrupt tyranny as a futile gesture, recommending instead the violent overthrow of the existing order. Although Leskov started out with some sympathy for the revolutionary, nihilist position, he very soon found himself overtaken by events, and arrived at a position where his mind was practically made up for him.

In St Petersburg, Leskov had quite a number of friends among the '*neterpelivtsy*', the impatient radicals who wished to transform Russian society at a single stroke by calling for a peasant uprising. These included the brothers Nikolai and Vasily Kurochkin, Pavel Yakushkin (the model for 'Musk-Ox'), the historian Platon Pavlov, and Nikolai Serno-Solovevich, a disciple of Herzen. In the spring of 1862, Leskov joined these and other leading St Petersburg radicals in taking control of a weekly magazine, *The Age*, which soon, however, ran into editorial squabbles and financial difficulties, and ceased publication. Another of Leskov's radical contacts in St Petersburg, a man with whom he was initially on very good terms, was a Ukrainian government official named Andrei Nichiporenko. Nichiporenko made a pilgrimage to Herzen's revolutionary headquarters in London, and in 1862 was sent by Herzen and Bakunin as a courier to Garibaldi. At the Austrian frontier he was searched, and the police discovered on his person a large file of revolutionary correspondence, of which they supplied copies to the Russian authorities. Nichiporenko was returned to St Petersburg and imprisoned in the fortress, where he informed on his radical colleagues. In the following year, he died. As a result of his informing, Leskov found himself summoned to give testimony. Although no charges were brought against him, he never forgave Nichiporenko for this betrayal.

Towards the end of 1861 Leskov found himself without a journal in which to publish his articles, having quarrelled with the editors of those in which he had previously been welcome. At this time a group of liberal intellectuals was taking control of a major daily newspaper, *The Northern Bee*, and Leskov joined them. The *Bee*'s political stance was somewhere midway between the liberal and radical positions, and it criticized the Right for being too reactionary and the Left for being negative and nihilistic. One of Leskov's associates on the newspaper was the cosmopolitan socialist Artur Benni. Benni had arrived in St Petersburg from London in the summer of 1861, having given up a well-paid position at the Woolwich Arsenal in order to come to Russia and work for the socialist cause. Benni was of very mixed background, being of Italian, Scottish, Polish, German and Jewish descent. (In 1871 Leskov published a lengthy and fascinating study of Benni's biography in *An Enigmatic Man*.) Benni was a naturalized British subject, an adherent of the Protestant faith, and was suspected in radical circles of being an agent of the 'Third Department', the Russian secret police.

During the afternoon of 28 May 1862, a fire destroyed the Apraksin and Shchukin markets in St Petersburg, and arson was suspected – a few days earlier, a group of revolutionary students had gone round the city distributing an extremist proclamation calling for the bloody overthrow of the Tsar. Such was the

wrath of the St Petersburg citizenry in the aftermath of the fire
that anyone identifiable as a university student was liable to be
assaulted – as many were. Leskov decided to use his editorial
capacity on *The Northern Bee* to defend the bulk of the students against the accusations that were being made against
them; in an editorial he called on the police to name the persons
they considered responsible for starting the fire, thus placing the
blame where it belonged. This was interpreted, not only by the
radicals, but also by many liberals, as tantamount to saying that
the revolutionaries were, in fact, the culprits, and as an attempt
to split the student body. Matters were further aggravated when
a 'deputation of the younger generation' turned up in the *Bee*'s
editorial offices, under the impression that Benni was the newspaper's editor. The deputation demanded that Benni announce
to the paper's staff that Leskov's accusation of arson would not
go unpunished. Leskov began to receive threatening letters. In
the end, Benni tried to put matters right by organizing volunteer
fire brigades drawn from the ranks of the students (to counter
their 'arsonist' image) – but this came to nothing, and merely
provoked the mockery of the radicals. Leskov and Benni were
now in public disgrace: in the eyes of 'progressive' opinion they
had committed the ultimate act of betrayal – they had behaved
as stool pigeons.

The *Bee* never managed to clear its name, and in the mind of
the Russian intelligentsia Leskov was forever afterwards associated with the 'betrayers of the revolution'. This was one of
the principal reasons why throughout the rest of the nineteenth
century his name was never held in the same esteem as those of
the other great Russian writers. For the rest of his life, Leskov
nursed a sense of bitter grievance against his former friends and
colleagues, the radicals – much in the terms of Dostoyevsky's
The Devils, he saw them as nihilistic demons, bent on destroy-
ing all that was true and honourable in Russia. In consequence,
he began to gravitate towards the political Right.

It was in the wake of this crisis that Leskov passed to the writing of fiction in earnest. Even before the fires, he had published
several journalistic sketches which, hovering on the border
between fact and fiction, describe the spiritual darkness of the

Russian peasantry, in a mode utterly alien to the fashionable 'narodnik' sympathies of the time. In *Musk-Ox*, written during a four-month stay in Paris and published in 1863, Leskov makes a statement about Russian society which recapitulates much of his own experience over the previous ten years. While the critique of radicalism and radicals is still quite gentle in this story – Musk-Ox (or Yakushkin) is seen as a tragic eccentric, quite out of touch with the grim reality and brutal backwardness of the Russian peasant classes, his attempt at inciting them to revolt doomed from the outset – the central message of despair is profound and intensely felt. The idyll of the Russian countryside, evoked in passages of exquisitely poetic writing, is contrasted with the murky, labyrinthine and seemingly infinite recesses of human nature, with its greed, stupidity, bigotry and cruelty. The monks and holy men who inhabit the hermitages in the forests are portrayed as lovable, quixotic, but essentially irrelevant to the needs of society. So intense is the idyll associated with them that one has the feeling that for Leskov their meditative impracticality is much to be preferred to the hard-nosed, Scott-like commercialism of a Sviridov, even though it is on men like the latter that Russia's future depends. Bogoslovsky's suicide, and the ingratiating words of the old peasant to Sviridov at the end of the story ('He'll rot, but you'll not, Liksandra Ivanych') are not exactly calculated to inspire the reader with hope. Yet the vitality of Musk-Ox, his extreme individualism, contains an element of redemption at an existential level – this is what Russia is good at producing, Leskov seems to be saying: it is wild, tragic and wholly useless, something on a level with a work of art.

Musk-Ox, with its first person narrative by a person who is not necessarily the author, its strongly delineated central character and its gallery of individual secondary portraits, set the model for many of Leskov's *povesti*, or 'tales'. It would be difficult here to give an adequate account of Leskov's prodigious output of fiction, which was to span the final third of the nineteenth century. Tales and other shorter and longer prose works (some of these are novels and quasi-novels) leapt from his pen with astonishing rapidity, and the last pre-revolutionary edition of his complete works comprises thirty-six thick volumes.

Faced with such a massive opus, the best we can do in this short introduction is to follow the remainder of Leskov's career with particular reference to the other four tales included in the present selection – each of these is, like *Musk-Ox*, in some way representative of a phase of Leskov's development, and may also be regarded as a high point in the author's progress as an artist.

In 1862 Leskov finally separated from Olga Vasilevna, and was left as a 'wifeless husband' – he could not obtain a divorce on the grounds that his wife was insane, since the Orthodox Church did not recognize such grounds. In Kiev, during the course of 1864, he met Katerina Bubnova, with whom he had a protracted romance, and who bore him a son, Andrei. It was while he was pursuing this affair, and writing the final instalments of his anti-nihilist novel about the 'banality of evil', *No Way Out*, that he produced the tale which is perhaps his best-known work – *Lady Macbeth of Mtsensk* (more correctly translated as 'A Lady Macbeth of the Mtsensk District'). The tale's title is clearly derived from Turgenev, who had published a story called *A Hamlet of the Shchigry District* as one of his *A Huntsman's Sketches*. As Hugh McLean has noted, 'the point of such titles is to juxtapose a Shakespearean archetype at a high level of psychological universalization with a specific, local, utterly Russian, and contemporary milieu. The effect on a Russian reader of that time was almost oxymoronic: how could there be a "Lady Macbeth", especially nowadays, in such a mudhole as Mtsensk? The truth to be demonstrated is that Shakespeare's universals know no boundaries of time or place or class.'[iv]

Much has been written about the tale, which occupies a unique place in Russian literature and indeed, perhaps, in world literature as a whole, as an example of the highest achievement to which the storyteller's art can aspire. As Walter Benjamin pointed out, Leskov is primarily a teller of stories, a journalist turned fiction-writer. It is often the exceptional, eccentric, tragically self-willed individuals, the Musk-Oxes, the Katerina Lvovnas, who fascinate him, and whose personalities seem to generate a wealth of stylistic nuances and associations through which they are transmuted into the stuff of fables and remain in the memory as legendary, heroic archetypes. The sensual and sexual energy of Katerina Lvovna, her violent thirst for power and freedom, are mirrored in the vivid, almost tactile descriptions of her natural surroundings, and find their sinister and destructive echo in the figure of Sergei, her empty and spiritless lover. The narrative means, almost operatic in their simplicity and dramatic intensity (it is not hard to see why Shostakovich selected the tale for musical development in his *Katerina Izmailova*), are entirely merged with the stormy, passionate nature of the heroine, and the accounts of the murders and their gruesome details are transformed into a quasi-expressionistic death-elegy by the neutral, dispassionate tone of the narration itself. There is nothing of this kind to be found elsewhere in nineteenth-century Russian literature, not even in Dostoyevsky, and it is small wonder that it was not until the twentieth century, after the experience of Symbolism and Russian modernism, that this tale, together with others by Leskov, came to be accepted and understood by readers in the country of its origin.

A work less controversial than *Lady Macbeth*, but one that was to prove a success in Leskov's own lifetime (it is nowadays considered a classic of Russian literature), was the 'chronicle of Old Town' which he began in 1866 and finally published in 1872 as the novel *Cathedral Folk* (*Soboryanye*). 'Stary Gorod', or 'Old Town', which in the final version of the novel became 'Stargorod' (in imitation of Gogol's 'Mirgorod'), is presented to the reader as a microcosm of Russian society past, present and future. The original title of the chronicle was 'Waiting for the Moving of the Water', a quotation from the Gospel according to St John which refers to the healing by the angel of the 'blind, halt and withered'. The novel in its published form represents only a carefully pruned selection from a vast and formless mass of material on which Leskov worked during these years, which was, in its basic conception, a kind of pot-pourri of chronicles, short stories and novel excerpts which presented a panoply of Russian provincial life, from the struggles of the eighteenth-century Old Believers, through the Katerina Lvovna-like drama of Platonida Deyeva, a young, beautiful woman married to a man twice her age, to a depiction of 'Old Times in the Village of

Plodomasovo'. Leskov was unable to carry this project through; *Cathedral Folk* represents those sections of the material which relate to the Russian clergy. In the characters of Father Savely Tuberozov, whose diary forms one of the book's main stylistic devices, Father Zakhariya Benefaktov and Deacon Akhilla Desnitsyn, the author manages to portray the lived reality of Orthodox belief, seen from the point of view of a sympathetic Protestant outsider, and shows how it concords with a warm and compassionate understanding of human nature. It is contrasted with the nihilistic emptiness of the radicals, such as Prepotensky, Bizyukina and Termosyosov. The language in which the novel – particularly those parts of it which purport to be Tuberozov's 'diary' – is written is a curious blend of nineteenth-century Russian, Old Slavonicisms and ecclesiastical jargon, and is extremely difficult to translate adequately into another tongue.

The same may be said of the linguistic texture of *The Sealed Angel* (1873), another literary work by Leskov which deals with ecclesiastical themes and problems, but treats a secular subject – the building of the first suspension bridge across the River Dnieper at Kiev, and the part played in it by a colony of Old Believers. In *Musk-Ox*, Leskov had given a negative portrayal of the Old Believers (the outlawed schismatics who did not accept the liturgical reforms introduced by Patriarch Nikon in the mid-seventeenth century) as being cruel and obsessed with the rigid observance of their faith. In 1863, Leskov had accepted a journalistic commission from the Tsarist Ministry of Education to investigate the secret schools of the Old Believers, who ran them illegally in defiance of the state authorities. The Tsarist government was considering a softening of its policy of persecuting the Old Believers, and Leskov was sent to Riga and Pskov to compile a first-hand report on the schools there. In his report, Leskov had pleaded for tolerance, claiming that the schism could only be overcome through education. In *Waiting for the Moving of the Water*, he had depicted a mass voluntary conversion of Old Believers to Orthodoxy, and throughout his life he was to return to the subject of their persecution. The plot of *The Sealed Angel*, which contains another, similar conversion, represents what is probably his most inspired treatment of the theme, and forms the basis of one of his finest and most gripping tales. As for the conversion itself, Leskov was criticized for this ending to the tale; at the time, many readers (including Fyodor Dostoyevsky, who reviewed the work in his *Diary of a Writer* for 1873) found that it lacked credibility. Yet read today, outside the context of nineteenth-century Russian religious and secular politics, the Old Believers' conversion to Orthodoxy has an undeniable rightness about it: it is Leskov's way of showing how the '*angel*', 'the angel in men's hearts' may be revealed, in opposition to the '*aggel*', or 'demon' which holds sway over human beings for most of the time.

In addition to a dramatic and exciting plot, *The Sealed Angel* displays a high degree of stylistic ornamentalism. This is mostly associated with the autodidactic speciality around which the action centres – the science of icon-painting. At the time the tale appeared, the study of Russian icons, whose beauty is nowadays universally appreciated, was still in its infancy, and Leskov was in many ways ahead of his time in taking a serious interest in them for their own sake. The studies and treatises which had appeared hitherto, such as the Slavist and folklorist Fyodor Buslayev's *General Concepts of Russian Icon-Painting* (1866), had viewed Russian icons almost solely as an expression of the national religious spirit; in his tale, Leskov writes of them as works of art, and demonstrates their living connection with the environment from which they spring. That he was able to do this was in no small part due to the fact that he had established a friendship with a living icon-painter, Nikita Savostianovich Racheiskov, who had a studio in St Petersburg. The 'isographer Sevastyan' (I have opted to preserve the old Graeco-Russian term *izograf*, meaning 'icon-painter') in *The Sealed Angel* derives his character and identity from Racheiskov, who lived entirely from the painting and restoration of icons. In a tribute to Racheiskov, published after the latter's death in 1886, Leskov claimed that 'on the publication of my Christmas story *The Sealed Angel* (which was entirely composed in Nikita's hot and stuffy studio), he received many orders for icons of angels'.

The Sealed Angel was first published in *The Russian Messenger*, a journal edited by the conservative Russian nationalist and publicist Mikhail Nikiforovich Katkov. Katkov had already published Leskov's long anti-radical novel, *At Daggers Drawn*, and during the years between 1870 and 1875, spurred on by Katkov's encouragement and generosity, Leskov produced a large number of major literary works – in addition to the two already mentioned, they included *Cathedral Folk, The Enchanted Pilgrim, A Decrepit Clan* and *At the Edge of the World*, and constitute the heart of Leskov's creation – nearly all of which appeared in the *Messenger*. Many of these works make use of the *skaz*, or spoken inner narrative, and their baroquely configured Russian speaks less of 'the individual' and his experience than it does of the mass of highly individual individuals who comprised the Russian people of Leskov's time. It is no exaggeration to say that in Leskov's writings we hear, as almost nowhere else apart from Gogol, the voice of Russia. This ethnocentric quality of Leskov's art seems to have impressed even those who were in charge of Russia's destiny: in 1873, S. E. Kushelev, a prominent statesman and general with influence at the Imperial Court, visited the author to tell him that *The Sealed Angel* had been read aloud to the royal family by Boleslav Markevich, and that the Empress Maria Aleksandrovna had expressed a wish to hear the tale read by Leskov himself. In her memoirs, Leskov's granddaughter, Natalya Bakhareva, relates that her mother inherited from her husband a diamond-encrusted gold watch and a gold snuffbox which were gifts from the Empress on the occasion of his reading *The Sealed Angel* at court.

As a result of this favourable interest in his work by highly placed individuals, Leskov was able, in early 1874, to acquire a modest government service position in the Ministry of Education, one he held for the next ten years. It was just as well for him that he was able to obtain it; after quarrelling with Katkov, he had found himself somewhat out on a limb with regard to the literary journals on which he depended for his livelihood (it was almost impossible for an author to live on the royalties of book publication in nineteenth-century Russia, so negligible were the amounts paid). Suspected by the liberals and left of having connections with the Russian secret police, and by the right of a 'literary' disregard for the principles of conservative nationalism (Leskov's quarrel with Katkov had centred on the latter's politically tinged editing of *A Decrepit Clan*), he had found himself with nowhere to go. The government service position provided him and his family with at least a basis of security, though the relatively meagre salary of a thousand roubles a year was not really sufficient for them to live on to any degree of comfort. The difficulties and uncertainties of Leskov's professional and public life at this time seem to have had their effect on his already strained unofficial marriage with Katerina Bubnova; in the spring of 1875, Leskov made an attempt to escape from his problems for a while, and set off for a second time through Europe for a visit to Paris. While there, he began to revise his attitudes towards Russian Orthodoxy. In particular, he met Louis Naville, the son of the Swiss Protestant theologian Ernest Naville: his conversations with Naville had a profound effect on him, precipitating a religious crisis, and, after a stay in Marienbad where he took the waters and mud baths, he returned to St Petersburg having exchanged his Orthodox convictions for what he termed a 'spiritual Christianity'. This bore many similarities to the form of Christianity soon to be propounded by Leo Tolstoy.

Leskov's first meeting with Tolstoy did not take place until 1887. In the twelve years before that time, Leskov had been steadily moving closer to Tolstoy's ideas in life as well as art. Indeed, in several respects Leskov may be said to have anticipated some of Tolstoy's positions. In 1877, he had quietly separated from Katerina Bubnova, and was henceforth to strive towards an ideal of celibacy, even though this ran counter to the strongly sexual component in his nature. For decades, he had regarded Tolstoy with an almost superstitious awe; *War and Peace* and *Anna Karenina* he had experienced not merely as great works of literature, but as spiritual watersheds – they had been a part of his own inner development. By the 1880s, both writers had arrived at a final repudiation of Orthodoxy. Yet while Tolstoy had proceeded to construct his own rationalized, 'Tolstoyan' version of Christianity, Leskov looked back towards the Protestant faith he had encountered at first hand in his childhood in the home of Alexander Scott, where there had been no icons, oil or candles, but only a practical, living desire to serve God and man. Even so, after his meeting with Tolstoy, Leskov became for a time a zealous convert to Tolstoyanism – on occasion his zeal was so strong that the master found it embarrassing.

With the assassination of Tsar Alexander II in 1881, a period of reaction began in Russian public and social life. It was the role played by the Orthodox Church, under the head of its Holy Synod, Konstantin Petrovich Pobedonostsev ('victory-bearer') – Leskov always referred to him as 'Lampadonostsev' ('lamp-bearer') – in supporting and reinforcing this reaction which finally persuaded Leskov that no good could be expected from the established Church. Before 1881, while turning increasingly towards Protestantism, he had continued to view the Church as a positive force in Russian life, and had hoped that somehow it might yet help to transform society. In a certain sense, it appears that Tolstoy's anti-ritualistic religion, with its intense faith in the Russian people, came to replace Orthodoxy in Leskov's spiritual cosmos; for Tolstoy was no Protestant – indeed, he regarded Protestantism with just as much suspicion and disgust as any other form of established, 'church' religion. Tolstoy appealed to the 'Old Believer' in Leskov – here was a larger-than-life character from one of his own tales, a religious heretic who possessed a demonic angelism which might save the Russian people and return it to the fold of righteousness.

Under Tolstoy's influence, Leskov began to examine the origins of the Christian religion, and its roots in both the Old and the New Testaments. The series of 'Synaxarion' tales on which he worked exclusively between 1886 and 1891 are didactic in the Tolstoyan manner, and look back to the lives of the early Christians. The *Synaxarion*, or *Prolog*, as it is known in Church Slavonic, is a short collection of *exempla*: lives of the early saints, ordered according to the ecclesiastical calendar. The first Slavonic translations of the *Synaxarion* date from the early Middle Ages, and they contain much material of a strange and flavoursome nature. The narrative style in which they are written is a primitive one, consisting to a great extent of long chains of sentences linked by the words 'and then'. These texts were especially cherished by the Old Believers, who did not accept the later editions prepared during the eighteenth and nineteenth centuries by the Holy Synod of the Church of Russia. In turning to them for inspiration, Leskov was also addressing the foundations of Russia's spiritual identity, and the tales he constructed from them must be seen as an attempt to draw the attention of his readers towards a recognition that the Orthodox Church had distorted the living message of this inheritance.

Pamphalon the Entertainer (1887), like the other *Prolog* tales, is set in the oriental world of Palestine, Egypt and Byzantium. This exotic background stimulated Leskov's imagination to many thoroughly un-Tolstoyan flights of imagery, and there are occasions when the reader suspects that, from a stylistic point of view at least, it is the Flaubert of *La Tentation de Saint Antoine* rather than the pedagogue of Yasnaya Polyana whom Leskov is seeking to emulate – as was indeed the case. Leskov had never travelled to the countries he describes in these narratives, and so his fantasy was able to roam freely, untrammelled by memory or fact. The tales are the purest of fictions, and in *Pamphalon* Leskov even invented a special form of 'spoken' Russian which is intended to convey the impression that the characters are talking Greek. This effect is almost impossible to bring across in translation, yet the tale deserves to be better known, as it is one of Leskov's liveliest and most succinct statements of his own *art poétique*. The carefree juggler and acrobat Pamphalon is contrasted with the morose, ascetic Hermius; yet through the agency of Christian love, Pamphalon is able to set Hermius's soul free from the bonds of 'self-conceit', and both are finally transformed into weightless spirits, beyond the reach of the earth and its snares.

Leskov's fascination with Tolstoy, though a powerful one, was not sufficient to mitigate the deep sense of anger, sorrow and despair he experienced towards the end of his life, as he saw that the mass of the Russian people were no more developed in a moral sense now than they had been fifty years earlier. *A Winter's Day*, written in the last year of his life, gives full vent to his emotions of grief and betrayal, and is one of the bleakest works in Russian literature. In the world that is evoked in this essentially dramatic composition, there is no hope, no redeeming feature to offset the universal panorama of greed, cruelty and stupidity which the author sees around him. Not even Gogol went so far in his denunciation of human nature as Leskov goes here. The Tolstoyans, while not condemned, are seen as powerless to affect the moral inertia of Russian society, while the radicals, though off-stage, lurk ready to add political tyranny to the general morass as their final contribution.

Leskov died early on the morning of 21 February 1895, after a return of the angina which had plagued him a year earlier. His funeral was held two days later on 23 February. In his 'Posthumous Plea' he had made the following request: 'I select no place of burial for myself, as that in my eyes is a matter of indifference, but I request that no one shall ever place on my grave any memento other than a plain, ordinary wooden cross. If this cross disintegrates, and there be found a person who wishes to replace it with a new one, let him do this and accept my appreciation for the remembrance. Yet if there should be no such well-wisher, that means that the time has passed for anyone to remember my grave.'

NOTES

i.   For a detailed account of Leskov's life and work, see Hugh McLean, *Nikolai Leskov, The Man and His Art* (Harvard University Press, 1977).
ii. McLean, op. cit., pp. 31–32.
iii. A. Leskov, *Zhizn' Nikolaya Leskova* (Moscow: 1954), p. 100.
iv. McLean, op. cit., p. 146.

Note on the Text

The Russian texts chosen for translation in the present volume are among those published in the thirty-six-volume *N. S. Leskov, Polnoye sobranie sochineniy* (St Petersburg, 1902–1903).

MUSK-OX

A Story

'It feeds on grass or, if there be insufficient of
this, on lichen.'

From a zoology treatise

I

When I first made Vasily Petrovich's acquaintance, he was already known as 'Musk-Ox'. People had given him this sobriquet because he really did look uncommonly like the musk-ox that is to be seen in the illustrated treatise on zoology by Yulian Simashko.[1] He was twenty-eight, but looked much older. While one could not have described him as athletic or Herculean, he was none the less a thoroughly strong and healthy individual – small in stature, thick-set and broad-shouldered. Vasily Petrovich's face was round and colourless; but it was indeed only his face that was round – his cranium displayed a curious deformity. At first sight it was reminiscent of a Kaffir's skull, but as one examined it and studied it more closely, one found oneself unable to place it within any straightforward phrenological system. He wore his hair in a fashion that made it look as though he wished to mislead everyone as to the actual shape of his 'upper storey'. The hair at the back of his head was cut very short, while at the front, over his ears, it fell in two long, thick, dark chestnut-coloured forelocks. Vasily Petrovich was in the habit of twisting these forelocks, and they forever lay on his temples like two rolled-up cylinders, while on his cheeks they curled, recalling the horns of the beast from which he had received his appellation. It was these forelocks which, more than anything else, made Vasily Petrovich resemble a musk-ox. There was, however, certainly nothing ridiculous about his physical appearance in general. A person meeting him for the first time would simply be aware that Vasily Petrovich was, as they say, 'poorly cut but firmly sewn' and, looking into his widely spaced, hazel-coloured eyes, would not fail to observe the will-power, determination and common sense which they contained. There was much that was unusual about the character of Vasily Petrovich. His primary distinguishing feature was an almost evangelical lack of concern about himself. The son of a rural deacon, who had grown up in bitter poverty and had, what was more, lost both his parents at an early stage in life, not only did he fail to manifest a concern for any lasting improvement in the conditions of his existence, but never even seemed to give a thought to the morrow. He possessed nothing which he might have given away, but was capable of stripping the last shirt from his body, and assumed a similar capability in everyone he came across – those who did not have it he customarily referred to, quite simply and plainly, as 'pigs'. When Vasily Petrovich was out of boots,[2] that is to say, when his boots had, to use his own expression, 'completely dropped their jaws', he would come to you or to me and without ceremony take your or my spare pair of boots, if they even so much as remotely fitted him, leaving his own cast-offs as a souvenir.

To Vasily Petrovich it was all the same whether you were at home or not: he would make himself at home in your quarters, take whatever he needed, always in the smallest quantities possible, and occasionally tell you when he met you later that he had borrowed your tobacco, or tea, or boots. More frequently, however, he would omit to say anything about such trivial matters. He could not abide modern literature, and read only the Gospels and the ancient classics. He would not hear a word on the subject of women, considered them all, without exception, 'halfwits' and quite sincerely regretted that his aged mother was a woman, and not some sexless being. Vasily Petrovich's selflessness knew no bounds. Never to a single one of us did he at any time indicate that he felt any affection for us; yet we were all well aware that there was no sacrifice which Musk-Ox would not make for each one of his associates and acquaintances. It never entered our heads to doubt his readiness to sacrifice himself for his chosen ideal – yet it was not easy to discover what that ideal might be. It was not so much that he poured ridicule on the many theories in which we then so ardently believed; it was rather that he nourished a deep and sincere contempt for them.

Musk-Ox was no lover of conversation: what he did, he did in silence, and it was always something which at any given moment he might least have been expected to do.

How and why he had become a member of the small circle of people to which I, too, belonged during the limited duration of my stay in our provincial capital, I do not know. Some three years before my arrival there, Musk-Ox had completed his studies at the Kursk theological seminary. His mother, who fed him on the crumbs she had scraped together 'in the name of Christ', was impatiently waiting for him to become a priest and settle down in a parish with a young wife. But the thought of a young wife had not even crossed her son's mind. Vasily Petrovich had not the slightest desire to get married. He had finished his course; his mother kept asking whether he had found a fiancée yet, but Vasily Petrovich would make no reply, and one fine morning he disappeared into nowhere. It was not until some six months later that he sent his mother twenty-five roubles and a letter in which he informed the impoverished old woman that he had reached Kazan and had enrolled at the ecclesiastical academy there. How he had reached Kazan, putting more than a thousand versts behind him, and by what means he had obtained the twenty-five roubles – all this remained a mystery. Musk-Ox said not a word about it in his letter. But hardly had the old woman had time to rejoice that her Vasya would one day be a bishop and that she would then be able to live with him in a little, light room with a little white stove and take tea and sultanas twice a day, then Vasya himself suddenly turned up, quite unexpectedly and mysteriously, out of the blue, in Kursk once again. Many times people asked him: 'What's this? How did you get back, and why have you come?' But they received little information. 'I didn't get along with them,' was all that Musk-Ox would say by way of reply, and more than that it was impossible to make him divulge. To only one person did he say slightly more: 'I don't want to be a monk,' and after that he clammed up completely.

The person to whom Musk-Ox said more than he told the others was Yakov Chelnovsky, a kind, good-natured fellow who would never have harmed a fly and who was prepared to render any service to his neighbour. Chelnovsky was related to some distant branch of my family. It was at his house that I struck the acquaintance of the thick-set hero of my story.

The events I shall describe took place in the summer of 1854. At the time, I was busy with some work in connection with a lawsuit that was taking place in the Kursk government offices.

I arrived in Kursk at seven o'clock on a May morning, and went straight to Chelnovsky's house. At this time Chelnovsky was working as a tutor, preparing young men for the university and giving lessons in Russian language and history in two boarding schools for girls, and making not a bad living out of it. He had a sizeable three-roomed flat with a vestibule, a rather good library, comfortable furniture, several exotic potted plants and a bulldog named Box which had grinning teeth, a thoroughly indecent posterior, and a walk that was slightly reminiscent of the cancan.

Chelnovsky was extremely glad to see me and made me promise I would stay with him for the whole of my time in Kursk. He was usually out all day, travelling around giving his lessons, while I would look in at the Civic Hall or wander aimlessly along the banks of the Tuskar or the Seym.[3] There are many maps of Russia on which you will not find the first of these rivers, while the second is renowned for its particularly tasty crayfish, though it has acquired an even greater fame by virtue of the system of locks which has been constructed along it, a system that has swallowed up vast quantities of capital without freeing the Seym from its reputation of being a river 'unsuitable for navigation'.

Some two weeks had passed since the day of my arrival in Kursk. There was never any mention of Musk-Ox in our conversation, and indeed I was unaware of the existence of such a strange creature within the bounds of our Black Earth region, so abundant in grain, beggars and thieves.

One day, at around two o'clock in the afternoon, I returned to Chelnovsky's house tired and exhausted. I was greeted in the vestibule by Box, who guarded our dwelling far more zealously than did the eighteen-year-old boy who acted as our valet. On the table in the reception-room lay a cloth cap, impossibly worn; a single man's suspender in the most filthy condition, with a little strap attached to it; a black, greasy kerchief which had been twisted into a plait; and a thin, hazelwood walking-stick. In the next room, which was stuffed with bookcases and rather showy study furniture, an impossibly dust-caked individual was sitting on the sofa. He was wearing a pink cotton shirt and a pair of bright yellow trousers which were worn through at the knees. The boots of this stranger were covered in a thick layer of white road-dust, and on his knees lay a fat tome which he was reading without lowering his head. When I entered the study, this dusty figure gave me a single cursory glance and once more fixed his gaze upon his book. In the bedroom everything seemed tidy enough. Chelnovsky's linen smock, in which he attired himself immediately upon his return home, hung where it usually did, bearing witness to the fact that the master of the house was not at home. I could not for the life of me think who this strange visitor, who had so unceremoniously settled himself down, might be. The normally truculent Box was looking at him as at a familiar, and did not go to be fondled for the sole reason that the dalliance and petting that are common to dogs of the French breed are not among the characteristics of specimens of the Anglo-Saxon canine race. I went back into the vestibule with two aims in view: first, to find out something about the visitor from the servant boy and, second, to provoke, by my appearance and departure, some words from the visitor himself. In neither respect was I successful. The vestibule was as deserted as it had been before, and the visitor did not even raise his eyes to look at me, but continued to sit calmly in the same position in which I had found him five minutes previously. There was only one thing for it: to address the visitor directly.

'I expect you're waiting for Yakov Ivanych?' I said, coming to a halt before the stranger.

The guest surveyed me lazily, then rose from the sofa, spat through his teeth, as only Great Russian *petits bourgeois* know how to spit, and said in a thick bass voice: 'No.'

'Who have you come to see, then?' I inquired, surprised by the man's strange reply.

'I've just dropped in for a bit,' the visitor replied, striding around the room and twirling his forelocks.

'May I have the honour of learning to whom I address myself?' I asked him, adding my name and informing him that I was a relative of Yakov Ivanych's.

'Oh, I'm just here,' the visitor replied, returning to his book once more.

There the conversation ended. Abandoning any attempt to solve the riddle of this personage's appearance in the house, I lit a cigarette and lay down on my bed with a book in my hands. When one comes in from the heat of the sun to a neatly made bed which awaits one, it is extremely easy to fall asleep. On the present occasion I cognized the truth of this by experience, not even noticing when the book slipped out of my hands. Through the sweet slumber that is enjoyed by those who are filled with hopes and aspirations, I heard Chelnovsky giving the servant-boy a ticking-off, something to which the lad had long ago become inured, and paid no attention to them. I only woke up properly when my relative went into the study and shouted:

'Ah! Musk-Ox! What fate brings you to us?'

'I've come,' the visitor replied to this unusual form of greeting.

'I know you have, but where from? Where have you been?'

'You can't see it from here.'

'Still the old joker, eh? Have you been here long?' Yakov Ivanych asked his guest, going into the bedroom. 'Oh, you're asleep,' he said, addressing me. 'Get up, old chap, I want to show you a beastie.'

'What sort of a beastie?' I asked, still not quite having returned to the state that is termed wakefulness from the state that is termed sleep.

Chelnovsky made no reply; instead, he took off his coat and threw on his smock, a process which took less than a minute, went back into the study and, dragging my stranger out of it by the hand, performed a comic bow; then he pointed to the visitor, who was leaning forward against his arm, and said:

'I have the honour to introduce to you – our Musk-Ox. It feeds on grass or, if there be not sufficient of this, it can eat lichen.'

I got up and extended my hand to Musk-Ox, who throughout the whole introduction kept his gaze trained placidly on the leafy lilac bough which screened the open window of our bedroom.

'I've already introduced myself to you,' I said to Musk-Ox.

'I heard you,' Musk-Ox replied. 'And I'm Vasily Bogoslovsky, a man of the Bible.'

'What's that you say? You've already introduced yourself?' said Yakov Ivanych. 'Have you two met somewhere before, then?'

'Yes, when I came back here I found Vasily . . . I'm afraid I don't know your patronymic?'

'It used to be Petrovich,' replied Bogoslovsky.

'That's what it used to be, but now you can simply call him "Musk-Ox".'

'You can call me what you like, for all I care.'

'Oh no, old chap! Musk-Ox you are by name, and Musk-Ox you are by nature.'

We sat down to table. Vasily Petrovich poured himself a glass of vodka, emptied it into his mouth, put his hand on his cheekbone for a few seconds and, having swallowed the vodka, gave the plate of soup which stood before him on the table a meaningful look.

'Isn't there a meat jelly?' he asked the master of the house.

'No, old man, there isn't. We weren't expecting such a special guest today,' Chelnovsky replied. 'And so none was made.'

'You could have had some of it yourselves.'

'We can drink soup just as well.'

'Milksops,' Musk-Ox added. 'And isn't there a goose?' he asked, with even greater astonishment, when we were served with meat pies.

'No, there's no goose, either,' the master of the house replied, smiling his affectionate smile. 'Tomorrow you shall have meat jelly, and a goose, and buckwheat porridge with goosefat.'

'Tomorrow isn't today.'

'Well, what can I do about it? I suppose you haven't eaten goose for a long time?'

Musk-Ox gave him a stony look and with an expression of some satisfaction said:

'You'd do better to ask if I've eaten *anything* for a long time.'

'Oh, I say!'

'Four days ago I ate a bun in Sevsk.'

'In Sevsk?'

Musk-Ox waved an arm in confirmation of this.

'And what were you doing in Sevsk?'

'I happened to be walking through it.'

'But what on earth took you there?'

For a moment, Musk-Ox held still the fork with which he was shovelling enormous chunks of meat pie into his mouth, gave Chelnovsky another stony look and, ignoring his question, said:

'Have you been taking snuff today?'

'Taking snuff? Why on earth do you ask that?'

Chelnovsky and I fell about laughing at Musk-Ox's strange question.

'Just because.'

'Because what? Do tell us, dear beastie!'

'Because your tongue's a bit on the itchy side today.'

'But how could I possibly fail to inquire? After all, you've been missing for a whole month.'

'Missing?' said Musk-Ox. 'My dear fellow, I don't go missing, and if I do, then I have my reasons.'

'All this preaching has eaten our country away!' Chelnovsky remarked in my direction. ' "O'erwhelming the desire, but cruel the fate." In our enlightened age we're not allowed to preach on the streets and squares; we're unable to join the priesthood, as that would mean "abjuring woman, the vessel of the serpent", and there's also something that prevents us from becoming monks. Though just what it is, I don't know.'

'It's just as well you don't know.'

'Why do you say that? The more one knows, the better.'

'Go and become a monk yourself, then you'll find out.'

'But don't you want to serve mankind by giving it the benefit of your experience?'

'Other people's experience is a waste of time, my friend,' said the eccentric, rising from his place at the table and using his napkin to thoroughly wipe his face, which was covered in perspiration from his exertions during the meal. Putting the napkin down, he went into the vestibule and there extracted from his coat a small clay pipe with a black, chewed mouthpiece, and a calico tobacco-pouch; he stuffed the pipe with tobacco, put the pouch in his trouser-pocket and then began to move further away into the vestibule.

'Why don't you smoke your pipe in here?' Chelnovsky asked him.

'It'll make you sneeze. You'll have headaches.'

Musk-Ox stood still, smiling. Never have I encountered a man who could smile as Bogoslovsky did. His face remained completely placid; not one feature of it moved, and in his eyes there was a deep, sad expression – yet at the same time one could see that those eyes were laughing, laughing that most good-natured laughter with which Russians sometimes make fun of themselves and their misfortunes.

'A new Diogenes!' said Chelnovsky, as Musk-Ox went out. 'He's forever looking for people who believe in the Gospels.'

We lit our cigars and, reclining on our beds, discussed various human foibles of which the eccentric behaviour of Vasily Petrovich had put us in mind. A quarter of an hour later, Vasily Petrovich returned. He put his pipe down on the floor beside the stove, squatted down on his heels next to Chelnovsky and, scratching his left shoulder with his right hand, said in an undertone:

'I was looking for a tutoring post.'

'When?'

'Just now.'

'Who did you ask?'

'People I met in the street.'

Again, Chelnovsky laughed; but Musk-Ox paid no attention.

'Well, and what did God provide for you?' Chelnovsky asked him.

'Not a sausage.'

'What a buffoon you are! Whoever heard of anyone seeking job vacancies out in the streets?'

'I knocked at some landowners' houses, and asked there,' Musk-Ox went on, in an earnest tone of voice.

'Well, and what did they say?'

'They wouldn't hire me.'

'No, of course they wouldn't – and they won't, either.'

Musk-Ox bestowed his stony gaze on Chelnovsky, and then, in the same monotonous tone of voice, asked:

'Why won't they?'

'Because no one will take a person he doesn't know into his house without an introduction.'

'I showed them my testimonial.'

'Is that the one that says "of fairly reasonable behaviour"?'

'Well, so what if it is? I tell you, my friend, it has nothing to do with that, it's because . . .'

'You're a Musk-Ox,' Chelnovsky said, prompting him.

'That's right, I am.'

'So what are you going to do now?'

'I'm going to have another pipeful of tobacco,' Vasily Petrovich replied, getting up and taking hold of his black-stemmed pipe.

'Have it in here.'

'I don't think so.'

'Go on: after all, the window's open.'

'I don't think so.'

'What's the matter with you, man? Anyone would think it was the first time you'd ever smoked your doobek⁴ in front of me.'

'He wouldn't like it,' Musk-Ox said, indicating me.

'By all means go ahead and smoke your pipe, Vasily Petrovich,' I said. 'I'm used to it: doobeks don't bother me.'

'You haven't seen my doobek when it's going – it'd make the Devil himself run away,' Musk-Ox replied, stressing the 'oo' in 'doobek', and the attractive smile flickered once again in his good-natured eyes.

'Well, I shan't run away.'

'So you're stronger than the Devil, are you?'

'On this occasion, yes.'

'He seems to have a pretty high opinion of the Devil's strength,' Chelnovsky said.

'Only woman, my friend, is more wicked than the Devil.'

Vasily Petrovich stuffed his pipe with *makhorka*⁵ and, exhaling a thin stream of acrid smoke, settled the burning tobacco with his index finger and said:

'I'll copy exercises.'

'What exercises?' Chelnovsky asked, putting his hand to his ear.

'Exercises, the exercises the seminary students have to write, I'll copy those. You know, pupils' exercise-books, don't you understand?'

'Now I do. That's pretty awful work, old chap.'

'I don't care.'

'You'll earn no more than two roubles a month doing that.'

'It's all the same to me.'

'Well, and what else will you do?'

'Find a tutoring post for me.'

'Is it to be in the country again?'

'Yes, I'd prefer the country.'

'And you'll walk out again after a week. Do you know what he did last spring?' Chelnovsky said, turning to me. 'I'd got him all set up in a post, on a salary of a hundred and twenty roubles a month, with board and lodging thrown in free; all he had to do was to get a boy ready to take the first year gymnasium exams. We bought him everything he needed, kitted the dear chap out. There, I thought: there's our Musk-Ox installed in a position! But a month later he turned up again on our doorstep as if he'd never left it. He'd taken up his studying again, and had left all his clean clothes back there.'

'Well, what of it? There was nothing else for it,' Musk-Ox said, frowning, and rose from his chair.

'And do you know why there was nothing else for it?' Chelnovsky said, turning to me. 'It was because they wouldn't allow him to pull the boy by the hair.'

'Tell me another,' Musk-Ox growled.

'Well, why was it, then?'

'It was because there was nothing else for it.'

Musk-Ox came to a halt in front of me and, after a moment's reflection, said:

'It was a thoroughly unusual business!'

'Sit down, Vasily Petrovich,' I said, moving along the bed a bit.

'No, I don't want to. A thoroughly unusual business,' he began again. 'The boy was nearly fifteen, and what's more he was your real gentry – a shameless rascal, in other words.'

'That's how it is in Russia!' Chelnovsky said, jokingly.

'Yes,' Musk-Ox went on. 'They had a male cook there, a young fellow named Yegor. He'd married a subdeacon's daughter from one of our impoverished clerical families. The young master of the house was up to all the tricks, and he set straight about murmuring small nothings in her ear. But the girl was young, and that wasn't her style; she complained to her husband, and he complained to the mistress. She had a word with her son, but he just carried on regardless. It happened a second time, and a third – the cook went to see the mistress, complaining that his wife was getting no respite – and again nothing happened. I started to get annoyed. "Listen," I said to him. "If you so much as give Alyonka another pinch, I'll beat the living daylights out of you." He flushed with anger; that was his noble blood playing up, you know. He flew off to his mother, and I followed him along. I looked: she was in an armchair, she was all flushed, too, and her son was complaining to her about me in French. As soon as she caught sight of me, she took him by the hand and smiled, the devil only knows why. "That's enough, my dear," she said. "Vasily Petrovich was probably only imagining things; he was joking, and you must show him that he was wrong." I could see she was giving me a sly look. My young charge went off and then, instead of having a word with me about her son, she said: "What a knight in shining armour you are, Vasily Petrovich! Don't you have a sweetheart?" Well, I can't abide talk about subjects like that,' Musk-Ox said, waving one hand energetically. 'I can't stay in the same room where things like that are said,' he repeated, raising his voice and beginning to stride about once again.

'Well, so did you leave the house immediately?'

'No – only six weeks later.'

'And you managed to live there peacefully?'

'Well, I didn't speak to anyone.'

'What about at mealtimes?'

'I used to have my meals with the clerk.'

'With the clerk?'

'Yes, in the servants' pantry. Well, I didn't mind. I mean, it's impossible to offend me.'

'Really?'

'Of course . . . anyway, what's the point of talking about this . . . Well, one day I was sitting near the window after dinner, reading Tacitus, and I could hear somebody shouting in the servants' room. Who was doing the shouting, I couldn't make out: but I could hear Alyonka's voice. That'll be the young master having a bit of fun, I thought. I got up and went along to the servants' room. I listened. Alyonka was weeping and shouting through clenched teeth: "You ought to be ashamed of yourself" and "You've no fear of God in you", and various other similar things. I looked. Alyonka was standing up in the attic at the top of the ladder, and my young charge was at the bottom, making it quite impossible for the girl to come down. It was quite simply shameful – well, you know how they carry on. And he kept on teasing her: "Come on down," he kept saying, "or I'll take the ladder away." I was seized by such a fit of anger that I took him out into the passage and boxed his ears.'

'So that the blood came spurting out of his ears and nose,' Chelnovsky broke in, with a laugh.

'As he so richly deserved.'

'What did his mother have to say about that?'

'I didn't see her again to find out. When I left the servants' room, I walked straight to Kursk.'

'How many versts was that?'

'A hundred and seventy; and even if it had been a thousand and seventy, it would have been all the same to me.'

If you had been able to see Musk-Ox at that moment, you would have been in no doubt that it really was 'all the same' to him how many versts he had to walk and whose ears he had to box if, according to his view of things, such a punishment appeared to be indicated.

A sweltering June set in. Vasily Petrovich would appear punctually in our house every day at twelve noon, remove his calico tie and his braces and, having said 'good day' to both of us, would settle down to reading his classical authors. In this manner he would pass the time before dinner; after dinner he would light his pipe and, taking up a position by the window, would usually inquire: 'Well, any tutoring posts?' A month had gone by since the day on which Musk-Ox had first put that question to Chelnovsky – each day since then he had repeated it, and each day throughout this entire month he had received the same dispiriting answer. There was not the faintest prospect of a post becoming available. Vasily Petrovich did not, however, seem to find this in the slightest upsetting. He ate with a hearty appetite, and was forever in the mood that was habitual with him. Only once or twice did I observe him a little more irritable than usual; but even this irritability was in no way connected with his personal situation. It proceeded from two entirely extraneous circumstances. On one occasion he encountered a woman who was sobbing fit to burst, and asked her: 'You foolish woman, what are you bellowing about?' At first the woman was afraid, but subsequently told him that her son had been press-ganged by the military and was to be taken off the next day to be a recruit. Vasily Petrovich recalled that the clerk at the recruiting office was an old friend of his from his days at the theological seminary. Early the next morning, he went to see the clerk and returned in an unusually disconcerted frame of mind. His petition had proved unsuccessful. On another occasion a party of young recruits[1] was being driven through

the town. At this period coerced inductions into the army were
frequent. Vasily Petrovich, chewing his upper lip and propping
his arms in rather a rakish fashion, stood looking attentively
out of the window at the transport of recruits that was going
by below. The waggons of the local inhabitants trundled slowly
along; carts, jolting from side to side along the municipal thor-
oughfare, swayed to and fro the heads of children, who were
clad in overcoats made of grey army material. The large, grey
caps which they wore pulled down over their foreheads lent a
horribly melancholy aspect to their pretty faces and intelligent
eyes, which looked with a mixture of anguish and childish curiosity at the unfamiliar town and the crowds of tradesmen's
boys who were skipping along behind the carts. Two female
cooks brought up the rear.

'I suppose they must have mothers somewhere?' said one of
the strapping, pock-marked cooks, as they drew level with our
window.

'I expect they have,' the other replied, thrusting her elbows
under her sleeves and scratching her arms with her fingernails.

'And I suppose they care for them even though they're just
little Jews?'

'Well, what else can a mother do?'

'Of course. But it's only because they're their mothers, isn't it?'

'Yes, it's because they're their mothers ... it's their own
flesh and blood ... They couldn't do any different ...'

'Of course not.'

'Silly fools!' Vasily Petrovich shouted to them.

The women stopped in their tracks and looked up at him
with astonishment. They both said, simultaneously: 'What are
you barking at, you old dog?' – and on they went. I felt I wanted
to go and see the manner in which these unhappy children were
unloaded outside the garrison barracks.

'Let's go over to the barracks, Vasily Petrovich!' I called to
Bogoslovsky.

'What for?'

'Let's go and see what they do with them over there.'

Vasily Petrovich made no reply; but when I reached for my
hat, he too got up and came along with me. The garrison

barracks to which the transiting party of young Jewish recruits were being taken was quite some distance from our house. When we arrived there, the carts were already empty and the children were standing in double ranks beside them. The party officer, together with an NCO, was carrying out a name-check on them. Onlookers crowded around the ranks of recruits. Near one of the carts several ladies were standing, and a priest wearing a bronze cross on a ribbon of St Vladimir. We went up to this cart. On it sat a boy who was evidently sick: he must have been about nine years old, and he was voraciously eating a cottage-cheese pie. Another boy was lying down, covered with an overcoat and paying no attention to anything; by his flushed features and his eyes, which burned with an unhealthy glitter, it could be deduced that he had a fever – possibly typhus.

'Are you ill?' one of the ladies asked the boy who was swallowing chunks of pie without even bothering to chew them.

'Ah?'

'Are you ill?'

The boy shook his head.

'You're not ill?'

Again the boy shook his head.

'Him no comprenay,' the priest observed, and then asked, almost immediately, 'Are you baptized?'

The lad thought about this, as if he had recognized something familiar about the question, and, once more agitating his head from side to side, said: *'Ne-ne.'*

'What a pretty boy he is,' the lady said, taking the lad by the chin and raising his comely face with its black-pupilled eyes.

'Where's your mother?' Musk-Ox asked him suddenly, giving the lad's overcoat a slight tug.

The lad trembled, looked at Vasily Petrovich, then at the people standing round, then at the NCO, and again at Vasily Petrovich.

'Your mother, your mother – where is she?' Musk-Ox repeated.

'Mama?'

'Yes, your mama, your mama?'

'Mama—' The boy waved his hand towards the distance.

'At home?'

The recruit thought for a bit and then nodded his head in agreement.

'He still has his wits about him,' the priest interjected, and asked: 'You have brothers?'

The child made a barely perceptible sign of negation.

'Boy lying, you lying – they no take only sons for recruits. Lying *nicht gut*, *nein*,' the priest continued, imagining that his pidgin Russian was making his side of the conversation more easily understood.

'I vagrantsir.'

'Wha – at?'

'Vagrantsir,' the boy said, more distinctly this time.

'Aha, a vagrantsir! In plain Russian that means he's a vagrant, given to a life of vagrancy. There's a law against them, against those Jewish lads, I've read about it . . . They're clamping down on vagrancy. Well, and quite right, too: a settled person has to stay at home, but it doesn't cost a vagrant a copeck to wander, and he can take holy baptism and mend his ways and end up a respected member of society,' said the priest. Just then, however, the name-check came to an end, and the NCO, pulling the horse by its bridle, tugged the cart with its load of recruits over to the front entrance of the barracks, where more young recruits were creeping forwards in a long line, trailing their kitbags and the skirts of their ungainly overcoats behind them. I began to look round to see if I could see my Musk-Ox; but there was no sign of him. Neither was there any sign of him that night, nor the following day, nor by dinner-time on the day after that. The servant-boy was sent to Vasily Petrovich's flat, where he lived together with some other seminarists – but he was not there either. The young seminarists with whom Musk-Ox lived had long since grown accustomed to not seeing Vasily Petrovich for whole weeks on end, and they had paid no attention to his disappearance. Chelnovsky was not in the slightest perturbed, either.

'He'll be back,' he would say. 'He's off wandering somewhere, or sleeping in some ryefield – that's all.'

To the reader it should perhaps be explained that Vasily Petrovich was, in accordance with a favourite expression of his, very fond of 'lairs', of which he had rather many. The bed-stead, with its bare boards, which stood in his room never held his body for long. Only now and again, when he called in at his home, would he lie down in it, compose a snap examination for the boys with some curious question or other at the end of each test, and then the bed would once again remain empty for a while. Only rarely did he sleep the night at our house, and then usually either on the porch or, if a heated discussion had begun during the evening and had not come to an end by bed-time, on the floor between our beds, with nothing underneath him but a thin floor-cloth. He would leave the house early in the morning and either go into the fields or to the cemetery. He visited the cemetery every day. There he would lie down on a grassy grave, open some paper-bound work by a classical Latin author, and proceed to read it; or he might roll the book up, put it under his head, and gaze up at the sky.

'You're a denizen of the graves, Vasily Petrovich,' Chelnov-sky's daughters, with whom he was on friendly terms, would say to him.

'Such silly nonsense you talk,' Vasily Petrovich would reply.

'You're a vampire,' the pale local schoolmaster, who had acquired the reputation of being something of a literary man ever since the local newspaper had published a learned article of his, would tell him.

'Such silly nonsense you write,' Musk-Ox would reply, and set off once again in the direction of his deceased friends.

Vasily Petrovich's eccentricities had accustomed the small cir-cle of his acquaintances not to be astonished by his escapades, and it was for this reason that no one was surprised by his swift and unexpected disappearance. He would have to come back again, and he would do so. No one was in any doubt about that: the only question was – where had he disappeared to? What part of the world was he wandering about in? What had caused him such irritation, and how would he get over it? These were questions the solution of which added some much-needed enlivenment to the tedium of my waking hours.

3

Another three days went by. The weather was magnificent. Our Russian nature, with all its might and generous splendour, came fully into its own. It was the time of the new moon. The hot days were followed by wonderful, light nights. At times such as these the inhabitants of Kursk would take delight in the singing of their local nightingales, which warbled to them for whole nights on end, as they in turn sat listening for whole nights on end in their large and leafy town gardens. Everyone went about softly and quietly, and only the young schoolmasters argued heatedly about 'emotions lofty and exalted', or about 'dilettantism in science.'[1] Heated, indeed, were those arguments. Even in the most remote flowerbeds of the old park one could hear the exclamations reverberating across through the air: 'That's a dilemma!', 'Oh, but you're mistaken!', 'You can't use *a priori* reasoning', 'Take an inductive approach!', and the like. Back then we still held arguments about matters such as these. Nowadays one never hears arguments of that type. 'To each season its bird, and to each bird its song.' Russian middle-class society is not at all the same nowadays as it was when I lived in Kursk at the period during which the events of my story took place. The questions that preoccupy us today had not even been raised back then, and in many a head romanticism reigned freely and powerfully; reigned, what is more, without any premonition of the new trends which would exact their claims on the Russian individual, and which the Russian individual of a certain level of personal development would accept in the way he accepts all things – not, that is to say, with unalloyed sincerity, but with passion, affectation, and a bit too much seasoning. In those days men were still not too embarrassed to talk about lofty and exalted emotions, and women were in love with ideal heroes, listened to the nightingales warbling in the dense shrubs of the flowering lilac, and drank in the words of the sombre wood-doves who escorted them, arm in arm, down shady, tree-lined alleys and solved with them the recondite enigmas of 'sacred love'.

Chelnovsky and I remained in the park until midnight, heard many fine things concerning exalted and sacred love, and at length retired to our beds feeling well-satisfied. Although all the lights had already been extinguished in our house, we did not fall asleep at once; as we lay there, we related to each other our impressions of the evening. The night stretched around us in all its immensity, and a nightingale chattered loudly right below our window, pouring out its passionate song. We were just getting ready to wish each other good-night when suddenly, from the other side of the fence that stood between the street and the small garden on to which our bedroom window gave, someone called:

'Chaps!'

'That's Musk-Ox,' Chelnovsky said, quickly raising his head from his pillow.

I said I thought it couldn't possibly be him.

'No, it's Musk-Ox, all right,' Chelnovsky insisted and, getting up from his bed, he went over and put his head out of the window.

All was quiet.

'Chaps!' the same voice called from down by the fence.

'Musk-Ox?' Chelnovsky called.

'Yes, it's me.'

'Come on in!'

'The gate's locked.'

'Try knocking, then.'

'Why wake anyone up? I just wanted to find out if you were asleep or not.'

Behind the fence several heavy movements could be heard, and then, like a sack of potatoes hitting the ground, Vasily Petrovich tumbled into the garden.

'What an old devil you are!' Chelnovsky said, laughing, as he watched Vasily Petrovich get up off the ground and start threading his way through the dense shrubs of acacia and lilac.

'Hullo there!' said Musk-Ox, cheerfully, appearing in the window.

Chelnovsky moved the small table on which our toilet things stood away from the window, and Vasily Petrovich put one of his legs inside. Sitting astride the windowsill, he then hauled his other leg in, and finally the whole of him appeared in our room.

'God, I'm exhausted!' he said, taking off his coat and shaking hands with us.

'How many versts have you travelled?' Chelnovsky asked him, lying down on his bed again.

'I've been in Pogodovo.'

'With the innkeeper?'

'That's right.'

'Will you have something to eat?'

'Yes, I will, if there is anything.'

'Go and wake the boy up, then.'

'Oh, leave him be, the milksop!'

'Why?'

'Let him have his sleep.'

'Still playing the holy fool, are you?' said Chelnovsky, then loudly bellowed: 'Moses!'

'Don't wake him up, I tell you: let him sleep.'

'Well, I'll never be able to find you anything to eat on my own.'

'Oh, it doesn't matter.'

'But you're hungry, aren't you?'

'It doesn't matter, I said. Look, I say, chaps, it's like this . . .'

'What, old fellow?'

'I've come to say goodbye to you.'

Vasily Petrovich sat down on Chelnovsky's bed and seized him cordially by the knee.

'Goodbye?'

'Haven't you ever heard of people saying goodbye before?'

'Where are you off to now?'

'Somewhere far away, dear chaps.'

Chelnovsky rose to his feet and lit a candle. Vasily Petrovich remained seated; in his face one could read calm, and even happiness.

'Let me take a look at you,' Chelnovsky said.

'By all means,' Musk-Ox replied, smiling his awkward smile.

'What's that innkeeper of yours up to these days?'

'Selling hay and oats.'

'And I suppose you and he talked about "falsehoods unpunished, and insults unbounded"?'

'We did.'

'And was it he who suggested you undertake a pilgrimage?'

'No, it was my own idea.'

'And pray, what Palestines are you bound for?'

'The ones in Perm.'

'Perm?'

'Yes, what's so unusual about that?'

'Forget something there, did you?'

Vasily Petrovich got up, strode about the room, twirling the forelocks at his temples, and muttered to himself: 'That's my business.'

'Oh, Vasya, you're playing the fool again,' Chelnovsky said.

Musk-Ox was silent, and so were we.

It was an oppressive silence. Both Chelnovsky and I realized that before us stood an agitator – a sincere and fearless agitator. Realizing that we had realized this, he suddenly shouted:

'What am I to do? My heart won't endure this civilization, this nobilization, this villainization! . . .' And he struck himself hard on the chest with one fist, and sank heavily into an armchair.

'But what will you do?'

'Oh, if only I knew what to do! Oh, if only I knew . . . I'm simply feeling my way.'

Neither of us said anything.

'Is it all right if I smoke?' Bogoslovsky asked, after a lengthy pause.

'Please go ahead.'

'I'll stretch out on your floor – it'll be my Last Supper.'

'Excellent.'

'Let's talk for a bit – you know … I can keep silent for so long, but then I feel like talking.'

'There's something worrying you, isn't there?'

'I feel sorry for the lads,' he said, spitting.

'What lads?'

'My lads, my Bible boys.'

'Why do you feel sorry for them?'

'Without me they'll go from bad to worse.'

'You don't exactly make them any better yourself.'

'That's not true.'

'Of course it is: they're taught one thing, and you teach them another.'

'Well, so what if I do?'

'They won't turn out well.'

A pause ensued.

'Look, I tell you what,' Chelnovsky said. 'You ought to find a woman and marry her, and then settle down with your old mother and be a good priest – that's the best thing you could possibly do.'

'Don't say that! Don't say that to me!'

'Well, it's up to you,' Chelnovsky retorted, with a wave of his arm.

Once again, Vasily Petrovich started to pace about the room. Coming to a halt beside the window, he declaimed:

> 'Stand alone before the storm,
> And call no wife unto your side.'[2]

'He knows some poetry, too,' Chelnovsky said, smiling to me and pointing at Vasily Petrovich.

'Only the sensible kind,' the latter replied, remaining over by the window.

'There's quite a lot of sensible poetry, Vasily Petrovich,' I said.

'It's all rubbish.'

'And are women rubbish, too?'

'Yes.'

'And what about Lidochka?'

'What about her?' said Vasily Petrovich, hearing mentioned the name of a very pretty and singularly unfortunate girl – the only female person in the town who paid him any attention at all.

'Won't you miss her?'

'What's that you say?' asked Musk-Ox, his eyes widening. He fixed them stonily on me.

'Just that. Won't you miss her? She's a pretty girl.'

'So what if she is?'

Vasily Petrovich said nothing for a moment. He knocked the contents of his pipe out on the windowsill, and reflected.

'Wretches!' he said, lighting another pipeful of tobacco.

Chelnovsky and I burst out laughing.

'What's got into you?' Vasily Petrovich asked.

'Is it the ladies you're calling wretches?'

'The ladies? No, the Jews.'

'What's put the Jews into your head all of a sudden?'

'The devil knows. I have a mother, and each of them has a mother,' Vasily Petrovich replied. Blowing out the candle, he lay down on his floor-cloth, his pipe stuck between his teeth.

'Haven't you got them out of your head yet?'

'I've a long memory, old chap.'

Vasily Petrovich sighed heavily.

'They'll die on the journey, the milksops.'

'Very likely.'

'And just as well, too.'

'That's a complicated kind of sympathy he has,' Chelnovsky said.

'No, it's you who're the complicated ones. With me, old chap, everything's simple, peasant-like. I can't make head nor tail of all your la-de-da's. The way you want it is for the sheep to be unharmed and the wolves to be fed – but that's not possible. Things just aren't like that.'

'How do you think the world ought to be run, then?'

'The way God proposes.'

'God doesn't intervene personally in human affairs.'

'No – of course, his servants, human beings, will do it all.'

'When they become servants,' Chelnovsky said.

'Oh, you clever dicks! To look at you, you'd think you knew it all, but you don't know a thing,' Vasily Petrovich exclaimed forcefully. 'You can't see further than the end of your gentrified noses. If you were in my shoes and had lived among the kind of people I meet on my travels you'd soon realize that it's no good whimpering and whining. How do you like that, he's got gentrified habits, too!' Musk-Ox said suddenly, getting to his feet.

'Who has?'

'The dog, Box. Who do you think?'

'What are his gentrified habits?' Chelnovsky inquired.

'He doesn't even close the door after him.'

Only now did we notice that there was indeed quite a draught in the room.

Vasily Petrovich got up, closed the door that gave on to the passage, and fastened it by its hook.

'Thank you,' Chelnovksy said to him when he returned and stretched out on his floor-cloth once more.

Vasily Petrovich was silent for a while. Then, after he had refilled his pipe and lit it, he suddenly asked:

'What are they lying about in their books?'

'Which books?'

'Those journals of yours.'

'Oh, people are writing all sorts of things, there's no end to it.'

'I bet they're still going on about progress, eh?'

'Yes, they are.'

'And the common people?'

'They write about the common people, too.'

'Oh, a plague on those scribes and Pharisees!' Musk-Ox said, uttering a sigh. 'They blab their heads off, yet they don't know a thing.'

'Vasily Petrovich, why have you got it into your head that no one knows anything about the common people except you yourself? It's just sheer plain vanity, old man.'

'No, it isn't. What it is is that I can see the rotten way in which everyone deals with that problem. It's all talk with them, but when it comes to action, there's nobody there. No, you should get on with the matter in hand, and stop telling lies. Otherwise all your love and compassion will just burn up and turn to smoke over dinner. Tales, they write. Short stories!' he added, after a brief pause. 'Ah, the scribes! The accursed Pharisees! I can guarantee you they never let themselves get carried away. They're afraid of choking on all that mealy stuff. But anyway, it's just as well they don't let themselves get carried away,' he added, after a short silence.

'Why so?'

'Because it's as I tell you: they'd choke on their mealy stuff, and then they'd have to be slapped on the back to give them their wind back, and they'd shout: "We're being beaten up!" Are those the sort of people to trust? No, what you ought to do,' he said, sitting up on his makeshift bed, 'is to try living the way I do, without coming to grief; try living on bread and water, keeping a stiff upper lip and never suffering fools gladly: then people will trust you. Curse your own soul so that others may see what sort of a soul you have, and stop playing around with paltry lies. People, my people! What would I not do for you? . . . People, my people! What would I not sacrifice for your sake?' Vasily Petrovich reflected for a moment, then raised himself to his full height and, stretching out his arms towards Chelnovsky and myself, said: 'My good fellows! Troubled days are approaching, troubled days! The hour cannot be far off, for the false prophets come, and I hear their accursed and hateful voices. In the people's name they will endeavour to lay snares for you and undo you. But do not fear their command and, if you feel not the strength of oxen in your backs, accept not the yoke upon them. It is not a question of numbers. You won't catch a flea with five fingers, but with one you will. I do not expect much of you. That isn't your fault – the flesh is willing, but the spirit is weak. I beg you, though, follow my one brotherly commandment: "Do not tell lies!" For I tell you, there is great harm therein. Yea, harm! Wherever you set your feet, you will pay the price – but for us Musk-Oxen,' he said, striking his breast, 'that is not enough. The retribution of Heaven will fall upon us if we rest content with that. "We are our own men, and our own will recognize us."'

Vasily Petrovich spoke powerfully and at length. Never before had he said so much, or expressed himself with such clarity. The dawn was already beginning to glimmer in the sky, and the room was noticeably acquiring a grey luminescence; but Vasily Petrovich was not done yet. His stocky figure was making energetic movements, and through the tears in his old cotton shirt we could see the prominent thrust of his hairy chest.

At around four we finally got to sleep. We awoke at nine. Musk-Ox had already gone, and we were not to see him again for three years to the day. The strange fellow set out that morning for a part of the world which had been recommended to him by his friend, the innkeeper at Pogodovo.

4

There are in our province a good many monasteries, which are situated in the forests and are known as 'hermitages'. My grandmother was a very religious old lady. A woman who belonged to an earlier age, she was inordinately fond of travelling around these hermitages. Not only did she know by heart the history of each one of these secluded monasteries – she was also familiar with all the legends associated with them, the history of their icons, the miracles which had been reported in them, the means commanded by each, what type of sacristy it had, and so on. She was a decrepit, but living guide to the ecclesiastical heritage of our part of the world. Everyone in the monasteries was likewise familiar with the old lady, and they would welcome her with unusual cordiality, in spite of the fact that she never made any donations more valuable than her patens, the embroidery of which would take her an entire autumn and winter, seasons when the weather prevented her from travelling. In the hospices of the hermitages at P— and L—[1] two rooms were always put at her disposal during the feasts of St Peter and the Assumption. They were swept and cleaned, and no one else was permitted to use them, not even on the eve of the feasts themselves.

'Aleksandra Vasilyevna's coming,' the Father Almoner would say to anyone who happened to turn up. 'I can't let you have her rooms.'

And, unfailingly, my grandmother would arrive.

On one occasion she was for some reason very late in arriving, and a large number of people had come to the hospice for the feast. Late in the night, just before matins, a general arrived, and demanded that he be given the best rooms available. The Father Almoner found himself in a difficult position. It was the first time that my grandmother had ever missed the tutelary feast at the hermitage chapel. 'The old woman must have died,' he reflected; but, taking a look at his pocket watch and observing that there were still two hours to go before matins commenced, he refused none the less to let the general have the rooms, and calmly repaired to his cell in order to recite his 'midnight vespers'. The great monastery bell tolled three times; in the chapel a taper glimmered, and by its light a lay brother could be seen fussing about in front of the iconostasis as he lit the candles. The common people, yawning a bit and making the sign of the cross over their mouths, were thronging inside, and my dear old grandmother, attired in a dapper grey dress and a snow-white cap of the type that was fashionable in Moscow during the year 1812, was already on her way in through the north door, piously crossing herself and whispering: 'Towards morning hear my voice, O my King and my Saviour.' By the time the hierodeacon started to intone his solemn 'Arise!', my grandmother had installed herself in a dark corner and was bowing to the ground in supplication for the souls of the departed. As he admitted the pilgrims to the crucifix at the end of the service in order to allow them to kiss it, the Father Almoner was not in the least surprised to see the old woman and, as he gave her the blessed bread from under his cassock, he said very calmly: 'Good evening, Mother Aleksandra!' In the hermitages it was only the young novices who called my grandmother 'Aleksandra Vasilyevna'; the older monks always addressed her as 'Mother Aleksandra'. At no time in her life, however, had our devout old lady been a hypocrite, and she never posed as a nun. Her fifty years notwithstanding, she unfailingly dressed as neatly as a heron. Her spotless grey or green cotton dress, her tall lace cap with its grey ribbons and her reticule with a dog embroidered on it – everything the good-natured old lady wore was fresh and guilelessly winsome. She trundled around the hermitages in a country-style springless hooded cart, drawn by a pair of old chestnut fillies of the very finest lineage. One of these – the mother – was called 'Fine Lady', and the other (the daughter) bore the name 'Surprise'. The latter had acquired her name from the circumstance of having arrived unexpectedly in the world. Both of these small horses of grandmother's were unusually docile, swift-legged and well-behaved, and to travel with the officious old lady and her most good-natured old companion the coachman Ilya Vasilyevich was one of the most intense delights of all my childhood years.

I had been one of the old lady's aides-de-camp from a very early age. When I was only six, I set off with her and her chestnut fillies, on the first such trip I had made, to visit the L— hermitage, and subsequently accompanied her on each of her excursions, until at the age of ten I was sent to attend classes at the local gymnasium. Those trips around the monasteries contained much that was very attractive to me. The old lady was able to impart an unusual degree of poetic awareness to her friends. We used to travel at a jog-trot. Everything around us was so lovely: the scent-laden air, the jackdaws hiding in the greenery, the people we encountered on the way, who would bow to us, and to whom we would bow back in return. When we came to woods, we would dismount and go through them on foot. My grandmother would tell me about the year 1812, about the gentry of Mozhaisk, about her flight from Moscow, about the arrogant manner in which the French conducted their advance, and about how they were subsequently driven out into the frosts without mercy and defeated. And then suddenly there would be an inn, innkeepers who knew us, women with fat bellies wearing aprons tied above their breasts, spacious common pastures where we could run about – all this used to captivate me, and possessed for me a fascinating charm. In her room my grandmother would begin to see to her toilet, and I would set off under the cool, shady canopy of trees to see Ilya Vasilyevich, lie down beside him on a bundle of hay and listen to the story of how Ilya had once driven the Emperor of All the Russias about the streets of Oryol. I would learn what a dangerous task this had been, how many carriages it had involved, and to what risks the Emperor's own coach had been exposed, when during his descent towards the River Orlik[2] the reins had snapped in the hands of the coachman and how thereupon he, Ilya Vasilyevich, had by his own quick thinking saved the life of the Emperor, who had been on the point of leaping from the conveyance. The Ithacans did not listen to Odysseus with half the attention I paid to Ilya Vasilyevich the coachman. In the hermitages themselves, I had friends. Two old men in particular were fond of me: the Father Superior of the P— hermitage, and the Father Almoner at the L— hermitage. The former was a tall, pale old man with a kind but stern face – he did not, however, enjoy my affection; the Father Almoner, on the other hand, I loved with all the ardour of my young heart. He was the most good-natured creature in all the sublunar world, a world of which, incidentally, he knew nothing; yet it seems to me that in this old man's very ignorance lay the foundation of his boundless love of humanity.

But in addition to these, as it were, aristocratic friendships with the leaders of the hermitages, I also had democratic relations with the monastic plebeians. I was very attached to the novices, that strange class of men in which, as a rule, two passions – laziness and vanity – predominate. In them, however, one sometimes encounters a store of cheerful unconcern and an authentically Russian indifference to the vicissitudes of their own fortunes.

'So did you feel a calling to enter a monastery?' you might ask one of them.

'No,' he would reply. 'There was no calling, I just went.'

'And will you take holy orders?'

'Certainly.'

Leaving the monastery is always something that seems to the novice quite impossible, even though he knows that no one will prevent him from doing so. As a child I was very fond of these men – they were cheerful, waggish, courageous and good-naturedly hypocritical. As long as a novice is merely a novice – or 'sluggard' – no one pays any attention to him, and consequently no one knows what sort of a person he is. But from the time that the novice dons his surplice and hood, there is a sudden alteration in both his character and his relation to those who are close to him. While he is a novice, he is an uncommonly sociable creature. What Homeric fistfights I remember in the monastery bakehouses! What daring songs were sung in an undertone on the hermitage walls, when five or six handsome novices were slowly walking along them and looking intently down across the river, on whose opposite bank the resonant, enticing voices of women were singing another song – one in which there sounded the winged calls of 'hurl yourselves, throw yourselves, into the green oak groves'. And I remember how the sluggards would hesitate when they heard these songs, and then, unable to restrain themselves, would rush off into the green oak groves. Oh, I remember all that so well! I have not forgotten one single lesson I learned: neither the singing of the cantatas which were composed on the most unusual of subjects, nor the gymnastics we did, not entirely facilitated by the high monastery walls, nor the acquisition of the ability to keep silent and to laugh while maintaining a serious expression on one's face. But most of all I loved the fishing in the monastery lake. My friends the novices also regarded an outing on the lake as something of a holiday. Within the framework of their monotonous lives, fishing was the sole occupation in the exercise of which they could let go for a while and try out the strength of their youthful muscles. And indeed, there was much in these fishing trips that was poetic. From the monastery to the lake it was a distance of some eight or ten versts, which had to be traversed on foot through a very dense deciduous forest. We generally used to set off on these fishing excursions before vespers. In the cart, which was drawn by a very fat old monastery horse, lay a sweep-net, several buckets, a barrel for the fish, and some hooks; no one sat in the cart, however. The reins would be tied to the cart's front edge, and if the horse wandered off the straight the novice who acted as driver would simply step up and give them a tug. But, in practice, the horse scarcely ever wandered off the road, and it would indeed have been impossible for him to do so, since there was only one road leading from the monastery through the woods to the lake, and it was such a winding one that the horse would never have felt like dragging the wheels out of the deep ruts. Sent along to keep an eye on us was the Elder Ignatius, a deaf and weak-sighted old monk who had once received the Emperor Alexander I in his

cell and who could never remember that Alexander I was no
longer on the throne. Father Ignatius travelled in a tiny cart of
his own, which was drawn by another fat horse that he drove
himself. As for myself, I always had the privilege of being
allowed to ride in Father Ignatius's cart, since my grandmother
had given special instructions that this should be so, and Father
Ignatius even let me drive the fat horse which was harnessed
between the abbreviated shafts of his cart; but I generally preferred to walk with the novices, who never kept to the road.
Very gradually, we would enter the woods, and would start by
singing: 'As a young monk was walking along, he met Jesus
Christ a-coming his way,' and then someone would break into
another song, and so we would sing them, one after the other.
Dear, careless time! A blessing on you, and a blessing on you
who gave me these memories. Only towards nightfall did we
approach the lake. There on the shore stood a small cabin in
which two old men who were cassocked novices lived: Father
Sergius and Father Vavila. They were both 'bookless', that is to
say, they could neither read nor write, and were executing a
vow of 'tutelary obedience' with regard to the wardenship of
the monastery lake. Father Sergius was an uncommonly skilful
handicraftsman. I still have in my possession a beautiful spoon
and an ornamental crucifix, both of his manufacture. He also
used to weave nets, and make peg-tops, bast and wicker baskets and various other similar items. He had a very skilfully
carved wooden statuette of some saint or other; but he only
showed it to me once, and then only on condition that I told no
one else about it. Father Vavila, on the other hand, did no form
of work. He was a poet, and 'loved freedom, laziness and rest'.
He was willing to remain looking out over the lake for hours
on end in a contemplative position, observing the flight of the
wild duck and the wading of the portly heron, which from time
to time pulled from the water the frogs who had managed to
persuade Zeus to make the heron their king. Immediately in
front of the cabin that belonged to the two 'bookless' monks
stretched a wide, sandy beach, and beyond it the lake. Everything inside the cabin was very clean: two icons stood on the
mantelpiece; there were two heavy, wooden beds, painted with

green oil paint; a table, covered with a plain cloth; two chairs; and along the walls, plain benches, as in a Russian peasants' *izba*. In the corner there was a small cupboard which contained a tea-service, and underneath the cupboard, on a special rest of its own, stood the samovar, which was kept polished as though it were the boiler of the Royal Yacht. Everything was very clean and comfortable. No one else lived in the cell of the 'bookless' fathers except for a marmalade cat which was called 'Captain', and whose only remarkable feature was that, bearing a masculine name and having been for a long time regarded as a male, he had suddenly, to the great consternation of all concerned, had kittens, and from that day forward had not ceased to multiply his progeny as befitted a proper she-cat.

Father Ignatius was the only member of our convoy who slept in the cabin of the 'bookless' fathers. I generally sought to decline this honour, and slept in the company of the novices out in the open, beside the cabin. We hardly really slept at all, however. We would light a fire, bring a pot of water to the boil, pour oatmeal flour into it to make a thin gruel, throw in a few dried carp, and then eat the mixture from a large wooden bowl. By that time it would already be midnight. But no sooner would we have lain ourselves down, than someone would immediately begin to tell a tall story, one which would be sure to be either extremely frightening or extremely shocking. From tall stories we would pass to true stories, and to these each narrator, as was the custom, would always 'add fables without number'. Frequently the night would pass in this fashion without any of us ever having had a wink of sleep. The subjects of the stories were usually wanderers and brigands. A particularly large repertoire of these stories was commanded by Timofey Nevstruyev, an older lay brother who enjoyed among us the reputation of being invincibly strong, and who was forever preparing to go off and fight in the war for the liberation of the Christians, and thus personally 'put all the heathens out of action'. He seemed to have traversed the length and breadth of all Russia, had even visited Palestine and Greece, and had observed that 'it wouldn't be so hard to cook their goose'. We would lie down on our sacking; the fire would still be smoking; the fat horses, which

had been tethered with their oatbags on, would snort as they
fed, and someone would start to tell another story. I have now
forgotten most of those stories, and recall only the ones I heard
on my last night which, thanks to my grandmother's leniency,
I was allowed to spend with the novices on the shore of Lake
P——. Timofey Nevstruyev was not really in the mood – he had
spent that day standing in prayer in the chapel as a penance for
having climbed over the wall of the Father Superior's orchard
during the previous night – and so Yemelyan Vysotsky, a young
man of about eighteen, began to tell a story. His family came
from Kurland; as a child he had been abandoned in our province and had become a novice. His mother had been a vaudeville
actress, and that was the only thing we knew about her; he had
been brought up by some merchant's wife who had taken pity
on the nine-year-old boy and placed him in the monastery as a
novice. The conversation began when, at the end of one of the
stories that had been told, one of the novices gave a deep sigh,
and asked:

'Why aren't there any good brigands nowadays, Brothers?'

No one ventured any reply, and this question began to torment me – it was one I had long been unable to permit myself.
In those days I was very fond of brigands and in my exercise-
books I used to draw pictures of them dressed in capes with red
feathers in their hats.

'There are still brigands, even now,' the Kurlandian novice
retorted in a reedy little voice.

'All right, tell us what they're like, then,' said Nevstruyev,
covering himself right up to his chin with his calico surplice.

'Well, when I used to live in Puzanikha,' the Kurlander
began, 'I once went with Mother Natalya of Borovsk, and
Alyona, another wandering pilgrim from Chernigov, on a pilgrimage to the icon of Nicholas the Devout of Amchensk*.'

'Which Natalya was that? The tall, fair-complexioned one?
Was it her?' Nevstruyev asked, interrupting him.

'Yes,' the narrator replied, hastily, and continued:

---

* i.e. of the town of Mtsensk, where there is a carved wooden icon of St Nicholas.
(Leskov's note.)

'Well, there's a village you pass through on the way there called Otrada. Twenty-five versts from Oryol. We arrived there towards evening, and asked some peasants if we could spend the night in their house – but they wouldn't let us; well, so we went to the inn, instead. At the inn we were only charged half a copeck each, but it was terribly overcrowded! All the guests were flaxbeaters. There must have been about forty of them there. They were drinking to get drunk, and there was so much foul language that we couldn't get out quickly enough. In the morning, when Mother Natalya woke me, most of the flax-beaters had gone. There were only three of them left, and they were tying their travelling-bags to their scutchers. We did up our bags, too, paid one-and-a-half copecks for our night's lodg-ings, and also left. When we were out of the village we looked behind us and saw that those same three flaxbeaters were on our tail. Well, if they were, they were. We thought nothing of it. Only Mother Natalya remarked: "That's funny! Yesterday," she said, "those same flaxbeaters said after they'd had their supper that they were headed for Oryol, yet today – look, they're following us to Amchensk." We continued on our way, and the flaxbeaters kept following us at a distance. And then we came to a small wood. As we approached it, the flaxbeaters began to catch up with us. We quickened our pace, but so did they. "What are you running for?" they said. "You won't get away from us." And then two of them grabbed Mother Natalya by the arms. She screamed in a voice that didn't sound like her own, and Mother Alyona and I made a run for it. As we ran, they roared after us: "Get them, get them!" All we could hear was their bawling, and the cries of Mother Natalya. "They've probably slit her throat!" we thought, and that made us feel even worse. Alyona's eyes were fairly popping out of her head, and my legs had given way under me. I realized I had no strength left, and so I threw myself under a bush. "What hap-pens now is God's will," I thought, as I lay there getting my breath back. I kept expecting them to fly at us, but nobody came. All I could hear was them still struggling with Mother Natalya. "She's a strong, healthy woman," I thought. "They won't be able to do her in." It was quiet in the woods, I could hear every single sound. Suddenly I heard Mother Natalya give another scream. "Well," I thought, "God rest her soul." As for myself, I didn't know whether to make a run for it or just lie there, and wait for some kind person to come along. Then I thought I heard someone coming close. I lay there more dead than alive, and peeped out from the bush. What do you think I saw, Brothers? It was Mother Natalya! Her black kerchief had fallen from her head; her light brown pigtail – it was a magnificent one – was all dishevelled; she was still clutching her bag, but she was stumbling. "I'll call out to her," I thought; and I did so, but only in an undertone. She stopped and looked at the bushes, and I called to her again. "Who's that?" she said. I jumped out to greet her, and she fairly gasped with surprise. I looked round – there was no one either behind us or ahead of us. "Will they catch up with us?" I asked her. "We'd better run, quickly!" But she just stood there as if she were frozen, and only her lips trembled. I took a look at her: her dress had been ripped to tatters, her arms were covered in scratches, right up to the elbows, and her forehead was also covered in scratches that looked as if they had been made by fingernails. "Let's be off," I said to her again. "Did they try to strangle you?" I asked her. "Yes, they did," she said. "Let's get out of here quickly." And off we went. "How did you manage to shake them off?" I asked her. But she wouldn't say anything more until we reached the village, where we met Mother Alyona.'

'Well, and what did she say when you arrived?' Nevstruyev asked. Like the others, he had preserved a deathly silence during the entirety of this narrative.

'All she would say was that they'd gone chasing after her, but that she'd kept praying and had thrown sand in their eyes.'

'And they didn't take anything from her?' someone asked.

'Not a thing. She only lost one of her shoes, and the amulet from around her neck. She said they kept looking to see if she had any money concealed in her bosom.'

'Oh yes, some brigands those were: all they cared about was getting at her bosom,' Nevstruyev said, following this remark by telling a story about some higher-class brigands who had given him a nasty scare in the district of Oboyansk. 'Now those,' he said, 'were real brigands.'

'I was once walking back from the fair at Korennaya,' he began. 'I'd gone there to fulfil a vow in connection with a toothache. All the money I had with me was a couple of roubles and a travelling-bag containing my shirts. En route I fell in with two chaps who said they were . . . tradesmen. "Where are you headed for?" they asked me. "For So-and-So," I said. "Oh," they said. "We're going to So-and-So, too. Let's travel together." "All right," I said. And off we went. We arrived at a village; it was already getting dark. "Come on," I said to them. "Let's sleep the night here." But they said: "This is a terrible place; let's walk another few versts: there's an inn further up the road, a big one, with all the conveniences." "I don't want your conveniences," I told them. "Come on," they said, "it's not as if it was very far." Well, on we went. And, true enough, five versts or so further up the road we came to an inn which could certainly not have been described as small – it looked like a staging-post. There was light in two of the windows. One of the tradesmen banged the knocker, the dogs in the hallway began to bark, but nobody came to the door. The tradesman knocked again. This time we heard someone come out of the interior of the house and call to us; we could tell it was a woman's voice. "Who are you?" she asked, and the tradesman said: "Friends." "Friends from where?" "Some from here and some from there." Then the door was unbolted. The hallway was pitch dark. The woman bolted the door behind us and led us into the interior. There were no men to be seen anywhere – there was only the woman who had let us in and another, pock-marked woman who was teasing flax. "Well, good evening, chieftainess!" the tradesman said to the one who had let us in. "Good evening," the woman replied, and suddenly she started giving me the eye. I looked back at her. She was a big, sturdy woman of about thirty; she was fair-complexioned, the rogue, with rosy cheeks and bossy eyes. "Where did you get this young fellow from?" she asked. That was me she was talking about, you see. "We'll tell you later," they said. "But first give us something to get our teeth around, or else they'll fall out from lack of use." We were served with pressed beef, horse-radish, some pies and a bottle of vodka. "Eat!" the tradesmen said to me. "No," I said, "I don't eat meat." "Well, have a cottage-cheese pie, then." I took one. "Have a glass of vodka," they said. I drank a glassful. "Have another," they said; and I had another. "How would you like to live with us?" they said. "How do you mean – live with you?" I asked. "Well, it's as you see: it's inconvenient for us being just the pair – if you join us on the road you can eat and drink with us, too . . . all you have to do is obey the chieftainess . . . How would you like that?" These men are up to no good, I thought. I've fallen into bad company. "No, fellows; I don't want to live with you." "Why ever not?" they asked. And they started to ply me with vodka again, and kept on at me, saying: "Drink, drink." "Do you know how to fight?" one of them asked me. "I never learned," I said. "Well, if you never learned, here's a lesson for you," one of them said, and landed me a whistling blow on the ear. The inn lady said not a word, and the other woman went on teasing her flax. "What was that for?" I asked. "Don't go poking your nose in where you're not wanted," the tradesman said, and landed me one on the other ear to match. Well, I thought, I've got nothing to lose, and I swung round and socked him one on the back of his neck. Knocked him fair and square under the table, I did. When he crawled out from under it he was groaning fit to burst. He pushed his hair back with one hand and then made straight for the bottle. "Do you want to meet your end right here and now?" he said. I saw that no one was saying anything, and that his mate was saying nothing either. "No," I said, "I don't want to meet my end." "All right, drink some vodka, then," he said. "I don't want to drink your vodka either," I replied. "Drink!" he said. "The Father Superior won't see, he won't make you do penance." "I don't want any vodka." "Well, go to the Devil then; pay for what you've drunk and go to bed." "How much do I owe you?" I said. "All you've got," he replied. "Ours is expensive stuff, lad – it's called 'the bitter Russian lot', and it's made from tears, water, pepper and the hearts of sons-of-bitches." I tried to make a joke out of it, but it was no good; no sooner had I taken my purse out than the tradesman snatched it from me and flung it over the partition. "Right, now, off you go to bed, monk," he said. "Where am I to sleep?" I asked. "The deaf woman'll show you," he replied. "Show him where he's to sleep!" he shouted to the woman who was teasing flax. I followed her into the passage, and from there out into the courtyard. It was a beautiful night, just like tonight – the Great Bear was gleaming in the sky and a breeze was playing in the woods like a squirrel. I was really beginning to long for my nice, quiet life in the monastery, but the woman opened the door to the cellar storeroom for me – "In you go, you sickly creature," she said; then she left. It was almost as if she felt sorry for me. I went in and felt around inside – there seemed to be something piled up in there, but what it was I couldn't make out. I felt the centre-post. "I've got nothing to lose," I thought – and I climbed up it. I got up as far as the ceiling beam and the lower roof beam, and began to move the rafters apart. My hands were soon rubbed raw, but I gradually managed to move five of the rafters. I began to dig my way through the straw thatching – and then suddenly I saw the stars. I continued my labours, made a hole, threw my bag out of it first, then crossed myself and finally somersaulted out myself. And I ran, Brothers, I ran, faster than I'd ever run in all my life.'

Many more of these stories would be told, and I found them so fascinating that I would listen to them all, and only barely manage to close my eyes towards dawn. But then Father Ignatius would prod us with his cane and say: 'Get up! It's time we were out on the lake!' The novices would get up and yawn; poor fellows, they were drowsy. They would pick up the sweep-net, take off their shoes and trousers, and go down to the boats. The monastery boats, black and ungainly as loons, were always kept moored to stakes some fifteen sagenes off shore, because there was a long sandbar running out from the beach, and the black boats sat very low in the water and could not pull in to the shore. Nevstruyev used to carry me in his arms all the way along the sandbar to the boats. Well I remember those wadings across, those carefree, good-natured faces. Even now I seem to see the novices wading into the cold water, straight from their slumbers. Jumping up and down, they would laugh and, trembling with cold, would drag the heavy net along, stooping down to the water to freshen their eyes which were still stuck together from sleep. I remember the fine mist that rose from the water, the golden carp and slippery turbot; I remember the exhausting noontides, when we would all flop down on the grass like dead men, refusing the amber-coloured fish soup which Father Sergius prepared for the 'bookless' monks. Even better, I remember the aggrieved, even hate-filled expression on everyone's face when the fat horses were being harnessed – the horses which would draw to the monastery the carts containing the carp we had caught and Father Ignatius, behind whom the 'sluggards' would have to march back within their monastery walls once more.

It was in these very same places, familiar to me from childhood, that I chanced yet once again, quite unexpectedly, to encounter the person of Musk-Ox, after his flight from Kursk.

A lot of water had flowed under the bridge since those days to which my memories relate, memories which have, perhaps, very little connection with Musk-Ox's grim destiny. I was growing up and becoming acquainted with life's sorrows; Grandmother had died; Ilya Vasilyevich, Fine Lady and Surprise were no more; the merry novices had turned into staid, respectable monks; I was sent to the gymnasium for a time, then transferred to the university of a town some sixty versts distant, where I learned to sing one Latin song, read some snippets of Strauss, Feuerbach, Büchner and Babeuf and, replete with knowledge, returned to my *lares* and *penates* once more. It was here that I formed the acquaintance with Vasily Petrovich which I have described. Another four years went by, years I spent in a rather miserable fashion, before finding myself once again beneath my native lime trees. At home during this time no change had taken place either in morals, views or trends of thought. The news was merely of the kind one would have expected: my mother had advanced in age and grown stouter, my fourteen-year-old sister had passed straight from the desk of a young ladies' boarding school to a premature grave, and several new lime trees had grown, planted by her childish hand. 'Can it really be,' I thought, 'that nothing has altered during this time in which I have experienced so much: acquired a faith in God, rejected Him and then rediscovered Him; loved my native land, been crucified with it and been among its crucifiers?' This seemed almost offensive to my youthful vanity, and I determined to carry out a verification of everything – myself and all that surrounded me in those days, when 'all the impressions of

existence were still new to me'.[1] Above all I wanted to see my
beloved hermitages, and one crisp morning I drove my droshky
to the P— hermitage, which lies some twenty or so versts distant from our home. The road was still in the same condition,
the jackdaws still hid in the thick winter crops, the muzhiks
still bowed from the waist, and the peasant women still begged
for alms as they lay in front of their thresholds. Everything was
as it had been in the old days. Here were the familiar hermitage
gates – there was a new gatekeeper now, the former one had
become a monk. But the Father Almoner was still alive. The
ailing old man had by now attained the ninth decade of his
life. There are many such examples of exceptional longevity to
be encountered in our monasteries. The Father Almoner no
longer performed his duties, however, and lived 'in retirement',
although he was still invariably referred to as 'the Father
Almoner'. When I was led in to him, he was lying on his bed;
not recognizing me, he began to grow agitated, and asked the
servant brother: 'Who's this?' Without replying to his question,
I went up to the old man and took him by the hand. 'Good day,
good day,' the Father Almoner muttered; 'Who are you?' I bent
forward, kissed him on the forehead, and spoke his name. 'Oh,
it's you, my little friend! Well, I never, good day!' the old man
said, growing agitated on his bed again. 'Kirill! Prepare the
samovar right away!' he said to the servant brother. 'I can't
walk any more, my friend. For more than a year now my feet
have been all swollen up!' The Father Almoner had dropsy,
which very frequently carries off monks who spend their lives
in prolonged standing in church and in other occupations
which make them susceptible to this illness.

'Tell Vasily Petrovich to come here,' the Almoner said to the
servant brother, when the latter placed the samovar and cups
on the bedside table. 'I have a poor fellow living here,' the old
man added, turning to me.

The servant brother left the room, and a quarter of an hour
later the sound of footsteps and of a distant bellowing could be
heard approaching down the flagstones of the outer passage.
The door opened, and before my astonished gaze appeared –
Musk-Ox. He was dressed in a short *svitka* of Great Russian

peasant cloth, coarse homespun trousers and a pair of tall, rather dilapidated Russian leather boots. By contrast, on his head he had a tall, black hat of the type worn by monastic novices. So little had his physiognomy changed that I recognized him at first sight.

'Vasily Petrovich! Is it you?' I said, going to greet my friend, and at the same time thinking: 'Oh, who better than you can tell me how the years of bitter experience have passed over the heads of those who live here?'

Musk-Ox appeared glad to see me, and the Father Almoner was astonished to see that we appeared to be old friends.

'Well, that's splendid, splendid,' he muttered. 'Pour the tea, Vasya.'

'You know perfectly well that I'm no good at pouring tea,' Musk-Ox replied.

'True, true. Perhaps our guest will pour it, then.'

I began to pour tea into the cups.

'Have you been here long, Vasily Petrovich?' I asked, handing Musk-Ox a cup.

He bit off a piece of sugar, threw it into his tea and, taking two or three gulps, replied:

'About nine months now.'

'Where will you go after this?'

'Nowhere for the meantime.'

'And may I ask where you came here from?' I asked, finding it impossible not to smile as I remembered the way in which Musk-Ox usually used to answer questions of this type.

'You may.'

'From Perm?'

'No.'

'Where, then?'

Musk-Ox drained his cup, set it down, and said:

'I've been everywhere and nowhere.'

'Did you see Chelnovsky?'

'No. I didn't go there.'

'Is your mother still alive?'

'No, she died in the almshouse.'

'Alone?'

'Who doesn't?'

'A long time ago?'

'About a year ago, they say.'

'Off you go and take a walk, boys – I want to have a nap until vespers,' said the Father Almoner, for whom any exertion was difficult.

'No, I want to drive over to the lake,' I replied.

'Aha! Well, off you go, then, and God be with you – you can take Vasya along with you: he'll show you the way.'

'Let's be off, Vasily Petrovich.'

Musk-Ox scratched himself, picked up his hat, and said:

'I daresay.'

We took our leave of the Father Almoner until the next day and went out. In the granary we harnessed up my little mare and drove off. Vasily Petrovich sat behind me, back to back, declaring he was unable to ride in any other fashion, as he could not get enough air if he was facing the back of someone's head. During the ride he got up to all sorts of odd tricks, although he was extremely untalkative, the only question he kept asking me being whether I had met any intelligent people in Moscow, and what had been their opinions. Having ceased to question me, he would begin to whistle – now like a nightingale, now like an oriole.

This continued throughout the whole of the drive.

Outside the cabin that had long been familiar to us we were met by the short, red-haired novice who had taken the place of Father Sergius – he had died some three years earlier, bequeathing his tools and prepared materials to the carefree Father Vavila. Father Vavila was not at home: following his custom, he was walking above the lake, watching a heron swallow some obedient frogs. Father Vavila's new companion was as delighted to see us as a country landowner's daughter is to hear the sound of sleighbells. He rushed to unharness our mare, prepared the samovar himself, and kept assuring us that 'Father Vavila will be back any minute now.' Musk-Ox and I listened to these assurances, sat down on the earth embankment beneath the wall, and both maintained an agreeable silence. Neither of us felt like talking.

The sun had already set behind the tall trees that surrounded the entire monastery lake in a dense thicket. The smooth surface of the water appeared to be almost black. The air was calm, but oppressive.

'We shall have a thunderstorm tonight,' Father Prokhor said as he hauled the bolsters of my racing droshky into the outhouse.

'Why worry about it?' I replied. 'It may not come this way.'

'It's all right, sir, I'm not really worried; but I'll take the mare over into the passage, too,' he said, re-emerging from the cabin.

'But why, Father Prokhor?'

'There's going to be a great storm; if she takes fright, she might break loose. No, sir, I'd better take her into the outhouse. She'll be all right in there.'

Father Prokhor untethered our mare and, going into the outhouse, pulled her by the reins, saying: 'Come on, old girl! Come on, you silly thing! What are you afraid of?'

'That's better,' he said, when he had found a place for the mare in a corner and had poured some oats into an old sieve for her. 'Father Vavila's been away a long time, that's for sure,' he said, walking round the corner of the cabin. 'And now it's beginning to cloud over,' he added, pointing to a greyish-pink cloud.

Outside it had grown quite dark.

'I'm going to take a look and see if I can see Father Vavila coming,' Musk-Ox said and, giving his forelocks a twirl, he strode off into the forest.

'Don't go: you'll never find him.'

'No doubt,' Musk-Ox replied, and with that he set off.

Father Prokhor took an armful of firewood and went into the cabin. Soon the windows were lit by the glow of the fire he had made in the stove, and the water in the billycan began to boil. There was no sign of either Musk-Ox or Father Vavila. Meanwhile the tops of the trees were beginning to sway from time to time, although the surface of the lake was still as smooth as lead. Only occasionally was it possible to observe the white splashes of a playful carp. The frogs, in chorus, kept up their single, monotonous, melancholy note. I continued to sit on the earth embankment, looking over at the dark lake and remembering my past years, which had flown away into the dark distance. Here, in those bygone days, had been moored those ungainly boats, to which the mighty Nevstruyev had carried me; here I had slept beside the novices, when everything had been so pleasant, so cheerful, so complete. Now it all seemed just the same – yet something was missing. My carefree childhood was gone, together with the warm, life-giving faith I had had in all the many things in which I had so secretly and hopefully placed my trust.

'I smell Russians! Where are our dear guests from?' cried Father Vavila, suddenly emerging from around the corner of the cabin in such a manner that I had completely failed to notice his approach.

I recognized him at once. All that was different about him now was that his hair had gone completely white; he still had the same childish gaze and the same merry features.

'Have you come far?' he inquired.

I mentioned a village some forty versts distant.

'Aren't you Afanasy Pavlovich's son?' he asked me.

'No,' I said.

'Oh well, it doesn't matter: come on, step inside my humble cell, or you'll get rained on.'

It had indeed begun to rain, and the lake's surface was beginning to be ruffled, even though there was hardly ever any wind in this hollow. There was nowhere for it to move around with any freedom. That was how quiet a place it was.

'What's your name?' Father Vavila asked me once we were inside his cabin.

I told him my name. Father Vavila looked at me, and a smile appeared on his shrewd, good-natured lips. I found myself smiling, too, in spite of myself. My attempt at mystification had failed: he had recognized me. I embraced the old man, and we exchanged several kisses in a row, the tears filling our eyes for no very good reason in particular.

'Let me take a closer look at you,' Father Vavila said, continuing to smile, and leading me over to the hearth. 'My, how you've grown!'

'And you've grown a little older, Father Vavila.'

Father Prokhor laughed.

'And there's him forever trying to make himself look younger,' Father Prokhor said. 'And that's an understatement.'

'That's just the way you see it,' Father Vavila retorted, summoning up some boldness, but almost immediately sitting down on a chair, and adding: 'No, Brother! The spirit is willing, but the flesh is weak. It's time I was off to join Father Sergius. I have terrible pains in my back today – I'll soon not be much good for anything any more.'

'Is it long since Father Sergius died?'

'It'll be two years come St Spiridon's day since he left us.'

'He was a good old man,' I said, remembering Father Sergius with his wooden sticks and his knife.

'Take a look over there, in the corner. The whole of his workshop's still there. Light a candle, Father Prokhor.'

'And is Captain still alive?'

'Oh, the cat, you mean . . . So you remember our cat Captain, do you?'

'Of course!'

'He crawled under our kneading-tub; its lid banged down on top of him one time when we were out. When we came back we searched for him high and low, but we couldn't find him. Then a couple of days later someone picked up the kneading-tub – we looked inside: he was there. We've got another cat now . . . you ought to see him: Vaska! Vaska!' Father Vavila began to call.

A large grey tom-cat emerged from underneath the stove and began to butt its head against Father Vavila's legs.

'How do you like that? The artful rascal.'

Father Vavila picked the cat up, placed it on his knees, belly up, and tickled its throat. It was just like a painting by Teniers:[2] the hoary old man with the fat, grey cat on his knees, the other, halfway to becoming an old man, fussing about in the corner; various domestic utensils, and the whole scene lit up by the warm, red glow of a burning hearth.

'Come on, light a candle, Father Prokhor!' Father Vavila said again.

'In a moment. I can't for the life of me find one.'

Father Vavila meanwhile made excuses for Father Prokhor, and told me:

'To tell you the truth we don't bother much with candles nowadays. We go to bed early.'

A candle was lit. The interior of the cabin appeared much the same as it had done twelve years earlier. The only difference was that Father Sergius's place by the stove had been taken by Father Prokhor, and that Father Vavila was amusing himself with the grey Vaska instead of the marmalade Captain. Even the knife and the stumpy wooden sticks which had been made by Father Sergius hung where the deceased monk had hung them, having fashioned them to meet some requirement or other.

'Well, the eggs are hard-boiled and the fish is ready, but there's no sign of Vasily Petrovich,' said Father Prokhor.

'Which Vasily Petrovich is that?'

'Vasily Petrovich the Wayward,' Father Prokhor replied. 'You didn't come here with him, did you?'

'Er, yes,' I said, guessing that the nickname referred to my Musk-Ox.

'Who on earth sent you here with him?'

'Oh, we're old friends,' I said. 'But tell me, why do you call him the Wayward?'

'He's wayward, my dear fellow. My, how he's wayward!'

'He's a good man.'

'Oh, I would never say he was bad; it's simply that that way-wardness of his has taken possession of him. He's turned into a ne'er-do-well: any sort of order displeases him.'

It was by now ten o'clock at night.

'Come on, let's have supper. I expect he'll turn up,' Father Vavila commanded, as he washed his hands. 'We'll have supper, and then sing a small liturgy . . . Agreed? Shall we sing a liturgy in memory of Father Sergius?'

Supper got under way. When it was over, we sang 'May he rest with the saints' for Father Sergius; but still Vasily Petrovich did not return.

Father Prokhor cleared the table of the dirty dishes, but left out a frying-pan with some fish in, a plate, the salt, the bread and five eggs. Then he went out of the cabin and, coming back in again, said:

'No, there's no sign of him.'

'Who is there no sign of?' asked Father Vavila.

'Vasily Petrovich.'

'If he were here, he wouldn't stand about outside the door. He must have felt like taking a walk.'

Father Prokhor and Father Vavila were both insistent that I should avail myself of one of the beds. With some difficulty I managed to talk them out of this idea, took one of the soft rush mats – the handiwork of Father Sergius – and lay down on the bench under the window. Father Prokhor gave me a pillow, snuffed the candle, went outside again and remained out there for some considerable time. He was evidently awaiting the arrival of 'the Wayward', but ran out of patience and on his return said simply:

'There's quite definitely a storm brewing.'

'It may not come to anything,' I said, in an attempt to allay my anxiety about the vanished Musk-Ox.

'Oh, it will: the weather was very oppressive today.'

'The weather's been that way for a long time.'

'My back's been aching something awful,' Father Vavila said.

'A housefly's been bothering me ever since this morning,' Father Prokhor added, ponderously turning over in his massive bed. At about that moment I think we all fell asleep. Outside it was awesomely dark, but it still had not rained.

'Get up!' Father Vavila said to me, giving me a shake as I lay on my mat. 'Get up! It's not good to sleep at such an hour. Unequal is the hour of God's will.'

Not understanding what the trouble was, I quickly sprang up into a sitting position on the bench. A slim wax taper was burning in front of the icon cabinet, and Father Prokhor was kneeling in nothing but his underwear, saying his prayers. A terrible clap of thunder, which detonated above the lake and went booming and reverberating over the forest, explained the reason for the alarm. Father Prokhor's housefly had evidently had good reason to bother him.

'Where's Vasily Petrovich?' I asked the old man.

Without ceasing to whisper his prayers, Father Prokhor turned his face towards me and indicated by a movement that Musk-Ox had still not returned. I looked at my watch: it was exactly one o'clock in the morning. Father Vavila, who was also dressed in nothing more than his underwear and a quilted calico bib, was looking out of the window; I joined him at the window, and began to look, too. By the constant flashing of the lightning, which brilliantly illuminated the whole of the expanse that was visible from the window, it could be seen that the ground was fairly dry. That meant that there had not been much rain since we had fallen asleep. But it was a fearful storm. Peal followed upon peal, each louder than the last, each more awe-inspiring than the last, and the thunder never died away even for a second. It was as though the heavens were yawning open and might fall to earth in an incandescent flood at any moment.

'Where can he be?' I said, finding my thoughts returning to Musk-Ox.

'You'd do better to think of something else,' Father Vavila said, remaining by the window.

'Do you think something's happened to him?'

'Why should anything happen to him? There aren't any wild beasts around these parts. Possibly a criminal or two – but there hasn't been a case like that for a very long time. No, I expect he's simply out walking. That's how his waywardness takes him.'

'Such a beautiful view,' the old man went on, admiring the lake, which the lightning was illuminating all the way to the opposite shore.

At that instant there was such a violent clap of thunder that the whole cabin shook; Father Prokhor fell to the ground, and Father Vavila and I were thrown back against the wall. Out in the outhouse something fell down and rolled against the door that led into the cabin proper.

'We're on fire!' Father Vavila cried; and, being the first to recover himself from the general state of numbed shock, he rushed to the door.

The door could not be opened.

'Let me try,' I said, perfectly convinced that the cabin was now ablaze, and with all my might I hurled myself, shoulder-first, against the door.

This time, to our extreme astonishment, the door opened freely and, unable to restrain myself, I rushed outside. The outhouse was in total darkness. I went back into the cabin, took one of the candles from the icon cabinet and returned with it to the outhouse. All the noise had been made by my little mare. Frightened out of her wits by the last fearful clap of thunder, she had tugged at the reins by which she had been tethered to a wooden support, had knocked over an empty cabbage press, on which had stood the sieve containing oats and, bolting to one side, had struck the door with the full weight of her body. The poor creature was moving her ears, rolling her eyes anxiously, and quivering in every limb. The three of us set about tidying up the mess, poured out another sieveful of oats, and went back inside the cabin again. Before Father Prokhor brought the candle in, Father

Vavila and I observed a faint glow which was coming through the window and being reflected off the wall. When we looked out of the window, we saw that directly across from us, on the opposite shore of the lake, an old, dead pine tree which had long stood on the bare, sandy hill, was burning like a colossal taper.

'Aha!' Father Vavila said in a long-drawn-out voice.

'The lightning has ignited it,' Father Prokhor whispered.

'And how wonderfully it's burning!' the artistic Father Vavila added.

'That is the fate to which it has been assigned by God,' replied the devout Father Prokhor.

'Come along, Fathers, let's back to bed: the storm's over.'

The storm had indeed completely died away, and only occasionally distant rolls of thunder could be heard; over the sky slowly crept the same endless black thunderclouds, seeming even blacker against the burning pine tree.

'Look! Look!' Father Vavila exclaimed, suddenly: he was still looking out of the window. 'There's our wayward friend!'

'Where?' Father Prokhor and I inquired in unison, both staring out of the window.

'Over there, beside the pine tree.'

And indeed, clearly delineated some dozen or so yards from the burning pine tree was a silhouette which could be recognized at first sight as being that of Musk-Ox. He was standing with his hands clasped behind his back; his head raised, he was observing the burning boughs.

'Shall I shout to him?' Father Prokhor asked.

'He won't hear us,' Father Vavila replied. 'There's still too much noise.'

'And he'll lose his temper,' I added, well acquainted with the character of my friend.

We continued to stand looking out of the window for a while. Musk-Ox did not move. We referred to him a few times as 'the Wayward', and then lay down in our respective sleeping berths. Vasily Petrovich's oddities had long ago ceased to astonish me; but on this occasion I felt unbearably sorry for my suffering friend ... As he stood there cutting such a melancholy figure beside the burning pine tree, I saw him as a tragic clown.

When I woke up it was already quite late. The 'bookless' fathers were no longer in the cabin. At the table sat Vasily Petrovich. He was clutching a large hunk of rye bread in his hands and gulping milk straight out of the jug that stood before him. Observing that I was awake, he glanced at me and silently continued his breakfast. I did not say anything to him. In this fashion some twenty minutes passed.

'Why are you lying there?' Vasily Petrovich said, at last, putting down the milk-jug which he had drained to the bottom.

'What do you suggest we do, then?'

'Let's take a stroll.'

Vasily Petrovich was in a most cheerful mood. Of this I was thoroughly glad, and I did not venture to question him about his nocturnal perambulations. As soon as we were out of the cabin, however, he began to tell me about them himself.

'What a night of storms that was!' Vasily Petrovich began. 'I simply can't recall one like it.'

'It didn't rain much, though.'

'It started several times, but it couldn't get going. I simply love nights like that.'

'I don't.'

'Why not?'

'Well, what's so marvellous about them? Everything gets twisted and broken.'

'Hm! That may not altogether be a bad thing.'

'Things get destroyed for no reason.'

'Yes, it's funny, isn't it?'

'That pine tree, for example.'

'It burned so beautifully.'

'Yes, we saw it.'

'So did I. It's a good life in the woods.'

'Except that there are rather too many mosquitoes.'

'Oh, you namby-pambies! The mosquitoes would eat you alive.'

'They annoy the bears, too, Vasily Petrovich.'

'Yes, and yet the bears never leave the woods. I've grown very attached to this way of life,' Vasily Petrovich continued.

'In the woods, you mean?'

'These northern woods are so lovely! They're thick, quiet – the leaves are blue – splendid!'

'But they don't stay like that for long.'

'It's good there in winter, too.'

'Oh, I'm not so sure about that.'

'I am.'

'What do you like about the woods in winter?'

'The quiet: there's a strength in quiet like that.'

'And what about the people?'

'What do you mean – what about the people?'

'What are their lives like, what expectations do they have?'

Vasily Petrovich thought for a while.

'You did spend two years among them after all, didn't you?'

'Yes, two years and a bit.'

'And were you able to fathom them?'

'What is there to fathom?'

'What's hidden in the people who live there?'

'A lot of nonsense, that's what.'

'But you didn't think that before?'

'I didn't think, full stop. Of what value are our thoughts? They're just built out of words. "Dissent", you hear – dissent, power, protest – and think you've discovered heaven knows what in them. You keep thinking that the right word is there somewhere, that they know it, and it's simply that they don't trust you, and that's why you can't get to the heart of the matter.'

'Well, so what are they really?'

'They're just dry-as-dust pedants.'

'But did you manage to get along with them?'

'How could I get along with them? I mean, I didn't go there in order to fool around.'

'But you must have managed somehow! I'm interested to know how you did it. Go on, please tell me!'

'It's very simple: I arrived, got myself hired as a labourer, and worked like an ox . . . I say, let's lie down above the lake, here.'

We lay down, and Vasily Petrovich continued his story, as was his custom, in short, jerky phrases.

'Yes, I worked. In winter I offered to copy books for them. I soon got the hang of writing in the old Slavonic characters. The devil only knows what the books they gave me were. At any rate, they weren't the ones I'd hoped for. It was a tedious life. Work and the singing of prayers – that was all there was. Nothing else. Then they started saying to me: "Come and live with us permanently!" I said: "It's all the same, I'm yours already as it is." "Why don't you find a nice girl and settle down in someone's household?" they said. You can imagine how much that idea appealed to me. "Oh well," I thought, "I'm not going to let this defeat me. So I joined a household."

'You?'

'Who else?'

'You got married?'

'I took a girl, and so – yes, I suppose I must have got married.'

I was dumbfounded with astonishment, and could not help asking:

'Well, and what came of that?'

'A lot of nonsense,' Musk-Ox said, his face displaying both animosity and vexation.

'What's the trouble – are you unhappy with your wife?'

'Do you think a wife is capable of affecting my happiness or unhappiness? No, I was deluding myself. I thought I'd find a pot of gold, but instead I found a stone.'

'Didn't the dissenters want to let you into their secrets?'

'They didn't have any to let me into!' Musk-Ox cried indignantly. 'Yet it was for the sake of their secrets that I'd gone and got mixed up with them in the first place! You know that phrase from the fairy tale: "Open Sesame!" Well, it didn't apply there. I know all their secrets, and they none of them merit anything but contempt. They gather together and you think they're going to resolve some weighty problem, but instead it's the devil only knows what – "our blessed honour and our blessed faith". They don't get any further than the blessed faith, and the blessed honour goes to the one who occupies the seat of honour. Nonsense and pedantry, leather whips and the cat-o'-nine-tails. If you're not of their creed, they don't want to have anything to do with you. And if you are one of them, you'll never get far, you'll just end up in the almshouse if you're old or infirm, and live in the kitchen on charity. The world will become a prison for you. They're forever commiserating, the confounded turkey-cocks: "There's not enough fear in the world. Fear's on the way out," they say. And here we've pinned all our hopes on them! ... the idiot sluggards, all they do is pull our legs with their secrecy.'

Vasily Petrovich spat indignantly.

'So do you consider our simple local muzhiks any better, then?'

Vasily Petrovich thought for a moment, then spat again and replied calmly:

'Better by far.'

'In what way, exactly?'

'Because they don't know what they want. Those dissenters reason this way, and that way, while the muzhiks only know one way of reasoning. They twist everything around their fingers. Take a simple bit of land, for example – or go and dig up an old weir. So what if it has been built by their hands? If there's brushwood in it – brushwood is what you'll find. And when you've pulled the brushwood out, there's just earth left, and earth that's been stirred up by fools, at that. So judge for yourself – which are better?'

'How did you manage to get away from them?'

'I just left. I saw there was nothing for me there, and I left.'

'What about your wife?'

'Why are you interested in her?'

'You didn't just leave her there, did you?'

'What would I have done with her?'

'Why, taken her with you and lived with her.'

'A fat lot of good that would have done me.'

'Vasily Petrovich – why, that's cruel! What if she was in love with you?'

'Stuff and nonsense! What kind of love is that: she reads a few lines out of the prayer-book and hey presto – she's my wife. But the very next day she gets a "dispensation" and goes to sleep in someone else's kitchen. And anyway, what business have I with a woman, what business have I with love? What business have I with all the women in the world?'

'But she's a human being,' I said. 'You ought at least to feel sorry for her.'

'I'll tell you in what sense you should pity a woman! . . . It's a very important matter, whose kitchen she crawls into. As if there were the time to spend moping over trifles of that sort! "Open Sesame, Open Sesame" – it's the one who knows the secret of "Open Sesame" we need!' Musk-Ox concluded, beating his breast. 'The man, give us the man whom passion has not enslaved, and for him alone shall we reserve the holiest recesses of our souls.'

The rest of my conversation with Vasily Petrovich did not go well. After taking dinner with the old monks, I drove him back to the monastery, took my leave of the Father Almoner and went home.

8

Some ten days after my parting with Vasily Petrovich, I was sitting with my mother and sister in the porch of our small house. It was beginning to get dark. All the servants had gone off to have supper, and there was no one about apart from ourselves. All around there was the most profound evening stillness; suddenly, in the midst of it, the two large watch-dogs which lay at our feet leapt up, rushed towards the gate and started to attack someone viciously. I rose to my feet and went over to the gate in order to take a look at the object of their immoderate aggression. Leaning against the fence was Musk-Ox, brandishing his stick in an attempt to ward off the two dogs which had fallen on him with an animosity that was almost human.

'They nearly ate me alive, the devils,' he said to me, after I had called the dogs off.

'Did you come on foot?'

'On Shanks's pony, as you see.'

Slung over Vasily Petrovich's back was the knapsack with which he generally travelled.

'Well, come on then.'

'Where to?'

'Why, back to the house, of course.'

'Oh no, I'm not going there.'

'Why ever not?'

'There are young ladies there.'

'Young ladies? There's only my mother and my sister.'

'All the same, I'm not coming.'

'You and your whims! They're ordinary, decent people.'

'I'm not coming!' Musk-Ox said, resolutely.

'Where am I going to put you, then?'

'Well, you'll have to put me somewhere – I've nowhere else to go.'

I remembered the bath-house, which in summer was unused and quite frequently served as a guest bedroom. Our house was a small one – '*szlachecki*' and not '*pański*'.[1]

Neither would Vasily Petrovich hear of walking through the yard, past the porch. It would have been possible to walk through the orchard, but I knew that the bath-house was locked, and that the key to it was in the possession of our old nurse, who was having her supper in the kitchen. I could not possibly leave Vasily Petrovich here on his own, as the dogs would have set upon him again – they had retreated only a few paces from us and were viciously barking. I leaned over the fence, behind which I was standing with Vasily Petrovich, and loudly hailed my sister. She came running, but stopped in bewilderment when she saw the eccentric figure of Musk-Ox in his peasant *svitka* and novice's cap. I sent her to fetch the key from the nurse and then, with the desired object at last in my possession, led my unexpected guest through the orchard and into the bath-house.

Vasily Petrovich and I talked together the whole night through. He could not return to the monastery from which he had come, as they would have thrown him out because of the things he had said to the pilgrims there. He had no plans of going to any other monastery. His lack of success had not sapped his courage, but it had temporarily upset his calculations. He spoke a great deal about the novices, about the monastery, about the pilgrims who had come there from every part of the country – all with a fair degree of coherence. While he had been living in the monastery, Vasily Petrovich had put into execution a most original plan. He had sought among the ranks of 'the insulted and the injured' of the monastic family those 'men whom passion has not made slaves' of his, and had aimed to open his Sesame with them, using them to influence the masses of the common people who arrived on their pilgrimages.

'No one will notice if I do it like that: it will catch them off their guard; the builders despise them, yet here there is something that deserves to be made the corner-stone,' Musk-Ox had reasoned.

As I called to mind the life of monasteries, a life with which I was well acquainted, and the people there who belonged to the ranks of 'the insulted and the injured', I could quite see that Vasily Petrovich's ideas were not without foundation.

My propagandist had, however, fallen on hard times. The first man he had discovered who, in his estimation, stood above his passions – this was none other than my old friend the novice Nevstruyev, who was presently known in his monk's career as Deacon Luka and had become a familiar of Bogoslovsky's – had hit upon the idea of doing something about his 'insult and injury': he had revealed to the monastic authorities 'what manner of man' Musk-Ox was, and Musk-Ox had been thrown out. At present he was homeless. In a week's time I was due to travel to St Petersburg, and then Musk-Ox would have nowhere to lay his head, as it would be impossible for him to remain there alone with my mother – and in any case, he himself did not want this.

'Find me a tutoring post again, I want to do some teaching,' he said.

I should have to find him a post. I made Musk-Ox promise to accept the post solely for its own sake, not for any ulterior motive, and began to seek shelter for him.

9

Our province contains a very large number of villages owned by small landowners. To adopt the parlance of the St Petersburg politico-economic commission, there is in our part of the world 'a rather widespread distribution of the separated farm economy'. The serf-owning *odnodvortsy*[1] had, after their peasants had been taken away from them, remained small farmers, while the small landowners had squandered their resources and sold their peasants off for resettlement in remote provinces, and their land either to merchants or to the now-prosperous *odnodvortsy*. In our neighbourhood there were five or six such farms, which had passed into the hands of commoners. A few versts from our own was Barkov Farm; it bore the name of its former owner, of whom it was said that he had once lived in Moscow

> Idly, gaily, richly
> And by various mothers
> Brought forty daughters to the world,

but who in his old age had embarked upon a legitimate marriage and had begun to sell off his estates, one by one. Barkov Farm, which had once been the private dacha on a large estate of an owner who had suffered financial ruin, now belonged to a man named Aleksandr Ivanovich Sviridov. Aleksandr Ivanovich had been born a peasant, had been taught to read and write and been given a musical education. From a young age he had played the violin in the landowner's orchestra, and at the age of nineteen had bought his freedom for five hundred roubles and become a distiller. Gifted with a clear, practical mind, Aleksandr Ivanovich had plied his trade in masterly fashion. He had begun by establishing himself as the best distiller in the district; having amassed a thousand roubles or so of spare cash, he had gone to Northern Germany for a year, and had returned from there such a brilliant construction engineer that his fame quickly spread far and wide. Aleksandr Ivanovich was well known in the three adjoining provinces, and people there vied with one another in commissioning building projects from him. He carried out the work with an extraordinary degree of precision, carefully taking into account the aristocratic foibles of his clients. He was a shrewd judge of character, and would laugh at them behind their backs, but he was not a bad man, and might even have passed for a good one. Everyone liked him – everyone, that is, except the local Germans, whom he was fond of making fun of whenever they set about trying to introduce civilized habits among people who were still half savage. 'He'll make a monkey of himself,' he would say – and sure enough, the German would go astray in his calculations and make a monkey of himself. Within five days of his return from Mecklenburg-Schwerin, Aleksandr Ivanovich had bought Barkov Farm from its owner, registered as a merchant in our district town, married off his two sisters and found a wife for his brother. Even before his departure for Germany, he had redeemed the family from its condition of serfdom, and it was now entirely supported by his agency. His brother and brother-in-law both worked for him and drew their salaries from him. He was in the habit of addressing them in a rather stern fashion. It was not that he insulted them; rather, he kept them in a state of fear. He treated the stewards and workmen in a similar manner. Not, again, that he wished to be shown deference; it was simply that he was convinced that 'servants should not be spoiled'. Having purchased the farm, Aleksandr Ivanovich bought from the same landowner a maidservant called Nastasya Petrovna, and married her. They lived together in the greatest of harmony. People used to say that they lived on 'love and counsel'. It was said that when Nastasya Petrovna had married, she had 'rounded out'. She had always been the very epitome of beauty, but after her marriage she blossomed like a sumptuous rose. She was tall, fair-haired, slightly on the plump side, but shapely; she had a high-coloured facial complexion, and large, kindly, blue eyes. Mistress Nastasya Petrovna was extremely good-looking. Her husband was seldom at home for as long as a week on end – he was constantly travelling about in connection with his building projects, and she would busy herself with the upkeep of the farm, detailing the stewards to their tasks and buying in timber and grain, if it were needed at any of the mills. She was Aleksandr Ivanovich's right hand in everything, and for this reason everyone took her very seriously and treated her with great respect, while her husband for his part had limitless confidence in her and refrained from extending to her his severe standards of behaviour. There was nothing he would have refused her. She, however, made no demands. By her own unaided efforts she taught herself to read, and she was able to sign her name. Aleksandr Ivanovich and she had only two children, two girls: the elder was nine, and the younger seven. They were given instruction by a Russian governess. Nastasya Petrovna would refer to herself, jokingly, as 'an illiterate noodle'. Yet in actual fact her knowledge was scarcely less extensive than that of many so-called 'educated ladies'. She knew no French, but devoured Russian books at a simply enormous rate. She had a fearfully long memory. I remember that she could recite Karamzin's *History* practically by memory. She also knew a countless number of poems off by heart. Lermontov and Nekrasov were particular favourites of hers. The latter she found especially sympathetic and easy of comprehension since, coming from a serf background herself, she had suffered much in times gone by. She would still frequently come out with peasant expressions in the course of her conversation, particularly if she happened to be talking heatedly; yet this demotic mode of discourse somehow suited her to a quite extraordinary degree. I recall that whenever she started to relate in this manner something she had read, it would lend her narrative such force that by the time she had finished one no longer felt it necessary to read the book. She was a very capable woman. Our local gentry would often call in at Barkov Farm, sometimes merely in order to sample a change of table, but more usually on business. Aleksandr Ivanovich's credit was universally good, while the landowners had almost none – people knew what bad payers they were. People would say of them: 'Oh yes, he's a real aristocrat – lend to him, and you'll scream for it a hundred times.' That was the sort of reputation they had. They would need grain, having nothing from which to distil vodka, and they would either have squandered all their money away or spent it on the repayment of old debts. So they would go and see Aleksandr Ivanovich, saying: 'Be my saviour! Stand security for me, there's a good fellow.' At that point they would kiss Nastasya Petrovna's hands – such unfeigning, tender hands she had. This would make her burst into paroxysms of laughter. 'Have you seen the *zhiristy*?'[2] she would say. Nastasya Petrovna had called the gentry '*zhiristy*' ever since the time a certain Muscovite lady, who was on her way back from her ravaged estate and was anxious to 'educate the little uncut diamond', had said: 'Do you not realize, *ma belle Anastasie*, that every country has its Girondistes?' All these men, without exception, kissed Nastasya Petrovna's hands, and she grew accustomed to their doing so. But there were also dashing young fellows who made her declarations of love and who propositioned her 'off to a shady nook'.[3] One Leib Hussar even told her she would be quite safe doing so, as long as she brought Aleksandr Ivanovich's leather wallet along with her. But

Their sufferings were to no avail.

Nastasya Petrovna knew how to behave herself with these devotees of beauty.

It was to these people – Sviridova and her husband – that I decided to appeal on behalf of my awkward friend. When I arrived to make my request, Aleksandr Ivanovich was as usual not at home. I found only Nastasya Petrovna, and I told her about the devil's urchin Fate had sent me. Two days later I took my Musk-Ox to the Sviridovs', and a week after that went to see them one final time in order to say goodbye.

'Why have you been leading my wife astray in my absence, old chap?' Aleksandr Ivanovich asked me, as he came out onto the porch to greet me.

'How have I been leading her astray?' I asked him in turn, failing to understand his question.

'Why are you getting her involved in philanthropy? Who's this clown you've landed us with?'

'Just listen to him!' a familiar, slightly harsh contralto voice shouted from the window. 'Your Musk-Ox is a fine man. I'm grateful to you for finding him for me.'

'No, but seriously, though – what kind of a beastie is this you've brought us?' Aleksandr Ivanovich asked me, when we had gone up into his draughting room.

'A Musk-Ox,' I replied, smiling.

'I can't make head nor tail of him, old chap!'

'Why not?'

'Well, he's so eccentric!'

'That's just when you first get to know him.'

'And I suppose later on he'll get even worse?'

I burst out laughing, and so did Aleksandr Ivanovich.

'Yes, old chap, it's all very well laughing, but what am I going to do with him? I've no room for a fellow like him.'

'Please provide him with some means of earning his bread.'

'I can't do it! It's not that I've any fundamental objection to the chap; but what sort of work could I give him? I mean, look what he's like,' Aleksandr Ivanovich said, pointing in the direction of Vasily Petrovich, who at that moment was walking about in the yard.

As I watched him striding about, one arm tucked into the front of his *svita* and the other engaged in twirling one of his forelocks, I myself thought: 'It's perfectly true: what kind of work could he do?'

'Why don't you let him supervise the woodfelling?' the lady of the house suggested to her husband.

Aleksandr Ivanovich laughed.

'Yes, let him do that,' I said.

'Oh you innocent little children! What would he do out there? Someone who isn't used to it would just hang himself from boredom. No, in my view, he ought to be given a hundred roubles to go where he likes and do what he wants.'

'No, don't throw him out.'

'No, you'll hurt his feelings,' Nastasya Petrovna said, backing me up.

'Well, where am I going to put him? All my men are muzhiks; I'm a muzhik myself; but he . . .'

'He's not a member of the gentry, either,' I said.

'Not a gentleman and not a peasant, and no good for anything at all.'

'Why don't you give him to Nastasya Petrovna to look after?'

'That's right, give him to me to look after!' Nastasya Petrovna said, intervening once more.

'Take him, take him, my dear!'

'Well, that's fine, then,' said Nastasya Petrovna.

And Musk-Ox remained in Nastasya Petrovna's hands.

In August, when I was already living in St Petersburg, I received, *poste restante*, a registered letter in which fifty roubles were enclosed. The letter said:

O Beloved Brother!

I am present at the destruction of the forests, which have grown as the birthright of all, but have fallen to the lot of the Sviridovs. As half a year's expenses I have been given the sum of sixty roubles, even though six months have not yet elapsed. Apparently, it is intended for my upkeep – but their generosity is in vain: I am in no need of this money. I have kept ten roubles for myself; please send the fifty enclosed herewith at once, *without any covering letter*, to the unmarried peasant woman Glefira Anfinogenova Mukhina in the village of Duba, X province. Do it so that no one will be able to tell who the money has come from. This unmarried woman is she who is supposed to be my wife: the money is for her, in case a child should have been born.

My life here is a repugnant one. There is nothing for me to do here, and all I have to console myself with is the thought that nowhere, ever, is there anything to be done in the neighbourhood but that which everyone does: talking well of one's parents and filling out one's trousers. Here everyone prays for Aleksandr Ivanovich – and for not a living soul besides. Everyone wants to be like him, but what sort of a creature is he, this man of the pocket?

Yes, today I have understood something, I have understood it. I have discovered the answer to the question: 'Russia, where are you striving to?' But be not afraid: I shall not leave this place.

There is nowhere for me to go. It is all the same, everywhere.
There's no getting away from the Aleksandr Petroviches.

Vasily Bogoslovsky

Olgina-Poyma,
3rd August, 185–

At the beginning of December I received another letter. It was
from Sviridov, and it informed me that in a day or two's time
he and his wife would be coming to St Petersburg; in the letter
he asked me to rent a small, comfortable apartment for them.

Some ten days after my receipt of this second letter, Aleksandr Ivanovich and his wife were sitting in their charming
little apartment opposite the Aleksandrinsky Theatre, warming
themselves with tea and my heart with their tales of that far-off
region

Where golden dreams were dreamt by me.

'But tell me,' I said, at last, seizing an opportune moment;
'How is my Musk-Ox faring?'

'He's kicking against the pricks, old chap.'

'How do you mean – kicking against the pricks?'

'Carrying on in that wayward way of his. He never comes to
see us – I suppose we're not good enough for him. No, he's
been spending all his time hob-nobbing with the labourers, but
now he's grown tired of that, too: he asked me to send him
somewhere else.'

'What about you?' I asked Nastasya Petrovna. 'We'd pinned
our hopes on you – that you'd domesticate him.'

'What's the good of hope? He runs away from that, too.'

I glanced at Nastasya Petrovna, and she at me.

'What can you do? I expect he thinks I'm hideous,' she said.

'But what's been going on? Tell me.'

'What is there to tell?' said Aleksandr Ivanovich. 'It's just
that he came to me and said: "Let me go." "Where will you
go?" I asked. "I don't know," he replied. "What's so bad about
being here with me?" I said. "Nothing," he said, "but let me go
all the same." "But what's the matter?" I asked. He wouldn't

say anything – just kept twirling those forelocks of his. "You ought to tell Nastasya if anyone does anything to upset you," I said. "No," he said. "Just send me to do some other kind of work." I felt too sorry for the poor fellow to be able simply to give him the sack like that, so I sent him to another woodfelling site, in Zhogovo, about thirty versts away. That's where he is, now,' Aleksandr Ivanovich added.

'How did you manage to upset him so badly?' I asked Nastasya Petrovna.

'Heaven only knows. I certainly never wanted to upset him.'

'She looked after him as if she were his own mother,' Sviridov said, supporting her. 'She sewed for him, clothed him, shod him. I mean, you know what a warm-hearted soul she is.'

'Well, and so what happened?'

'He just took against me,' Nastasya Petrovna said, laughing.

I settled down to a right royal existence in St Petersburg with the Sviridovs. Aleksandr kept bustling about on business, while Nastasya Petrovna and I did nothing but 'idle around'. Nastasya Petrovna found the city thoroughly to her liking; she was especially fond of the theatre. Each evening we would visit one of these, and we never grew tired of this diversion. The time passed swiftly and agreeably. During this period I received yet one more letter from Musk-Ox, in which he had some dreadfully bitter things to say about Aleksandr Petrovich. 'In my opinion,' he wrote, 'even brigands and foreigners are to be preferred to these Russian moneybags! Yet everyone is for them, and my entrails heave when I reflect that that's as it should be – that everyone should be for them. I saw a curious thing. I saw that he, this Aleksandr Ivanov, was in my way, even before I became acquainted with him. That's who the enemy of the people is – that kind of well-fed brute, a brute who feeds his movable paupers on the crumbs from his table, to prevent them from expiring on the spot and to keep them working for him. That type of Christian is particularly in keeping with our national Russian character, and one day he will conquer us all unless we give him his comeuppance. With me holding the ideas I do, it's impossible for the two of us to live in this world. I yield to him, as he is their darling. He may be of some use to a few, while my ideas, I see, are of no good whatsoever. It's not for nothing that you gave me the name of some beast or other. No one wants to be my friend, and I've never met anyone whom I wanted to be my friend.' He went on to ask me to write and let him know how I was keeping, and how Nastasya Petrovna was.

At this time two coopers of Aleksandr Ivanovich's who had travelled with a consignment of vodka from the distillery in Vytegra arrived in St Petersburg and called on their master. I put them up in my spare kitchen. I knew both of them quite well. We got talking about one thing and another, and eventually came on to the subject of Musk-Ox.

'How is he getting along with you?' I asked them.

'Oh, all right,' said one of them.

'He's active,' the other man volunteered.

'But does he do any work?'

'Well, what kind of work could you expect him to do? I don't know why the master keeps him on, really.'

'How does he pass the time?'

'He wanders about in the forest. He's supposed to be a sort of steward, keeping a record of the number of trees that have been felled, but he doesn't even do that.'

'Why not?'

'Who knows? The master spoils him.'

'But he's strong, you know,' the cooper went on. 'Sometimes he picks up an axe, and when he starts to swing it – Lord! The sparks fairly fly!'

'The other thing he's been doing is night-watchman duty.'

'What sort of night-watchman duty?'

'The local people started putting a rumour around that there were runaway serfs in the neighbourhood, and he began to disappear for whole nights at a time. The lads started to get the idea that he might be mixed up with these runaways, and that they ought to keep an eye on him. So whenever he set off, three of them would tail him. They'd see him go straight to the farmhouse. Well, nothing came of it, though – nothing except a lot of nonsense. They said they saw him sit down under a shrub, right outside the master's windows, call the dog, Sultanka, over to his side and sit there until dawn; when day broke he'd get up and move on to another place. And so it went on, a second and a third time. The lads would rush after him to see what he was doing. It went on like that until autumn. But one night after the Feast of the Assumption some of the lads were getting ready to turn in, and they said to him: "That's enough of that, Petrovich – don't you go off on night-watchman duty no more! Why don't you turn in like the rest of us?" He didn't say anything, but two days later we heard that he'd asked for leave of absence: and the master had him transferred to another dacha.'

'But did your lads like him?' I asked.

The cooper gave this some thought, and then said:

'I don't think they had any feelings one way or the other.'

'But, I mean, he's a good-natured fellow.'

'Oh yes, he never did any of us any harm. They used to say that whenever he started talking about Filaret the Merciful or some other holy father, he'd turn everything to the subject of goodness, and deliver stirring words against Mammon-worship. A lot of the lads used to listen to what he had to say.'

'And did they like what they heard?'

'They liked it, all right. Sometimes he could even make them laugh.'

'What did he say that was so comical?'

'Well, for example, he'd talk for ages about God – and then suddenly you'd realize it was the higher-ups he was talking about. He'd take a handful of peas, select the biggest, juiciest ones, and plant them out on his *svitka*. "Now the biggest one," he'd say, "is the Tsar; this smaller one here is his ministers and princes; this even smaller one is the lords and merchants and fat-bellied priests; and lastly, these ones –" here he'd point to the whole handful – "these are us, the tillers of the soil." And then he'd throw these tillers of the soil among the princes and the priests: and it would all even out. There would just be a great pile of peas. Well, of course, the lads used to hoot with laughter. "Let's see that show again," they'd say.'

'That was him – always playing the fool,' the other man muttered.

We felt obliged to be silent for a while.

'What is he, anyway?' the second cooper asked. 'Is he an actor?'

'What gave you that idea?'

'It's what folk used to say. Mironka used to say it.'

Mironka was a quick, nimble little muzhik who had travelled everywhere with Aleksandr Ivanovich for as long as anyone could remember. He was renowned as a singer, storyteller and cracker of jokes. Occasionally he would stir up absurd rumours, putting them into circulation in the most expert fashion among the credulous peasants and taking pleasure in the fruits of his inventiveness. It was evident that Vasily Petrovich had become not only an enigma to the woodfellers, but also the object of idle gossip; Mironka had taken advantage of this circumstance, and had made of my hero a retired actor.

It was Shrovetide. Nastasya Petrovna and I had managed, only just, to obtain tickets for an evening performance at the theatre. It was a performance of *Esmeralda* which she had long wanted to see. The show went very well and, in accordance with Russian custom, ended very late. The night was a fine one, and Nastasya Petrovna and I walked home together. As we went, I noticed that my distiller's wife was in a very reflective state of mind, and that many of her replies were *non sequiturs*.

'What's on your mind?' I asked her.

'How do you mean?'

'Well, you don't seem to hear what I say to you.'

Nastasya Petrovna laughed.

'So what do you suppose I'm thinking about, then?'

'It's hard to say.'

'Well – for example?'

'Esmeralda.'

'Yes, you're warm: but it isn't Esmeralda herself who's on my mind – it's that poor Quasimodo.'

'You feel sorry for him?'

'Terribly. That's the real misfortune: to be the kind of person no one can love. And you feel sorry for him, you'd like to be able to take his pain away, but it's impossible. That's terrible! And it really is impossible – quite impossible,' she continued, meditating.

When we sat down to have tea, expecting Aleksandr Ivanovich to return in time for supper, we had a very long talk. Aleksandr Ivanovich did not show up.

'Ah! Thank God that people like that don't really exist.'

'People like what? Quasimodo?'

'Yes.'

'What about Musk-Ox?'

Nastasya Petrovna slapped the table with the palm of her hand, and said quietly:

'You know, you're right!'

She moved the candle closer to her and began to look intently into its flame, slightly narrowing her beautiful eyes.

The Sviridovs remained in St Petersburg until the summer. Day by day they had postponed their departure on the pretext that they had business still to attend to. They persuaded me to travel together with them. Together we drove to our local district town. There I ascended a post-chaise and rode to my mother's house, while they went home, having first exacted from me a promise that I would come to see them in a week's time. Immediately upon his return home Aleksandr Ivanovich planned to ride off to Zhogovo, where the woodfelling was proceeding, and where Musk-Ox now resided, promising to be home again within a week. As for myself, my people had not been expecting to see me, and they were delighted at my arrival . . . I said I would go nowhere for a week; my mother invited my cousin and his wife to stay with us, and various bucolic amusements got under way.

In this fashion some ten days went by. At the crack of dawn on the morning of the eleventh – or possibly the twelfth – day, my old nurse entered my room in a somewhat agitated frame of mind.

'What's the matter?' I asked her.

'The master's sent someone to see you,' she said.

A boy of about twelve came into the room and, without bowing, passed his cap from one hand to the other several times, cleared his throat, and said:

'The mistress says you're to come and see her at once.'

'Is Nastasya Petrovna all right?' I asked.

'I think so. I don't know.'

'And Aleksandr Ivanovich?'

'The master's not at home,' the boy replied, clearing his throat again.

'Where is he?'

'In Zhogovo. There's been an incident there, you see.'

I had one of my mother's trace-horses saddled, dressed quickly, and rode off to Barkov Farm at a brisk trot. It was only five in the morning, and everyone in our house was still asleep.

When I arrived at my destination, all the windows of the little farmhouse – apart from those of the nursery and the governess's room – were already open, and at one of them stood Nastasya Petrovna, wearing a large blue silk scarf tied round her head. Distractedly she returned my bow, and while I was tethering my horse to the post, she beckoned to me twice, signalling to me to hurry up.

'It's a disaster,' she said, meeting me right on the threshold.

'What on earth's happened?'

'Aleksandr Ivanovich went away to Turukhtanovka the day before yesterday, and at three o'clock this morning this note arrived from the woodfelling site at Zhogovo by express messenger.'

She gave me a crumpled letter which up until now she had been clutching in her hands. The letter was from Sviridov.

Nastya!

Send someone immediately to M with a cart and pair, and give him letters for the doctor and the district police officer. That queer fish of yours has played us a proper caper, and no mistake. Only last night I was talking to him, and this morning he's gone and hanged himself. Send someone with a bit of intelligence who'll buy all that's needed and see to it that a coffin's brought in as soon as possible. I've no time to bother about such things at the moment. Please be quick, and explain to whoever you send what he's to do with the letters. You know how precious time is, and there's a dead body here.

Yours
Aleksandr Sviridov

Ten minutes later, I was riding to Zhogovo at a fast trot. As I zigzagged along the various country byways I very soon lost the right road, only reaching the forest at Zhogovo, where the woodfelling was taking place, as night was falling. I had completely exhausted my horse, and was myself worn out by the long, hot ride. As I entered the clearing where the watch-hut was, I caught sight of Aleksandr Ivanovich. He was standing on the porch in his waistcoat and shirtsleeves, clutching some bills in his hands. His face was as usual calm, but its expression was slightly more serious than normal. In front of him stood a crowd of some thirty muzhiks. They were bare-headed, and had axes stuck in their belts. Some way to their side stood the steward Orefich, with whom I was acquainted, and standing still further away was the coachman, Mironka.

Here, too, unharnessed, stood a pair of Aleksandr Ivanovich's stocky little horses.

Mironka pranced over to me and, taking my horse, said with a cheerful smile:

'My, what a lather he's in!'

'Walk it, walk it properly!' Aleksandr Ivanovich shouted to him, still clutching his fistful of bills.

'Is that all right?' he asked, addressing the peasants who stood before him.

'S'pose it'll have to be, Aleksandr Ivanych,' several voices replied.

'Well, that's settled then,' he said to the peasants, shook hands with me and, giving me a long look in the eye, said:

'So, old chap.'

'What?'

'So what's he gone and done to himself? Eh?'

'He's hanged himself.'

'Yes. Who told you?'

I told him how I had found out.

'That woman showed some sense in sending for you; I must confess I'd never have thought of it. What else do you know?' Aleksandr Ivanovich asked me, lowering his voice.

'Nothing. Is there something else to know?'

'What? My dear fellow, he used to cause havoc around here such as you'd never believe. He used to thank me for my hospitality. It's Nastasya Petrovna and you *I've* got to thank for landing me with that worn-out bag of tricks.'

'What are you getting at?' I said. 'Speak plainly.'

By now I had a thoroughly unpleasant sensation.

'My dear chap, he started interpreting the Scriptures in his own curious way – and, I'll tell you this, it wasn't any decent sort of way, it was a damned stupid one. He started going on about the publican, and poor Lazarus, and who could get through the eye of a needle and who couldn't – and he landed it all on me.'

'You mean he turned against you?'

'What? . . . Yes, he did, to the point where he put me in the category "merchant equals grasping paw" and told the tillers of the soil that they ought to give me a hammering.'

All was now plain.

'Well, and so what did the tillers of the soil do, then?' I asked Aleksandr Ivanovich, who was giving me a meaningful look.

'The lads? Oh, nothing, of course.'

'You mean they made a clean breast of it?'

'Of course. The wolves!' Aleksandr Ivanovich continued, with a sly smile. 'They'd forever be saying to him, as if they'd never given it a moment's thought: "You must be right, Vasily Petrovich. Now when we see Father Peter, we'll ask him about that, too." But to me they'd talk about it more as a sort of joke: "He keeps saying things that aren't in accordance with the law." And they'd repeat the things he told them straight to my face.'

'Well, and so then what happened?'

'I used to try to let on that I didn't understand it, either. Well, but now, after this terrible happening, I called them together as though my purpose was just to check their bills, but on the side I threw in a bit about all that being a lot of hot air, that they'd better get it out of their heads and keep very quiet about it.'

'It'll be as well for them if they stick to that.'

'They'd better stick to it – nobody fools around with me.'

We went inside the hut. On Aleksandr Ivanovich's bench lay a large piece of brightly coloured Kazan felt and a red Morocco cushion; the table was covered by a clean cloth, and on it a samovar merrily bubbled.

'What on earth got into him?' I said, as I sat down at the table with Sviridov.

'Nothing gets into a man if he has enough intelligence. I can't stand those seminarists.'

'You said you talked to him the day before yesterday?'

'That's right, I did. Nothing unpleasant passed between us. The labourers came here, I treated them to vodka, talked to them a bit, gave money to those who'd asked for it in advance; but at that point he slipped away. In the morning he wasn't to be found, and some girl came to the labourers. "Look in the forest behind the clearing here," she said. "There's a man hanged himself." The lads went rushing off, but the poor fellow was already stiff with *rigor mortis*. He must have hanged himself the previous evening.'

'And nothing unpleasant had passed between you?'

'Not a thing.'

'Are you sure it wasn't something you said to him?'

'What will you think of next?'

'Did he leave no letter?'

'None.'

'Have you had a look through his papers?'

'He doesn't appear to have had any.'

'I'd still like to take a look, until the police get here.'

'By all means.'

'Did he have a suitcase?' Aleksandr Ivanovich asked the cook.

'The dead man, you mean? Yes, he did.'

A small suitcase with no lock was brought in, and opened in the presence of a steward and the cook. It contained nothing except two changes of underwear, a grubby volume of extracts from the works of Plato, and a bloodstained handkerchief wrapped in a piece of paper.

'What's this handkerchief?' Aleksandr Ivanovich inquired.

'Oh, that was when he cut his hand when the mistress happened to be present, and she bandaged it up with her handkerchief,' the cook replied.

'Yes, it's the very same one,' the woman added, inspecting the handkerchief more closely.

'Well, that's that, then.'

'Let's go and take a look at him.'

'Yes, let's.'

While I was waiting for Sviridov to get dressed, I carefully examined the piece of paper in which the handkerchief had been wrapped. It was completely blank. I turned over the pages of the Plato volume – not the slightest sign of a note anywhere, only passages underlined by fingernail. I read the underlined passages:

'The Persians and the Athenians lost their equilibrium, the former by distributing too widely the rights of the monarchy, and the latter by extending too far their love of freedom.'

'It is not an ox that is made a leader of oxen, but a human being. May genius reign.'

'The type of power closest to nature is the power of the strong.'

'When the old men are without shame, the young men will certainly also be without shame, too.'

'It is impossible to be absolutely good and absolutely wealthy. Why? Because whoever acquires by both honest and dishonest means acquires twice as much as he that acquires solely by honest means, and whoever makes no sacrifice to goodness expends less than he that is ready to make sacrifices.'

'God is the measure of all things, and their most important measure. In order to resemble God one must be moderate in all things, even one's desires.'

Here, in the margin, were some words, faintly written in Musk-Ox's hand in something that resembled bortsch. With difficulty I made out: *'You fool, Vaska! Why aren't you a priest? Why have you shorn the wings of your words? A teacher with no robes – a clown to the people, a disgrace to yourself, a destroyer of the idea. I am a thief, and the further I go, the more I will steal.'*

I closed Musk-Ox's book.

Aleksandr Ivanovich put on his long-skirted coat, and we walked to the clearing. When we got there, we took the right fork, and walked through a dense pinewood; we crossed an opening, from which the woodfelling was being started, and then entered another large clearing. Here stood two large stacks of last year's hay. Aleksandr Ivanovich stopped in the middle of the clearing and, taking a deep breath, shouted in a loud voice: 'Hallo!' There was no answer. The moon lit the clearing brightly, and the two haystacks threw long shadows.

'Hallo!' Aleksandr Ivanovich shouted, a second time.

'Hallo-a!' some voices echoed from the right of the wood.

'There they are!' said my companion, and we set off in a rightward direction.

Ten minutes later, Aleksandr Ivanovich gave another shout, which was answered immediately, and then we caught sight of two muzhiks: an old man and a young lad. When they saw Sviridov, both of them removed their caps and stood there, leaning on their long sticks.

'Hallo, Christians!'

'Hallo, Liksandra Ivanych.'

'Where's the dead man?'

'Right here, Liksandra Ivanych.'

'Show us where he is: I didn't spot the place.'

'Here he is.'

'Where?'

'Right here, sir!'

The peasant smiled ironically, and pointed to our right.

Musk-Ox hung only three paces from us. He had hanged himself with a thin peasant belt, having tied it to a bough no higher than head height. His knees were bent, and only barely touched the ground. It was as though he were kneeling. His hands were stuck in the pockets of his *svitka*, as they usually were. He was in shadow, but through the branches the pale radiance of the moonlight fell on his head. That poor head! Now, at last, it was at rest. Its forelocks still protruded like ram's horns, and the turbid, stupefied eyes surveyed the moon with the same expression that remains in the eyes of a bull that has been struck several times on the forehead with the butt of a butcher's knife, and which has then, immediately after, had the blade drawn across its throat. It was impossible to read in them the dying thoughts of a voluntary martyr. Neither did they say what his quotations from Plato or his handkerchief with its red stain had revealed.

'That's it: a man lived, and now he's gone,' Sviridov said.

'He'll rot, but you'll not, Liksandra Ivanych,' said the old man in an obsequious, saccharine voice.

Musk-Ox had also said that he would rot, but that the Aleksandr Ivanoviches of this world would not.

It felt airless in this dark corner of the forest which Musk-Ox had chosen as the place in which his torments should cease. But in the clearing it was light and cheerful. The moon bathed in the azure of the heavens, and the pines and fir-trees slumbered.

Paris
28 November 1862

LADY MACBETH OF MTSENSK

A Character Sketch

'The first song should be sung with a blush'
Russian Proverb

I

In these parts one occasionally comes across individuals of such character that, no matter how many years may have passed since one's last encounter with them, one can never recall them without experiencing an inward tremor. An example of this type was Katerina Lvovna Izmailova, a merchant's wife who once enacted a drama so awesome that the members of our local gentry, taking their lead from someone's light-hearted remark, took to calling her 'Lady Macbeth of Mtsensk'.

Although Katerina Lvovna was not a beautiful woman, she did have a very pleasing appearance. She was approaching twenty-four; she was short, but slender, her neck looked as though it had been sculpted from marble, her shoulders were full and round, her bust firm, her nose straight and delicate, and her eyes black and lively; she had a white, high forehead, and so black was her hair that it possessed an almost bluish tint. She had married one of our local merchants, a man named Izmailov from Tuskar in the province of Kursk, not because she loved him or was in any way attracted to him, but because he had sought her hand and she, being a girl from a poor family, could not afford to be choosy. The house of Izmailov was certainly not among the least in our town: the Izmailovs traded in white flour, rented a large mill in the district, owned a profitable orchard in the suburbs and a handsome residence in town and were, in short, rather well-to-do. What was more, the family was by no means a large one: there were only Katerina Lvovna's father-in-law, Boris Timofeich Izmailov, a man of nearly eighty who had long been a widower; his son Zinovy Borisych, Katerina's husband, who was also getting on a bit, being over fifty; and Katerina Lvovna herself. Although Katerina Lvovna and Zinovy Borisych were in the fifth year of their marriage, they had no children. Neither did Zinovy Borisych have any children by his first marriage, even though he had lived with his first wife for twenty years before she had died and he had married Katerina Lvovna. He had fervently hoped that God would, by this second marriage, at least grant him an heir to the family fortune and a little capital; but in these respects Katerina Lvovna had brought him no better luck than his first wife had done.

This state of childlessness was a cause of great inward suffering to Zinovy Borisych; it was also a source of considerable sadness to old man Boris Timofeich, and even to Katerina Lvovna herself. For one thing, the unrelieved monotony of life in the merchant's barred and bolted tower of a house, with its high staked fence and loose watch-dogs, occasionally depressed the young woman to the point of stupefaction; how glad she would have been, God knows how glad she would have been to have a little child to make a fuss of. For another, she was tired of hearing the reproaches that were constantly levelled against her: 'Why on earth did you ever get married? What did you go and get yourself hitched up to a man for if you're unable to have children?' – as though she were guilty of some crime against her husband, her father-in-law and the whole of their honest merchant family.

In spite of all its ease and affluence, the life that Katerina Lvovna led in the house of her father-in-law was an intensely tedious one. She seldom went out visiting, and even on those odd occasions when she did accompany her husband on his rounds of the local merchantry, she derived little pleasure from it. They were such a strict set of people: they would observe the way she sat down, the way she walked, the way she rose to her feet. Katerina Lvovna, on the other hand, had a passionate nature and, having grown up in poverty, was used to simplicity and freedom: running down to the river with her pails, bathing in her chemise by the landing-stage or scattering the husks of sunflower seeds over the gate in the direction of any handsome young swain who happened to be passing. Here, however, it was all rather different. Her husband and father-in-law would rise at the crack of dawn, drink tea together at six o'clock, and then be off about their business, while she would be left to wander idly about from room to room. Wherever she went it was clean, quiet and empty; lamps burned before the icons; but nowhere in all the house was there a living sound or a human voice.

Katerina Lvovna would pass to and fro through the empty rooms, start to yawn from boredom and then climb the stairs to the conjugal bedchamber, which had been installed in a small, high-up attic. Here she would sit, gaping absent-mindedly at the granary, where hemp was being weighed or flour being poured into sacks – and again she would feel like yawning. She would steal an hour or two's nap, but awake from it once again to that peculiarly Russian boredom, the boredom which reigns inside the houses of merchants, and which, it is said, makes even the thought of hanging oneself seem a cheerful prospect. Katerina Lvovna was no great reader, and besides, apart from the Kiev Lives of the Holy Fathers, there were no books in the house.

It was a tedious life that Katerina Lvovna had lived in her rich father-in-law's house, for the five long years of her marriage to a husband who showed her little affection. But, as is so often the case, no one paid the slightest attention to the boredom that was wearing her down.

During the sixth spring of Katerina Lvovna's marriage, the dam at the Izmailovs' water-mill gave way and burst. This happened at the very time when activity at the mill was at its most hectic, and the burst was a major one: the water was gushing out under one of the crossbeams of the timber wall, and at such a rate that not even the swiftest hand could stop it. Zinovy Borisych travelled round the entire neighbourhood chasing people together who could help, and spent practically all his time down at the mill; the old man took care of the town side of the business on his own, and Katerina Lvovna languished at home with not a soul in sight for days on end. At first she found that her husband's absence made the tedium even worse than usual, but after a while this passed, and she started to feel better than she generally did: being alone increased her sense of freedom. She had never really had any deep affection for her husband, and with him gone there was one less person to boss her around.

One day Katerina Lvovna was sitting at her attic window, yawning dreadfully and thinking of nothing in particular, when she suddenly felt ashamed of herself and stopped yawning. After all, the weather outside was so beautiful: it was warm, bright and cheerful, and through the green wooden trellis of the orchard she could see the fruit-trees and the birds fluttering from bough to bough.

'What am I doing, sitting here yawning my head off like this?' Katerina Lvovna thought to herself. 'I could at least get up and take a walk in the yard, or go down into the orchard for a bit.'

Katerina Lvovna threw on an old damask jacket and left the house.

Outside it was brilliantly sunny; the air was such that one wanted to take deep breaths of it, and the sound of merry laughter was coming from the gallery outside the granaries.

'What are you laughing at?' Katerina Lvovna inquired of her father-in-law's stewards.

'Oh, Katerina Lvovna, ma'am, we've been weighing a live sow,' an old steward replied.

'Which sow?'

'It's that sow Aksinya, ma'am, the one that had a son called Vasily and never invited us to the christening,' said the bold, cheerful voice of a sturdy young lad with a cheeky red face that was framed by coal-black curls and the beginnings of a beard.

At that moment, from the measuring vat that was suspended from the beam of the scales appeared the fat and rubicund features of the cook, Aksinya.

'You devils, you horrible devils!' the cook was cursing, trying to grab hold of the iron scale-beam and clamber out of the swaying vat.

'She weighs eight puds[1] before dinner, and if she eats a large basketful of hay there won't be weights enough to measure her,' said the handsome young lad, continuing his explanation. Then, giving the vat a shove, he tipped the cook out on to a large nine-pud flour sack that was lying in the corner.

The peasant woman, whose cursing was mostly in jest, began to straighten her dress.

'All right then, how much do I weigh?' said Katerina Lvovna in a humorous tone of voice and, seizing hold of the rope, jumped on to the weighing board.

'Three puds seven,' replied the handsome lad, whose name was Sergei, throwing weights into the weighing pan. 'Amazing!'

'What's amazing?'

'That you only weigh three puds, Katerina Lvovna. A man couldn't ask for better than to carry you around in his arms all day: not only would the fellow not get tired – he'd have a really wonderful time!'

'Do you think I'm some kind of disembodied spirit, or what? Of course you'd get tired,' replied Katerina Lvovna who, being unused to this kind of talk, found herself blushing slightly. She felt a sudden desire to let her hair down and say a lot of roguish and diverting things.

'I wouldn't, you know! I could carry you all the way to blessed Arabia,' Sergei said in answer to her remark.

'You've got it wrong, you know, young fellow,' said the muzhik who was pouring the flour. 'What does our weight matter? Do you think it's important what we weigh? The weight of our bodies doesn't matter at all – it's how strong we are, our strength – that's what matters.'

'Yes, when I was a young girl I was ever so strong,' said Katerina Lvovna, once again unable to restrain herself. 'There were even some men who couldn't get the better of me.'

'All right then, let's put our hands together and see if that's true,' said the young man.

Katerina Lvovna was somewhat put off her stride by this request, but she extended her hand all the same.

'Ouch! Leave my ring alone: that hurts!' cried Katerina Lvovna, as Sergei gripped her hand in his, and with her free hand she pushed him in the chest.

The young man let go of his mistress's hand and went flying a couple of paces sideways from the force of her push.

'Well now, that's some woman for you!' said the muzhik in wonderment.

'Come on, let me try a wrestling hold on you,' said Sergei, making it sound like some official challenge.

'Very well,' Katerina Lvovna replied and, by now in a thoroughly good humour, raised her elbows.

Sergei put his arms around the young mistress and pressed her firm bosom against his red shirt. Katerina Lvovna scarcely had time to make a move before Sergei lifted her from the floor, held her in his arms, gave her a hug and put her gently down on the upturned measuring vat.

Katerina Lvovna did not even get a chance to exercise the strength of which she had boasted. Red and flushed, she sat on the measuring vat, adjusted her jacket, which had slipped off her shoulders, and quietly left the granary, while Sergei gave an energetic cough and shouted:

'Right, you fools of the Heavenly Tsar! Pour, and don't slack, give your shovels their whack; whatever's to spare is ours, and so there!' just as if nothing had happened.

'That Sergei's a devil for the lasses!' said Aksinya the cook as she trudged along behind Katerina Lvovna. 'The cheeky thief's got all that it takes – the face, the height and the looks. Any woman he wants he has her right away, the villain – he'll flatter her and flatter her and lead her into sin. And he's fickle, the villain, fickle-fickle-fickle!'

'By the way, Aksinya,' said the young mistress as she walked on in front, 'is that little boy of yours still alive?'

'Of course he is, ma'am – what else? It's always the little ones as aren't wanted that goes on living.'

'Tell me again, how was it you came to have him?'

'Oh, I just had him, ma'am. From having a good time. Us peasant women get about a bit, you know. From having a good time.'

'What about that young fellow, has he been with us long?'

'Who do you mean, ma'am? Sergei?'

'Yes.'

'About a month, ma'am. Before he came here he was working over at the Kopchonovs' place, but old man Kopchonov kicked him out.' Aksinya lowered her voice, adding: 'They do say that he and the missus were carrying on together . . . though his soul be three times damned, he's a bold one, and no mistake!'

A warm, milky twilight floated over the town. Zinovy Borisych had still not returned from the water-mill. Neither was Boris Timofeich, Katerina's father-in-law, at home: he had gone to the name-day celebration of an old friend, saying he would not be back until after supper. For want of anything better to do, Katerina Lvovna had her supper early, opened the small windows of her attic bedroom and, leaning against the windowpane, spent her time shelling sunflower seeds. The servants took their supper in the kitchen and went off to various places in the yard in order to sleep: some to the woodsheds, others to the granaries and others to the tall, fragrant haylofts. Sergei was the last to leave the kitchen. He strolled about the yard, unleashed the watch-dogs, whistled for a bit and then, as he passed beneath Katerina Lvovna's window, looked up at her and gave her a deep bow.

'Hullo,' Katerina Lvovna said to him softly from her attic, and the yard fell as silent as the grave.

Two minutes later, outside Katerina Lvovna's locked door, someone said: 'Ma'am?'

'Who is it?' Katerina Lvovna asked, fearfully.

'Don't be afraid: it's me, Sergei,' the steward's voice replied.

'What do you want, Sergei?'

'I just wanted to have a word with you about something, Katerina Lvovna. It isn't really very important, but I wondered if you could do me a small favour; may I come in and see you for a moment?'

Katerina Lvovna unlocked her door and let Sergei in.

'What is it you want?' she asked, retreating to the window.

'Oh, Katerina Lvovna, I've come to ask you if you might have a book you could lend me to read. Things are so boring just now.'

'I haven't any books, Sergei: I don't read them,' Katerina Lvovna replied.

'But everything's so boring!'

'I like that, coming from you.'

'How can it fail to be boring? I'm a young chap, and yet we live the life of monks in a cloister here, and when I look into the future I sometimes think I'll be stuck in this lonely way of life until my grave. Sometimes I get really desperate.'

'Why don't you marry, then?'

'That's easier said than done, ma'am. Who would I marry? I'm not one of your bigwigs: there's no master's daughter who'd have me, and as for the poorer girls, well, you know yourself, Katerina Lvovna, they're such an uncultured lot. You can't expect them to have any proper understanding of what love is. There isn't even much of that among the better-offs. If you'll pardon me saying so, ma'am, you'd be the joy and consolation of any normal man's life, any man who had feelings – yet he keeps you cooped up here like a canary in a cage.'

'Yes, I'm bored, too,' Katerina Lvovna burst out, suddenly.

'How can you fail to be bored, ma'am, living the life that you do? Even if you had a man on the side, as it were, the way other married women do, you'd never be able to see him.'

'Now I think you're . . . going a little too far. No, it's just that I think I'd be happier if I were to have a baby.'

'Yes, but if you'll pardon me, ma'am, babies don't just spring out of thin air – they're the consequence of certain goings-on between people. You know, I've lived a lot of years among the masters, and I've seen the kind of life the merchants' wives lead – do you think I don't know what goes on? There's a song you sometimes hear, it goes: "When your sweetheart's gone, sadness catches on" and, if you'll forgive me, ma'am, that sadness is lying so heavy on my own heart that I'd like to cut it out of my breast with my damask steel knife and throw it at your little feet. I'd feel so much better then – a hundred times better . . .'

Sergei's voice began to tremble.

'Why are you telling me all this, Sergei? It has nothing to do with me. Now off you go . . .'

'No, please, ma'am—' said Sergei, who was now quivering all over. He took a step towards Katerina Lvovna. 'I know it and I see it and I feel it: your life's no happier than mine, only now –' he said in a single breath, 'now, at this very moment, it's all in your hands, it's all in your power.'

'What's in my power? What is it you want? Why have you come to me? I'll jump out of the window,' said Katerina Lvovna, feeling herself becoming overwhelmed by an indescribable sense of terror, and clutching with one hand at the windowsill.

'My matchless darling! Don't be so silly!' Sergei whispered, unabashed, and, making a grab at her, snatched her off the windowsill and held her in a tight embrace.

'Oh! Oh! Let go of me!' Katerina Lvovna moaned softly, her resistance softening under Sergei's passionate kisses as, in spite of herself, she pressed herself against his powerful body.

Sergei picked his mistress up like a child and carried her off in his arms to the dark sleeping recess.

Silence ensued in the room, broken only by the regular ticking of Katerina Lvovna's husband's pocket watch, which hung above the headboard of her bed; but that proved little of a disturbance.

'Go now,' said Katerina Lvovna, half an hour later, avoiding Sergei's eyes as she rearranged her dishevelled hair in front of the small mirror.

'Now why should I go at a time like this?' Sergei replied happily.

'My father-in-law will lock the doors.'

'Oh, sweetheart, sweetheart, what kind of men have you been living among, who only know how to reach a woman by way of a door? I can find doors both to you and from you wherever I look,' the young gallant replied, pointing to the wooden supports of the gallery.

4

Zinovy Borisych stayed away from home for another week in a row, and his wife spent every night of that week indulging in pleasure with Sergei.

Much, on those nights in the bedchamber of Zinovy Borisych, was the drinking of wine from Katerina Lvovna's father-in-law's wine cellar, the gorging of sweetmeats, the kissing of the mistress's sugary lips, the fondling of black curls on soft pillows. Not all roads are, however, equally smooth: from time to time there are also roughnesses in the way.

On one of the nights in question, Boris Timofeich was unable to get to sleep: the old man kept wandering about the house in his striped cotton nightshirt, going first to one window, then on to another, looking and looking, when suddenly what should he see but the red shirt of that young gallant Sergei moving softly, softly down one of the gallery supports beneath his daughter-in-law's window. That was a sight he hadn't seen before! Boris Timofeich leapt out on to the gallery and seized the young gallant by the legs, whereupon Sergei swung round in order to land the old man a hefty blow on the ear, but refrained from doing so at the last moment, having evidently decided that it would cause too much trouble.

'Out with it,' said Boris Timofeich. 'Where have you been, you thieving villain?'

'Where have I been, Boris Timofeich?' Sergei replied. 'Why, sir, I've been where I no longer am.'

'Have you been sleeping with my daughter-in-law?'

'Well now, master, I know where I've been sleeping; and all I can tell you is that it's no good crying over spilt milk. Don't bring shame on the house of a merchant by your carrying-on. Tell me, what is it you want of me? What satisfaction do you desire?'

'I'll tell you what I desire, and that's to give you five hundred strokes of the lash, you viper,' Boris Timofeich replied.

'The guilt is mine – the will be thine,' the young blood admitted. 'Just say the word, tell me where I'm to go, and you may fatten yourself on my distress to your heart's desire.'

Boris Timofeich led Sergei down into his storeroom dungeon and lashed him with a whip until he had no more strength. Sergei did not utter so much as a groan, even though he bit half of his shirtsleeve away.

Boris Timofeich left Sergei in the storeroom until such time as his flayed back had healed; he shoved an earthenware jug of water under his nose, locked the storeroom with a heavy iron padlock, and sent a messenger off to fetch back his son.

But even in the Russia of today a journey of a hundred versts takes some considerable time, and Katerina Lvovna was already beginning to feel that she could not live another hour without Sergei. Quite suddenly, the full force of her newly awoken character burgeoned out, and she grew so determined that there was no stopping her. She found out where Sergei was, spoke to him through the iron door and rushed off to look for the keys. 'Let Sergei out of there, Father-in-law,' she said.

The old man turned fairly green with rage. Not in all his born days had he expected such brazen impudence from his daughter-in-law who, though he knew her to be no angel, had at least remained obedient until now.

'How dare you talk to me like that, you . . .' he said, beginning to put Katerina Lvovna to shame.

'Let him out of there,' she said. 'I swear to you on my conscience that nothing bad has passed between us.'

'Nothing bad!' he said, fairly grinding his teeth in fury. 'What have you been doing with him all those nights? Putting new covers on your husband's pillows?'

But Katerina Lvovna kept up the pressure, demanding that he do as she wanted: 'Let him out, go on, let him out!'

'Very well then,' said Boris Timofeich. 'If that's the way you want it, when your husband comes home we'll haul you off to the stables with our bare hands and I'll personally see to it that that villain goes to gaol tomorrow.'

Thus did Boris Timofeich decide: but it was a decision that came to nothing.

Before he retired for the night, Boris Timofeich ate a supper of pickled mushrooms and kasha, and consequently began to suffer from heartburn. All of a sudden he was taken ill in the pit of his stomach; terrible heavings rose within him, and towards morning he met with exactly the same kind of death as that experienced by the rats in his granaries, rats for whom Katerina Lvovna was in the habit of preparing a special kind of food containing a noxious white powder that had been entrusted to her care.

Katerina Lvovna let her Sergei out of the old man's storeroom dungeon and, without stopping to worry about what people might think, she put him to bed to rest between her husband's sheets so that he might recover from the beating he had received from her father-in-law. Old man Boris Timofeich was buried according to Christian ritual, and no one suspected a thing. It never occurred to anyone to wonder whether there might have been anything unusual about the affair; Boris Timofeich had died, and he had died as a result of eating pickled mushrooms, just as many others had died before him. They buried Boris Timofeich in a hurry, not even waiting for his son to return, as the weather was warm. In any case, the messenger who had been sent to bring back Zinovy Borisych had not found him at the mill; Zinovy Borisych had happened to learn of some timber that was being sold off cheap at a place some hundred versts away: he had gone to inspect it, and had told no one about his precise destination.

Once she had attended to this matter, Katerina Lvovna completely let herself go. She was no coward, and there was no knowing what might be on her mind; she strutted about giving orders to everyone in the house, and would not let Sergei out of her sight. All of this was much to the wonderment of the servants, stewards and workmen, but Katerina Lvovna was lavish with her tips, and the wonderment very quickly faded away. 'The mistress and Sergei are having a bit of a doo-dah together, that's all,' people would say with a nod and a wink. 'It's her business, and she's the one who'll stand to account for it.'

Meanwhile Sergei grew better, straightened up and once more stalked around Katerina Lvovna like a gerfalcon; once again they resumed their amorous relations. But not for them alone did time roll on: after a long absence Zinovy Borisych, the wronged husband, came hurrying home.

That afternoon the heat was sweltering, and the nagging flies unbearably irksome. Katerina Lvovna closed the bedroom shutters and draped a woollen shawl over them; then she lay down beside Sergei on the merchant's bed to rest. She dozed fitfully, but was so tormented by the heat that her face streamed with perspiration and her breathing was hot and shallow. She felt that it must be time for her to be up and about again, time to go into the orchard and drink tea – but try as she would, she could not get up. At last the cook came to the door and knocked. 'The samovar under the apple tree's going out,' she said. With an effort, Katerina Lvovna turned over on her side and found herself stroking a cat. The cat was rubbing itself between Sergei and her, such an enormous, handsome grey tom-cat, as fat as fat could be . . . and with whiskers like those of a country rent-collector. Katerina Lvovna began to run her fingers through its fluffy fur, and it pressed its animal's face against her; pushed its soft, round muzzle against her resilient breasts, maintaining all the while a quiet, musical purr, as though it were declaring its love for her. 'How on earth did this big cat get in here?' Katerina Lvovna wondered. 'And I left the cream out on the windowsill too: it's sure to gobble it all up, the scoundrel. I must chase it out,' she decided, and she tried to seize hold of the cat and throw it out; but it slipped through her fingers as though it were made of thin air. 'Oh, where has this cat come from?' Katerina wondered in her nightmare. 'We've never had any cat in our bedroom before, and just look at the size of the one that's got in!' Once again she tried to catch hold of the cat, but once again there was no cat there. 'Oh, what is this? Is it a cat, or isn't it? she thought. She was suddenly overcome by a sense of utter confusion which completely jolted her out of her state of drowsiness and dispelled the dream altogether. Katerina Lvovna looked round the bedchamber – there was no cat anywhere to be seen, and only the handsome Sergei lay there pressing one of her breasts to his hot face with a powerful arm.

Katerina Lvovna got up, sat down on the bed, covered Sergei in kisses, caressed him, straightened the rumpled eiderdown, and then went out into the orchard to drink tea; by this time the sun had completely set, and a beautiful magical evening was descending on the hot, baked land.

'I overslept,' Katerina Lvovna said to Aksinya, as she sat down on the carpet which had been spread underneath the flowering apple tree to drink tea. 'What do you think this means, Aksinya?' she asked the cook, as she wiped a saucer for herself with the tea-towel.

'What, ma'am?'

'It wasn't a dream: there was a cat in my bedroom. It came and rubbed itself against me.'

'Sakes, ma'am, what *are* you talking about?'

'It's true, a cat got into my bedroom.'

And Katerina Lvovna told the story of the cat that had got in.

'And why did you stroke it?'

'How should I know why I stroked it?'

'It's a strange thing, sure enough!' the cook exclaimed.

'I just can't get over it.'

'What it probably means, ma'am, is that somebody's going to come and press themselves against you, or that something else will come of it.'

'But what, exactly?'

'My dear mistress, *exactly* what it is no one can tell you – only that something will happen.'

'I kept dreaming about the moon, and there was this cat,' Katerina Lvovna went on.

'The moon means a little one, ma'am.'

Katerina Lvovna blushed.

'Shouldn't I perhaps tell Sergei to come to you out here?' Aksinya inquired, evidently anxious to become Katerina Lvovna's confidante.

'Well, why not?' Katerina Lvovna replied. 'Yes, go and tell him to come out here; tell him there's some tea for him if he wants it.'

'Just so, ma'am. It's the right thing to do – I'll tell him to come here,' Aksinya said in a decisive tone, and waddled off towards the orchard gate, for all the world like an enormous duck.

Katerina Lvovna told Sergei about the cat, too.

'It was just a dream you had,' was Sergei's response.

'But why have I never had that dream before, Sergei? Answer me that.'

'There are a lot of things that have never happened before! The time was when I used to pine just at the sight of you – yet now I possess the whole of your white body.'

Sergei embraced Katerina Lvovna, whirled her around in mid-air, and laughingly threw her down on the fluffy carpet.

'Oh, my head's spinning,' said Katerina Lvovna. 'Sergei, come here for a moment; sit down here beside me,' she called, stretching voluptuously, and taking up a languorous posture.

The young gallant stooped down and came in under the low-hanging apple tree, which was covered in white blossoms, and sat down on the carpet at Katerina Lvovna's feet.

'So you used to pine for me, did you, Sergei?'

'How could I have failed to pine for you?'

'What sort of pining was it? Describe it to me.'

'How do you describe a thing like that? Can a man explain to a woman how he pined for her? I just longed for you, that's all.'

'Why did I never feel that you were pining for me? They say a woman can feel that sort of thing.'

Sergei was silent.

'And why were you always singing, if you were so miserable without me? What about that? I think I used to hear you singing in the gallery, didn't I?' Katerina Lvovna went on, persisting with her questioning of Sergei, while continuing to caress him.

'What of it? The gnat spends its whole life singing, but it doesn't do it because it's happy,' Sergei observed, coldly.

There ensued a pause. Katerina Lvovna was filled with the most extreme delight at these confessions of Sergei's.

She felt like talking, but Sergei sat looking gloomy, and said nothing.

'Look, Sergei – isn't this simply heavenly?' Katerina Lvovna exclaimed, looking up through the apple tree's thickly blossomed branches which covered her, at the cloudless dark-blue sky in which a bright, full moon was shining.

As it penetrated the leaves and the flowers of the apple tree, the moonlight played over the face of the supine Katerina Lvovna, and over her entire body. The air was quiet. Only a light, warm zephyr barely ruffled the drowsy leaves, wafting the delicate fragrance of flowering grasses and trees. There was a breath of something languorous, something that predisposed one towards laziness, sweet bliss and dark desires.

Receiving no answer, Katerina Lvovna again fell silent, and continued to look up at the sky through the pale pink blossoms of the apple tree. Sergei, too, was silent; but the sky did not interest him. He sat hugging his knees with both arms, staring hard at his boots.

What a golden night it was! It was still and light and fragrant and benignly, enliveningly warm. Far away beyond the ravine, behind the orchard, someone began to sing in a rich, resonant voice – in the dense cherry thicket by the fence a nightingale chattered and then burst into loud carolling; on a tall pole in a cage, a quail sang in drowsy delirium; a sleek horse sighed languorously on the other side of the stable wall, and on the other side of the orchard fence a boisterous pack of dogs went shooting out across the common grazing land without any sound whatsoever, and vanished in the misshapen shadow cast by the old, half-ruined salt warehouses.

Katerina Lvovna raised herself on one elbow and looked at the grass of the orchard. How it glittered in the moon's radiance, which splashed against the blossoms and the leaves of the trees! It was all being turned to gold by these intricate, dappled patches of light, and how they flickered and quivered over it like living butterflies of fire, or as if all this grass under the trees were so many fish caught by the moon's net and tossing from side to side.

'Oh, Sergei, how lovely it is!' Katerina Lvovna exclaimed, as she looked around her.

Sergei let his eyes rove around indifferently.

'What's wrong, Sergei? Why are you so sad? Have you grown tired of my love already?'

'Don't be silly,' Sergei replied coldly and, leaning down, he gave Katerina Lvovna a lazy kiss.

'You're a deceiver, Sergei,' Katerina Lvovna said in a jealous voice. 'You're shallow.'

'I don't accept those words as referring to myself,' Sergei replied calmly.

'Then why don't you kiss me properly?'

This time Sergei fell completely silent.

'It's only husbands and wives who kiss like that, to brush the dust off each other's lips,' Katerina Lvovna went on, as she fondled his curls. 'I want you to kiss me so that the young blossoms on this apple tree above us fall to the ground. Look, like this, like this,' Katerina Lvovna whispered, twining herself around her lover and kissing him with passionate tenderness.

'Listen, Sergei, there's something I want to ask you,' Katerina Lvovna began a short while later. 'What is it that makes everyone say the same thing about you – that you're a deceiver?'

'What is it that makes people tell lies about me?'

'It's what they say.'

'Well, perhaps I may sometimes have deceived girls who were completely unworthy.'

'And why did you get involved with girls who were unworthy, you silly idiot? You shouldn't go making love to girls who are unworthy.'

'It's all very well for you to talk! Do you think it's the sort of thing a man plans beforehand? It's temptation that does the work, that's all. Without any intention of doing it, you break the commandments with her, and all she does is put her arms round your neck. That's love for you!'

'Now listen here, Sergei! I don't know anything about those other women of yours, and I don't want to; all I know is that it was you who seduced me into this love affair of ours, and you yourself know how much I entered it because I wanted to and how much because of your cunning – so, Sergei, if you deceive me, if you throw me over for anyone else, anyone else at all, then bear this in mind, my darling friend: I won't part from you alive.'

Sergei gave a start.

'Wait, Katerina Lvovna. Light of my day,' he said, 'you can see for yourself the way things stand between us. Just now you remarked that I seemed broody today, but you don't reflect that I may not be able to help it. It may be that my heart has drowned in its own blood.'

'Tell me about it, Sergei. Tell me about what's troubling you.'

'What is there to tell? Very soon, the next thing you know, your husband's going to show up and then he'll say: "Right you are, Sergei Filipych, off you go, round to the backyard and get those musicians ready to play." And there I'll have to sit, looking up from the woodshed at the candle burning in Katerina Lvovna's bedroom and see her plumping up her featherbed and lying down in it together with her lawful husband, Zinovy Borisych.'

'It won't happen!' said Katerina Lvovna in a lazy, laughing voice, waving her arm.

'What do you mean, it won't happen? The way I see it, there's absolutely nothing you can do to prevent it from happening. But I have a heart, too, Katerina Lvovna, and I can foresee the suffering that's in store for me.'

'Oh come, that's enough of all that.'

This manifestation of Sergei's jealousy pleased Katerina Lvovna and, laughing, she resumed her kisses.

'But I must say,' Sergei went on, quietly freeing his head from Katerina Lvovna's arms, which were bare to the shoulders, 'I must say that my station, even though it be the lowliest imaginable, causes me to do a lot of thinking, one way and another. I'll tell you this, Katerina Lvovna, that if I were your equal, if I were some master or merchant or other, I'd never part with you, not ever in my life. Well, but surely you can see for yourself what sort of a man you have before you? When very soon now I see your husband take you by your white arms and lead you to the bedchamber, I will have to endure it within my heart, and will despise myself because of it ever afterwards, Katerina Lvovna! You see, I'm not like other fellows who'll put up with anything just as long as they get their pleasure from a woman. What I feel is real love, and I feel it sucking at my heart like a black viper . . .'

'Why are you saying all these things to me?' said Katerina Lvovna, interrupting him.

She had begun to feel sorry for Sergei.

'Katerina Lvovna! How can I help saying them to you? How can I help it? When it may well be that it's all been described to your husband in the most vivid detail, when – never mind about at some distant date in the future – tomorrow there may not be so much as a shadow of a ghost left of your Sergei in this establishment.'

'No, no, don't say such things, Sergei. I tell you it just won't happen – I won't be left alone without you,' Katerina Lvovna said, calming him with the same caresses as before. 'If it ever comes to that . . . either he will die, or I will; but you are going to stay with me.'

'That can never be, Katerina Lvovna,' Sergei replied, shaking his head sadly and mournfully. 'My life's no joy to me on account of this affair of ours. If I'd chosen someone who wasn't my social superior I'd have been all right. You don't seriously suppose that this can last, do you? I mean, it doesn't exactly do you credit to be my mistress, does it? I'd like to be your husband, marry you in church: then, even though I'd still consider myself your inferior, I'd at least be able to demonstrate to everyone the respect I have for my wife . . .'

Katerina Lvovna was quite overcome by these words of Sergei's, by his jealous possessiveness and his desire to marry her – a desire which is always pleasing to a woman, even if her relations with the man before marriage have been of the very briefest. Katerina Lvovna was now ready to follow Sergei through hell and high water, come what may. So much in love with him had he made her that her devotion to him knew no limits. She was in an ecstasy of happiness; her blood was aroused, and she would listen to no more of what Sergei had to tell her. Quickly, she pressed the palm of one hand against his lips and, pressing her head against his breast, she said:

'Anyway, I know now how I can make you a merchant, too, and live with you in an entirely proper fashion. All I ask is that you don't make me feel sad to no purpose, before we've had a chance to straighten things out.'

And once again their kissing and caressing resumed.

The old steward who was sleeping in the woodshed began to be aware, through his heavy slumber, that the silence of the night was being broken, now by whispering and quiet laughter, as though somewhere children were discussing how best they might make a fool of the puny old man, and now by bursts of resonant, high-spirited laughter, as though the wood-sprites were tickling someone. All these sounds were emanating from where Katerina Lvovna, splashing in moonlight and rolling over on the soft carpet, was playing and disporting herself with her husband's young steward. The fresh, white blossoms kept falling, falling from the leafy apple tree, and then at last stopped falling. And meanwhile the brief summer night had passed, the moon concealed itself behind the rounded roofs of the tall granaries and gave the earth a sidelong look, growing paler and paler; then spitting was heard, followed by angry hissing, and two or three tom-cats fell noisily scrabbling off the roof down a pile of planks that had been placed against it.

'Let's go to bed and sleep now,' Katerina Lvovna said slowly, as though her appetite for lovemaking had grown jaded, and getting up from the carpet just as she was, wearing nothing but her shift and white petticoat, she walked across the quiet – even deathly quiet – yard into the merchant's house. Sergei picked up the carpet and the blouse which she had playfully thrown off, and followed her inside.

As soon as Katerina Lvovna had blown out the candle and lain down, almost completely naked, on the soft featherbed, she sank into a deep slumber. So sound was her sleep after all her wanton pleasure that her legs and arms lost all sensation; but then once again through her sleep she seemed to hear the door opening, and the same tom-cat which had recently made its appearance fell on to her bed like a heavy old boot.

'Why has this cat been sent to plague me?' Katerina Lvovna thought, wearily. 'I took good care to lock the door, the window's closed – yet here it is again. I'll have to throw it out again.' She tried to get up, but her drowsy limbs would not obey her; and meanwhile the cat walked all over her, making a strange purring noise that sounded like human speech. And wherever the cat walked on it, Katerina Lvovna's body was covered in gooseflesh.

'No,' she thought, 'there's nothing for it: I shall have to sprinkle the bed with holy water tomorrow, for this is a very strange cat that's taken to visiting me.'

The cat continued to purr, right next to her ear now, butting her with its muzzle. Suddenly it said: 'I'm not a cat! Where did you get that idea? You know perfectly well, Katerina Lvovna, that I'm not a cat, but the prominent merchant Boris Timofeich. It's just that I'm in rather a bad way at present on account of some stuff my daughter-in-law gave me to eat.' Then it purred: 'That's what's made me shrink in size, so that I look like a cat to those who don't know who I am. Well, Katerina Lvovna, how are you getting along in our house these days?

Still keeping to your marriage vows, are you? I thought I'd just nip over from the cemetery for a while to watch you and Sergei Filipych keeping your husband's bed warm. Purr, purr, but I can't see a thing, you know. You don't need to be afraid of me: you see, my eyes fell out because of that stuff you gave me to eat. Look into my eyes, my dear, don't be afraid!'

Katerina Lvovna looked, and then began to scream at the top of her voice. Once again the cat was lying in between her and Sergei, but this time it had the head of Boris Timofeich, bloated and swollen as it had been on his corpse, and instead of eyes it had two fiery circles that kept spinning and spinning in opposite directions.

Sergei woke up, calmed Katerina Lvovna, and then went back to sleep again; but she was wide-awake now – and that was just as well.

As she lay there with her eyes open she suddenly heard something that sounded like someone climbing over the gate. The dogs began to rush about, but then grew quiet – as if they were fawning on someone. Another minute went by, and then the iron latch on the front door downstairs gave a click, and it opened. 'Either I'm imagining things, or that's Zinovy Borisych come back,' thought Katerina Lvovna, and she gave Sergei a hurried shove.

'Listen, Sergei!' she said, sitting up on one elbow and straining her ears.

And indeed, someone was quietly climbing the stairs, treading cautiously, step by step, in the direction of the bedchamber with its locked door.

Clad only in her shift, Katerina Lvovna quickly leapt from the bed and opened the window. At that same moment Sergei jumped out on to the gallery in his bare feet and threw his legs around the support down which he had slid so many times in the past after leaving his mistress's bedchamber.

'No, don't, don't! Find somewhere to lie down, and don't go far away,' Katerina Lvovna whispered. Out of the window she threw Sergei his shoes and clothes, and then plunged back under the coverlet, waiting.

Sergei did as Katerina Lvovna told him; instead of slipping down the support, he took refuge under some bast which had been used to cover the floor of the gallery.

Meanwhile Katerina Lvovna could hear her husband approaching the door and listening, as he held his breath. She could even hear the quickened beating of his jealous heart; it was, however, not with pity, but with malicious laughter that she was convulsed.

'You're on a wild-goose chase,' she said to him mentally, her smile and breathing as pure as those of a newborn infant.

This state of affairs continued for some ten minutes: but finally Zinovy Borisych got fed up with standing outside the door listening to his wife sleeping. He knocked.

'Who's there?' Katerina Lvovna called, after a slight pause, and in a voice that was meant to sound sleepy.

'A friend,' Zinovy Borisych replied.

'Is that you, Zinovy Borisych?'

'Of course it's me! Don't you know my voice?'

Katerina Lvovna sprang up, just as she was, wearing nothing but her shift, let her husband into the room and dived back into the warm bed.

'It seems to get cold before dawn,' she said, pulling the covers up around her.

As he entered, Zinovy Borisych looked around him, said a few prayers, lit a candle and then took another look round.

'How have you been keeping, then?' he asked his wife.

'Oh, all right,' Katerina Lvovna replied. Sitting up, she began to put on a buttonless, open cotton blouse.

'Do you want me to put the samovar on?' she asked.

'It's all right, shout for Aksinya, let her do it.'

Katerina Lvovna kicked on her shoes, not bothering to put on stockings, and ran out of the room. She did not return until half an hour later. During this time she lit the samovar herself, and slipped out on to the gallery to see Sergei.

'Stay where you are,' she whispered to him.

'How long for?' he asked her, also in a whisper.

'Oh what a blockhead you are! Stay where you are until I give the word.'

And Katerina Lvovna made him crawl back into his hiding-place again.

From the gallery Sergei could hear everything that was going on in the bedchamber. Again he heard the sound of the door banging, and of Katerina Lvovna going back to her husband. Every word was audible.

'What's taken you so long?' Zinovy Borisych inquired of his wife.

'I've been lighting the samovar,' she replied, calmly.

A pause ensued. Sergei could hear Zinovy Borisych hanging his frock-coat on the coat-rack. Next came the sound of him washing himself, snorting and splashing water in all directions. There he was, asking for a towel. Once more the talking resumed.

'So you buried Father, did you? How did that come about?' her husband inquired.

'That's right, we did,' said his wife. 'He died, so we buried him.'

'It was rather an odd thing to happen, wasn't it?'

'Perhaps it was and perhaps it wasn't,' Katerina Lvovna replied, putting the cups down with a rattle.

Zinovy Borisych paced mournfully about the room.

'Well, and how did you pass the time while I was away?' he asked, keeping up his questioning of his wife.

'Everyone knows what there is by way of entertainment here: we don't go to balls and we don't go to the theatre.'

'It seems to me that you don't find having your husband back particularly entertaining either,' Zinovy Borisych said, giving her a sidelong look.

'Well, it's not exactly as if we were young lovers, you and I, that we should go out of our minds every time we meet after an absence. What more can I do to show you I'm pleased to see you? Here I am fussing around, running at your beck and call.'

Once again Katerina Lvovna ran out of the room, this time to fetch the samovar, and again she paid a flying visit to Sergei, tugged his arm and said: 'Whatever you do, don't doze off!'

Sergei had no idea of where all this was leading to, but he kept himself on the alert all the same.

When Katerina Lvovna returned, she found Zinovy Borisych kneeling on the bed. He was hanging his silver watch above the headboard by its bead chain.

'Why is the bed made up for two when you've been on your own here, Katerina Lvovna?' he suddenly asked his wife, in a tone of subtle inquiry.

'I spent all the time waiting for you,' Katerina Lvovna replied, surveying him calmly.

'I'm grateful for that, I'm sure ... And what about this object lying on the bed, how did it get here?'

Zinovy Borisych picked up Sergei's woollen belt from the sheet and held it up by one end in front of his wife's eyes.

Katerina Lvovna did not hesitate for a moment before replying.

'I found it in the garden and used it to tie my skirt with,' she said.

'Is that so?' said Zinovy Borisych, giving his words a peculiar emphasis. 'Yes, I've been hearing a few things about your skirts, too.'

'What have you been hearing?'

'Oh, about all the fine things you've been up to.'

'I haven't been up to anything.'

'Well, we shall see, we shall see,' Zinovy Borisych replied, pushing his empty teacup towards his wife.

Katerina Lvovna said nothing for a while.

'We shall bring all that you've been up to out into the open, Katerina Lvovna,' said Zinovy Borisych, after another long pause, beetling his brows at his wife.

'Your Katerina Lvovna isn't easily frightened,' his wife replied. 'Not easily frightened at all.'

'What? What?' cried Zinovy Borisych, raising his voice.

'Nothing, forget it,' his wife replied.

'Well, you'd better watch out, that's all I can say. You seem to have an awful lot to say for yourself all of a sudden!'

'And why shouldn't I have a lot to say for myself?' said Katerina Lvovna.

'You ought to look to yourself.'

'I've no reason to look to myself. As if it weren't enough for loose tongues to go wagging a lot of nonsense in your direction, I have to put up with all your innuendoes as well. That's a fine state of things, isn't it?'

'It's not loose tongues that are to blame – the truth about your amours is out, that's what.'

'What amours?' screamed Katerina Lvovna, flaring up in earnest now.

'I know what ones.'

'All right, come to the point, then, and tell me about them!'

Zinovy Borisych said nothing for a bit. Once again he pushed his empty cup towards his wife.

'It's evident there's nothing for you to tell!' Katerina Lvovna said with contempt, throwing a teaspoon excitedly into her husband's saucer. 'Well, tell me: what have people been saying about me? Who's this lover I'm supposed to have?'

'You'll find out soon enough – don't be in such a hurry.'

'It's Sergei, isn't it? They've been telling you lies about him.'

'We shall see, we shall see, Katerina Lvovna. No one has robbed me of my power over you, and no one is going to do so . . . You shall tell me yourself . . . '

'Ugh! I can't stand this,' shrieked Katerina Lvovna, grinding her teeth in rage. Her face was now as white as a sheet. She suddenly leapt up, and vanished out of the door.

'Very well, here he is,' she said as she came back into the room a few moments later, leading Sergei by the sleeve. 'Go ahead. Ask us both about whatever it is you think you know. Perhaps you'll learn more than you bargained for.'

By now, Zinovy Borisych had thoroughly lost his head. He looked now at Sergei, who was leaning against the doorway, and now at his wife, who had sat herself calmly down on the bed with her arms folded, and could not for the life of him think where all this was leading.

'What have you been up to, you snake in the grass?' he barely managed to articulate, riveted to his armchair.

'Go on, ask us about whatever it is you think you know so well,' said Katerina Lvovna, cheekily. 'You think you can frighten me with the threat of a beating,' she continued, giving him a meaningful wink, 'but you'll never be able to do that. I decided how I would deal with you even before you made those threats of yours, and now I'm going to carry out my plan.'

'What's this? Get out of my house!' Zinovy Borisych shouted to Sergei.

'Well I never!' Katerina Lvovna said, teasingly.

Nimbly, she locked the door, put the key away in her pocket and once again lolled back on the bed in her open blouse.

'Now then, Sergei, come to me, come over here, my darling,' she said to the steward, enticing him with her charms.

Sergei tossed back his curls, and boldly sat down beside his mistress.

'Good Lord! What is this? What are you doing, you savages?' cried Zinovy Borisych, turning purple as he rose from his armchair.

'There! Don't you think he's handsome? Look, look at my fine young eagle, look how splendid he is!'

Katerina Lvovna burst out laughing and kissed Sergei passionately in front of her husband.

At that same instant a deafening slap set her cheeks aflame, and Zinovy Borisych rushed towards the open window.

8

'Aha! So that's how you want it . . . Very well, my dear friend – thank you. That's all I've been waiting for!' screamed Katerina Lvovna. 'Now I know how things stand . . . we'll do this my way, not yours . . .'

In one single movement she thrust Sergei away from her; then she hurled herself at her husband and, before Zinovy Borisych had time to make a leap for the window, with her slender fingers she seized hold of him by the throat from behind and threw him to the floor as if he were a sheaf of hemp.

When Zinovy Borisych went noisily lumbering over, and the back of his head struck the floor with full force, he really went to pieces. This sudden dénouement was the last thing he had been expecting. This first show of violence against him on the part of his wife was enough to indicate to him that she was prepared to stop at nothing in order to be rid of him, and that the situation in which he now found himself was an extremely dangerous one. Zinovy Borisych grasped all this in a single flash at the moment of his fall and uttered no cry, realizing that no one would be able to hear him and that to make a fuss would only make matters worse for him. He cast his eyes around in silence, and finally brought them to rest on his wife, whose slender fingers firmly gripped his throat, with an expression of malevolent hostility, reproach and suffering.

Zinovy Borisych made no attempt to defend himself. His arms with their tightly clenched fists lay extended, twitching convulsively. One of them was completely unhindered; the other was pinned to the floor by one of Katerina Lvovna's knees.

'Keep him there,' she instructed Sergei in a cold-blooded whisper, turning to look at her husband.

Sergei sat down on top of his master and pinned down both his arms with his knees. As he was about to put his hands around the master's throat where Katerina Lvovna's had been, however, he emitted a dreadful yell. At the sight of his old *bête noire*, a lust for bloody revenge had rallied all the last vestiges of Zinovy Borisych's strength: he made a terrible exertion, jerked his entrapped arms out from under Sergei's knees and, using them to grab Sergei by his black curls, sank his teeth into the steward's throat. This state of affairs did not last for long, however; a second or two later Zinovy Borisych uttered a dreadful groan, and his head fell back.

Pale and scarcely breathing at all, Katerina Lvovna stood over her husband and her lover. In her right hand she clutched a heavy cast-iron candlestick by its upper end, the heavy base downward. A fine thread of vermilion blood was trickling down one of Zinovy Borisych's temples, and also down one of his cheeks.

'Send for a priest,' groaned Zinovy Borisych dully, throwing his head back in loathing as far as he could from Sergei, who was still sitting on top of him. 'I want to take confession,' he said, even less distinctly, starting to tremble and squinting sideways at the warm blood that was clotting thickly under his hair.

'You'll do fine just the way you are,' Katerina Lvovna whispered.

'That's enough messing around with him,' she said to Sergei. 'Grab him by the throat, properly.'

Zinovy Borisych began to make a wheezing sound.

Katerina Lvovna leaned down and pressed her hands on top of Sergei's where they clenched her husband's throat, and placed her ear against her husband's chest.

Five minutes later she got to her feet and said:

'That's enough, he'll do now.'

Sergei also got up, panting and puffing. Zinovy Borisych lay dead; he had been throttled, and there was a gash in one of his temples. Under his head, on the left side, there was a patch of blood which had, however, stopped flowing; it originated from a small wound which had already hardened and congealed under the matted hair.

Sergei carried the body of Zinovy Borisych down into a cellar of the same storeroom dungeon in which Boris Timofeich had only so recently locked him up, and then climbed the stairs back to the attic again. Meanwhile, Katerina Lvovna, who had rolled up the sleeves of her blouse and had rolled up the hem of her skirt high above her knees, was giving the patch of blood that Zinovy Borisych had left on the floor of his bedchamber a thorough scrub with soap and bast. The water in the samovar from which Zinovy Borisych had drunk his seigniorial cups of tea was still quite warm, and the stain washed away easily without a trace.

Katerina Lvovna picked up a brass slop-basin and a soaped piece of bast.

'Right, then: hold the candle for me, so I can see,' she said to Sergei, as she walked over to the door. 'Hold it lower down, a bit lower,' she said, attentively examining every one of the floorboards over which Sergei had had to drag Zinovy Borisych's corpse all the way to the coal cellar.

In only two places on the painted floor there were two tiny spots the size of cherries. Katerina Lvovna scrubbed them with her piece of bast, and they disappeared.

'Take that!' she said in the direction of her husband's body where it lay in the dungeon. 'That'll teach you to go creeping up on your wife like a thief, lying in wait for her like that.'

'That's enough now,' said Sergei, trembling at the sound of his own voice.

As they were on their way back into the bedchamber, a thin band of red erupted in the east and, lightly gilding the apple trees which were clothed in radiance, stared briefly through the green stakes of the orchard fence into Katerina Lvovna's room.

Crossing himself and yawning, a sheepskin jacket covering his shoulders, the old steward was trudging his way from the woodshed across the yard to the kitchen.

Katerina Lvovna cautiously tugged one of the cords that opened the shutters and studied Sergei attentively, as though she were trying to see into his soul.

'Well, there you are: you're a merchant, too, now,' she said, putting her white hands on his shoulders.

Sergei made no reply.

His lips were trembling, and the rest of him was shaking as if with a fever. Katerina Lvovna's lips, on the other hand, were cold.

Two days later, large calluses, raised by the crowbar and heavy shovel he had used to bury Zinovy Borisych, appeared on Sergei's hands. This was, however, compensated for by the fact that Zinovy Borisych lay so neatly tidied away in his dungeon that without the help of his widow or her lover it would have been impossible to find him until the day of the resurrection of the dead.

Sergei went about with a crimson kerchief wound round his throat, complaining that there was something stuck in it. But before the marks which Zinovy Borisych had left on Sergei's throat had had time to heal, people began to notice the absence of Katerina Lvovna's husband. Indeed, Sergei himself began to talk about him more frequently than anyone else. He would sit on the bench by the gate of an evening with the young swains of the house and start the ball rolling with gambits like: 'You know, lads, I really wonder where our master can have disappeared to all this time . . .'

And the other swains would also express their bewilderment.

Then the news came from the mill that the master had hired some horses and set off for his house a long time ago. The cabby who had driven him said that Zinovy Borisych had seemed to be in a distraught frame of mind, and had paid him off in a rather odd fashion, some three versts outside town; near the monastery he had dismounted from the cart, taken his bag and walked away. When they heard this story, people began to wonder even more.

Zinovy Borisych had gone missing, that was the plain fact of it.

Searches were conducted, but nothing was discovered: it was as if the merchant had vanished into thin air. In his deposition, the cabby, who had been arrested, merely said that the merchant had dismounted from the cart on the other side of the river, near the monastery, and had walked away. The case remained unsolved, and meanwhile Katerina Lvovna proceeded to live with Sergei as a widow, unmolested. People hazarded guesses that Zinovy Borisych might be in such-and-such or such-and-such a place, but he did not come home, and Katerina Lvovna knew better than anyone else that it was quite impossible that he should ever do so.

In this way a month went by, then another, then yet another, and suddenly Katerina Lvovna realized that she was pregnant.

'We'll get the capital, Sergei: I've an heir now,' she told him, and went to the local Duma to make a complaint, saying that she was with child, trade was practically at a standstill: she should be allowed to take everything over.

A commercial enterprise such as this could not just be allowed to go to the wall. Katerina Lvovna was her husband's lawful wedded wife; there were no debts in the offing, and so it seemed as though she might as well be allowed to take over. And so she did.

Katerina Lvovna threw herself entirely into the running of the place, and lorded it over everyone; because of her importance, Sergei was now addressed as Sergei Filipych. Then suddenly, without warning, a fresh misfortune arrived. The mayor received a letter from Livny[1] which said that Boris Timofeich's business had been founded not on his own capital alone; in addition to his own money, he had also made use of funds belonging to his nephew, a minor named Fyodor Zakharov Lyamin, that the case should be investigated and that the business was not to be entrusted to the exclusive care of Katerina Lvovna. This news had only barely arrived, and the mayor had only just had time to tell Katerina Lvovna about it when some three weeks later, bang out of the blue, an old woman arrived from Livny together with a small boy.

'I'm the cousin of the deceased, Boris Timofeich, and this is my nephew, Fyodor Lyamin,' she said.

Katerina Lvovna asked them both to come in.

When Sergei, who was out in the yard, observed their arrival, and saw Katerina Lvovna ushering the visitors into the house, he turned as white as a sheet.

'What's the matter with you?' his mistress asked him, noticing his deathly pallor as he followed the visitors into the house and stood still in the hallway, looking them up and down.

'Oh, nothing,' the steward replied, turning from the hallway into the outside passage. 'I was just thinking what a strange and wonderful place Livny is,' he said with a sigh, closing the passage door behind him.

'Well, what are we going to do now?' Sergei Filipych asked Katerina Lvovna as they sat by the samovar together after dusk. 'Now all our plans have come to nothing.'

'Why do you say that, Sergei?'

'Because the whole place will be divided up now. And what'll be the point of owning a paltry bit of it?'

'Surely you'll get your fair share, Sergei?'

'That's not the point; the point is that I doubt very much whether we'll get much joy out of this state of affairs.'

'Why not? Why do you say that?'

'Because, I swear by my love for you, Katerina Lvovna, I'd like to see you a real lady, who doesn't have to live in the way you've lived up to now,' Sergei Filipych replied. 'And now, what with the reduction in the capital, it looks as though we'll be even worse off than we were before.'

'But surely you don't think I care about that, Sergei?'

'That's just it, Katerina Lvovna. It may be of no interest to you, but it is to me, because I hold you in esteem, and there's also the fact that it will look very bad in the eyes of the common folk, who are envious and mean-spirited. You're entitled to feel as you please, of course, but the way I see it is that I'll never be able to be happy with things as they are at present.'

And Sergei went on and on to Katerina Lvovna about how Fedya Lyamin had made him the most wretched man in the whole world, having deprived him of the chance of exalting and distinguishing her, Katerina Lvovna, before all the merchants of Russia. Time and time again, Sergei would return to his assertion that, were it not for this Fedya, she, who would give birth to a son less than nine months after her husband had gone missing, would get all the capital, and there would be no limits to their happiness.

And then suddenly Sergei stopped talking about the co-inheritor. No sooner, however, had the name of Fedya Lyamin ceased to fall from Sergei's lips, than it ensconced itself firmly in Katerina's mind and heart. She became pensive, and even grew cold towards Sergei. In her sleep, on her rounds of the business, or as she said her prayers, the same thought kept nagging at her: 'How can I let this happen to me? Why should I be deprived of the capital because of him? After all the suffering I've been through, after all the burden of sin I've taken on to my own two shoulders. Then he comes along and takes everything from me just like that, as easy as winking . . . I mean, if he were a grown man, that would be different – but he's just a boy, a mere child . . .'

The first frosts of autumn set in. Hardly surprisingly, no word of Zinovy Borisych had been received from any quarter. Katerina Lvovna grew larger and went about as pensively as ever, and tongues began to wag all over the town as people wondered how it could be that the young Izmailov woman, who had so far failed to have any children and had spent her time wasting away and getting thinner and thinner, could possibly have started to swell out in front. And all the while the boy co-inheritor, Fedya Lyamin, dressed in his light squirrel coat, amused himself in the yard by smashing the ice that had formed in the wheel-ruts.

'Well now, Fyodor Ignatich! Is that any way for a merchant's son to be carrying on?' Aksinya the cook would shout at him as she crossed the yard. 'Loitering about in puddles – whatever's got into you?'

And the co-inheritor, who was causing such annoyance to Katerina Lvovna and her amour, would go kicking about as serenely as a young billy-goat, would sleep, even more serenely, in bed opposite the grandmother who had brought him up, and never once suppose or reflect that he might be standing in anyone's light or spoiling anyone's happiness.

Eventually, Fedya went down with chicken-pox, aggravated by a chest catarrh, and the lad was put to bed. At first he was treated with herbs and grasses, but then a doctor was sent for.

The doctor began to make house calls, and he prescribed various medicines, which the old woman would administer hourly to the boy. Sometimes she would ask Katerina Lvovna to do it.

'Katerinushka,' she would say, 'you're soon to be a mother yourself, you give me a hand.'

Katerina did not refuse to do her bidding. When the old woman went to all-night service to pray for 'the boy Fyodor, who lieth upon a bed of sickness', or to early-morning matins to have a particle taken out for him,[1] Katerina Lvovna would sit by the patient's bedside, give him water to drink and administer his medicine when it was time for him to take it.

On one occasion, at the Feast of the Induction, in November, the old woman went to vespers and all-night service, asking her 'Katerinushka' to look after her 'Fedyushka'. By this time the lad was already getting better.

Katerina Lvovna went in to Fedya, who was sitting on his bed wearing his squirrel coat, reading the *Lives of the Holy Fathers*.

'What are you reading, Fedya?' Katerina Lvovna asked him as she sat down in the armchair.

'I'm reading the *Lives*, Auntie.'

'And is it a good book?'

'Yes, Auntie, it's a very good book.'

Katerina Lvovna sat propping her face in her hands and began to stare at Fedya's moving lips. Suddenly it was as if all the demons in hell had broken loose within her: in a flash all her old thoughts returned to take possession of her, and she reflected on all the harm this boy was doing her and how good it would be if he were not there at all.

'Wait a moment,' thought Katerina Lvovna. 'He's ill, isn't he? He's taking medicine, after all . . . A lot of things can happen to people when they're ill . . . All I have to do is say the doctor gave him the wrong medicine.'

'Is it time for you to take your medicine, Fedya?'

'Yes, please, Auntie,' the lad replied. When he had swallowed a spoonful of the stuff, he added: 'It's a really good book, Auntie. It tells you all about the saints.'

'Well, carry on reading then,' breathed Katerina Lvovna. Casting a cold glance about the room, she brought it to rest on the windows, which were covered in frost-patterns.

'We must tell them to draw the shutters,' she said, and went into the drawing room. From there she went into the reception hall, then upstairs to her own room, where she sat down.

Some five minutes later, Sergei followed her upstairs and went in; he was wearing a Romanov sheepskin coat which was trimmed with downy sealskin.

'Have the shutters been drawn?' Katerina Lvovna asked him.

'Yes,' Sergei replied curtly, trimming the candle with a pair of scissors. He took up a standing position beside the stove.

A silence ensued.

'Do you think the service will go on for a long time tonight?' Katerina Lvovna asked.

'Tomorrow's one of the great feasts; it'll last for ages,' Sergei replied.

Again there was a pause.

'Someone ought to go down and see Fedya: he's on his own in there,' Katerina Lvovna said, getting up.

'On his own?' Sergei inquired, giving her a distrustful look.

'That's right,' she replied in a whisper. 'What of it?'

For a second a charge of lightning seemed to leap from one pair of eyes to the other. Neither one of them said anything further after that.

Katerina Lvovna went downstairs and walked through the empty rooms. All was quiet; the lamps burned tranquilly before the icons; her own shadow glided here and there over the walls; the film of ice on the recently shuttered windows was now beginning to melt, and the panes were weeping. Fedya sat reading, as before. When he saw Katerina Lvovna, all he said was:

'Auntie, please take this book and give me the one that's on the icon table.'

Katerina Lvovna did as her nephew asked and gave him the book.

'Wouldn't you like to go to sleep now, Fedya?'

'No, Auntie, I'm waiting for gran to come back.'

'Why do you need to wait for her?'

'She promised to bring me a consecrated wafer from the service.'

Katerina Lvovna suddenly went pale. For the first time, her own child had just stirred within her, and she felt a sensation of cold pass through her. She stood still for a moment in the middle of the room, and then went out, rubbing her chilled hands together.

'Right!' she whispered, quietly going into the bedchamber and finding Sergei still standing in the same position beside the stove.

'What is it?' Sergei asked in a voice so faint he almost choked.

'He's on his own.'

Sergei waggled his eyebrows and began to breathe heavily.

'Let's get on with it,' Katerina Lvovna said, turning abruptly towards the door.

Quickly, Sergei took off his boots, and asked:

'What should we take with us?'

'Nothing,' Katerina Lvovna replied in a single breath, and quietly led him forward by the hand.

When Katerina Lvovna came into his room for a third time, the convalescent boy gave a start and lowered his book on to his lap.

'What's wrong, Fedya?'

'Oh, I got a fright, Auntie,' he replied, smiling uneasily and nestling up against the corner of the bed.

'What were you afraid of?'

'Who was that who came into the room with you, Auntie?'

'What are you talking about? No one came in with me, dear.'

'Are you sure?'

The boy craned over to look under the legs of the bed, peered narrowly in the direction of the doorway through which his aunt had entered, and then grew calmer.

'I probably just imagined it,' he said.

Katerina Lvovna stood still, leaning her elbows on the head-board of her nephew's bed.

Fedya looked at his aunt and said he thought she looked awfully pale.

In answer to this remark, Katerina Lvovna gave a forced cough and gazed expectantly at the door of the drawing-room. Nothing much happened, except that one of the drawing-room floorboards gave a creak.

'You know, Auntie, I'm reading the life of my guardian angel, Theodore the Warrior. He really did all he could to please God.'

Katerina Lvovna just stood there, not saying a word.

'Sit down if you like, Auntie, and I'll read it aloud to you,' her nephew said, touching her affectionately.

'Yes, all right; but you must wait a moment, while I set right the icon-lamp in the reception hall,' replied Katerina Lvovna, and she made a hurried exit.

From the drawing-room the very quietest of whispers began; but amidst the general silence it reached the boy's sensitive hearing.

'Auntie! What's going on? Who are you whispering to in there?' the boy cried, with tears in his voice. 'Come back, Auntie: I'm frightened,' he called, a moment later, even more tearfully. He heard Katerina Lvovna in the drawing-room say 'Right!', and thought she must be speaking to him.

'What are you scared of?' Katerina Lvovna asked him in a voice that was somewhat hoarse, coming into the room with a bold, determined stride, and stopping beside his bed in such a way that the door to the drawing-room was concealed from the invalid by her body. 'Get into bed,' she said.

'But I'm not tired yet, Auntie.'

'Now listen to me, Fedya, and do as I say: get into bed, it's time now. Get into bed,' Katerina Lvovna repeated.

'Why are you going on at me like this? I'm not tired one little bit!'

'Get into bed and lie down,' Katerina Lvovna said. Her voice had changed again – it was shaky now. Seizing the boy under the arms, she forced him down crosswise over the head of the bed.

At that moment Fedya gave a violent scream: he had seen Sergei, pale and bootless, coming into the room.

Katerina Lvovna quickly put her hand over the mouth of the terrified boy, and shouted:

'Be quick about it: keep him flat so he can't struggle!'

Sergei seized hold of Fedya's arms and legs, and with a single movement Katerina Lvovna covered the invalid's childish face with a large feather pillow and leaned on it hard with her powerful, resilient bosom.

For a space of some four minutes the room was as silent as the grave.

'He's dead,' Katerina Lvovna whispered. Barely had she risen in order to put everything back in order, when the walls of the quiet house, which had covered up so many crimes, were suddenly shaken by deafening blows: the windows rattled, the floors shuddered, the chains of the hanging icon-lamps quivered, and fantastic shadows went leaping over the walls.

Sergei began to tremble, and took to his heels as fast as he could. Katerina Lvovna went rushing after him, and noise and uproar followed in their wake. It was as if unearthly powers were rocking the guilty house to its foundations.

Katerina Lvovna was afraid that Sergei, driven by terror, might run outside and give himself away by the state of panic he was in; but he rushed straight up to the attic.

As he was running up the stairs in the dark, Sergei struck his head on a door which was halfway open, and went flying back down again with a groan, having completely lost his head from superstitious terror.

'Zinovy Borisych, Zinovy Borisych!' he muttered, as he flew head over heels down the staircase, knocking Katerina off her feet and taking her with him as he fell.

'Where?' she asked.

'Look, he's flying over us with a sheet of iron,' Sergei shouted. 'Look, look, there he is again! Oh! Oh! There he goes, clanking and clattering!'

It was now plainly obvious that a large number of hands were knocking at the window from outside, and that someone was trying to force the door.

'You fool! Get up, you fool!' Katerina Lvovna cried, and with these words she darted back to Fedya, placed his lifeless head on the pillows to make him look as though he were asleep and then resolutely opened the door, through which a large group of people was trying to force an entry.

It was a fearsome spectacle. Katerina Lvovna looked over the heads of the crowd which had laid siege to the porch, and observed entire legions of people she had never seen before scaling the enclosure into the yard, while the street outside was filled with the hubbub of voices.

Katerina Lvovna had hardly had time to put two and two together, when the crowd which had surrounded the porch forced her back and threw her inside the house again.

Now all this alarm had been raised in the following manner: on the evening of 20th November, all the churches in the town where Katerina Lvovna lived – though it was only a regional centre, it was quite large, and contained a fair amount of industry – were packed full of people for the all-night service preliminary to the Feast of the Presentation on the 21st; and in the grounds of the church in which there was to be an altar feast the following day there was not even room for an apple to fall from the trees that grew by its surrounding fence. In this church on such occasions there usually sings a choir which is composed of the merchants' young swains, and which is conducted by a special precentor, an amateur singer like the rest.

The folk in our part of Russia are a devout lot, zealous in all matters relating to the church. What is more, they have an artistic sense that is all their own: ecclesiastical grandeur and euphonious, 'organ-like' singing constitute the most exalted and purest of their enjoyments. Wherever a church choir is singing, there you are sure to find practically half the town, especially the younger folk from the trading professions: stewards, boys, hands, artisans from the mills and factories, even the owners themselves and their 'better halves' – all will crowd into a single church, each of them desirous of the chance to stand on the parvis for a while, to listen underneath a window in the blazing heat or biting frost and hear the thundering of an octave or a show-off tenor pouring out his whimsical *'varshlaki'*.*

* This is how singers in the province of Oryol refer to *forshlagi* [= 'gracenotes', tr.]. *Leskov's note.*

In the parish church of the Izmailov family there was an altar dedicated in honour of the presentation of the Virgin Mary in the temple, and for this reason on the evening before the feast – at the very same time as the events concerning Fedya Lyamin, just described, were taking place – the youth of the entire town was packed into it. As they left it in a noisy crowd, they discussed the respective merits of one or two of the tenors, and the occasional awkwardnesses of one of the basses.

Not all of them, however, were occupied by these finer points of the vocal art: some members of the crowd had other matters of interest to discuss.

'Hey, lads, there are some fine stories going the rounds about the young Izmailov woman,' said a young machinist who had been brought from St Petersburg by a certain merchant to look after his steam-mill, as they drew near to the Izmailovs' house. 'They say that she and their steward Sergei are having it off with each other every moment they can manage . . .'

'Everyone knows about that,' a man in a nankeen-covered sheepskin replied. 'She wasn't in church today, either.'

'What would she be doing in church? That nasty little bitch has rolled around in the muck for so long that she's not afraid of God, her conscience, or the eyes of other people any more.'

'See, there's a light on in their place,' the machinist observed, pointing to the crack of light between the shutters.

'Go on then, take a look through and see if you can see what they're doing,' several voices urged impatiently.

The machinist supported himself on the shoulders of two of his companions and had no sooner put his eye to the gap between the shutters than he yelled at the top of his voice:

'Here, mates! They're smothering somebody in there! Somebody's being smothered!'

And the machinist began to pummel the shutters with both fists. About a dozen other men proceeded to follow his example; jumping up to the window, they also set to work with their fists.

With every moment that passed the crowd was growing larger, and there ensued the siege of the Izmailovs' house which we have already described.

'I saw it myself, I saw it happen with my very own eyes,' the machinist said in testimony later, as he stood over Fedya's corpse. 'The boy had been knocked over, he was lying on the bed and the two of them were smothering him.'

That same evening, Sergei was taken down to the police station, while Katerina Lvovna was locked up in her attic room, with two policemen set outside to guard her.

In the Izmailovs' house it was unbearably cold: the stoves were not lighted, and the front door was perpetually open, as one dense throng of curious townsfolk gave way to another. Everyone wanted to see Fedya lying in his coffin, and the other large coffin, the lid of which was covered by a capacious pall. On Fedya's forehead lay a white corolla of satin, concealing the red scar which the autopsy of his skull had left behind. The autopsy had revealed that Fedya had died of suffocation; and indeed, when Sergei was led before the corpse, the very first words of the priest about the Last Judgement and the punishment of the unrepentant were enough to make him burst into tears. Not only did he frankly confess to having murdered Fedya – he also begged that the body of Zinovy Borisych, which he had so unceremoniously buried, be exhumed. It turned out that he had buried it in dry sand, and it had not completely decomposed: it was disinterred and laid in a large coffin. To the universal horror of all concerned, Sergei named the young mistress of the house as his accomplice in both these crimes. All Katerina Lvovna would say in reply when they questioned her was: 'I know absolutely nothing about any of that.' Sergei was made to confront her at a specially arranged interview designed to expose her. When she had finished listening to his confession, Katerina Lvovna looked at him in speechless bewilderment, but without anger, and said, indifferently:

'If he can find it in him to tell all that, why should I keep my lips sewn? I admit it: I killed them.'

'Why?' she was asked.

'I did it for him,' she replied, pointing at Sergei, who was hanging his head in shame.

The criminals were sent to prison, and the horrific case which had attracted such general attention and outrage was very soon laid to rest. At the end of February Sergei and the third-guild merchant's widow Katerina Lvovna were informed in the criminal court that they had each been sentenced to be flogged with whips in the market square of their town, and were then to be sent into exile to do penal servitude. On a cold, frosty morning at the beginning of March, the executioner counted off the appointed number of blue-and-crimson weals on Katerina Lvovna's exposed white back, then lashed Sergei's shoulders with the relevant portion and imprinted his handsome face with three penal brands.

For some reason, during all this time, Sergei aroused far more public sympathy than Katerina Lvovna. Bloodied and begrimed, he stumbled and fell as he was descending the black scaffold; Katerina Lvovna, on the other hand, made her descent quietly, taking care only to try to prevent the coarse cloth of her convict's *svita* from touching her lacerated back.

Even when later, in the prison hospital, she was presented with her baby, she merely said: 'Oh drat and blast him!' and, turning to the wall, threw herself face down on the hard prison bunk without the slightest murmur of complaint.

The group of convicts in which Sergei and Katerina Lvovna
had ended up set out for its place of exile at a time of year when
it is only spring on the calendar, and when the sun, in the words
of the folk proverb, 'shines briefly up aloft, but warms nor man
nor beast'.

Katerina Lvovna's child had been given into the care of the
old woman, Boris Timofeich's sister, since, being considered the
lawful son of the felon's murdered husband, the infant was now
the sole inheritor of the entire Izmailov fortune. This arrangement came as a great relief to Katerina Lvovna, and she gave her
child into the care of the old woman quite without any feelings
one way or the other. As is often the case with over-passionate
women, her love for the father did not carry over to the child by
one iota.

The fact was, though, that for her there was neither light nor
dark, nor good nor bad, nor joy nor sorrow; she perceived
nothing, and loved no one, not even herself. She lived only in
the impatient expectancy of the moment when the group would
set out on the road, where she hoped she might meet her Sergei
again, and she relinquished all thought of the child.

Katerina Lvovna's hopes did not deceive her: fettered with
heavy chains, disfigured with brand-marks, Sergei was in the
little group of convicts with whom she trudged out through the
prison gates.

There is no situation, however loathsome, to which a human
being cannot grow accustomed, and in each and every one of
them he retains, so far as is possible, his ability to pursue his meagre joys; but Katerina Lvovna needed to make no adjustment: she

could see her Sergei again, and in his presence even the road of penal servitude would blossom with happiness.

Small was the number of valuables Katerina Lvovna had brought with her in her brightly coloured cotton bag, and even smaller the amount of ready cash. But before she had gone even a little way along the road to Nizhny, she had given both cash and valuables away to the NCOs of the escort in exchange for being allowed to walk beside Sergei during the journey and stand embracing him for an hour or so in the darkness of night, hidden away in some cold recess of a narrow transit-prison corridor.

The only trouble was that Katerina Lvovna's branded lover had become thoroughly unaffectionate towards her: whenever he spoke to her, he did it curtly; he did not seem to place any value on their secret rendezvous, in order to arrange which she had gone without food and drink and parted with the last quarter-copeck from her slender purse. On a few occasions he even said:

'You ought to have let me have that money, instead of giving it to that NCO.'

'It was only a quarter-copeck, Sergei,' Katerina Lvovna would say, attempting to justify herself.

'It makes no difference, it's money, isn't it? You've picked up a lot of those quarter-copecks on the journey, and you've thrown a lot of them away, too.'

'But at least it's made it possible for us to see each other.'

'Yes, and what kind of a happiness for us is it to see each other after all the misery we've been through? I feel like cursing my life, not having rendezvous.'

'I don't care about all that, Sergei: all I care about is being able to see you.'

'That's just a lot of stupid nonsense,' Sergei would reply.

At times these replies would make Katerina Lvovna bite her lip until the blood came; at others, her normally dry eyes would well with tears of rage and resentment in the darkness of their nocturnal rendezvous; yet she endured it all, refrained from answering back, and tried to deceive herself.

In this manner, with this new form of relationship established between them, they arrived at Nizhny. Here the group with which they were marching joined up with another party of convicts that was headed for Siberia along the high road from Moscow.

In the female section of this large group, which contained all kinds of people, there were two particularly interesting women: one was a soldier's wife from Yaroslavl called Fiona, a splendid, beautiful woman, tall, with a thick black mane of hair and warm, languorous eyes hung with a bridal veil of thick eyelashes; the other was a small, sharp-featured blonde of seventeen with delicate, rose-coloured skin, a tiny mouth, dimples on her fresh cheeks and reddish-gold curls that spilled out capriciously on to her forehead from under her multicoloured convict's headscarf. To the members of the group this girl was known as Sonetka.

The beautiful Fiona was of a gentle, lazy disposition. Everyone in the group knew her, and none of the men were ever particularly pleased when they were successful with her, just as none of them were particularly miffed when they observed that she had favoured another aspirant with similar success.

'Our Fiona's a good girl, she never turns a man down,' the convicts would unanimously agree, in jest.

But Sonetka was something else entirely.

Of her they would say:

'She's a slippery one: she comes near you, but you can't catch her.'

Sonetka had special tastes: she liked to pick and choose, and was really rather fussy. She wanted passion to be served up to her not in its raw, uncooked state, but simmered in a spicy, piquant sauce of suffering and sacrifice. Fiona, by contrast, was a simple Russian peasant woman, who could not even be bothered to say 'go away' to a man, and who knew only one thing: that she was a woman.

The appearance of these two women in the group that now attached itself to the one to which Sergei and Katerina belonged was to have a tragic outcome for Katerina Lvovna.

From the very first days of the combined groups' progress from Nizhny to Kazan, Sergei began to make approaches to Fiona the soldier's wife in the most obvious fashion. Fiona, languorous beauty that she was, did not repulse Sergei's advances any more than, in the goodness of her heart, she ever repulsed those of any man. At the third or fourth stopping-place along the way, Katerina Lvovna arranged a rendezvous with her Sergei by means of bribery, and then lay, unable to sleep a wink, waiting for the duty NCO to come in, gently nudge her, and whisper: 'Make it snappy.' The door opened once, and a woman darted out into the corridor; the door opened again, and another woman quickly jumped down from the plank bed and likewise disappeared in the wake of the duty NCO; finally someone tugged at the *svita* with which Katerina Lvovna had covered herself. The young woman rapidly got up from the plank bed, which was worn shiny from the bodies of innumerable convict women, threw the *svita* over her shoulders and nudged the NCO who was standing in front of her.

As Katerina Lvovna was making her way along the corridor, which was lit, in one place only, by a dimly flickering lampion, she ran into two or three couples whom it would have been impossible to observe from any distance. As she passed the men's section she heard muffled laughter coming through the spyhole that had been cut in the door.

'Dirty pigs,' growled the NCO who was leading her and, taking hold of her shoulders in order to prevent her from going any further, he shoved her into a corner and went away.

Feeling about with one hand, Katerina Lvovna found herself touching a *svita* and a beard; her other hand came into contact with a woman's hot face.

'Who's this?' she heard Sergei's voice ask in an undertone. 'Why are you here? Who's that with you?'

In the darkness, Katerina Lvovna tugged the headscarf off the head of her rival. The woman slipped to one side, took to her heels and, tripping over someone in the corridor, made off at top speed.

From the men's section came a burst of appreciative laughter.

'Villain!' Katerina Lvovna whispered, and she struck Sergei about the face with the ends of the headscarf she had torn from the head of his new paramour.

Sergei was about to raise his hand against Katerina Lvovna, but she fled lightly away along the corridor and heaved open the door to her own section. The guffawing from the men's section resumed as she went, and it was so loud that the sentry who was standing apathetically opposite the lampion, spitting at the toecap of one of his boots, raised his head and roared:

'Quiet!'

Katerina lay down in silence and stayed there in the same position until morning. 'I don't really love him anyway,' she kept telling herself, yet felt that she loved him even more ardently than before. And in her eyes she kept picturing, picturing the palm of one of his hands quivering under that *other woman's* head, as his other hand had embraced her hot shoulders.

The poor woman began to weep and found herself helplessly crying out for that same palm of his to be under her own head at that very moment, and for his other hand to embrace her hysterically quivering shoulders.

'Here, give me back my headscarf,' said Fiona the soldier's wife, wakening her next morning.

'Oh, so it was you, was it?'

'Give me it back, please.'

'Why are you trying to come between us?'

'How am I coming between you? It's really not anything to get worked up about.'

Katerina Lvovna thought for a moment, and then took out from under her pillow the headscarf she had snatched the previous night. Throwing it to Fiona, she turned her face to the wall.

She was beginning to feel better.

'Pah!' she said to herself. 'Am I really going to start being jealous of that painted washtub of a woman? To blazes with her. Even comparing myself to her leaves a nasty taste in my mouth.'

'Listen here, Katerina Lvovna,' Sergei said to her as they were on the move again the following day. 'Please get two things straight; firstly, I'm no Zinovy Borisych, and secondly you're not the wife of an important merchant any more – so do me a favour and don't go giving yourself airs. Beggars can't be choosers.'

Katerina Lvovna made no reply to this, and for the rest of the week she trudged along beside Sergei without ever exchanging a single word or glance with him. As befitting a woman who had been insulted, she kept up a firm front and was unwilling to take the first step towards reconciliation in this, her first quarrel with Sergei.

Meanwhile, during this time in which Katerina Lvovna was angry with Sergei, he began to plume himself and make advances to Sonetka the blonde. He would bow to her 'with my especial compliments' or smile to her or, if he was together with her, he would try to embrace her and press her close to him. Katerina Lvovna saw all this, and it only made her heart seethe even more.

'Perhaps I ought to make it up with him,' she thought, as she stumbled along, hardly conscious of the ground beneath her feet.

But now even more than before, her pride would not permit her to go up to him and take the first step towards reconciliation. And all this time Sergei was becoming more and more closely involved with Sonetka, and it was becoming apparent to everyone that the inaccessible Sonetka, who normally wriggled away like a slippery loach, and could not be caught, was suddenly losing all her shyness.

'You complained about me,' Fiona said to Katerina Lvovna one day. 'But what did I do to you? I had my chance, and now it's gone; but I'd watch out for that Sonetka, if I were you.'

'The devil take my pride; I swear I'll make it up this very day,' Katerina Lvovna decided, her one thought being of how best to tackle the delicate matter of a reconciliation.

From this difficult situation she was rescued by none other than Sergei himself.

'Hey, Lvovna!' he called to her during one of their halts. 'Come over and see me for a minute tonight: there's something we ought to talk about.'

Katerina Lvovna said nothing.

'What, are you still angry with me? Don't you want to come?'

Again Katerina Lvovna made no reply.

But Sergei, like everyone else who was observing Katerina Lvovna, saw her draw close to the senior NCO as they were approaching the transit prison and slip him seventeen copecks which she had collected as alms in the villages they had been passing through.

'As soon as I've got some more, I'll slip you a ten-copeck bit,' Katerina Lvovna said, wheedlingly.

The NCO put the money in the cuff of his coat and said:

'Very well.'

When these negotiations were at an end, Sergei grunted and gave Sonetka a wink.

'Oh, Katerina Lvovna!' he said, embracing her on the steps of the transit prison as they went in. 'Lads, there's no woman in all the world who can hold a candle to this one.'

Katerina Lvovna blushed and gasped with happiness.

Night had scarcely fallen when the door opened quietly, and she came darting out: as she groped for Sergei in the dark corridor she trembled.

'My Katya!' Sergei said, as he embraced her.

'Oh my wicked, wicked man,' Katerina Lvovna replied through tears, and put her lips to his.

A sentry came down the corridor, halted, spat on his boots and continued on his way; the snoring of weary convicts came from behind the door; a mouse nibbled at a feather; under the stove, vying with one another, crickets shrilled at the tops of their voices – but Katerina was still in the seventh heaven of happiness.

These transports of delight subsided, however, and prose took over.

'I'm in such damned pain all the time: my legs are fairly shrieking, all the way from my ankles to my kneebones,' Sergei complained as he sat next to Katerina Lvovna on the floor of the corridor niche.

'What else do you expect, Sergei?' she said, huddling up beneath the skirts of his *svita*.

'Do you think I should ask to be transferred to hospital in Kazan?'

'Oh, come, it's not that bad, is it, Sergei?'

'It is, I'm fairly dying of the pain.'

'So you'll just stay behind, while I'm driven onwards, is that it?'

'What else can I do? The rubbing's so bad, I tell you, that the chain's practically eating into the bone. Maybe if I had some woollen stockings to put on it'd be better,' Sergei said, a moment later.

'Stockings? I've a pair, Sergei – new ones.'

'You have?'

Without saying a further word, Katerina Lvovna plunged along to the women's section, emptied out the contents of her bag on the plank bed and came leaping back to Sergei holding a pair of thick navy-blue Bolkhov woollen stockings with brightly coloured arrows on the sides.

'Now I won't feel a thing!' Sergei said as he took his leave of Katerina Lvovna and accepted her last pair of stockings.

Happy, Katerina Lvovna went back to her plank bed and fell fast asleep.

She did not hear Sonetka come out into the corridor after her arrival, and neither did she see her come back from there shortly before dawn.

This happened only two days before the group of convicts arrived in Kazan.

A cold, inclement day of gusting wind and rain that was turning to snow met the convict group as it left the gates of the
airless transit prison. Katerina Lvovna stepped outside cheerfully enough, but as soon as she joined the ranks of marching
convicts she began to shake all over and turned deathly pale.
Everything went dark before her eyes; every joint in her body
began to ache and grow feeble. What she saw before her was
Sonetka, in those all-too-familiar woollen stockings with their
brightly coloured arrows.

Katerina Lvovna embarked upon the journey like a woman
who was already dead. The only sign of life in her was in her
eyes, which fixed Sergei with a dreadful stare that never once
shifted from him.

At the next halt she approached Sergei calmly, whispered
'villain' at him, and then spat in his face.

Sergei would have hurled himself upon her, but was
restrained from doing so by the others.

'Just you wait!' he said, as he wiped himself down.

'You've got it made – she goes for you like a real she-devil!'
the convicts laughed, making fun of him. Sonetka's laughter
was the merriest of all.

The minor intrigue in which she now found herself caught
up was entirely to Sonetka's taste.

'I won't forget this,' Sergei told Katerina Lvovna, threateningly.

Exhausted by the bad weather and the perpetual marching,
Katerina Lvovna slept uneasily on the plank bed of the new
transit prison, and did not hear the two men who entered the
women's section.

As they came in, Sonetka raised herself from the bed, pointed silently to Katerina Lvovna, lay down again and huddled up beneath her *svita*.

At that very same moment, Katerina Lvovna's *svita* flew over her head, and on her back, which was covered only by her brown Holland shift, wielded with the full might of a peasant's strength, landed the thick end of a double plaited rope.

Katerina Lvovna shrieked; but her voice was inaudible under the *svita* that enveloped her head. She attempted to jerk herself free, but this was to no avail, either; a sturdy convict was sitting on her shoulders, holding her arms tightly.

'Fifty,' a voice counted at last, a voice which no one would have had much difficulty in recognizing as that of Sergei, and in a trice the nocturnal visitors disappeared out of the doorway.

Katerina Lvovna succeeded in freeing her head and leapt to her feet: there was no one to be seen. Somewhere close by someone was tittering gloatingly from under a *svita*. Katerina Lvovna recognized Sonetka's laugh.

There were no bounds to the sense of personal outrage Katerina Lvovna now experienced; there were no bounds, either, to the feelings of spite and anger that seethed up within her at this moment. Staggering forwards, she collapsed unconscious on the breast of Fiona, who had caught her as she fell.

On this ample bosom, which had so recently gratified Katerina Lvovna's unfaithful lover with the delights of lewdness, she now sobbed out her intolerable grief and, like a child to a mother, pressed herself close to her slow and feckless rival. Now they were equal: they had both been cheapened, and both been discarded.

They were equal! . . . Fiona, who gave in to the first passing fancy, and Katerina Lvovna, who had enacted the drama of love!

By this time, however, there was nothing that was capable of insulting Katerina Lvovna. Having shed all her tears, she stood stock-still, and prepared with wooden impassivity to go out for roll-call.

The drum was beating: *trat trat-a-trat trat*. Fettered and unfettered, the convicts came trailing out into the yard: Sergei, Fiona, Sonetka, Katerina Lvovna, a schismatic chained to a Jew, and a Pole chained to a Tartar.

They all huddled together, then somehow managed to sort themselves out into a kind of order, and set off.

It was a most dismal picture: the little group of people, estranged from the world and deprived of the faintest hope of a better future, trudging through the thick black mud of an earth road, under a grey sky, their only witnesses the wet, leafless willows and the crows that sat with ruffled feathers in their exposed branches. And all the while the wind moaned and raged, wailed and roared.

In these hellish, soul-destroying sounds, which complemented the full horror of the picture, one could hear an echo of the counsel offered to Job by his wife: 'Curse the day that thou wast born, and die.'

Those who do not wish to pay heed to these words, those to whom the thought of death, even in this sorry situation, appears not a blessed release but a cause for fear, must try to drown out these wailing voices with something even uglier than they. The ordinary man understands this perfectly: at such times he gives free rein to all his brutish ordinariness and proceeds to act stupidly, jeering at his own feelings and at those of other people. Not particularly soft-hearted even at the best of times, he now becomes positively nasty.

'Good morning, madam merchant: I trust your ladyship is in good health?' Sergei said to Katerina Lvovna, as soon as the group had lost sight, behind a green knoll, of the village in which it had spent the night.

As he spoke, he turned quickly towards Sonetka, covered her round with the open flaps of his coat, and began to sing in a high falsetto:

> At the window in the shadow flits a red-haired head,
>   Don't you sleep, my torment, don't you sleep, my little rogue,
>   I'll protect you with my coat, so no one will see.[1]

With these words Sergei embraced Sonetka, kissing her loudly in front of the entire group . . .

Katerina Lvovna saw all this, but without taking it in: she was moving forward like one who was no longer of this earth. Members of the group began to nudge her and point out to her the way Sergei was carrying on with Sonetka. Katerina Lvovna became the object of their derision.

'Leave her alone,' Fiona said, protectively, when one of the group tried to make fun of the stumbling Katerina Lvovna. 'Can't you see that the woman's been taken poorly, you devils?'

'She must have got her feet wet,' a young convict wisecracked.

'Well, she's from a merchant family: she had a soft upbringing,' Sergei replied.

'Of course, if she had a pair of warm stockings to wear, she'd be fine,' he went on.

Katerina Lvovna seemed to snap out of her dream-like state.

'You vile snake!' she said, unable to endure these taunts. 'Go on, you villain, laugh until you kill yourself!'

'Oh, but I'm not saying that just for a laugh, madam merchant; it's just that Sonetka here's got some real nice stockings to sell and the thought occurred to me that perhaps our madam merchant might like to buy them.'

A number of the group burst out laughing. Katerina Lvovna kept striding onwards like a clockwork automaton.

The weather continued to get worse. From the grey clouds that covered the sky, wet flakes of snow began to fall, melting almost before they touched the ground and making the deep mire even deeper. At last a dark, leaden band became visible, the other side of which was lost from view. This was the Volga. Above the river a stiffish wind was blowing, which made its dark, voracious, slowly heaving waves lunge to and fro.

The drenched and shivering group of convicts slowly approached the crossing-point and came to a standstill, waiting for the ferry.

A wet, dark ferry boat drew in at the moorings; its crew began to show the convicts to their places.

'They say that someone on this ferry keeps a barrel of vodka handy,' observed one of the convicts, as the ferry boat, surrounded by flakes of wet, driving snow, unmoored from the bank and began to pitch and roll on the waves of the thawing river.

'Yes, we could do with a drop of that,' Sergei replied. Still teasing Katerina Lvovna for the amusement of Sonetka, he said: 'Madam merchant, won't you give us a drop of vodka for old times' sake? Don't be mean, now. Remember our former love, my darling, remember how we used to enjoy ourselves, my joy, how we used to sit together on those long autumn nights, how we dispatched your kinsfolk to eternal rest without the assistance of priest or deacon.'

Katerina was shivering all over. But other forces besides the cold, which had penetrated through her drenched clothing to the very bone, were at work in Katerina Lvovna's organism. Her head was burning as if it were on fire; the pupils of her eyes were dilated, lit by a sharp, intermittent glitter, and were motionlessly fixed on the surging waves.

'Well, I wouldn't mind a drop of vodka, either, it's awfully cold,' Sonetka shrilled in a ringing voice.

'Come on now, madam merchant, won't you give us some?' said the voice of Sergei, who continued to needle Katerina Lvovna.

'You ought to be ashamed of yourself,' said Fiona, shaking her head.

'It does you no credit,' said a convict named Gordyushka, in support of the soldier's wife.

'Even if you've no conscience in front of her, you ought to have some in front of the rest of us, seeing how poorly she is.'

'Shut up, you communal snuffbox!' Sergei shouted at Fiona. 'You're the one who ought to have a conscience, if anyone should. Why should I have any conscience about her? I don't think I ever loved her, anyway – all I know is that I get more pleasure out of one of Sonetka's down-at-heel shoes than I do from Katerina Lvovna's ugly mug, the scraggy feline; what have you got to say to that? Let that Gordyushka with his crooked gob love her, or else . . .' At that moment he looked round and caught sight of a shrimp of an officer who happened to be riding by in a felt cloak and a military cap with a cockade, and added: 'or else let her go and cuddle up to a transit officer: at least the rain won't get in through his felt cloak.'

'And everyone would start calling her madam officer, then,' Sonetka shrilled.

'Of course they would! . . . and she'd get plenty of money for stockings, just for the asking,' Sergei said, to round this off.

Katerina Lvovna made no attempt to defend herself: she gazed at the waves ever more fixedly, and her lips moved. Interspersed with Sergei's foul-mouthed tirade she seemed to hear a groaning, rumbling sound that came from the heaving, crashing breakers. And then suddenly, in one of the breaking waves she fancied she saw the blue, swollen head of Boris Timofeich, and in another the swaying form of her husband, peeping out at her and embracing Fedya's hanging head. Katerina Lvovna tried to remember a prayer, and she moved her lips, but all her lips could whisper were the words: 'how we used to enjoy ourselves, how we used to sit together on those long autumn nights, how we dispatched your kinsfolk to a cruel death in broad daylight . . .'

Katerina Lvovna shivered. Her intermittent gaze focused itself, and became wild. Once, twice her arms stretched out towards some unknown point in space and fell back again. Another minute passed – and suddenly she began to rock and sway and, without taking her eyes off the dark waves, she bent down, seized hold of Sonetka by the legs and in one single movement hurled herself with her over the side of the ferry.

Everyone froze in amazement.

Katerina Lvovna appeared on the crest of a wave, then disappeared under the water; another wave brought Sonetka to the surface.

'A boathook! Throw them a boathook!' people shouted from the ferry.

A heavy boathook on a long rope went flying out and fell into the water. There was no sign of Sonetka now. A couple of moments later, she came into view again, raising her arms in the air as the current carried her swiftly away from the ferry; but just then Katerina Lvovna rose from another wave, almost waist-high out of the water, lunged at Sonetka like a muscular pike at a soft-feathered roach, and neither of them was ever seen again.

THE SEALED ANGEL

I

It happened at Yuletide, on the eve of the Feast of St Basil.[1] The weather was terrible. A ferocious blizzard, of the kind for which the winters on the left bank of the Volga are famous, had driven many people into a solitary inn which stood like a lonely old man in the midst of the smooth and boundless steppe. Here, thrown together higgledy-piggledy, were noblemen, merchants and peasants, Russians, Mordvins and Chuvashes. In such cramped quarters it would have been impossible to observe the niceties of social rank and distinction; wherever one turned there was overcrowding: some people were drying themselves, others were trying to get warm, yet others were searching for some corner, however tiny, in which they might take shelter. The air of the dark, low-ceilinged *izba* was stuffy and thick with the steam from damp clothing. Not an empty space was visible anywhere: on the stove, on the planks above it, on the benches and even on the dirty earth floor – everywhere people lay. The landlord, a surly muzhik, was deriving satisfaction neither from his guests nor from the money he was making out of them. Angrily slamming the gate shut after the last sleigh to arrive in his yard, carrying two merchants, he locked it and, hanging the key above the icon-case, said firmly:

'All right. It doesn't matter who else comes now; they can beat their brains out against the gate, for all I care: I won't open up.'

But hardly were these words out of his mouth, and hardly had he had time to take off his capacious sheepskin coat, cross himself broadly with two fingers,[2] and prepare to clamber on to the hot stove, than someone began a timid knocking at the windowpane.

'Who's there?' the landlord called in a loud, displeased voice.

'It's us,' came the muffled answer from the other side of the window.

'Well, and what do you want?'

'Let us in, for Christ's sake. We've lost our way . . . We're fair frozen.'

'Are there many of you?'

'No, not many, not many – there are only eighteen of us, eighteen,' said the man on the other side of the window; he was stammering, his teeth were chattering, and he was obviously chilled to the very bone.

'I've nowhere to put you, the whole place is packed full.'

'Just let us in to get warm for a bit, then.'

'What sort of folk are you, anyway?'

'We're draymen.'

'With loads or without?'

'With loads, dear fellow. We're carting furs.'

'Furs? You're carting furs and you're asking to spend the night in an *izba*? Russia has some strange people. Be off with you!'

'But what are they to do?' asked a traveller who was lying under a bearskin coat on the upper row of planking.

'Pile up their furs and sleep underneath them, that's what,' replied the landlord who, after directing a further stream of abuse at the draymen, lay down on the stove and remained there, motionless.

From under his bearskin coat the traveller began to rebuke the landlord for his cruelty in tones of lively protest, but the landlord did not deign to make the slightest answer. Indeed, the person who finally replied was not the landlord at all, but a short, ginger-haired little man with a pointed, wedge-shaped beard who was sitting over in the far corner.

'Don't be so hard on the landlord, kind sir,' he said. 'He's talking from experience and what he's suggesting is quite correct – they'll be quite safe under their furs.'

'Are you sure?' the traveller asked dubiously from under his bearskin coat.

'Absolutely, sir. And in fact, it'll be better for them if he doesn't let them in.'

'How is that?'

'Because now they'll get some useful experience, and if anyone who's really in a spot should turn up, there'll be room for him.'

'Yes, who else is the Devil going to send us?' said the bearskin coat.

'Listen here, you,' the landlord retorted. 'Don't go shooting your mouth off about things you know nothing of. Do you think it's the Devil who sends people somewhere where there are so many holy objects? Haven't you seen that there's an icon of Our Saviour here, as well as an image of Our Lady?'

'It's true,' the ginger-haired man said in support. 'A man who's been saved is led not by the dark one, but by his guiding angel.'

'Well now, I can't say as I've ever observed that, and since I'm not having a particularly nice time in this place, I don't want to believe it's my angel who's led me here,' the loquacious bearskin coat replied.

The landlord merely spat angrily, and the little ginger-haired man said in good-natured tones that the paths of angels are not visible to everyone and that only first-hand experience could give one an understanding of this.

'You speak of it as though you yourself have had such first-hand experience,' said the bearskin coat.

'Yes, sir, I have.'

'What? You mean you saw an angel, and it led you?'

'Yes, sir, I saw one, and he guided me.'

'Is this a joke, or are you trying to make a fool of me?'

'God forbid that I should ever make jokes about a matter like that!'

'All right, so what did you actually see? How did your angel show himself to you?'

'That, kind sir, is a long story.'

'You know what? It's really impossible to get to sleep here, and it would do us a power of good if you'd tell us that story right now.'

'Certainly, sir.'

'Well, carry on then, please: we'll listen. Only what are you kneeling for over there? Come over here to where we are, we'll squeeze up somehow and make room for you to sit down.'

'No, sir, but thank you kindly, sir! Why should I make you squeeze up? And anyway, the tale I'm going to tell you is better told kneeling, because it's a very holy tale, and it's also a terrible one.'

'Well, as you wish. Only hurry up and tell us how it was you saw an angel, and what it did for you.'

'Very well, sir, I will begin.'

'As you are doubtless able to tell just by looking at me, I'm a thoroughly insignificant fellow; I'm nothing more than a muzhik, and I received the kind of education usual for a person of my social standing – a truly rural one. I'm not from these parts – I come from far away. I'm a stonemason by trade, but I was born into the old Russian faith. Because I was an orphan, from my earliest years I went with my fellow villagers to do seasonal labour in various places, but always in the same *artel'*, which was run by one of our peasants, Luka Kirilov. This Luka Kirilov is still alive today; he's our number one subcontractor. His farm was ancient, and had been cultivated by his fore-fathers. He didn't let it run to waste, but increased its value and created a large and abundant granary for himself. He was and is a fine man, giving no one cause for any offence. And where didn't we go with him? We seemed to traverse the length and breadth of Russia, and nowhere did I encounter a better or a more decent master. We lived with him in the most peaceful form of patriarchal relationship – where our trade was con-cerned he was our subcontractor, and where our faith was concerned he was our preceptor. We followed him to where there was work like the Jews in their wanderings with Moses; we even used to take our own tabernacle with us, and we never let it out of our sight: it was our own special "blessing from God". Luka Kirilov was passionately fond of holy icons and, my dear sirs, he had the most wonderful specimens of the art: they were really old, really exquisite – either real Greek ones or ones by the earliest Novgorod or Stroganov isographers.[1] It wasn't their frames that shone so much as the clarity and fluency of their amazing artistry. I've never seen such exalted stuff anywhere else!

'And, Lord, what *Deises*[2] there were, and an image of the Saviour with wet hair,[3] surely not of any human making, and saints and martyrs and apostles – and, most wondrous of all, multi-figured icons depicting episodes from the Bible: the "Indict",[4] the "Saints",[5] the "Heavenly Host",[6] the "God the Father",[7] the "Week",[8] the "Benefice",[9] the "Septenary"[10] with supplicants, the Trinity with Abraham worshipping the Lord by the tree in the plains of Mamre . . . In short, there was such splendour as it would be impossible to describe. They don't paint icons like that anywhere nowadays, neither in Moscow, nor in St Petersburg, nor in Palikhov;[11] as for Greece, it doesn't even come into question: the art fell into neglect there long ago. We loved all those holy things of ours passionately, and we burned the holy oil before them together, and we kept a horse and waggon at the *artel*'s expense for the especial purpose of carting those blessings of God around with us everywhere we went. There were two icons in particular we liked to have with us: one of them had been executed on the Greek model by the old Muscovite masters of the Tsar,[12] depicting Our Lady praying in an olive-grove, with all the olives and cypresses bowing to the earth before her;[13] the other showed a guardian angel – it was a work of the Stroganov school. You have simply no idea of what art there was in those two holy objects! When you looked at Our Lady and saw those inanimate trees bowing before her purity, your heart would melt and quiver; when you looked at the angel . . . what joy! That angel was truly indescribable. His face – I can see it before me now – was so divinely radiant and so compassionate; his gaze was tender; there were thongs[14] above his ears, a sign of his universal power of hearing; his raiment burned, mottled all over with gold pendants; his armour was like fishes' scales, and his shoulders were heavily girdled; at his breast he bore a round icon of the boy Emmanuel; in his right hand there was a cross, in his left a fiery sword. Wonderful! Wonderful! . . . His hair was red and curly, and it wove upwards from his ears, each fine thread of it attached to the other as if by a needle. His wings were vast and white as snow, with the azure blue sky behind them, and each feather, each little tuftlet of feather, fitted closely with the next. You would look at those wings, and all your fear would vanish: "Protect me," you would pray, and in an instant you would grow calm, and peace would enter your soul. That was what kind of an icon it was! And you know, sirs, those two icons were to us what the Holy of Holies is to the Jews, the tabernacle adorned by the wondrous artistry of Bezaleel. We used to cart all the icons I mentioned earlier around in a special chest on a horsedrawn cart, but we never put those two in with the others – they were carried. Luka Kirilov's wife Mikhailitsa always used to take care of Our Lady, while Luka himself kept the depiction of the angel on his breast. He had a brocade satchel lined with dark canvas which had been made especially for this icon; the satchel had a button fastener; on its front side there was a scarlet cross of proper[15] cloth, and it had a thick green silken cord sewn to the top of it, so he could wear it around his neck. Kept on Luka's breast in this way, the icon went before us wherever our steps took us, as if the angel himself were preceding us. We would tramp from place to place through the steppes, always in search of new work; Luka Kirilov would wave a notched surveyor's rod instead of a walking-stick, Mikhailitsa would follow behind him in the cart with the icon of Our Lady, and we, the *artel'*, would bring up the rear. Oh, the grass would be green in the fields, the flowers would be bright in the meadows, here and there flocks would be grazing, and the shepherd would be playing his reed-pipes . . . in other words, a delight to the heart and mind! Everything went swimmingly for us, and we had the most marvellous success in each and every one of our endeavours: we invariably found good work; harmony prevailed among us; and the news from those we had left at home put our minds at rest. For all this we blessed our angel who went before us, and I think we would have found it easier to surrender our very own lives than to part with this miraculous icon.

'Indeed, could anyone have possibly imagined that by any chance of fate we could be deprived of this our most precious and holy possession? Yet such a bitter loss lay in store for us, and it came about, as we later discovered, not because of any human perfidy, but by the agency of the very guide we were guarding. He it was who wished insult upon himself, so as to let us know sorrow in holy fashion and thereby point out to us the true path, before which all the paths we had previously trodden were as a dark and trackless labyrinth. But tell me, does my tale interest you? Am I not troubling your attention in vain?'

'No, how can you possibly think that?!' we exclaimed, thoroughly fascinated by this narrative. 'Please continue!'

'Very well, sirs, I shall obey you and will, as best as I am able, begin to set before you the miraculous happenings that befell us on account of our angel.'

'We arrived outside a large town on a large river, the Dnieper, in order to undertake a large project – here we were to build a large stone bridge,[1] which is nowadays very famous. The town stands on the right bank, which is a steep one, but we stood on the left bank, which is meadowy and sloping, and before us appeared the whole landscape: the ancient churches, the holy monasteries with their many sacred relics; the dense orchards and the trees that looked like the ones in the headpieces of old books – sharp-crested poplars. You would look at all that, and it would feel as if someone were pulling at your heartstrings, it was that beautiful! As you know, of course, we're just simple folk – but we feel the exquisiteness of the nature created by God all the same.

'And so strongly taken were we with that place that on that very first day we began to build a temporary shelter for ourselves. First we drove tall piles into the ground, as this place was low-lying, right beside the water; then on top of the piles we set about constructing our prayer-room, with a storeroom next to it. Into the prayer-room we put all out holy possessions, as the law of our fathers instructs us to do. Along one entire wall we spread out our folding iconostasis, which had three levels; the first for prayer, on which we placed the large icons, and above it two more shelves for the smaller ones. We made the staircase lead up to the icon depicting the crucifixion, as is prescribed by Church law, and we placed the "Angel" on the lectern from which Luka Kirilov read the Scriptures. Luka Kirilov and Mikhailitsa moved into the storeroom, and we partitioned off a small barracks for ourselves next door to it. When they saw what we had done, others who had come to work here for a long period built themselves similar quarters, and before we knew where we were we had our own flimsily built little town on stilts facing the great, solidly founded city. We set to work, and everything went perfectly! We were paid in cash on the nail by the Englishmen who ran the office; God sent us such good health that not one person fell sick all summer; and Luka's Mikhailitsa even started to complain that she was getting fat. We Old Believers found it particularly pleasing that, whereas everywhere else at that time we were subjected to persecution for our ritual, here we could do as we pleased; there were no municipal authorities, no district commissioner, no priest; we saw no one, and no one was affected or disturbed in any way by our religion ... We prayed as much as we liked; when we had finished work for the day we would go to our prayer-room, and there would be such a brilliant radiance from all the many icon-lamps there that one's heart, too, seemed to catch light. Luka Kirilov would bid the opening blessing; and then we would catch up the refrain, and we'd sing the praises of the Lord so loudly that in quiet weather our voices could be heard far beyond the settlement. And no one was troubled by our form of Christianity; in fact, I think many people got quite used to it, and it seemed to please not only the simple people, who were inclined towards Russian forms of worship, but also those of other religious persuasions. Many churchgoers who were pious by nature but had no time to attend the church on the other side of the river used to stand underneath our windows and listen, and then they would begin to pray. We never tried to stop them doing this: it would have been impossible to drive them all away, because sometimes even foreigners who were interested in the old Russian ritual came and listened to our singing with approval. The English master-builder, Yakov Yakovlevich, even used to come and stand under our window with a piece of paper and was forever trying to transcribe the chants we sang; afterwards, he would go off to inspect the work-sites, droning away to himself in imitation of us: "O Lord, appear thou to us" – except that, of course, in his mouth it sounded rather different, as those chants are notated by the

Byzantine "hook" method,[2] and it's impossible to catch them completely using modern Western notation. To do them all credit, though, the English are devout, reliable folk; they were very fond of us, thought we were good people and praised us. In other words, the angel of the Lord had brought us to a good place, had opened the hearts of men towards us and revealed to us the whole of nature's landscape.

'In this peaceful fashion we lived, after the manner I've described to you, for nigh on three years. Everything went as well as it possibly could, success showered down upon us as from the horn of Amaltheia, when all of a sudden we perceived that among us there were two vessels chosen by God for our punishment. One of these was the blacksmith Maroy, and the other was the tally-clerk Pimen Ivanov. Maroy was a complete simpleton, practically illiterate, something that was rare among us Old Believers; but he was a peculiar fellow; he was clumsily built, like a camel, and he was as plump as a wild boar, just one big belly, and his forehead was covered all over with thick shaggy hair that made him look like an ant-lion[3] of ancient times, and he had a tonsured patch on the top of his head. His speech was slow and incoherent, he kept champing his lips, and he had such a poor, lumbering intelligence that he wasn't even able to learn his prayers by heart, but could merely keep repeating the same word over and over again; but he was gifted with the sixth sense, was able to prophesy future events, and could give hints that came in useful. Pimen, on the other hand, was a foppish sort of chap; he liked to go around swaggering and saying things that had such a cunning twist to them that you could only marvel at his words; but he had a fascinating, aerial temperament. Maroy was an elderly man of over seventy, while Pimen was elegant and middle-aged; he had curly hair which was parted in the centre; his eyebrows were bushy, his face was ruddy-cheeked – he was a Belial, in short. It was in these two vessels that the sourness of the harsh beverage we were to drink to the dregs began to ferment.'

'The bridge, which we were building on eight granite piers, had already risen high above the water, and in the summer of the fourth year we started to fix iron chains on to those pillars. There was, however, one slight impediment; when we were assembling the chains and fitting steel rivets through each link, many of the riveting bolts turned out to be too long – we would have to cut them down to the right size. Each bolt – in English they're called "bars", and they're all made in England – was cast of the strongest steel, each one the thickness of a grown man's arm.[1] We couldn't heat them, because that would have tempered the steel, and there was no instrument that could have sawn through them. Our blacksmith Maroy, however, suddenly hit on the following method; he would smear the place where the bolt needed to be cut off with a mixture of thick cart axle-grease and coarse sand, shove the bolt into the snow, sprinkle salt around it, and turn it and twirl it; then he would quickly whip it out and throw it on to the red-hot forge, and when he struck it with his hammer it would crack like a wax candle, as if he had cut it with a pair of scissors. The English and Germans came to watch this cunning procedure of Maroy's – they would look, and look, and then suddenly burst out laughing and say, first to one another in their own language, and then in ours:

' "That's the way, Russky! Your fellow knows his physics!"

'But what sort of physics could Maroy have known? He hadn't a clue about science, but did simply as his Lord instructed him.

'Our Pimen Ivanov went off to boast about this event. That meant we got the worst of both worlds: some people ascribed our success to science, of which Maroy had no knowledge, while others said that God's visible abundance was performing miracles above us, which we had never observed. And this latter assertion was even more bitter to us than the former. As I have told you, Pimen Ivanov was a weak man and a voluptuary, but I shall now explain why we kept him in our *artel'*. He was the one who went into the town to get our provisions and buy whatever articles we needed. We used to send him to the post-office to dispatch our passports and money to our farms, and he brought us back new passports. In general, he managed all that kind of thing, and I must say that in this respect he was necessary and even useful to us. Any genuine, self-respecting Old Believer always shuns such trivial business, of course, and avoids all contact with government officials, the reason being that we've never had anything but trouble from them. But Pimen was glad of this trivial occupation, and in the town on the opposite bank he formed an amazing number of acquaintances; everyone, both the traders and the masters with whom he had dealings in connection with *artel'* business, knew him and regarded him as our top man. Of course, we used to joke about that: he really was inordinately fond of having tea with the masters and talking to them in a pompous fashion. They would call him our foreman, and he would just smile and stroke his beard. A frivolous fellow, in other words! This style of living took our Pimen to see a certain not unimportant person who had a wife from our part of the world; she was a teacher, and she'd read some new books that had been written about us – we didn't know what was in them – and I don't know why, but she suddenly decided she was very much in favour of Old Believers. There was a remarkable thing: what she had been chosen to be a vessel for! Well, she went on being in favour of us, and whenever our Pimen came to see her husband, she would immediately sit him down to have tea, and he'd accept with pleasure, and unroll his scrolls in front of her.

'On she'd go, prattling away in her woman's voice about how us Old Believers were this and that – holy, righteous, many-blessed; and our Belial would narrow his eyes, put his head on one side, oil his beard, and say in a sugary voice:

' "Of course, mistress! We observe the law of our fathers, and keep such-and-such and such-and-such precepts and see to it that each of us leads a pure life."

'And, in short, he would say to her all the kind of things that were completely out of place in conversation with a woman of worldly background. Yet, just imagine: she was actually interested!

' "I have heard," she said, "that God's blessing appears to you in visible form."

' "Of course, ma'am," he replied. "In very plain form indeed."

' "But visibly?"

' "Yes, ma'am," he said. "Visibly. Why, only the other day one of our men was snapping mighty bars of steel as if they were cobwebs."

'At this, the lady fairly threw up her hands in astonishment.

' "Goodness!" she said. "How interesting! Oh, I do so love miracles – and I have faith in them! I tell you what," she said. "Please ask your Old Believers to say a few prayers for me and ask God to send me a daughter. I've two sons, but I really do want a daughter as well. Do you think that's possible?"

' "Naturally, ma'am!" Pimen replied. "Why ever not? It's perfectly possible. Of course," he said, "in a case like that you'd have to have us burn some holy oil in your name."

'And, as pleased as Punch, she gave him ten roubles to spend on oil, and he put the money in his pocket, and said:

' "Very well, ma'am, you can rely on me: I'll have a word with them."

'Now, of course, Pimen never did have a word with us – but the lady had her daughter.

'Phew! She made such a fuss that she'd hardly recovered from the birth than she was summoning our light-minded fellow and singing his praises, as if he himself were the miracle-worker – and he lapped it all up. That's the degree to which a man can grow vain, his intelligence blunted and his feelings frozen. A year later, the mistress came to our God with another request – this time she wanted her husband to rent her a dacha for the summer. And again everything went according to her wishes, Pimen received offerings for candles and holy oil, pocketing the money and never letting any of it come our way. The most amazing miracles kept on occurring. This lady had an older son who was at a training school: he was a villain of the first order, and a lazy loafer, what's more, who never did any studying. But when it was time for his exams, she sent for Pimen and asked him to say some prayers so that her son would get into the next grade. Pimen said:

' "That's a hard one: I'll need to get all my men together for prayers and we'll have to be up all night until dawn, burning candles and singing and wailing."

'But she wasn't going to let that stop her; she gave him thirty roubles, just as long as they'd say those prayers! And what do you suppose? That prodigal son of hers did so well that he got into the top class. The lady nearly went crazy with joy, so nicely was our God treating her! She started to ply Pimen with request after request, and he managed to wangle the whole works out of God for her: health, an inheritance, a higher rank for her husband, and so many medals that there wasn't room on his chest for them all – they say he used to carry one of them around in his pocket. A sheer miracle, and all along we knew nothing about it. But the time came when all this had to be exposed, and these wonders be replaced by others.'

'Some trouble had arisen concerning the trading operations in a certain Jewish town in that province. I really don't know what it was all about: whether counterfeit money had been used, or there had been dealings in contraband; at any rate, the authorities wanted the matter cleared up, and they were offering a generous reward. So the lady sent for our Pimen and said:

' "Pimen Ivanovich, here are twenty roubles for candles and oil; tell your men to pray as hard as they can for my husband to be sent on this assignment."

'What did our Pimen have to lose? By now he could hardly imagine life without his oil-money, and he replied:

' "Very well, ma'am, I'll have a word with them."

' "But see that they do it properly," she said, "because this is really important to me!"

' "Ma'am, they won't dare to be slack in their praying if I'm giving the orders," Pimen said to her reassuringly. "I won't let them have anything to eat until they've finished." Then he took the money, and off he went, and that very same night the lady's husband got the assignment he wanted.

'Unfortunately, however, this latest stroke of good fortune had the effect of turning the lady's head, and she began to be dissatisfied with our prayers; she felt that she absolutely must come and glorify our holy icons herself. She told Pimen about this, and he took fright, as he knew that our men would never allow her anywhere near their icons; but the lady wouldn't give up.

' "As you wish," she said. "I shall take the boat this very evening and come to your settlement together with my son."

'Pimen tried to persuade her that it would be better for the men themselves to do the praying. "We have a guardian angel," he said. "If you'll make a donation for oil, we'll see to it that your husband doesn't come to any harm."

' "Why, that's marvellous," she replied, "marvellous; I'm so glad you have an angel of that kind; here's something for his oil. Now be sure you light three icon-lamps in front of him, and I shall come and watch."

'Pimen felt uneasy. He came and apologized to us, saying: "I didn't want to go against her wishes, the filthy Greek, because her husband's useful to us," and spun us a long yarn still without ever telling us all that he'd been up to. Well, even though we didn't like the idea, there wasn't much we could do about it: we quickly took our icons down from the walls and put them away in their chests; from the same chests we took out some substitutes which we kept in case of a raid by the authorities, put them on the iconostasis and waited for our guest. When she arrived, she was all dressed up fit to kill: she swept along with her long, wide skirts and kept looking through her lorgnette at our substitute icons, asking: "Tell me, please, which one of these is the angel who works the miracles?" We didn't know how to get her off the subject.

' "We haven't any angel like that," we said.

'And no matter how hard she tried, and no matter how much she kept telling Pimen off, we didn't show her the angel and quickly ushered her away to have tea and what snacks we were able to provide.

'We didn't like her one little bit, I don't really know why: there was something repulsive about the way she looked, even though she was supposed to be beautiful. She was tall, you see, long-legged, like, as thin as a steppe goat, and she had these big eyebrows.'

'Don't you find that sort of beauty attractive?' asked the bearskin coat, interrupting the narrator.

'Well, begging your pardon, sir, but what's attractive about a woman who looks like a snake?' he replied.

'So what passes for beauty among your sort? I suppose you want a woman to look like a tuft of grass!'

'A tuft of grass?' the narrator repeated, smiling and taking no offence. 'Now why do you think that? We true Russians have our own ideas about what a woman should look like; they're far better than any of your modern, light-minded notions, and they have nothing to do with tufts of grass. The point is that we're not interested in long legs – no, we like a woman's legs to be strong and stout, so she won't go straying off, but roll along everywhere like a ball and keep pace with us: those long-legged women run, but then they stumble. That snakelike thinness doesn't command much respect with us, either; we want a woman to be plump, with a good fat belly, for although that may not look very elegant, it underlines the motherliness in her; and although the faces of our true Russian women are a bit fleshy and meaty, they're soft and they show more warmth and cheerfulness. The same is true of their noses: they're not curved, they're straight as pipes, but a pipe like that is much nicer to have around the house than a dry, snooty nose. And especially the eyebrows: the eyebrows are what open a face up, and so a woman's eyebrows shouldn't be close together, but open, like arches, for it's easier for a man to talk to a woman like that; she makes you feel at home. But of course the modern taste has left that kindly type behind, and what it approves of in the female sex is airy ephemerality – but that's just a lot of nonsense. Anyway, I notice that we've strayed off the subject. I'd better continue.

'As a man who was used to a fair bit of fuss, our Pimen observed that when we were seeing our guest off we began to voice some criticisms of her, and he said:

' "What's the matter with you? She's a nice lady."

'But we replied: "What's nice about her when she's not even nice to look at? But God be with her: let her be as she is, we're just glad we've seen her off and we've started to give the place a good dose of incense to get rid of the smell of her perfume."

'After that, we swept the room clean of all traces of our guest; we put the substitute icons back in their chest on the other side of the partition, and got the genuine ones out again; we placed them on the iconostasis, just as they had been before, and sprinkled them with holy water; we said a blessing, and then each of us went off to his bed to turn in for the night. Only for God knows what reason, none of us could get much sleep that night – we felt uneasy, with an ominous sense of foreboding.'

'In the morning we all went off to work and did our tasks, but there was no sign of Luka Kirilov. Knowing his love of punctuality, this was surprising; but I was even more surprised when he finally arrived at about eight o'clock, pale and distraught.

'Aware that he was a man of self-control who didn't easily show his emotions, I drew his attention to this, and asked: "What's wrong, Luka Kirilov?" "I'll tell you later," he replied.

'But I was a young chap in those days, and terribly inquisitive; what's more, I'd suddenly had a premonition from somewhere that it was something unpleasant connected with our faith; I had a great reverence for our faith, and had never been an unbeliever.

'For this reason I was unable to put up with the uncertainty for long, and under some pretext or other I abandoned my work and ran off home; "I'll find out something about it from Mikhailitsa before the others get back," I thought. Although Luka Kirilov didn't unburden himself to her, she knew what went on inside him, in spite of her simple ways. And she wouldn't hide anything from me, because I'd been an orphan since childhood, and had grown up in their home. I was like a son to them; and Mikhailitsa was like a second mother to me.

'So, good sirs, I went to see her, and there she was sitting in the porch in an old, unfastened quilted jacket, looking sad, ill, and sort of green in the face.

' "Why are you sitting out there, Mother?" I asked.

'And she replied:

' "Where else can I sit, Marochka?"

'My name's Mark Aleksandrov; but she, with her motherly feelings for me, called me Marochka.

' "What's this?" I thought to myself. "Why is she talking this nonsense about there being nowhere for her to sit?"

' "Why don't you go and lie down in your storeroom?" I said.

' "I can't," she replied. "Marochka, old man Maroy's praying in the big room in there."

' "Aha!" I thought. "So it *is* something to do with our faith." And Mikhailitsa went on:

' "Marochka, my child, do you know what happened here last night?"

' "No, Mother," I said. "I don't. Tell me."

' "Oh, I don't know whether I can."

' "Come on," I said. "Tell me. I'm as good as a son to you, not a stranger, after all."

' "I know," she replied. "It's just that I'm not sure whether I'm able to put it into the right words, as I'm a stupid, feeble woman. Why don't you wait until your uncle comes back after his work-break, I expect he'll tell you everything."

'But I couldn't wait; I kept on at her, saying: "Tell me, tell me right now what's happened."

'Then I saw that she kept blinking and blinking, and her eyes were soon full of tears. She wiped them with a handkerchief, and then whispered to me, softly:

' "My child, our guardian angel came down among us last night."

'This revelation threw me into a state of turmoil.

' "Tell me," I begged her, "tell me at once: how did this miracle take place, and who witnessed it?"

' "Nobody knows how it took place," she said. "And there were no witnesses apart from myself, because it happened in the very dead of night, and I was the only one who wasn't asleep."

'And then, good sirs, she told me the following story:

' "After I'd said my prayers that night," she said, "I fell asleep. I don't know how long I slept for, all I know is that suddenly I had a dream about a fire, a big fire: I saw our home and all our possessions burning down, and the river swirling the ashes away into the eddies near the piers of the bridge, sucking and swallowing them down into the depths." Mikhailitsa saw herself jumping out in nothing but a tattered shift that was covered in holes, and standing at the edge of the water; opposite her, on the other bank, was a red pillar, and on the top of the pillar a small white cockerel was flapping its wings. She said: "Who are you?" because she seemed to sense that this bird was prophesying something. And this little cockerel suddenly said, in a human voice: "Amen," and flew down, and then was gone, and around her there was silence and such a thinning of the air that she got scared and couldn't draw her breath; then she woke up and found herself lying in bed. She could hear a lamb bleating outside the door. She could tell by its bleat that it was a very young lamb which still had its first fleece intact. Its silvery little voice was chiming away as clear as a bell – "beh-eh-eh", and Mikhailitsa suddenly realized that it was in the prayer-room, she could hear its little hooves scampering about the floorboards, "chock-chock-chock", and it seemed to be looking for someone. "Lord Jesus!" she thought to herself. "What's this: not one of the sheep in our new settlement has produced a single lamb so far, so where has this little suckling sprung from?" And at the same time she wondered: "How did it get inside, anyway? We must have forgotten to lock the front door after all the commotion yesterday. Thank the Lord," she thought, "that it's only a lamb that's got in, and not a dog from the yard that might have gone for the icons." Well, and so she woke Luka: "Kirilych," she shouted, "Kirilych! Get up quickly, dear, our door's open and a little lamb's got in." But Luka Kirilov was still sound asleep, as if that were his intention. No matter how hard she tried to rouse him, he wouldn't wake up: he'd just mumble, without getting any words out. The harder she shook him and moved him, the louder he'd mumble, and that was all. She began to beg him "to wake up in Jesus' name", but no sooner had she uttered that name than there was a squealing in the prayer-room, and at that moment Luka leapt up from his bed, and was about to rush forward, when all of a sudden he was flung back as if by a wall of brass. "Blow out the candle, woman! Quickly, blow it out!" he shouted to Mikhailitsa, not moving from the spot. She snuffed out the candle and ran over to him; he was as pale as a man who's been condemned to death, trembling so badly that not only was his neck-fastener moving – even his trousers were shaking. Again the woman spoke to him. "Winner of our bread," she said, "what's wrong with you?" But all he could do was point with one finger, to show her that in the spot where the angel had been there was now just an empty gap, and the angel was lying beside Luka on the floor.

'Luka Kirilov immediately went to Maroy and told him what his wife had seen and what had happened, and asked him to come and look. Maroy came and knelt down before the icon of the angel that was lying on the floor, and stayed there motionless for a long time looking down at it like a marble tombstone, and then, raising his arm, scratched the shaven patch on the crown of his head and said quietly:

' "Bring twelve fresh bricks."

'Luka Kirilov lost no time in fetching the bricks. Maroy inspected them, saw that they were all fresh, straight from the furnace, and told Luka to lay them one on top of the other. In this fashion they erected a pillar, covered it with a clean table-cloth, and stood the icon on it. Then Maroy threw himself to the floor and declaimed:

' "Angel of the Lord, may thy steps lead thee wheresoever thou wilt!"

'No sooner had he said these words than there was a sudden "knock-knock-knock" at the door, and an unfamiliar voice called:

' "Hey, you, schismatics: who's your boss?"

'Luka Kirilov opened the door and saw a soldier with a medal standing there.

'Luka asked him what sort of boss he wanted to see, and he replied:

' "The one who's called Pimen and went to see the lady."

'Well, Luka immediately sent his wife to fetch Pimen, and asked: "What's it about? Why have they sent you at night in search of Pimen?"

'The soldier said:

' "I don't really know, but there's a rumour that the Jews have done something unpleasant to the master over there."

'But what it was he was unable to relate.

' "I heard," he said, "that the master sealed them up and that they sealed him up in return."

'But as to how this mutual sealing-up had taken place, the soldier was unable to offer any cogent explanation.

'At that point Pimen arrived and, like a Jew, started to turn his eyes this way and that: he evidently didn't know what to say. Luka said:

' "What sort of a *spielmann* have you turned into? Now go and play your *spiel* to its end."

'The soldier and Pimen got into the soldier's boat, and off they went.

'An hour later our Pimen returned, boasting that he felt fine; but it was obvious that he was badly out of sorts.

'Luka started to question him:

' "You'd better tell us the whole story, you windbag: what have you been up to over there?"

' "Nothing," he said.

'Well, that seemed to be the end of it – but it wasn't, not by a long chalk.'

'An extraordinary thing had happened to the master for whom Pimen had said the prayers. As I was telling you, he'd gone to the Jewish town, arriving there late at night, when no one was expecting him, and had sealed up each and every shop in the place; then he had let the police know that in the morning he would be helping them to conduct an official government inspection. The Jews found out about this immediately, of course, and that very night they went to try to do a deal with him – for they had a huge amount of contraband goods in their possession. When they arrived, they lost no time in thrusting ten thousand roubles under the master's nose. He said: "I can't accept your money, I'm a senior official, invested with trust, and I don't take bribes"; but the Jews got together, did a bit of argy-bargying, and then offered him fifteen thousand. Again he said: "I can't accept it"; and they offered him twenty thousand. "What's the matter with you?" he said. "Don't you understand that *I can't accept your money*; I've already told the police that I'll be conducting an inspection with them tomorrow." And again they did some argy-bargying, and said:

' "Ah, your excellency, that's all right that you've told the police, ve'll give you twenty-five thousand, and in return you give us your seal and go to bed quietly and sleep: that's all ve vont."

'The master thought hard: although he considered himself a big shot, it was clear that even the heart of a big shot wasn't made of stone. He accepted the twenty-five thousand, gave the Jews the seal he used for marking goods as being the property of the government, and then went to bed. During the night the

Jews, of course, hauled all their stuff out of their vaults and sealed it using the master's seal; he was still asleep when they came cackling in his hallway. Well, he let them in; they thanked him and said:

'"Ah, your excellency, now you can proceed with the inspection."

'Well, he pretended not to hear that, and said:

'"Give me back my seal."

'But the Jews replied:

'"You give us our money back then."

'"What?" the master said.

'And the Jews began to argue:

'"Ve left our money with you as security," they said.

'The master said:

'"What do you mean, security?"

'"Just that," they said. "Security."

'"Oh no you don't," he said. "You're villains, sellers of Christ: you certainly didn't leave that money with me as security."

'The Jews nudged one another and laughed.

'"*Hörsch-du*," they said. "Listen, ve think ve did . . . Hm, hm! *Ay-vay*: d'you really think ve're so stupid, like muzhiks with no politics, that ve'd try to slip a *khabar* to such a big shot as you?" (*Khabar* in their lingo means 'a bribe'.)

'Well, sirs, what better line could you imagine than that one? If the gent had given the money back, that would have been the end of the matter – but he went on making a fuss, because he didn't want to part with the money.

'The morning came; all the shops in the town were shut; people walked around, marvelling; the police demanded the seal back, but the Jews wailed: "*Ay-vay!* Vot kind of a government is this? The powers-that-be vont to ruin us!"

'What a to-do! The master sat behind locked doors and couldn't make up his mind what to do; towards evening he summoned those crafty Jews and said: "All right, you cursed lot, take your money – but give me back my seal!" But they wouldn't agree to that now, and said: "Ah, how is that possible? None of us here in town have done any business today: now we want fifty thousand roubles from your excellency."

You see how things were going! And the Jews threatened him, saying: "If you don't give us fifty thousand roubles today, tomorrow it'll cost you twenty-five thousand more!"

'The master lay awake all night; in the morning he sent for the Jews again, returned all the money he had accepted from them and, in addition, wrote out a promissory note, and managed somehow to proceed with his inspection: he didn't find anything, of course, and went speeding back to his wife in a right old rage, asking: "Where can I get twenty-five thousand roubles so I can redeem the promissory note I gave those Jews? You'll have to sell the village you got as a dowry." But his wife said: "Not for anything in the world will I sell it: I'm very attached to it." "It's all your fault," he said. "It was you who had all those prayers said by those schismatics in order to get me this commission; you told me their angel would help me, and look where he's landed me." And she replied: "You're the one whose fault it is for not having the sense to arrest those Jews and for not telling the authorities that they'd stolen your seal; but forget about all that: you just do as I say, and I'll set the matter right and make others pay for your foolishness." And suddenly in a raucous voice she shouted to whoever happened to be there: "Quickly, this instant," she said, "go over to the other side of the Dnieper and bring me the schismatics' leader." Well, of course, a messenger went and fetched our Pimen, and the mistress said to him, without beating about the bush: "Listen," she said, "I know you're an intelligent man and will understand what I want: my husband has met with a slight unpleasantness – some villains have robbed him ... Jews ... you understand; we've really got to find twenty-five thousand roubles this very day, and I really don't know where I can get my hands on that much money in so little time; but I've summoned you, and am confident that you can help me, as you Old Believers are rich and clever and, as I've had occasion to experience, God helps you in all things – so please let me have twenty-five thousand roubles, and in return I'll tell all the ladies in town about your miracle-working icons, and you'll get a lot of money for oil and candles." Well, kind sirs, I don't expect you'll have much difficulty in imagining what our *spielmann* felt at such a turn of events? I don't know exactly what he told her in so many words, but I can assure you that he began to curse and swear that we were far too poor to raise such a sum – but she, like a latter-day Salome, wouldn't listen. "I know perfectly well," she said, "that you schismatics have plenty of money; twenty-five thousand roubles is just chicken-feed to you. When my father served in Moscow, the Old Believers often lent him larger sums than that; twenty-five thousand is a trivial amount." Pimen naturally tried to explain to her that "those Muscovite Old Believers were men of substance, while we were just simple labouring peasants – how could we hope to match the power and wealth of Muscovites?" But her time in Moscow had evidently taught her a thing or two, and she suddenly brought him up short, saying: "Stop it, stop trying to tell me that! Do you think I don't know about all those miracle-working icons you have? You've told me yourself about all the money you're sent for oil and candles from all over Russia? No, I don't want to hear your objections; I want the money at once, or else my husband will go to see the governor this very day and tell him about your praying and putting temptation in folk's way, and then you'll know all about it."

'Poor Pimen nearly fell off the porch, he was that flabbergasted; he arrived back home, as I've told you, and all he could say was "never mind", over and over again; he was red all over, as if he'd just come out of a bath-house, and kept moping around in corners blowing his nose. Well, Luka Kirilov finally asked him a few questions about what had happened, but he didn't reveal everything; he did, however, tell him the gist of it, saying: "This lady wants me to lend her five thousand roubles." Well, of course, Luka Kirilov let fly at him even just for that: "Oh, you *spielmann*, you *spielmann*," he said. "You would go and get involved with folk like that, and lead them to our door! What do you think we are, rich men, to have money like that in our coffers? And why should we give it away? Where is it, anyway? . . . Since you've landed yourself in this mess, you can get yourself out of it again. We've nowhere we can get five thousand roubles from."

'With that, Luka Kirilov went off to his place of work and arrived there, as I told you, as pale as a man who's been condemned to death, because the event he'd witnessed in the night had given him a premonition that something unpleasant was lying in store for us; but Pimen set off in a different direction. We all saw him row his little boat out through the reeds and cross over to the town side of the river; and now, after Mikhailitsa had told me the whole story in sequence of how he had come begging for five thousand roubles, I guessed that he was probably hurrying back to try to propitiate the lady. Reflecting in this fashion, I stood beside Mikhailitsa and wondered whether some harmful consequences might not come of this for us, and whether we ought not to be taking some measures to prevent this evil from taking place, when I suddenly observed that it was too late to do anything, because a large boat was coming in alongside the bank, and over my shoulder I could hear the sound of many voices. Turning round, I caught sight of several uniformed government officials, together with rather a large number of gendarmes and soldiers. Before Mikhailitsa and I had time to exchange glances, they had all gone thronging straight past us into Luka's prayer-room, posting two sentries with drawn sabres outside the door. Mikhailitsa began to throw herself at these sentries, not so much because she wanted them to let her in, as because she wanted to do a bit of suffering; they, of course, began to shove her away, but she would hurl herself at them even more furiously, and so heated did the battle become that one of the gendarmes finally dealt her a savage blow, so that she rolled back down the porch steps like a peg-top. I was about to rush across the bridge to fetch Luka, but then I saw Luka running towards me with the whole of our *artel'* in his wake; they were all in a tremendous state of agitation, and each man wielded the implement he had been working with – some had crowbars, others mattocks: they were all coming to defend their holy place . . . Those who had been unable to get into the boat that was available, having no other means of getting to the right part of the bank, had leapt off the bridge still wearing their workclothes, and were swimming one after the other across the icy waves . . . I couldn't believe my eyes, and began to be afraid for how it was all going to end. The government patrol was made up of a couple of dozen men, but even though they were all kitted out in various dashing forms of fighting gear, there were over fifty of our men, and every one of them was inspired with lofty, ardent faith. They came swimming across the water like sea-lions, and you could have knocked their heads in with hammers, but still they would have reached their holy possessions on the opposite bank; wet as they were, they suddenly all marched forward, like a living wall, indestructible as stones.'

'Now, you'll recall that while Mikhailitsa and I were holding our conversation, old man Maroy was praying in the big room. Well, the government officials and their henchmen caught him there. He told us afterwards that when they came in they immediately slammed the door shut behind them and rushed towards the icons. Some of the men went round snuffing out the icon lamps, and others tore the icons off the walls and put them on the floor. They shouted to Maroy: "Are you the priest?" "No, I'm not," he said. "Who's your priest?" they wanted to know. "We don't have any priest," he replied. To which they said: "What do you mean, you haven't any priest? How dare you say that you haven't any priest!" At this point Maroy was about to explain to them that we don't have priests in our faith, but so incoherent was his speech – he would keep champing his lips – that they, not understanding a word, merely said: "Tie him up and place him under arrest!" Maroy submitted to being tied up: it didn't much matter to him if some platoon private bound his hands with a piece of rope; accepting it all as a consequence of his faith, he stood watching to see what would happen next. Meanwhile, the officials had lit candles and were sealing the icons: some of them applied the seals, others wrote up inventories, yet others bored holes with drills and strung the icons on iron rods like doughnuts. Maroy observed this sacrilegious outrage without even a shrug of his shoulders, reasoning that no doubt God had wished to allow such barbarous behaviour. At that moment, however, old Maroy heard one of the gendarmes give a shout, and then another: the door flew open, and our sea-lions came still wet with the water from which they had clambered and were into the prayer-room like a shot. Fortunately, Luka Kirilov managed to maintain his lead on them. All at once he shouted:

' "Wait, men of Christ, don't be too bold!" And, turning to the icons which had been strung together on rods, he said: "Why are you harming our holy possessions in this way, gentlemen of the authorities? If you are within your rights to take them from us, then take them – we are no enemies of the government; but why harm the precious art of our fathers?"

'But the husband of the lady Pimen had been seeing was in charge of the government patrol, and he shouted at our Luka:

' "To heel, you villain! Do you dare to raise your voice against us?"

'And Luka, even though he was a proud muzhik, tamed his pride and answered quietly:

' "All right, your excellency, we know the form: we've got about a hundred and fifty icons in this room of ours, and we'll give you three roubles for each of them, just as long as you leave the art of our forefathers alone."

'The master's eyes flashed and he thundered:

' "Be gone!" But in a whisper he added: "Give me a hundred roubles each for them, otherwise I'll burn the lot."

'Luka could not even consider paying such a large sum, and he said:

' "Well, if that's the way it's got to be, go ahead and destroy them – we haven't got that kind of money."

'The master burst out angrily:

' "You bearded goat, how dare you mention money in our presence?" And he suddenly started to rush around, gathering all the icons he could see into sheaves; then nuts were screwed onto the ends of the rods and seals applied, so that it would be impossible either to remove the icons or replace them with substitutes. When they had finished doing this, the patrol made ready to leave: the soldiers hoisted the skewered sheaves of icons on to their shoulders and carried them to the boats. In the meantime, Mikhailitsa, who had followed the men into the prayer-room, managed to sneak the icon of the angel from the lectern; just as she was about to carry it under a cloth off to the storeroom, her hands began to shake so badly that she dropped it. Goodness gracious, how the master let fly! He called us thieves and swindlers, and said:

' "Aha! You swindlers thought you could filch that one so it didn't get put on a rod; well, if it's not going in with the rest, this is what I'll do to it!"

'And, heating his stick of sealing-wax so that it smoked, he thrust its burning, seething resin right in the angel's face!

'Good sirs, please don't be annoyed with me, but I couldn't even begin to describe to you what happened when the master splashed the angel's face with a stream of bubbling sealing-wax and what is more, cruel man, raised the icon aloft in order to boast of the means he had found of outraging us. All I remember is that the angel's divine countenance was red with sealing-wax, and that beneath the seal the drying-oil, which had begun to melt ever so slightly under the fiery pitch, was trickling down his cheeks in two streams, like bloodstained tears . . .

'We all gasped and, covering our eyes with our hands, fell prostrate and began to groan as though under torture. Such was our wailing that it continued into the dead of night; as we howled and mourned for our sealed angel in the darkness and silence of our desecrated holy place, an idea came to us: we would find out where our protector had been taken. We vowed to steal him back, even though our lives might be put at risk in the process, and to unseal him. The young lad Levonty and I were chosen to put this plan into execution.

'This Levonty was still just a lad of no more than seventeen years, but he was powerfully built and good-hearted; he had been a devout Christian since childhood, and was as dutiful and well-behaved as a keen white stallion in a silver harness.

'I could have wished for no better helper and fellow conspirator for such a risky undertaking as the tracking-down and reappropriation of our sealed angel, the spectacle of whose blinded sight was quite simply intolerable to us.'

'I won't weary you with the details of how I and my fellow conspirator passed through the eyes of needles, penetrating everywhere, but will simply tell you about the grief by which we were overcome when we discovered that after boring holes in our icons and stringing them in sheaves on iron rods, those government officials had dumped them in the crypt of the consistory – that was it, they were as good as buried, and we had no hope of ever seeing them again. The only mitigating factor was that the bishop, who himself was said to have disapproved of such barbarity,[1] had inquired: "What's the good of this?" and had even intervened on the side of the old works of art, saying: "These are antiquities, they ought to be preserved!" But the bad part of this was that hardly had the disaster caused by the officials' disrespect had time to recede in our memories than another, even greater one now threatened us from the actions of this pious man: the bishop – with good intentions, one must suppose – picked up our sealed angel and spent a long time examining it, after which he looked to one side and said: "What a sorry sight! How dreadfully they have disfigured him! Don't put this icon in the crypt, but leave it in the window behind my altar." The bishop's servants did as he commanded them, and I must admit to you that while on the one hand we found it very pleasant to receive such attention from an ecclesiastical hierarch, on the other we saw that all our plans of stealing back our icon had been rendered useless. There was another method open to us: that of bribing the bishop's servants and with their assistance substituting in place of the angel another icon which was a cunningly painted likeness of it. Our

Old Believers have had a number of successes in this field, but it is a craft that demands above all the skilled and experienced hand of an isographer, who is able to make an exact copy of an icon, and we had no hope of finding such an isographer in those parts. From the moment of that realization a redoubled sense of depression descended on us, and it passed over us like the dropsy: in the prayer-room, where before only hymns of praise had been heard, now there were nothing but sobs, and within a short space of time we had all sobbed our hearts out, unable to see the ground in front of us for the tears that filled our eyes; it may or may not have been because of this that an eye disease took hold among us, and it began to affect everyone. People who had never suffered this way before were now stricken: there were no limits to the number of cases! Among the labourers a rumour went round that there was more to it than there seemed: it had to do with the Old Believers' angel: "He was blinded with the seal, and now we're all going blind," they said, and this interpretation caused unrest not only among our folk, but among all the other church folk as well, and no matter how many doctors our English masters brought in, no one would go to them, nor would they take any medicine, but simply kept wailing:

' "Bring us the sealed angel, we want to pray to him, for he alone can heal us."

'Yakov Yakovlevich, the Englishman, who had inquired into this matter, went to see the bishop and said:

' "Whichever way you look at it, your grace, faith is a great thing, and whoever has faith yields to faith: so please return the sealed angel to us who live on the other side of the river."

'But the bishop would not listen, and said:

' "We must not pander to their foolishness."

'At the time these seemed like hard words to us, and we said a lot of damning things about the bishop in the course of idle talk. Later on, however, it was revealed to us that all this happened not because of cruelty but as a result of God's supervision.

'Meanwhile, the omens showed no sign of ceasing, and on the other side of the river the accusing finger began to point to the chief culprit in the whole affair – Pimen, who, following the disaster, had fled from us and had rejoined the Church. I once ran into him in the town, and he bowed to me; I bowed back. He said:

' "I have sinned, Brother Mark, in diverging from your faith."

'I answered:

' "The matter of what faith a man belongs to lies in God's hands; but I think it's a poor show that you've sold your birthright for a mess of pottage, and if you'll forgive me, I don't mind telling you so – in brotherly fashion, as the prophet Amos commands us."

'This mention of a prophet fairly made him quiver.

' "Don't talk to me about prophets," he said. "I know the Scriptures, and I know that 'prophets torment the living on the earth'; I even bear the marks of this truth on my own person . . ." And he complained to me that the other day he had taken a dip in the river and that after it his body had become covered in irregularly shaped spots. He undid his shirt and showed me his chest, and true enough, there were irregular blotches, like those on a skewbald horse, running from his chest up across his neck.

'Sinful man that I am, it was on the tip of my tongue to say to him that "God marks the scoundrel", but I refrained from doing so, and said merely:

' "Well, offer up a prayer and be glad that you've been given such titles of abbreviation; perhaps at second liturgy you'll be a plain text."

'Again he began to moan about his misfortune and about the hardship he would suffer if the spots rose to his face, because the governor himself had apparently been pleasantly struck by how handsome Pimen was when he had joined the Church, and had instructed the mayor that whenever important personages were passing through the town Pimen was to be stationed in front of everyone else, holding a silver plate. Well, and would they put a man with spots to the fore like that? But I'd had enough of listening to his Belial-like vanity and frivolousness, and I turned and walked away.

'And with that we parted. His "titles of abbreviation" became ever more clearly discernible, and as for ourselves – well, the succession of omens showed no signs of abating. At the end of the autumn the river had no sooner frozen than a sudden thaw set in; all the ice that had formed split up and started to do damage to the buildings we had constructed. Disaster followed disaster, until suddenly one of the granite piers was washed away, and all the work of many years, costing many thousands of roubles, was swallowed up by an abyss . . .

'This event made an impression on our English masters, and their leader Yakov Yakovlevich received word from someone that in order to obtain deliverance from such calamities it would be necessary to drive us Old Believers away; but since Yakov Yakovlevich was a kindly soul, he ignored this advice, and instead summoned Luka Kirilov and myself, saying:

' "Tell me yourselves what I should do: isn't there anything I can do to help you and bring you consolation?"

'But we replied that while the countenance of the angel, who went before us everywhere, remained beneath its seal of pitchy wax, there was nothing that could console us – we were pining away with sorrow.

' "What do you plan to do?" he asked.

' "Eventually we plan to unseal and restore his pure countenance, which has been singed by the godless hand of a government official."

' "But why is this angel so dear to you?" he asked. "Can you really not get hold of another one like it?"

' "He's dear to us," we replied, "because he has protected us, and we can't get another, for he was painted in the good old days by a pious hand and was consecrated by an ancient priest according to the Euchologion of Metropolitan Peter;[2] but nowadays we have neither priests nor the Euchologion."

' "But how will you be able to unseal him, when his face has been burned away by sealing-wax?" he asked.

' "Oh, don't worry yourself on that account, your honour: all we have to do is get him back in our hands again, and he'll do the rest, our guardian will. He's not the work of one of those commercial artists, he's a genuine Stroganov, and the Stroganov drying oil, like the Kostroman, is boiled so it's not afraid of fiery wax and won't let it reach the delicate paint."

' "Are you sure of that?"

' "Yes, sir: that drying-oil is as resilient as our old Russian faith."

'Here he let fly a string of oaths at people who didn't know how to look after artistry of that kind, gave us his hand, and said:

' "Well, be of good heart: I'm here to help you, and we'll get your angel back. Do you need him for a long time?"

' "No," we said. "We only need him for a short time."

' "Well, I tell you what: I shall make a rich, golden mounting for your angel, and when they give me him, we'll substitute another icon in his place."

'We thanked him, but said:

' "Only don't do it either tomorrow, or the day after tomorrow, sir."

' "Why do you say that?" he asked.

' "Because, sir," we replied, "it's very important that the icon we use as a substitute be as like the original as to make no difference, and there aren't any such masters to be found either here or anywhere in the neighbourhood."

' "Nonsense!" he said. "I shall bring an artist here from the town; he's not only a master of copying, but is a magnificent portrait painter, too."

' "No, sir," we replied. "Please don't do that, because first, a secular artist like that might start improper rumours circulating, and second, no artist could ever possibly execute such a work."

'The Englishman did not believe us, and I intervened in order to explain the difference to him: that artists nowadays didn't practise the same kind of art – they used oil paints, whereas in olden times the colours were delicate, dissolved in egg-yolk; in modern paintings the paint is daubed on, so as to give a natural effect only at a distance, while in the old art the strokes of paint are smoothly applied and distinct even very close to; I told him that a secular artist could not hope to be able to copy the graphic outlines of the original, because he would have been trained to depict that which is contained in the earthly human body, attached to worldly life, while what is depicted in holy Russian icon-painting is an aethereal type of person, of which materially limited man can have no conception.

'My words interested the Englishman, and he asked me:

' "Are there any masters anywhere who *do* understand this special type?"

' "They're very rare nowadays," I told him. (Even in the old days they lived in the strictest secrecy.) "There is," I said, "in the settlement of Mstyora³ a certain master Khokhlov. He's a man of very advanced years, though, and he wouldn't be able to undertake a long journey; and there are two men in Palekh, but they'd hardly make the journey either – and anyway," I added, "neither the masters of Mstyora nor of Palekh would be any good to us."

' "Why is that?" he asked.

' "Because," I replied, "they have the wrong manner: those little Mstyoran icons with their large-headed figures are painted in dim colours, and the tone of the Palekhs is turquoise, reminiscent of whortleberries . . ."

' "So what can we do?"

' "I don't really know," I said. "I've heard tell that in Moscow there's another fine master called Silachov: he's renowned throughout the whole of Russia among our folk, but he's better at doing work in the Novgorod and Muscovite Tsarist styles; the only person who could paint us an icon in our Stroganov style, in the brightest, richest colours, is master Sevastyan from the lower reaches of the Dnieper – but he's passionately fond of travelling around: he traverses the whole of Russia doing repair work for the Old Believers, and no one knows where he is."

'The Englishman listened with pleasure to all this information, and smiled. Then he replied:

' "You're remarkable folk, and no mistake," he said. "Listening to you, one has a pleasant feeling that you know about everything which affects your lot, and are even capable of understanding art."

' "Why shouldn't we understand art, sir?" I said. "It's a matter of divine art, and among us there are connoisseurs – the very simplest of muzhiks – who are not only able to distinguish all the various schools from one another by their styles: the

Ustyugan from the Novgorodian, the Muscovite from the Vologdan, the Siberian from the Stroganov. They are even able to distinguish unerringly between the work of certain old Russian masters within one and the same school."

' "Can that really be?" he asked.

' "It's like the way you distinguish the handwriting of one man from that of another. They simply have to take one look, and they can tell who the artist was: Kuzma, Andrey or Prokofy."

' "What are the distinguishing marks they look for?"

' "There's always a difference in method and form: and also in the type of paint used, the blank spaces, the facial expressions and the texturing."

'He listened to it all; I told him what I knew about the painting of Ushakov[4] and Rublyov,[5] and about Paramshin,[6] the earliest Russian painter, whose icons our pious Tsars and princes gave as a blessing to their children, and instructed their priests to guard more closely than the apple of their eye.

'The Englishman immediately got out his notebook and asked me to repeat the name of this artist and to tell him where he could see his icons. But I replied:

' "You'll go looking in vain, sir: there's not a trace of them left anywhere."

' "Where have they been put?"

' "I don't know," I said. "They've either been screwed up and made into chibouks or been exchanged for tobacco from the Germans."

' "That cannot be," he said.

' "On the contrary," I replied. "It happens all the time, and there are notable examples of it: in the Pope's residence in the Vatican there is a folding tripartite icon which was painted by our Russian isographers Andrey, Sergey and Nikita in the thirteenth century.[7] This many-figured miniature is said to be so remarkable that even the greatest foreign painters go into ecstasies over such wonderful artistry."

' "But how did it end up in Rome?"

' "Peter the Great made a gift of it to some foreign monarch, who sold it."

'The Englishman smiled and thought for a while, then quietly said that in England every painting was preserved from generation to generation, thereby showing to which family it belonged.

' "Yes, I suppose our methods of education are a bit different; the connections with the traditions of our forefathers have been broken, so that everything should seem as new as possible, as though the entire Russian race was only hatched out yesterday by a moorhen from under a nettle-patch."

' "Well, if that's the case, your educated ignoramuship," he said, "why is it that you in whom the love of your birthright has been preserved don't make an effort to maintain your natural artistic ability?"

' "There's no one to maintain it for us," I replied. "In the modern schools of painting there has developed a universal corruption of sentiment and the mind obeys vanity's dictates. The type of lofty inspiration has been lost, and everything centres around the earthly, and breathes with earthly passion. Our most recent artists began by using Prince Potyomkin of Taurida as a model for the Archangel Michael, and they've even gone so far as to depict Christ the Saviour as a Jew.[8] What more may one await from such people? Their uncut hearts may still be depicting abominations and asking us to consider them divine: after all, in Egypt people considered a bull and a red-feathered bow as divinities. But we won't worship alien gods and we won't accept a Jew's face as the countenance of the Saviour; we view these depictions, no matter how exquisite they may be, as manifestations of unnecessary ignorance, and we turn away from them in accordance with the tradition of our fathers, which says that 'the diversion of the eyes sullies the purity of the reason, even as a damaged fountain spoils the water'."

'With this, I brought my discourse to a close. The Englishman said:

' "Continue: I like your manner of reasoning."

'I replied:

' "I've said all I have to say."

'But he said:

' "No, you haven't; tell me what you understand by an inspired depiction."

'Now that, good sirs, was a pretty tricky question for a simple fellow like myself to answer, but there was nothing for it: I plunged in and began telling him about the way the starry heavens are painted in Novgorod,[9] and then proceeded to describe the Kievan icon in the Church of St Sofia, in which seven winged archangels are depicted standing on either side of the God of Sabaoth, none of whom resemble Prince Potyomkin, naturally; at the thresholds of the canopy, prophets and forefathers; a stage lower, Moses with the tablets; a stage below that, Aaron with his mitre and rod; on the other stages, King David wearing his crown, the prophet Isaiah with his charter, Ezekiel with the closed gates, Daniel with the stone, and around these supplicants, who were showing the way to Heaven, whose gifts which the man who follows this glorious path may attain: the Book of the Seven Seals, representing the gift of holy wisdom; the seven-pronged candlestick, representing the gift of reason; the seven eyes, representing the gift of wise counsel; the seven trumpets, representing the gift of strength; the right hand amidst the seven stars, representing the gift of vision; the seven censers, representing the gift of piety; the seven lightning bolts, representing the fear of God. "There," I said, "that's the kind of depiction that's uplifting!"

'But the Englishman replied:

' "I'm sorry, old chap, but I don't understand why you consider all that uplifting."

' "Because a depiction like that tells a man in no uncertain terms that the duty of Christians is to pray and yearn to be exalted from the earth to realms of unspoken glory."

' "But anyone can understand from the Scriptures and the Orthodox prayers."

' "Certainly not," I replied. "It isn't given to everyone to understand the Scriptures, and for those who don't understand, there are obscure passages in the prayers as well: some people hear the prayer about the 'great and rich mercies', immediately assume it's about money, and get down on their knees with avid zeal. But when he sees before him a depiction of heavenly glory, he thinks about the higher things of life and comes to understand how this goal may be reached, because here everything is

simple and sensible: if a man prays first of all for the gift of the
fear of God to enter his soul, that soul of his will immediately
pass, made lighter, from stage to stage, appropriating with each
new step a super-abundance of higher gifts – at times of prayer
such as those, money and all earthly glory will appear to a man
as nothing other than baseness before the Lord."

'Here the Englishman rose from his seat and said in a cheerful voice:

' "And what about you strange lot? What do you pray for?"

' "We pray for a Christian end to our lives, and that we
may give a good account of ourselves at the Last Judgement,"
I replied.

'He smiled and then suddenly tugged at a gilt tassel which
opened a green curtain; behind this curtain his English wife sat
in an armchair, knitting with long knitting-needles by the light
of a candle. She was a marvellous, good-natured lady, and
although she couldn't speak much Russian, she understood
everything we said and had probably wanted to listen to our
conversation with her husband on the subject of religion.

'And what do you suppose? When the curtain that concealed
her was tugged open, she at once got up, almost trembling, and
came towards Luka and myself, stretching out both her arms
towards us; there were tears in her eyes, and she said:

' "Good people, good Russian people!"

'For these kind words, Luka and I kissed both her hands,
and she placed her lips against our muzhiks' heads.'

The narrator paused and, covering his eyes with his sleeve,
wiped them quietly and said in a whisper: 'That woman fairly
touched my heart!' Then, regathering himself, he continued:

'After these tender actions of hers, this Englishwoman began
to say something to her husband in her own language which we
couldn't understand; from her voice, though, it was fairly obvious that she was pleading for us. And the Englishman – he, of
course, was pleased by this display of kindness in his wife –
looked at her, and fairly beamed with pride. He kept stroking
her head, and cooing away like a dove in that language of
theirs: "Good, good," or whatever it is they say, and we could
see that he was praising her and assuring her of something.

Then he went to his writing desk, took out two hundred-rouble notes, and said:

"Here's some money for you, Luka: go and find the skilled isographer you need, let him do what's necessary for you and paint it in your style for my wife – she wants to give an icon like that to her son, and she'll pay you for all the trouble and expense involved."

'And she smiled through her tears, saying quickly:

' "No, no, no: that's just from him – I've got my own." And with that, she fluttered out through the doorway and came back holding a third hundred-rouble note.

' "My husband gave this to me to buy a dress – but I don't want the dress, and I'm donating the money to you," she said.

'We naturally began to refuse, but she would not hear of it, and ran off, and he said:

' "No, don't dare to refuse her; take what she's giving you." And then he, too, turned away, saying: "And now go, you strange lot, be off with you!"

'We were not at all offended at being shown the door in this manner, however, because although the Englishman had turned his back on us, we could see he had done it in order to conceal the fact that he was visibly moved.

'Well, good sirs, our own folk weren't too pleased with us, but the English nation had brought us comfort and lent our souls such fervour that it was as if we had taken a regenerative baptism!

'It's at this point, kind sirs, that the middle part of my story begins, and I shall give you a brief account of how, taking with me my silver-harnessed Levonty, I went to see the isographer, an account of the places through which we travelled, of the people we saw, what fresh wonders were revealed to us and what, at last, we found and what we lost, and what we returned with.'

'For a man on a long journey, the nature of his travelling companion is of the first importance. With a good, intelligent companion it's easier to bear both cold and hunger, and I had received this blessing in the person of that wonderful youth Levonty. He and I set off on foot, taking with us knapsacks and a sufficient sum of money; in order to guard it and our lives, we took an old-fashioned short-bladed sabre with a broad handle, which we kept permanently ready in case of danger. We travelled as tradesmen do, living each day at a time, all the while, of course, keeping a constant look-out for anything that might be to our advantage. Right at the outset we visited Klintsy and Zlynka, and then called on some of our own people in Oryol, but this brought no useful results. We couldn't find any good isographers anywhere, and eventually we reached Moscow. But what can I say? Alas, Moscow! Alas, glorious empress of the Russias! We, the Old Believers, were not favoured by you.

'It's hard to know whether one should talk about it, or whether it's best to keep quiet about it, but the spirit we encountered in Moscow was not the one we were thirsting for. We discovered that the ancient traditions were no longer supported by love of goodness and piety, but only by bigotry; as, day by day, Levonty and I became more and more convinced that this was so, we began to feel embarrassed, for we both saw things which were offensive to any peaceful follower of the faith: in our embarrassment, however, we refrained from discussing any of this with each other.

'There were, of course, isographers to be found in Moscow, and highly skilled ones at that; but what was the point of

seeking them out when none of them possessed the spirit of
which the traditions of our fathers relate to us? When, in olden
times, the devout icon-painters had set about their holy art,
they had prayed and fasted, and had produced the same high
quality of work for any fee, whether large or small, as the honour of their exalted task demanded. These modern painters – well,
some of them work in *reft'*,[1] and others work in white oil,[2] but
only for short periods of time, never for the whole of their lives;
the primers they use are weak, chalky ones, never alabaster,
and they add water to the paints they use in a lazy fashion, all
in one go, and not, as in olden times, in as many as four or even
five separate stages, producing colours that were as fluid as
water, and which lent their work its wonderful delicacy, a delicacy nowadays unattainable. And it's not just a matter of their
technical clumsiness: they themselves have grown slack in their
behaviour. They will boast in front of one another, or one of
them will drag the name of another in the muck, in order to
humiliate him; or, what is even worse, they form into gangs
and prepare the most cunning deceptions together, gather in
inns, drink vodka and sing the praises of their own artistry
with conceited haughtiness, blasphemously calling the work of
another "hell-painting"; always hovering around them, like
sparrows following owls, are the junk-shop owners, who pass
various old icons from hand to hand, changing them, copying
them, faking them, blackening them in their chimneys to make
them appear older, trying to give them a fragile appearance and
putting "worm-holes" in them; they make brass icon-screens
using the old chiselled models; they will cover an Old Testament genre-painting with enamel glaze; they make fonts out of
basins and put ancient imperial eagles, of the kind there were
in the days of Ivan the Terrible, on top of them, and sell them
to credulous folk as genuine Ivan the Terrible fonts, even
though there are countless such fonts all over Russia, and all
this is a deception and a shameless lie. In a word, all these
people deceive one another in the matter of holy objects like
gypsies trading in horses, and all this with a mode of address
that makes you feel embarrassed, as all it reveals is sin,

temptation and blasphemy. People who have grown used to this shamelessness remain indifferent to it; but among the Muscovite art-lovers there are many who are even interested in this dishonourable work of forgery and who boast about it: so-and-so has made a real spitting likeness of a *Deisis*, or so-and-so's made an incredible St Nicholas, or a base forgery of an icon of Our Lady. All this is grist to their mill, and in one another's presence they discuss how best to trick inexperienced believers out of God's blessing. But to Levonty and me, who were just simple country folk, all these seemed so intolerable that we both felt depressed and were gripped by a sense of fear.

' "Is this really what it's come to now, our unlucky old faith?" we thought. But even though I thought this, and Levonty bore the same thought in his wounded heart, we didn't talk about it to each other, and I merely observed that he seemed forever to be looking for a secluded spot.

'On one occasion I looked at him, and wondered: "Perhaps his embarrassment has put some peculiar thought into his head?" And I said:

' "What's the matter, Levonty? Is something grieving you?"

'But he replied:

' "No, Uncle, it's all right: it's just the way I'm made."

' "Let's go to Bozhenin Street," I said, "and see if we can't do business with the isographers at the Yerevan Inn. Two of them promised to bring some ancient icons along today. I've already obtained one by barter, and I want another."

'But Levonty replied:

' "No, Uncle, you go alone. I don't want to."

' "Why is that?" I asked.

' "I just don't want to," he replied. "I don't feel quite myself today."

'Well, I counted one, and I counted two, and on the count of three I said:

' "Come on, Levonty, my boy, let's be on our way."

'But he merely gave me a charming bow, and said:

' "No, Uncle, my white dove: let me stay at home."

' "But listen, Levonty, you came along as my partner, yet all you do is sit at home all the time. I'm not getting much help from you, son."

'He replied:

' "Oh, Uncle, oh kinsman, oh Mark Aleksandrych, sir, don't ask me to go to that place where they eat and drink and tell stupid stories about things that are holy, or I may be seized by temptation."

'These were his first conscious words concerning his feelings, and they struck right to my heart; but I didn't try to argue with him, and went alone. That evening I had a long conversation with the two isographers, and had a horribly unpleasant experience at their hands. It's dreadful to relate what they did to me! One of them let me have an icon for forty roubles, and left, and the other said:

' "You'd better not pray to that icon, my man."

' "Why ever not?" I said.

' "Because it's a hell-painting," he replied, and with that he scratched it with his fingernail. A layer of the paint fairly jumped off, and on the priming underneath it there was a drawing of a devil with a tail! He scratched the paint in another place, and there under the base of the icon was another devil.

' "Lord!" I wept. "What does this mean?"

' "What it means," he said, "is that you'd better order your icon from me, and not from that fellow."

'By this time I had realized that they were both in the same gang, and intended to treat me in an unpleasant and dishonourable fashion. Leaving the icon with them, I left them, my eyes full of tears, thanking God that my Levonty, whose faith had been shaken, had not witnessed this event. But just as I was approaching the house where we were staying, I saw that there was no light in the windows of the room we had rented, and at the same time I became aware of a thin, tender singing voice wafting from in there. I knew at once that it was Levonty's pleasant voice, singing with such feeling that every word seemed bathed in tears. I entered quietly, so he wouldn't hear me, stood outside the door and listened as he sang the lamentation of Joseph:[3]

> To whom I waft my sorrow,
> Him do I summon to sobbing.

'This verse, as you may know, is already so piteous that it is impossible to hear it with equanimity; Levonty was singing it, weeping and sobbing as he did so that

> You sold me, my brethren!

'He wept and wept, singing of how he could see his mother's coffin, and summoning the earth to mourning for the sin of his brethren!

'These words are always capable of stirring a man; I was particularly susceptible to their influence at that time, when I had only just fled from the brother-baiters. So deeply was I moved by them that I myself began to sob, and when Levonty heard this he stopped singing and called me:

' "Uncle! Hey, Uncle!"

' "What is it, good lad?" I asked.

' "Do you know who this mother of ours is who appears in the song?" he asked me.

' "It's Rachel," I answered.

' "No," he said. "In ancient times it was Rachel, but now we have to interpret it mystically."

' "How do you mean, mystically?" I inquired.

' "Well, it's said to be connected with the Transfiguration."

' "Listen, lad: are you sure you're not thinking along dangerous lines there?"

' "No," he replied. "I feel in my soul that the Saviour crucifies us for not seeking Him with united mouths and united hearts."

'I grew even more alarmed, wondering where his thoughts were leading him, and I said:

' "You know what, Levonty? Let's leave Moscow and go to Nizhegorod and look up the isographer Sevastyan – he's there just now, I've heard."

' "All right, let's," he replied. "Here in Moscow there's some kind of irksome spirit that's sorely bothering me, but there there are woods, the air is purer, and there, too," he said, "I've heard that there's a certain Elder Pamva, an anchorite completely without envy or wrath – I should like to see him."

' "The Elder Pamva's a servant of the ruling Church," I said sternly. "What do you want to go and see him for?"

' "What harm can it do?" he said. "I'd just like to see him so I can find out what the grace of the ruling Church is like."

'I gave him a good scolding, saying, "What kind of grace can there be there?", but feeling as I did so that he was more in the right than I, because he wanted to find out about the matter for himself; whereas I, knowing nothing about it, rejected it, merely growing harder in my resistance and saying stupid things to him.

' "Church folk," I said, "don't even look at heaven with faith; instead they look into *The Gates of Aristotle*[4] and chart their course at sea by the star of the pagan god Remphan; is that what you want to do?"

' "You're making up a lot of stories, Uncle: there's no god Remphan, nor has there ever been, and everything is created by the One Great Wisdom."

'His words seemed to make me even more stupid, and I said:

' "Church folk drink coffee!"

' "What's so bad about that?" Levonty replied. "Coffee's a bean, and it was brought to King David as a gift."

' "Where do you get all this knowledge from?" I asked.

' "I've read it in books," he said.

' "Well, let me tell you that not everything is written in books."

' "What's not written there?" he said.

' "What? What's *not* written there?" I didn't know what to say in reply to that, and I blurted out:

' "Church folk eat hares, and hares are unclean."

' "Don't revile God's creatures," he replied. "It's a sin to do that."

' "How can one not revile hares," I said, "when they're unclean, when they have the temperament of donkeys and are hermaphroditic and give human beings thick, melancholic blood?"

'But Levonty burst out laughing and said:

' "Go to sleep, Uncle, you're showing your ignorance!"

'I will confess to you that at that time I hadn't really cottoned on to what was taking place in the soul of this grace-inspired youth, but I was very glad when he showed no signs of wishing to pursue the conversation, as I knew very well that I really didn't know what I was talking about. I, too, fell silent, lay in my bed, and thought:

' "No; it's just the sorrow that has put this doubt into his heart. Tomorrow we'll get up and be on our way, and it'll all disappear." But just to make sure, I decided that for some of the time I would stay silent as we travelled, to show him I was very angry with him.

'The only trouble was that, having a capricious character, I completely lack the strength of will to pretend to be angry, and Levonty and I soon began talking to each other again – not about divine matters this time, however, as he was far too erudite for me, but about the surrounding countryside, which hour by hour supplied a pretext for such conversations in the shape of the enormous, dark forests through which our path lay. I tried to put the entire conversation I had had with Levonty in Moscow out of my mind, and decided merely to take care that we didn't run up against this anchorite, the Elder Pamva, whom Levonty so much admired and about whose exalted life I had heard from Church folk the most amazing things.

' "Anyway," I thought to myself, "there's no great need to worry. If I'm running away from him, he's not going to find us!"

'And so we walked on together in peace and harmony and at last, when we had reached a certain district, we heard a rumour that the isographer Sevastyan was indeed travelling around in these parts, and we set off in search of him from town to town, from village to village. Just when we would think we were hot on his trail and were about to track him down, it would turn out that we were as far from tracking him down as ever. We hunted for him like pack-dogs, going for twenty or thirty versts without a break, only to be told upon reaching our destination:

' "Yes, he was here, but he just left about an hour ago!"

'On we would rush, but we still couldn't catch him.

'Then, on one of these journeys, Levonty and I began to quarrel. I said we ought to turn right, but he thought we should turn left, and he jolly well nearly out-argued me, but I insisted we take my direction. Well, we walked and walked and finally I realized that I didn't know where we were; there was neither a path nor a trail.

'I said to the lad:

' "Let's go back, Levonty!"

'But he replied:

' "No, Uncle, I can't walk any further. I've no more strength."

'I grew concerned, and said:

' "What's the matter, Son?"

'And he replied:

' "Can't you see that I've got the ague?"

'And true enough, I saw that he was shaking all over, and his eyes were moving this way and that. I was amazed, good sirs, at how suddenly it had happened. One moment he wasn't complaining of anything, marching cheerfully along, and the next he sat down on some grass in the forest, laid his head against a rotten tree-stump, and said:

' "Oh, my head, my head! Oh, my head's on fire! I can't walk; I can't go another step further!" And he stooped towards the ground, and fell down.

'This happened towards evening.

'I was terribly scared, and as we waited there to see if his illness might pass, night started to fall; it was autumn, the place was dark and unfamiliar, around us there were only mighty pines and firs, like the cedars of Arkath, and the lad was practically dying. What was I to do? With tears in my eyes, I said to him:

' "Levonty, Son, if you could make an effort, we might manage to get some shelter for the night."

'But his head drooped like a cut flower, and he said fever-ishly, as though in his sleep:

' "Don't touch me, Uncle Marko; don't touch me and don't be afraid."

'I said:

' "Forgive me, Levonty, but how could one not be afraid in such deep backwoods?"

' "The Lord will preserve him that does not sleep but stays awake."

'I thought: "Heavens! What's the matter with him?" Even though I was afraid, I started to keep an ear open, and I seemed to hear a cracking sound far away in the undergrowth ... "Merciful Lord!" I thought. "That's probably a wild beast, and in a moment it'll be tearing us to pieces!" I stopped trying to exhort Levonty, because I saw that he had gone floating and wandering off somewhere beyond himself, and I merely prayed: "Angel of Christ, watch over us in this terrible hour!" But the cracking noise got nearer and nearer, and then it was right next to us ... Here, sirs, I must confess to great baseness of character: so frightened was I that I left the sick Levonty where he lay, and leapt up into a tree more nimbly than a squirrel, drew my sabre and sat on a branch to see what would happen, my teeth chattering like those of a startled wolf ... And suddenly, sirs, I observed in the darkness, to which my eyes had become accustomed, that something was emerging from the forest; it was something which at first was quite formless – it was impossible to see whether it was a wild beast or a brigand; gradually, however, I began to look more closely, and I saw that it was neither a wild beast nor a brigand, but a very little old man wearing a cap. I could even see that he had an axe tucked into his belt, and that he was carrying a large bundle of firewood on his back. He came out into the clearing, his breath coming in short gasps, as though he were gulping in air from every side; then he threw down his bundle of firewood and, as if sensing the presence of another human being, walked straight towards my companion. He approached, bent down, looked into Levonty's face and took him by the arm, saying:

' "Get up, Brother!"

'And what do you suppose? I saw him raise Levonty from the ground and lead him straight towards his bundle; this he placed on Levonty's shoulders, and then he said:

' "Carry my bundle and follow me!"

'And Levonty did as he commanded.'

'You can imagine, good sirs, how frightened I was by such a wondrous happening! Where had this imperious old man come from, and how was it possible that my Levonty, who only a moment ago had been on the point of death, unable to raise his head, should now be carrying a bundle of firewood?

'I quickly leapt down from the tree, slung my sabre over my back on its string, made myself a stick from a healthy, sturdy sapling, set off after them and soon caught up with them. I saw that the old man was striding in front, and that he was exactly as he had appeared to me at first sight: small and hunchbacked, with beard showing at the sides of his face in tufts like soap-suds. Behind him marched my Levonty, cheerfully in step, and turning round to look at me. No matter how much I accosted him and touched him with my arm, he paid not the slightest heed, and kept marching along as though in his sleep.

'Then I ran up alongside the old man and said:

' "My goodly fellow!"

' "What do you want?" he replied.

' "Where are you leading us?"

' "I'm not leading anyone anywhere," he said. "It's the Lord who leads us!"

'And, so saying, he suddenly halted. In front of us were a low wall and a gate, and in the gate there was a small door. The old man began to knock at this door, and shout:

' "Brother Miron! O Brother Miron!"

'An insolent voice answered coarsely from inside:

' "He's come crawling here at night again. Go and spend the night in the forest! I'm not letting you in."

'But the old man began to beg and wheedle again:

' "Let us in, Brother!"

'The insolent fellow suddenly unbolted the door, and I saw he was wearing a cap like that of the old man. But he was a stern and forbidding churl of a fellow, and hardly had the old man put his foot over the threshold, than this ruffian gave him such a shove that he nearly fell to the floor.

' "May God bless you, my brother, for your kind service," was the old man's response to this.

' "Lord!" I thought. "Where have we landed ourselves?" And suddenly an illuminating realization struck me like a bolt of lightning.

' "Merciful Saviour!" I conjectured inwardly, "this old man must be Pamva the wrathless! I'd have done better," I thought, "to have perished in the labyrinths of the forests, or been savaged by wild beasts, or been carried off to a den of brigands than to come in under his roof."

'And no sooner had he led us into some little hovel and lit a yellow wax candle, than I immediately guessed that we really were in a sylvan monastery. Unable to control my patience any longer, I said:

' "Forgive us, pious man. I ask you: is it right for my companion and myself to remain here, where you have brought us?"

'But he replied:

' "All the earth is God's, and blessed are all the creatures in it. Lie down, and sleep!"

' "No," I said. "Permit us to inform you that we are of the Old Faith."

' "We are all members of the one body of Christ!" he said. "He gathers us all unto Him."

'And with this he led us to a corner where a lowly bast bed had been made up on the floor, with a log of wood covered with straw at its head, and again he said to us:

' "Sleep!"

'And would you believe it? My Levonty, like the obedient lad he was, immediately lay down. Still harbouring some uneasy feelings, I said:

' "Forgive me, man of God, but I have just one more question . . ."

'He replied:

' "Why ask questions? God knows everything."

' "No," I said. "Please tell me – what your name is?"

'To this he replied in a womanish falsetto that was completely at odds with his appearance:

' "Some call me Luck, some call me Duck!" And with these frivolous words he started to crawl with his candle into some little storeroom or other, as cramped as a wooden coffin; but from the other side of the wall the insolent fellow suddenly shouted:

' "Don't you dare to burn a candle in there: you'll burn the place down! Say your prayers from the book in the daytime; at night you can say them in the dark!"

' "Oh, certainly, Brother Miron, certainly," he replied. "God bless you!"

'And he blew out the candle.

' "Father!" I whispered. "Who was that man who so rudely threatened you?"

'He replied:

' "That was my servant Miron . . . He's a good man, he looks after me."

' "Well, that's good enough for me," I thought. "This is the anchorite Pamva, sure enough. No one else is as devoid of envy and wrath as he. What a terrible thing to happen! Now he's got us in his clutches, and he'll rot us away like gangrene eating through flesh. There's only one thing for it: early tomorrow morning I'll have to get Levonty out of here, and we'll have to make a run for it somewhere where he won't find us." With this plan in mind, I decided not to go to sleep, but to wait for first light, when I would wake the lad and we would flee together.

'In order to keep myself awake, I lay there and said my "Credo", as our old faith instructs us; and when I had said it once, I immediately wailed: "This Holy Catholic, this Apostolic, this Universal faith affirm", and began all over again. I don't know how many times I recited this prayer, in order not to fall asleep, but it must have been a fair number. Meanwhile the old man continued to pray in his coffin-like room. Light filtered towards me through the cracks in the planking, and I could see him prostrating himself. Then I seemed to hear a conversation ... a conversation of a most inexplicable kind: what seemed to happen was that Levonty went into the elder's room, and they talked about religious faith together, yet they used no words – merely looked at each other and understood. This went on for a long time. I stopped saying my "Credo", and seemed to hear the elder say to the lad: "Go and purify thyself." "Yes, Father," I seemed to hear him reply. I don't know whether it really happened or whether I dreamed it, all I know is that then I slept for a long time, and when I woke up it was morning, completely light, and the elder, our host, the anchorite, was sitting picking with a needle at a bast shoe. I began to study him more closely.

'Oh, how pleasing he was! How aethereal! It was as if an angel were sitting before me weaving bast shoes, for the greater peace of his soul.

'As I watched him, I saw him look at me and smile, and he said:

' "That's enough sleep, Mark. It's time to serve the cause now."

' "What cause have I to serve, O pious man?" I said. "Or do you know everything?"

' "I do," he said. "I do. What man undertakes a long journey without a cause? Every man and woman seeks the Lord's way, Brother. May He help you in your humility!"

' "What humility have I, O holy man?" I asked. "You possess humility, but I live a vain and empty life!"

'But he replied:

' "Oh no, Brother, no; I possess no humility: I am full of overweening pride, for I wish for a share in the kingdom of heaven."

'And suddenly, having confessed to this crime, he folded his arms and burst into tears like a little child.

' "Lord!" he prayed. "Do not be angry at me for this wilfulness; send me to the nether regions of hell and command the demons to torment me as I deserve."

' "Well," I thought. "This can't be the wise anchorite Pamva after all, it must simply be some elder who's gone soft in the head." I reasoned this way because who in his right mind could renounce the kingdom of heaven and pray the Lord to send him to be tormented by demons? I had never in all my life heard anyone express such a desire and, regarding it as a mark of insanity, turned away from the elder's lamentation as from an idolatrous outrage. Well, at last I pulled myself together: "What am I lying here for, it's time to get up," I thought. But then I suddenly saw the door open and my Levonty, whom I had practically forgotten all about, come in. He went straight to the feet of the elder and said:

' "Father, I have done all that you commanded: now give me your blessing!"

'The elder looked at him, and replied:

' "Peace be unto you: now rest!"

'And again I saw my lad prostrate himself, get up and go out. The anchorite resumed the weaving of his bast shoe.

'At that point I leapt up and thought:

' "No; I'll go and get Levonty, and we'll flee from this place without a backward glance!" I went out into the passage and saw my lad lying there on his back atop a wooden bench, with no pillow for his head, his arms folded on his chest.

'So as not to raise the alarm, I said to him in a loud voice:

' "Can you tell me where I can get some water with which to wash my face?" Then I whispered to him: "In the name of the living God, let's get out of here as quickly as we can!"

'But when I looked at him more closely, I saw that he wasn't breathing . . . He'd departed . . . Died!

'In a voice not my own, I howled:

' "Pamva! Father Pamva! You've killed my lad!"

'But Pamva came out slowly across the threshold and said in a joyful tone of voice:

' "Our Levonty's flown away!"

' "Yes," I replied through tears. "He's flown away. You let his soul escape, like a dove from a cage!" And, throwing myself at the feet of the departed, I groaned and wept until evening. Then some monks came from the monastery, laid out his corpse, put it in a coffin and carried it off, as that very morning, while I, lazy fellow, had been asleep, he had joined the Church.

'Not another word did I say to Father Pamva; and indeed, what could I have said to him? If I were rude to him, he would bless me, if I beat him, he would prostrate himself before me – a man with humility like that was invincible! What could strike fear into his heart, when he himself asked to be sent to hell? No: not for nothing had I gone in dread of him, fearing that he would rot us away like gangrene eating through flesh. With his humility he would drive all the demons out of hell – either that or convert them to Christianity! They'd start tormenting him, and he'd beg them: "Torture me more cruelly, for I have deserved it!" No, no! Not even Satan would be able to hold out against humility like that. He'd keep cutting his hands on him and, breaking his claws on him, come to recognize his power-lessness before the Author who had created such love, and be overcome with shame.

'So it was that I made up my mind that this elder with the bast shoe had been created for our ruin! All night I roamed about the forest – I don't know why I didn't just go somewhere far away – and kept thinking:

' "What sort of prayers does he say – how does he say them, and what books does he recite them from?"

'I remembered that, with the exception of a cross made from sticks bound together with pieces of bast, I had not seen a sin-gle holy image in his retreat; there had been no bulky volumes, either . . .

' "Lord!" I found myself thinking. "Were there to be but two such men in the Church we should be lost; this man is entirely filled with love."

'I couldn't get my mind off him, and suddenly, towards dawn, I conceived a fierce desire to see him for a moment before I departed from that place.

'No sooner had this thought come into my head, than again I suddenly heard the same cracking in the undergrowth and Father Pamva emerged once more with his axe and his bundle of firewood, and said:

' "What's been keeping you? Was Babylon built in a day?"

'That seemed a cruel thing to say, and I retorted:

' "Why do you reproach me with such words, elder? I am building no Babylon; indeed, I keep myself apart from all Babylonian abominations."

'But he replied:

' "What is Babylon? A pillar of conceit. Don't be conceited about the truth, or the angel will leave you."

' "Father," I said. "Do you know why I am walking about?"

'And I told him about our misfortune. He listened hard to the whole story, and then replied:

' "The angel is quiet, the angel is modest, he dresses in the apparel ordained for him by God; what God instructs him to fulfil, he fulfils. That is the angel! He lives in the souls of men, sealed with wisdom, but love can break the seal . . ."

'So saying, the old man walked away from me. I couldn't take my eyes off him and, unable to master myself, fell down and prostrated myself in his direction. When I lifted my face, I saw that he was no longer there. He had stepped behind some trees, or . . . Lord knows where he had gone.

'At that point I began to run over in my head the words he had spoken: "The angel lives in the souls of men, but is sealed, yet love will free him," and I suddenly thought: "What if he's the angel, and God has commanded him to appear to me in another guise: I will die, like Levonty!" I don't remember much after that: with that conjecture in mind, I ferried myself across the river on a tree-stump and rushed to escape: I walked for sixty versts without a break, in constant terror of setting eyes on the angel. Suddenly I reached a certain village, and there I found the isographer Sevastyan. We came to an arrangement at once, and decided to set off the very next day. But we remained on rather formal terms, and this formality marked our progress on the journey, too. Why was that? For one thing, the isographer Sevastyan was a pensive man, and for another – this was, perhaps, even more to blame – I wasn't really myself: the shadowy figure of the anchorite Pamva kept flitting about in my soul, and my lips kept whispering the words of the prophet Isaiah, that "the spirit of God is in the nostrils of this man".

'The isographer Sevastyan and I made the journey back swiftly. Arriving at our settlement after nightfall, we found everything in order. After we had announced ourselves to our own people, we at once went off to see Yakov Yakovlevich, the Englishman. He, being an inquisitive fellow, was fascinated to meet a real, live isographer, and kept looking at Sevastyan's hands and shrugging his shoulders; this was because Sevastyan's hands were like enormous rakes and, what was more, were black – he indeed resembled nothing so much as a swarthy gypsy. Yakov Yakovlevich said:

'"I'm amazed that you can paint with those big hands of yours, Brother!"

'But Sevastyan replied:

'"Why? What's wrong with my hands?"

'"Well," said the Englishman, "I mean: you couldn't do fine details with them."

'"Why not?"

'"Because the flexibility of your fingers wouldn't permit you to."

'Sevastyan retorted:

'"That's nonsense! Do you think my fingers are capable of permitting me or not permitting me to do something? I'm their master, and they are my servants and obey me."

'The Englishman smiled.

'"Does that mean you'll do our sealed angel for us?"

'"Why," he said, "I'm not one of those masters who are afraid of work, in fact it's the work that's afraid of me; I'll do it so that you won't be able to distinguish it from the original."

' "Good," said Yakov Yakovlevich. "We shall immediately try to get you the original icon, and in the meanwhile, show me your art so as to allay my doubts: paint an icon of my wife in the old Russian style, and make it one that will please her."

' "What will I call it?"

' "Oh, I don't know," he said. "Paint some subject that's familiar to you. It's all the same to her – just make it something she'll like."

'Sevastyan thought for a bit, and then asked:

' "What does your wife pray God for most of all?"

' "I don't know, my friend," he said. "I don't know, but I should think she prays mostly about the children – that our children should grow up to be honest people."

'Sevastyan thought some more, and then replied:

' "Very well, sir, I'll do it with that sort of a flavour."

' "And how will that look?"

' "I'll do it so it will provoke contemplation and contribute to the greater spiritual intensity of your wife's prayers."

'The Englishman gave instructions for Sevastyan to be provided with every convenience in the turret of his house. Sevastyan, however, did not begin his work there, but sat down by the window in the garret above Luka Kirilov's prayer-room and set about his activity.

'But as to what he intended to produce, my good sirs, of that we had not the slightest idea. Since children had been mentioned, we thought he would depict Romanus the miracle-worker, to whom prayers are said in cases of infertility, or the slaying of the infants in Jerusalem, which is always a subject pleasing to mothers who have lost a child, as Rachel is seen weeping inconsolably for her children; but this wise isographer, having learned that the Englishwoman had children and that she said prayers not for them to be gifted but to be of righteous morality, went off and painted something quite different, which was even more suited to her purposes. For this he selected a small old board with the span of a human arm, and began to exercise his talents on it. First, of course, he primed it well with strong, Kazan alabaster, to make the priming as tough and smooth as ivory; then he divided it into four equal areas, each one forming the space for a separate, smaller icon, united them by putting a gold border on the drying-oil between them, and began to paint. In the first area he painted the birth of John the Baptist – eight figures, a newborn child, and chambers; in the second, the birth of the Holy Virgin Mother – six figures, a newborn child, and chambers; in the third, the immaculate birth of the Saviour, with the manger, the crib, and Mary and Joseph praying – here, too, were the Wise Men, and Solomia,[1] and beasts of all kinds: oxen, sheep, goats and asses, and the cormorant, which is forbidden to the Jews, and of which it is written in Leviticus that it proceeds not from Judaism but from the God who is the Creator of all things. Depicted in the fourth section was the birth of Nicholas the Devout, and here again we saw the holy divine in his infancy, and chambers, and many people gathered round, praying. How edifying it was to see before one's eyes the educators of such good children, and what artistry was involved: all the figures were pin-sized, yet the life and movement of each one of them was clearly evident. In the scene depicting the nativity, for instance, the prophetess Anna was reclining on a couch, as specified by the original Greek; before her stood timbrel-playing maidens, some holding gifts, some sunflowers, some candles. One of the women was supporting Anna's shoulders; Joachim was looking at the upper chambers; a woman was bathing the Holy Mother of God in a font up to the waist: at one side a maiden was pouring water into the font from a vessel. The chambers were all arranged in a circle, the upper ones bluish-green, and the lower ones crimson-purple, and in this lower circle sat Joachim and Anna on the throne. Anna was holding the Holy Mother of God, and all around, between the chambers, there were stone pillars, bright red widths of cloth and a white and yellow wall ... Sevastyan had depicted all this wonderfully, wonderfully, and had expressed in each tiniest face the most complete religiosity. He inscribed the icon "The Good Children", and brought it to the English couple. They looked at it, began to examine it, and threw up their hands in delight: never had they expected such power of imagination; never before had they encountered

such microscopically fine painting. They even looked at the
icon through a magnifying lens, and even then they couldn't
find any mistakes. They gave Sevastyan two hundred roubles
for the icon, and said:

' "Can you paint even more finely than that?"

' "Yes, I can," Sevastyan replied.

' "Then make me a portrait of my wife that I can wear on a
ring."

'But Sevastyan said:

' "No, I can't do that."

' "Why not?"

' "Well," he said. "In the first place I haven't ever tried anything like that, and in the second place I couldn't degrade my
artistic skill by doing such work without falling subject to the
condemnation of the Holy Fathers."

' "What nonsense!"

' "Not a bit of it," he replied. "It isn't nonsense. We have a
patriarchal law which dates from time immemorial. It says:
'For whosoever shall be considered worthy of doing such
holy work as the painting of icons, such an isographer, be he of
reputable ways, must not paint anything other than holy
icons.' "[2]

'Yakov Yakovlevich said:

' "But what if I give you five hundred roubles for such a piece
of work?"

' "You can promise me five hundred thousand, but they'll
still remain in your pocket."

'The Englishman beamed and said to his wife, jokingly:

' "How do you like that? He thinks painting your face would
be degrading for him!"

'In English, he added in her ear: "Oh, here we have character!" But in conclusion he said:

' "Look, lads, we're going to take a break from work now. I
can see that you have rules for everything, so nothing is left out
or forgotten which could interfere with the harmony of the
whole."

'We replied that we foresaw nothing like that happening.

' "Well, look," he said. "I'm going to get started." And he went to the boss saying that he wanted to busy himself with gilding a mounting for the sealed angel and adorning a crown for him. The boss was non-committal: neither refused his permission nor gave it; but Yakov Yakovlevich kept up the pressure and finally got his way. As for us, we could hardly wait.'

'Permit me to remind you, sirs, that some considerable time had elapsed since this plan had got under way, and Christmas was now practically upon us. But you can't compare the Christmases they have down there with the ones they have here. There the seasons are capricious: sometimes Christmas is accompanied by real wintry weather; but other years, you'd be hard put to it to say what time of year it was – it's wet and rainy; one day there'll be a slight frost, and by the next it'll have melted away; one day the river will be covered in ice, and the next it'll be rushing swollen, with ice-floes in it, as if the spring floods had arrived . . . In short, it's a most unpredictable time of year; in those parts they don't say "weather" but "wetter" – and wetter's the right name for it.

'In the year from which my story dates, this unpredictable quality of the weather was of the most irritating kind. When I returned with the isographer, I could not have told you how many times our lads had worked according to the winter regulations, and how many according to the summer regulations. But to judge from the way the work had gone, the weather must have been of the very warmest, for all seven of our piers were already in place, and chains were being fitted from one bank to the other. The masters, of course, wanted these chains connected up as quickly as possible, so that by the time the spring floods came it would be possible to construct at least a temporary bridge on them, over which building material could be brought, but this hadn't worked: no sooner had the chains been stretched across than such a terrible frost set in that it was impossible to do any bridge-building. So that was the way it remained: the chains hung there, but there was no bridge. However, our God created another bridge: the river froze, and our Englishman crossed the Dnieper on the ice to attend to the business of our icon; when he came back he said to Luka and me:

' "Give me till tomorrow, boys, and I'll have your treasure back for you."

'Lord, what didn't we feel at that moment! At first we intended to keep quiet about it and only tell the isographer, but the heart of man knows no patience! Instead of keeping it a secret, we went round all our men, knocking on everyone's windows and whispering to one another, and running like wildfire from hut to hut, for the night was light and magnificent, the frost sparkled on the snow like diamonds, and the star Jasper burned in the pure heavens.

'Having spent the night in such joyous running, we greeted the day in the same state of enraptured expectation. From morning onwards we remained in the company of our isographer, and were ready to do anything for him, since the hour had now arrived in which everything depended on his artistry. Whatever he instructed us to give him or carry for him, we flew off by the dozen to get, exerting ourselves so much that we almost fell over one another in our eagerness. Even Uncle Maroy took part: he ran so much that he tripped up and tore one of the heels of his boots. The isographer alone was calm, because this wasn't the first time he had undertaken such a commission, and he spent the time unhurriedly getting ready all the thing he needed: he mixed egg-yolk with kvas, inspected the drying-oil, prepared a primed canvas, laid out some small, old boards which were about the right size for icons, prepared a sharp little saw, the string-like blade of which was set in the curve of a strong hoop of metal, and sat near the window, grinding the paints he deemed would be necessary with his fingers in his palm. Meanwhile, we washed in hot water from the stove, put on clean shirts and stood on the riverbank, looking at the town of sanctuary, from whence our light-bearing guest was to come to us; our hearts rose and sank alternately . . .

'Oh, what moments those were! They lasted from early dawn right up until evening, and then suddenly we saw the

Englishman's sleigh rushing across the ice from the town straight towards us ... A tremor passed over us all, we all threw down our caps and prayed:

' "Lord God, Father of spirits and of angels, have mercy on thy servants!"

'And with this prayer we fell prostrate on to the snow and eagerly stretched out our hands, and suddenly we heard the Englishman's voice above us, crying:

' "Hey! Old Believers! Here you are!" And he gave us a little bundle wrapped in a white cloth.

'Luka took the bundle and froze: he could feel that it was something small and light! He lifted a corner of the cloth and saw that it was just the silver mounting of our angel – the icon itself wasn't there.

'We rushed towards the Englishman and wailed at him:

' "They've tricked you, sir; there's no icon here, just the silver mounting!"

'But the Englishman was no longer disposed towards us in the way he had been previously: probably this long affair had started to get on his nerves, and he shouted at us:

' "Why do you muddle everything up? You yourselves told me you wanted the mounting back, and I've got it back for you; I don't think you know what you want!"

'Observing his anger, we began carefully to explain to him that we needed the icon in order to make an imitation of it. But he would not listen to us, and shooed us away; the only concession he made to us was to send for the isographer. Sevastyan went to him, and became the object of the same anger.

' "Your muzhiks don't know themselves what it is they want," he said. "First they asked me to get them the mounting, saying that you just needed to take the dimensions and contours, and now they're roaring that it's no use to them. But I can't do anything more for you, because the bishop won't part with the icon. You'd do better to make a quick imitation of the thing, then we'll cover it with the mounting and give it to him, and meanwhile my secretary will steal the old one from him."

'But Sevastyan, being a man of discretion, charmed him with soft words, replying:

' "No, if you please, sir; our muzhik fellows know what they are about, and we really do need the genuine original. It's just something that's said to do damage to our reputation when people claim that we paint from models as though they were stencils. Our law-book does prescribe certain things, but their execution is left to the freedom of the artist's imagination. According to the law-book, for example, the Saints Zosima and Gerasim are supposed to be shown together with a lion – but the artist may depict that lion in any way his imagination suggests, and for this reason I'm unable to know how the angel I need to copy has been depicted."

'The Englishman listened to all this and then shooed both Sevastyan and ourselves away, and no further decision came from him. We sat, dear sirs, above the river like crows on a ruin, not knowing whether to despair utterly, or whether to wait and see if he would say something else. What was even worse, the weather began to join in our mood: a dramatic thaw set in, it began to rain, the sky was the colour of black smoke even during the day, and at night it was so dark that not even the star Hesperus, which in December never sets in the heavens, was visible, and never once made an appearance . . . It was, quite simply, a prison for the soul! And in this fashion Christmas arrived: on Christmas Eve there was a clap of thunder, a downpour began, and it rained and rained without cease for two, three days: the snow was all washed away and carried into the river, and the river-ice began to turn blue and to swell up, and suddenly, on the second-last day of the year, the ice broke up and started to move . . . The water rushed up over it and hurled floe after floe into a dark flood, and the whole river seemed to be jammed against our building works; floe piled on top of floe, leaping and clanking, Lord forgive me, like demons . . . How the bridge managed to withstand that incredible pressure of ice, I shall never comprehend. Millions of roubles' worth of material might have been destroyed, but we didn't care about that, for Sevastyan, seeing that there was no work for him, had rebelled – he had packed his belongings, and intended to go to another part of the country, and there was nothing we could do to hold him back.

'And the Englishman didn't care either, because during this spell of bad weather he almost went out of his mind. It was said that he kept going around asking everyone: "What am I to do? What is one to do?" And then he finally regained control of himself, summoned Luka and said:

' "I tell you what, muzhik: how about you and I going and stealing your angel back?"

' "It's a deal," Luka replied.

'Luka noticed that the Englishman seemed almost eager to undertake some risky enterprise; he proposed that the following day he go to the bishop at the monastery, taking the isographer with him, pretending the latter was a goldsmith. The isographer would ask to see the icon, saying he wanted to examine its contours so he could make a mounting for it; meanwhile he would study it as closely as possible and make an imitation of it when he got home. Then, when the real goldsmith had our mounting ready, it would be brought to us on the other side of the river, and Yakov Yakovlevich would return to the monastery, saying that he wanted to see the bishop's festive service; he would go up behind the altar and stand there beside the window ledge where our icon was kept, in the darkness, wearing his overcoat. Then he would hide it inside his coat, give the coat to his servant, saying he was too hot, and ask him to take it outside. Outside the church our man would immediately take the icon out from under the coat and run as fast as his legs would carry him over to this side of the river, and here, while the all-night service was going on, the isographer would remove the old icon from its board and substitute the copy, cover it with the mounting and send it back in such a manner that Yakov Yakovlevich was able to put it back in the altar window, just as though nothing had happened.

' "All right," we said. "We're ready for anything!"

' "But be careful," he said. "Bear in mind that I'll be acting like a thief: I want to be sure you won't give me away."

'Luka Kirilov replied:

' "Yakov Yakovlevich: we are not the kind of people who deceive a benefactor. I'll take the icon and bring both of them back for you – the genuine one and the fake."

' "And what if something interferes with your plan? ...
Well, say you were to meet a sudden death – say you drowned,
for example."

'Luka thought: why should I meet an obstacle like that? But
on reflection, he had to admit it was true that on occasion the
spade of a man digging for treasure strikes a rock, and the man
going to market encounters a rabid dog, and he replied:

' "In such a case, sir, I would leave my servant with you. If I
met with some mishap, he would take all the guilt upon himself
and would go to his death without giving you away."

' "And who is this servant on whom you place such
reliance?"

' "Maroy the blacksmith," Luka replied.

' "That old man?"

' "Yes, it's true he's not young."

' "But he's a numbskull, isn't he?"

' "It's not his intelligence we stand in need of, sir; and besides,
he possesses a worthy spirit."

' "What kind of spirit can a numbskull possess?" said the
Englishman.

' "The spirit, sir," Luka replied, "has nothing to do with the
intellect: the spirit wafts where it wishes. It's like hair: on one
man it grows long and thick, on another thin and meagre."

'The Englishman thought for a bit, and then said:

' "Good, good: those are interesting notions. Well, and how
is he going to get me out again, say I manage to get in?"

' "This is what we'll do," Luka replied. "Once you're inside
the church you'll go and stand by the altar window; Maroy will
be standing outside, below the window, and if I don't appear
with the icons by the time the service finishes, he'll break the
glass, climb in through the window and take all the blame on
himself."

'The Englishman thought this was an excellent idea.

' "It's curious, though," he said. "Curious. Why should I trust
this spirited numbskull of yours not to run away himself?"

' "Well, sir, it's a matter of mutual trust."

' "Mutual trust," he repeated. "Ahem, ahem, mutual trust, is
it? I get hard labour for the sake of a numbskull muzhik, or else

he suffers the knout for my sake. Ahem, ahem! If he keeps his word . . . under the knout . . . that I'd like to see."

'They sent for Maroy and explained to him what it was all about, and he said:

' "All right, I'll do it. So what?"

' "Well, won't you run away?" the Englishman asked him.

' "Why would I do that?" Maroy replied.

' "So you won't be flogged and sent to Siberia."

'To this, Maroy said:

' "Whatever next?" – and after that remained silent.

'The Englishman was pleased as Punch: he really livened up.

' "Wonderful," he said. "Truly wonderful." '

'Immediately after this conspiratorial meeting, our plan moved into action. The very next morning, we oared up the master's big longboat and ferried the Englishman over to the town side of the river. There he and the isographer Sevastyan got into a carriage and drove to the monastery. A little over an hour later we looked and saw our isographer running, with a sheet of paper containing a copy of the icon in his hands.

'We asked him:

' "Did you see it, kinsman, and will you be able to make an imitation of it now?"

' "Yes, I saw it," he replied. "And I'll make the imitation, only it might be a bit too lively; but that doesn't matter, for when the original gets here it'll only take me a minute to tone down the brightness of the colours."

' "Do your best, good fellow," we implored him.

' "Don't worry," he said. "I will."

'And when we brought him the icon he settled down to work at once, and by twilight had produced an angel on his canvas who was a spitting likeness of our own sealed angel, except that his colouring seemed slightly fresher.

'Towards evening the goldsmith sent a new frame, as it had been ordered earlier, together with the mounting.

'The most dangerous hour of our project had arrived.

'We had, of course, made all our preparations. Before evening we said our prayers, and waited for the prearranged moment. As soon as the first bell pealed from the other side, summoning the faithful to the all-night service, the three of us – old man

Maroy, Uncle Luka and myself – got into a small boat. Old man Maroy took with him an axe, a chisel and a length of rope, so as to appear more thief-like, and we rowed straight up to the monastery wall.

'Darkness fell early at that time of year, of course, and the night – even though this was the time of the full moon – was of the very darkest, a real thieves' night.

'When we got over to the other side, Maroy and Luka, leaving me in the boat under the overhang of the riverbank, stole into the monastery. I shipped the oars, used the end of the rope as a temporary mooring, and waited impatiently for Luka to return; as soon as he set one foot in the boat, I was ready to row us away immediately. The time seemed to pass terribly slowly, as I kept worrying about the outcome of our plan: would we be able to conceal our thievery while the vespers and the all-night service took place? It seemed to me that already aeons had passed; the darkness was fearful, the wind was gusting, the rain had given way to wet snow, the boat had started to sway a bit, and I, faithless servant, gradually succumbed to the warmth of my *svita*, and began to doze.

'Suddenly something landed in the boat, making it rock violently. I started up, and saw Luka standing in it. In a choked voice, not his own, he said:

' "Row!"

'I seized the oars, but couldn't for the life of me fit them into the rowlocks, I was that scared. By an effort of will I regained my composure and pushed off from the bank. Then I asked:

' "Did you get the angel, Uncle?"

' "I've got it with me, now row as hard as you can!"

' "Tell me how you got it," I asked.

' "We stole it, as we arranged."

' "And will we have time to return it?"

' "We should do: they've only got as far as the Great Prokimenon. Row! Where are you taking us?"

'I looked round: Oh Lord! He was right: I was going the wrong way. I was rowing upstream, as I was supposed to, but there was no sign of our settlement. This was because of the snow and the terrible gale; my eyelids were stuck together, and all around us there was a roaring and heaving, and the surface of the water seemed to be filming over with ice.

'But, by the mercy of God, we got there. We both leapt out of the boat and set off at a run. The isographer was ready. He acted coolly, but firmly: first he took the icon in his hands, and then, after everyone had fallen down before it, prostrating themselves, he allowed each man to approach the sealed countenance and cross himself before it. Meanwhile he surveyed it, comparing it with his imitation, and said:

'"I didn't do too badly. Only I'll have to tone it down a bit with earth and saffron!" Then he took the icon out of its frame, set it in a vice, stretched tight the sawblade which he had fixed in the metal hoop, and . . . began to saw away. We all stood watching, thinking he would surely damage the icon. It was a scary sight, sirs! Can you imagine: with those big ungainly hands of his he sawed it off a board as thin as the very thinnest sheet of writing paper . . . He could so easily have made a mistake: if the saw had gone squint by as much as a hair's breadth, he would have ripped the angel's face and gone clean through! But Sevastyan the isographer completed the whole process with such coolness and skill that as you watched him you felt calmer and calmer with each minute that passed. And lo and behold, he sawed the painting in one very thin layer, then in the space of a minute cut this layer out round the edges, and then stuck the edges back on the same board. Then he took his imitation and crushed and crumpled it in his fist, now slapping it against the edge of the table, now rubbing it between the palms of his hands, as though he wanted to tear it and destroy it; finally, he held it up to the light, and saw that this new copy was covered all over in a sieve of tiny cracks . . . Having done this Sevastyan took the copy and stuck it on to the old board, fitting it in between the edges. Taking some dark, coloured substance in his palm, he mixed it, using his fingers, with some old drying-oil and saffron to make a kind of putty, and then rubbed the mixture as hard as he could with the flat of his hand into the crumpled copy . . . All this he did swiftly, and the freshly painted copy now looked quite old, for all the world like the original.

Then the imitation was treated with drying-oil for a minute or two, and then some of our men began to put it in its frame. The isographer set the original, sawed icon on to a specially prepared board and asked for some old felt hatting material.

'Now began the most difficult part of the unsealing.

'A felt hat was brought to the isographer, and he immediately tore it apart at the seams on his knee. Then, covering the sealed icon with it, he shouted:

' "Bring me the hot iron!"

'On the stove, according to his earlier instructions, lay a heavy, heated, tailor's iron.

'Mikhailitsa picked the iron up with her oven prongs and held it towards Sevastyan; wrapping its handle in a rag, he picked the iron up, spat on it, and dashed it over the hatting material . . . Immediately there was a horrible stink of burning felt; the isographer gave the felt a rub and suddenly whipped it away. His hand darted like lightning, the smoke from the felt rose in a column, and he continued to apply the heat intermittently; while turning the felt slightly with one hand, with the other he wielded the iron, each time pressing it more firmly and for a longer interval. Then suddenly he threw down both iron and felt, and held the icon up to the light. The seal had practically disappeared: the powerful Stroganov drying-oil had held, and the sealing-wax had all come off – on the angel's face there remained the merest fiery-red dew, but that divine and radiant countenance was entirely visible . . .

'At this point some of us prayed, others wept, yet others got down on their knees and kissed the isographer's hand; but Luka Kirilov did not forget the matter in hand and, remembering that every minute was precious, gave the isographer the fake icon and said:

' "Right, now finish your work quickly."

'But the isographer replied:

' "My work's done; I've fulfilled my part of the bargain."

' "But you've still to put the seal on."

' "Where?"

' "On the face of the new angel, just like the one on the old one."

'But Sevastyan shook his head and replied:

' "No, I'm not a government official. I wouldn't dare take on a task like that."

' "So what are we going to do now?"

' "I don't know," he said. "You'd have needed a government official or a German for that, so if you've gone and overlooked them, you'll have to do it yourselves."

'Luka said:

' "What are you thinking of? We wouldn't dare to do a thing like that!"

'But the isographer replied:

' "Well, I wouldn't dare to, either."

'During these brief moments there arose such a hubbub among us that Yakov Yakovlevich's wife came rushing into the room as pale as death, saying:

' "Aren't you ready yet?"

'We said we were ready and yet we weren't ready: we'd done the essentials, but couldn't manage the details.

' "What are you waiting for?" she said in a mixture of broken Russian and her own language. "Can't you hear what's happening outside?"

'We listened, and then turned even paler than she was: so absorbed in our concerns had we been that we had paid no attention to the state of the weather, and now we could hear a rumbling sound: the ice was moving!

'I leapt up and saw that it was already disintegrating over the entire width of the river, like some enraged wild beast, hurling floe upon floe so that they twisted together, booming and breaking.

'Oblivious to all thoughts except that of escape, I rushed towards the boats: but not one of them was left, they had all been carried away ... My tongue grew as stiff as an old boot in my mouth, so that I couldn't move it, and the ground seemed to open up gradually under my feet ... I stood there, unable to move or to make a sound.

'While we were all rushing about in the darkness, the Englishwoman, who had remained behind in the *izba* with Mikhailitsa and had discovered the cause of the delay, seized the icon and . . . came running out a moment later on to the porch with it, holding a lamp, and shouting:

' "Here you are, it's ready!" '

'We looked: there was a seal on the face of the new angel!

'Luka immediately stuffed both icons under his belt and shouted:

' "Get me a boat!" '

'I explained to him that there weren't any boats, that they'd all been carried away.

'Meanwhile, the ice, I tell you, was thronging the river like a herd of horses, cracking against the starlings and shaking the bridge itself so badly that you could hear the chains, each of which was as thick as a good-sized floorboard, rumbling and clanking.

'When the Englishwoman had taken this in, she threw up her hands, screamed "James!" in a voice that was scarcely human, and fell senseless to the ground.

'As for ourselves, we stood there, the only thoughts in our minds being: how would we keep our word? What would happen to the Englishman now? What would happen to Uncle Maroy?

'Just then, the third peal of bells started to toll from the monastery.

'Uncle Luka suddenly started and exclaimed to the Englishwoman:

' "Wake up, mistress, your husband's going to be all right, and maybe only our old man Maroy will have his feeble hide tortured by the executioner and his goodly, decent face dishonoured by the brand, but that'll only be over my dead body!" And so saying, he made the sign of the cross over himself, walked solemnly away, and left.

'I shouted:

' "Uncle Luka, where are you going? Levonty perished, and so will you!" And I rushed after him to make him turn back, but he picked up from under his feet the oar which I had thrown down as I had arrived and, waving it at me, shouted:

' "Be off with you, or I'll beat you to death!" '

'Sirs, in the story I'm telling you I have been fairly frank with you about my cowardice – as on the occasion when I left the deceased youth Levonty lying on the ground, and climbed a tree – but, as the Lord's my witness, I swear to you that I would have braved that oar and faced up to Uncle Luka, but ... believe me or not, as you will ... no sooner had Levonty's name flashed into my mind, than in the darkness between myself and Uncle Luka there was outlined the figure of Levonty, shaking his fist. The fear this inspired was too much for me and I recoiled backwards, but Luka was already standing on the end of one of the chains, and suddenly, as he established his foothold on it, he shouted through the storm:

' "Sing a catabasis!"[1]

'Our choir-leader Arefa was standing there, and he immediately obeyed, intoning: "I shall open my lips ... "; the others joined in, and we chanted the catabasis, pitting our voices against the howling of the storm. Then Luka, as if immune to the fear of death, began to walk across the bridge-chain. Within the space of a minute he had crossed the first span, and was lowering himself on to the second ... And then? Then the darkness wrapped him round, and we couldn't see whether he was still moving across or whether he had fallen in and been gimleted into the abyss by the accursed ice-floes; we didn't know whether to pray that he be saved, or to lament him, that his honest, upright soul be granted rest.'

'Now what was happening on the opposite bank? His Most Holy Reverence the Bishop was performing the all-night service, according to his custom, in the main church, completely unaware that there was a thief in his altar-room; it had pleased our Englishman, Yakov Yakovlevich, to stand in the altar-room, which gave on to the altar proper, steal back our angel and send it out of the church hidden in an overcoat, as he had planned, and Luka had darted off with it; meanwhile, old man Maroy had kept his word and remained standing outside underneath that very same window, waiting until the very last moment when, if Luka had not returned, the Englishman would depart, and Maroy would smash the window and climb into the church with a crowbar and chisel, like a real villain. The Englishman kept a constant eye on him, and observed that old man Maroy was punctiliously fulfilling his vow; as soon as he noticed the Englishman pressing his face against the window to survey him, he immediately nodded, as if to say: "Here I am – I'm a good, responsible thief."

'Thus both men showed each other nobility of spirit, and this prevented either one of them from exalting himself above the other by reason of his version of the Christian faith. Towards these two faiths a third was moving; but as yet they had no knowledge of what that third faith would bring about . . . At any rate, when the last bell of the all-night service had died away, and the Englishman quietly opened the casement window a little way so that Maroy could climb in, and was himself on the point of leaving, he suddenly saw old man

Maroy turn away from him, paying him no attention, but instead staring fixedly out over the river and saying over and over again:

' "May God carry him across, may God carry him across, may God carry him across!" And then he leapt in the air and started to dance like a man intoxicated, shouting: "God has carried him across, God has carried him across!"

'Yakov Yakovlevich was seized by the greatest dismay, thinking:

' "Well, it's all up with us: the old man's lost his wits, and I shall perish." And then suddenly, as he looked, he saw Maroy and Luka embracing each other.

'Old man Maroy said, in his champing voice:

' "I saw you had lamps to light your way over the chain."

'But Uncle Luka replied:

' "I had no lamps with me."

' "Where did the light come from, then?"

'Luka replied:

' "I don't know. I didn't see any light, I just ran across and I don't know how it was that I didn't fall in . . . it was as if someone were supporting me by both arms."

'Maroy said:

' "That was the angels. I saw them, and for that I won't live much longer, but will die before the day is halfway done."

'Since Luka didn't have time to do much talking, he refrained from replying to the old man, but quickly handed the Englishman the two icons through the open window. The Englishman took them, but then handed them back.

' "What's this?" he said. "There's no seal on it."

' "Isn't there?" Luka replied.

' "No, there isn't."

'Well, at that point Luka crossed himself and said:

' "Well, it's all up with us, then! There's no time to put it right now. It's a miracle wrought by the angel of the church, and I know what purpose it's meant to serve."

'And Luka immediately rushed into the church, managed to squeeze his way into the altar-room where the bishop was being disrobed and, falling to the bishop's feet, said:

' "I've committed sacrilege, I've done this and I've done that: have me put in fetters and thrown in prison."

'The bishop listened, as befitted a man of his honour, and then replied:

' "It must by now be apparent to you where faith is more effective: you removed the seal from your angel by means of a scoundrelly trick, but ours removed it from itself, and brought you here."

'Uncle Luka said:

' "I see it, O Bishop, and I tremble. Please have me flogged at once."

'But the bishop replied with a word of absolution:

' "With the power given me by God I forgive you and absolve you, my son. Prepare yourself to partake of the most pure body of Christ at matins."

'Well, sirs, I don't think there's really much more to tell you. Luka Kirilov and old man Maroy returned in the morning, and said:

' "Fathers and Brothers, we have seen the glory of the angel of the ruling Church, and the divine care for that Church as revealed in the kindness of its bishop; we ourselves have been anointed into that Church with holy oil, and have this day received communion, partaking of the flesh and blood of the Saviour."

'And again I felt the urge, which had been with me ever since we had stayed with the elder Pamva, to be animated with the soul of all Russia, and for all of us I exclaimed:

' "We're with you, Uncle Luka!" And then we all crept up to his side in one flock, like lambs in the charge of a single shepherd, and it was only then that we began to understand to what it was and where it was our sealed angel had led us, first moving where it pleased him to place his steps, and then unsealing himself for the sake of the mutual human love that had been revealed in that terrible night.'

The narrator concluded his tale. The listeners remained silent for a while, but finally one of them cleared his throat and observed that everything in the story could be rationally explained – Mikhailitsa's dreams, the vision she had had while still half asleep, the fall of the angel, which a stray cat or dog must have knocked to the floor, the death of Levonty, who had been ill even before his meeting with Pamva; the enigmatic things Pamva had said could all be explained as chance verbal coincidences.

'It's also clear why Luka crossed the chain holding an oar: bricklayers are well known for their skill in being able to walk and climb anywhere, and the oar acted as a balancing instrument. It's clear, too, why old man Maroy saw the light near Luka, the light he thought was angels. A man who's frozen with cold may very easily see dots in front of his eyes, caused by excessive strain. I wouldn't even have been surprised if, for example, old man Maroy had died before the day was halfway done, as he himself predicted . . .'

'Yes, he did die, sir,' Mark replied.

'There you are, you see! There's nothing remarkable about an old man of eighty dying after all that excitement, and catching cold; but what I'm completely at a loss to explain is: how could the seal have disappeared from the new angel, which the Englishwoman had sealed?'

'Why, that's the simplest part of all, sir,' Mark replied merrily; and he told them that shortly thereafter they had found the seal in between the icon and the mounting.

'How could that have happened?'

'Like this: the Englishwoman hadn't dared to risk damaging the angel's face either; she'd made the seal out of paper, and had slipped it under the edge of the frame ... She did it very cleverly and skilfully, but while Luka was carrying the icons, they moved about under his belt, and so the seal fell off.'

'Well, I suppose that accounts for it all very neatly, then.'

'Yes, that's what many people think: that there was nothing at all unusual about what happened. And it's not just educated people who've heard the story who think that way, but even some of our own brethren, who've remained schismatics and who laugh at us for being pushed into the established Church by an Englishwoman with a bit of paper. But we don't argue when people talk that way: everyone must judge according to his belief, and for us it's all the same by what paths the Lord seeks out a man and from what vessel he gives him to drink, just as long as he does seeks him out and slakes his thirst to be united with his Fatherland. But there are those louts of muzhiks crawling out from under the snow. They've obviously had a good rest, and they'll be off in a moment or two. Maybe they'll give me a ride. St Basil's Eve has passed. I've been a bother to you and have tried your patience sorely. But I wish you a Happy New Year. In the name of Christ, forgive me: I'm just a poor, ignorant soul!'

PAMPHALON THE ENTERTAINER

'Weakness is all, strength is insignificant. When a man is born, he is weak and yielding; when he dies, he is strong and hard. When a tree begins to grow, it is yielding and tender, and when it is dry and tough, it dies. Hardness and strength are the concomitants of death. Pliancy and weakness express the freshness of existence. Therefore, that which has grown hard will not prevail.'

Lao-Tse

I

During the reign of Emperor Theodosius the Great there lived at Constantinople a certain nobleman, a 'patrician and bishop' named Hermius. Rich, high-born and distinguished, he possessed a forthright and honest character. He loved truth and detested insincerity, an attitude that ill concorded with the times in which he lived. In those far-off times there were in Byzantium (or Constantinople as it is called nowadays), just as there were in every part of the Byzantine Empire, a great many arguments about faith and piety, in the course of which the passions of men would become aroused; discord and quarrels would ensue, with the result that although everyone was preoccupied with questions of piety, there was in reality neither godliness nor peace. Indeed, among the lower orders of society at this time there prevailed a state of moral turpitude such as was too embarrassing even to be talked of, while the higher orders were characterized by a universal and dreadful hypocrisy. Everyone pretended to be God-fearing, but lived in a fashion that was thoroughly un-Christian: there were backbiting, mutual hatred, and an absence of compassion for the poor people at the lower end of the scale; the rich drowned in luxury and felt not the slightest pangs of shame that the common people should, at the very same time, be suffering the most crushing needs. People who became impoverished were taken into servitude or slavery, and it not seldom happened that poor people actually died of hunger outside the houses of feasting nobles. Moreover, the plebeians knew that these eminent folk were constantly warring among themselves, and that they were frequently the cause of one another's undoing. Not only did they make slanderous reports about one another to the Emperor – they were even in the habit of poisoning one another at feasts or in their own homes, bribing the cooks or other minions to do their dirty work for them.

At both its upper and lower levels, the entire state was filled with vice.

Hermius's soul was a *peaceful* one. What was more, he had strengthened it with a love of human beings, as taught by Christ in His Gospels. Hermius wanted to see genuine piety, not some simulated version of it that brought no one any benefit, but merely served as a pretext for vainglory and deceit. Hermius would say: 'If we believe that the Gospels are divine and reveal to us how we must act in order to annihilate the evil in the world, we must act in the way the Gospels show us, and not merely pay lip-service to them: such, for example, as to recite the words "and forgive us our debts, as we forgive our debtors", and then forgive no one anything, but instead wax wrathful at the slightest offence and claim back what is owed by one's neighbour, sparing him neither life nor limb.'

Because of this, all the other nobles began to make jokes about Hermius and poke fun at him; they would say to him: 'No doubt you want us all to become beggars and stand around stark naked throwing our shirts to one another. Behaviour like that's simply not acceptable in a civilized state.' To which he would reply: 'I'm not talking about civilized states, I'm talking about how it may be possible for us to live according to the teaching of Christ, a body of doctrine which you have termed divine.' They would retort: 'That's all very well, but it's impossible!' And they would proceed to argue with him. Eventually, however, they started making depositions about Hermius to the Emperor, claiming that he had lost his wits and was no longer suitable to hold office.

Hermius began to notice this, and he fell into reflection. How difficult was it, he wondered, to retain one's standing in society and yet live one's life according to Christ's teaching?

No sooner had Hermius begun to deliberate this notion in depth, than it appeared to him that it was quite impossible to do both of these things at the same time; one would have to choose either the one or the other: either turn one's back on Christ's teaching or turn one's back on the nobility, for there was no way that they would fit together, and if at any time you were to try to fit them together by force, they would not concord for long, but would once again diverge, even further than before. 'You'd get rid of one devil, but he'd only come back again and bring another seven with him,' he thought. Looking at the matter from another point of view, however, Hermius reasoned that if he were to start pointing an accusing finger at everyone and arguing with all and sundry, he would end up in everyone's bad books, and the other nobles would then slander him to the Emperor, call him a traitor to the state, and bring about his downfall.

'I can't please everyone,' he thought. 'If I side with the schemers I'll ruin my soul, yet if I side with the guileless I won't be of any assistance to them but will only create a lot of trouble for myself. I'll be said to be a man of evil intent, who is out to sow unrest, and it might come to pass that I would lose patience with all the tales they told about me and would begin to justify myself; if that were to happen, my soul would grow brutalized – I would start accusing my accusers and become every bit as nasty as them. No, things had better not work out like that. I don't want to shame anyone or reproach anyone, because all that is repugnant to my soul; the best thing would be for me to give up all this; go to the Emperor and ask him to permit me to relinquish all the power that I have, and live out the rest of my days in peace somewhere, as an ordinary person.'

Hermius did as his reflections prompted him. When he went to see Emperor Theodosius, he made no complaints or accusations about anyone, but merely asked to be relieved of his duties. At first the Emperor tried to persuade him to remain at his post, but then gave in. Hermius was allowed to take full retirement ('Give up all power').

At this very same time Hermius's wife died, and the former noble, now left on his own, began to reflect in a different way. 'May this not be a sign to me from above?' he wondered. 'The Emperor has freed me from the cares of my post, and the Lord has freed me from marriage. My wife has died, and there is no one in my family for whose sake I must try to increase my substance. Now I can walk faster and further towards the aim that is outlined in the Gospels. What good is wealth to me? It brings nothing but worry, and even though I've given up my official position, wealth would compel me to worry about it and draw me into the kind of activities that are unsuitable for someone who wants to be a disciple of Christ.'

But Hermius owned a very great deal of wealth ('for he had great possessions') – he had a house, a village, slaves and all kinds of treasures.

Hermius set all his slaves free. As for the rest of his 'great possessions', he sold them and distributed the proceeds among poor people who were in need.

He acted in this way because he wanted to 'be perfect', and because to those who wanted to attain perfection, Christ had clearly and concisely pointed out a single path: 'Go and sell all that thou hast . . . and come and follow me.'

Hermius followed this instruction very precisely, leaving himself without a farthing to his name, and he rejoiced that he in no way found it grievous or difficult. It was only at the outset that it cost him something of an effort; after a while he took pleasure in giving everything away, so that nothing should ensnare him or hinder him from travelling lightly towards the loftiest aim of the Gospels.

4

Having thus freed himself from power and riches, Hermius left
the capital in secret and set off to look for a secluded spot where
no one would prevent him from keeping himself pure and holy,
and from leading a life that was pleasing in the eyes of God.
After a long journey, which he made barefoot, Hermius reached
the remote town of Edessa,[1] and quite unexpectedly came across
'a certain pillar' for himself. 'Here it is,' thought Hermius.
'Here's a place all ready for me.' And he immediately clambered
on to his 'pillar' by means of a frail piece of timber which someone had placed against the rock, and then pushed the timber
away. It rolled far away down the precipice and broke in pieces;
but Hermius remained standing where he was, and continued to
stand there for thirty years. During all that time he prayed to
God and tried to forget about the hypocrisy and other evils
which he had seen and which had pained and angered him.

The sole item of personal property which Hermius had taken
with him on to the rock was a long piece of rope which he had
used to hang on by during his climb; it was to prove useful in
another respect, too.

On one of the first few days of his sojourn on the rock, when
he had not yet remembered to remove the length of rope, it was
observed by a boy goatherd who had come there to graze his
goats. The goatherd began to tug at the rope, and Hermius
called to him, saying:

'Please fetch me some water: I'm very thirsty.'

The boy hooked his water-gourd to the length of rope and
said:

'Here you are: you can keep the gourd, if you like.'

He also gave Hermius his basket, which contained a handful of black, sharp-tasting berries.

Hermius ate the berries, and said:

'God has sent me a provider.'

As soon as the boy had arrived back in his village with his herd of goats that evening, he at once began to tell his mother of how he had seen an old man on the rock. When the boy's mother went down to the well, she proceeded to inform the other women about what her son had told her, and it was in this fashion that people came to learn about the existence of the new stylite. The villagers flocked to see Hermius, and brought him more lentils and beans than he was able to eat. So it went on. Scarcely would Hermius have lowered the wicker basket and the gourd on the long rope than the villagers would be putting cabbage-leaves and dry, uncooked pulses into the basket and filling the gourd with water. And this was the diet on which the Byzantine noble and plutocrat Hermius was to live for the next thirty years. He ate neither bread nor anything that had been prepared over a flame, and he forgot the taste of cooked food. According to the perceptions of those days, this was thought pleasing in the eyes of God. Hermius never once regretted having given away his wealth – indeed, it passed from his memory altogether. He talked to no one, and appeared stern and austere, in his silence imitating the prophet Elijah.

The villagers believed that Hermius was capable of performing miracles. This conviction was not based on anything he had said to them, but they held it none the less. Those who were sick would come to stand in his shadow, which the sun cast from the rock on to the ground, and would go away feeling that this had brought them relief. But he continued to remain silent, concentrating his mind in prayer, or reciting by memory the three million lines of Origen and the two hundred and fifty thousand lines of Gregorius, Pierus and Stephanus.

Thus Hermius passed the days, and sometimes, in the evening, when the scorching heat subsided and his face was refreshed by the coolness, he would bring his prayers and meditations about God to a close and think instead about human beings for a while. He would reflect on how during the course of those thirty years the evil in the world must be increasing and on how, under a veil of bigotry and sanctimoniousness that had replaced the true doctrine with its own inventions, all authentic virtue had probably withered away in people and become a mere form without content. So unfavourable were the impressions which the stylite had taken with him from the smooth-tongued capital he had left behind that he was in a state of despair concerning the entire world, and failed to perceive that through this despair he was degrading the aim and purpose of creation, while considering himself the most perfect of men. He would recite the works of Origen to himself, all the while thinking: 'Well – perhaps it is so: perhaps the world really is here for the sake of eternity, and the people in it are like the pupils in a school preparing to take their examinations in eternity, and show the progress they have made. But what kind of progress can they hope to be able to show when their lives are full of vanity and spite, and they learn nothing from Christ, but go on living according to the old pagan habits? What good will eternity be to them?' It was all very well for Origen to reassure everyone that it was impossible for the Creator to have fallen into error concerning His Creation, since he had seen 'that it was good', and would have been well aware if there had been anything wrong with it; to Hermius it nevertheless seemed that 'the whole world lay in sin', and it was in vain that his intelligence sought to ascertain the presence of 'those who were pleasing to God and deserving of Eternity'.

Hermius found it quite impossible to imagine a human being who might be worthy of eternity – to his eyes, everyone seemed wicked, everyone had arrived in life with an inclination towards evil already installed in him, and during the course of his life upon earth merely went from bad to worse.

And the stylite was at last seized by the desperate certainty that eternity was quite empty, since there was no one worthy of entering it.

One evening, as night was lowering her veils, and the stylite was 'endeavouring with all his might to learn who are they that are pleasing in the sight of God', he inclined his head to the edge of the precipice on which he perched, and a strange thing happened to him: he felt a gentle, even breeze wafting towards him, and at the same time heard the following words:

'Hermius, your grief and horror are in vain: there are indeed those who earn God's pleasure, and whose names are written in the book of eternal life.'

The stylite was overjoyed to hear the sweet voice, and he said:

'Lord, if I have acquired grace in your eyes, let there be revealed to me just one such person – then my mind will be put at rest regarding the whole of earthly creation.'

Once again the gentle breathing wafted to the ear of the aged monk:

'In order for that to come about you must forget all the people you have known, come down from your pillar and go and see my servant Pamphalon.'

With that, the breathing faded, and the monk leaned forward, wondering whether he had really heard these words, or whether it had only been a dream. Another cold night passed, and then another hot day; then twilight fell once more, and again Hermius leaned over, and heard the voice say:

'Come down to earth, Hermius, you must go and see Pamphalon.'

'But who is he, this Pamphalon?'

'One of the people you want to see.'

'And where does he live?'

'In Damascus.'

Again Hermius gave a start, uncertain whether he was dreaming or not. Then he decided he would put the matter to the test: if yet a third time he were to hear this clear voice speaking of Pamphalon, he would cast all doubt to the winds, come down from the rock and walk to Damascus.

He determined, however, to make detailed inquiries as to what sort of man this Pamphalon was, and how he was to seek him out in Damascus.

Another hot day went by, and when the cool of the evening arrived, the name of Pamphalon sounded once more on the delicate breeze.

This time the mysterious voice said:

'Why are you being so slow, elder? Why aren't you coming down to earth and walking to Damascus to see Pamphalon?'

The elder replied:

'How can I go and look for someone I don't know?'

'You know his name.'

'I know his name's Pamphalon – but in a great city like Damascus there must surely be many men of that name. Which of them shall I approach?'

The voice on the delicate breeze said:

'That is not your concern. All you need do is come down quickly from your pillar and walk to Damascus: there everyone knows the Pamphalon you want to see. Ask the first person you meet – they'll show you the way. Everyone knows him.'

Now, after the third such conversation, Hermius was no longer in any doubt that this was the voice which must be obeyed. As for the question of which Pamphalon he was to see in Damascus, it ceased to trouble him. This Pamphalon whom everyone knew must doubtless be some famous poet or warrior, or possibly a well-known noble. In short, Hermius had no more grounds for hesitation; in order to obtain the fulfilment of his request, he must go and bring it about himself.

And so it was that after thirty years of standing in the same place, Hermius had to climb down from his rocky precipice and walk to Damascus . . .

It might, of course, seem a strange thing for such a complete recluse as Hermius was to go and look for a man who lived in Damascus, as in those times the city of Damascus was, with regard to moral purity, on a level with present-day Paris or Vienna – cities which are not renowned for the holy lives led by their inhabitants, but have the reputation of being nests of vice and sin; in ancient times, however, there was, in fact, nothing particularly strange about such an occurrence: the emissaries of piety were often expressly sent to those places where it was most absent.

He must walk to Damascus! At this point, however, Hermius remembered that he was naked: the rags in which he had arrived thirty years ago had rotted away and fallen from his bony frame. His skin was tanned black by the sun, his eyes were wild, his hair was bleached and tangled, and his fingernails were as long as the talons of a bird of prey . . . How, looking like that, was he to show himself in the big, prosperous city?

But the voice continued to guide him, resounding from afar:

'It's all right, Hermius, on you go: your nakedness will find you a covering.'

Hermius took his basket containing its dried pulses and the water-gourd and threw them down to the foot of his pillar. Then he himself clambered down by means of the very same rope which he had used to haul up the supplies of food he had been brought.

The stylite had by this time grown so emaciated that the thin and semi-rotten rope was able to take his weight. True, it creaked a bit, but that did not deter Hermius: he landed safely at the foot of his pillar and set off, tottering like a young child, as his legs had grown unused to movement and had lost their steadiness.

Hermius trudged across the hot, uninhabited desert for a very long time; on his way he encountered not a single person, and so had no cause to be ashamed of his nakedness; as he was approaching Damascus, he came across a dried-up, skeletonized corpse lying in the sand, and beside it a tattered goatskin of the type worn in those days by monks who lived in communal dwellings. Hermius covered the corpse with sand, put the goatskin over his shoulders, and rejoiced, seeing in this a provision that had been especially made for him.

The sun was already beginning to set as Hermius drew near to Damascus. The elder had been slightly vague as to his plans, and now did not know which he should do: quicken his pace, and hurry, or take his time and wait for the morning. To his eyes there seemed only a short distance left to go, but his legs were aching. He decided to try to get there while it was still light, and entered the city just as the red sun was falling behind the horizon, the dusk was thickening and everything was becoming enshrouded in gloom. It was as if he were sinking in unfathomable sin.

Hermius grew afraid – he felt like turning back ... And again the thought came into his head: was not all he had heard about his journey merely a dream, or even a temptation? What righteous man could be found in this noisy city? What source of righteousness could there be here? Would it not be better if he were to retrace his steps, climb back into his rocky cleft, and remain standing there for good?

He had already turned round, but his legs would not carry him, and in his ears once again he heard the 'delicate breeze' saying:

'Go quickly and kiss Pamphalon in Damascus.'

The old man turned round again to face Damascus, and his legs carried him forward. He arrived at the city wall just as the sentinel was closing the gates.

With some difficulty the poor old man managed to persuade the gatesman to let him through, though in exchange for this he had to part with his basket and gourd, a transaction which left him defenceless in the midst of a city which was totally unfamiliar to him and which seemed to him quite terrifyingly sinful.

In the south the nights fall quickly; there is scarcely any twilight, and the darkness is so intense that it is impossible to see anything. The events described here took place at a time when oriental cities were as yet without street lighting, and their inhabitants locked up early in the evening. The streets were a very dangerous place after dusk, and so the householders barred all the entrances to their houses very securely, so that no evil-doer should sneak in under cover of darkness and rob them, or murder them and burn down their property. At night they would either not open up at all, or would open up only to friends or members of their domestic staff who had been delayed, and even then only when they had satisfied themselves that the person knocking really was someone they ought to let in.

The only doors that remained open late were those of the prostitutes, who were available to everyone and who, the more visits they received, the better they were pleased.

Having arrived at Damascus in total darkness, the Elder Hermius was completely at a loss as to where he should seek shelter until the morning. There were, of course, inns in the city, but Hermius could not go and knock at the door of an inn, as there he would be requested to pay for his night's lodging, and he had no money with him.

Hermius came to a halt. After he had given some thought to the question of what a person in his situation might do, he decided to ask to be allowed to spend the night at the first house he came to.

Thus following his inner promptings, he approached the house nearest to him and knocked at its door.

From behind the door a voice asked:

'Who's that knocking?'

Hermius replied:

'A poor pilgrim.'

'Oh, one of those! There's a lot of your sort gadding about. What do you want?'

'I need shelter for the night.'

'Well, you've come to the wrong house. Go to an inn.'

'I've no money, and I can't pay for an inn.'

'That's too bad. Well then, go to the house of people who know you; perhaps they'll let you in.'

'No one knows me here.'

'If there's no one who knows you here, you'd do better to stop wasting your time knocking at our doors and go away as quickly as possible.'

'I'm asking in the name of Christ.'

'Oh, please don't mention that name. There's a whole bunch of you going around: you're forever going on about Christ, but all you do is tell lies and use that name to cover up all your evil doings. Go away, there's no shelter for you here.'

Hermius approached a second house, and here again he began to knock.

And here again a voice from behind the closed door asked:

'What do you want?'

'I'm a poor pilgrim who's exhausted . . . Please let me rest in your house!'

But again he received the same answer: go to an inn.

'I've no money,' Hermius said. He uttered the name of Christ, but it earned him nothing but reproof.

'That's enough, don't come shouting that name again,' replied the voice from behind the door of the second house.

'Nowadays all the villains and layabouts use it to cover up their misdeeds.'

'I beseech you,' Hermius said. 'Please believe me: I've done nobody any harm and I have no intention of doing so. I've just come in from the desert.'

'Well, if you're from the desert, you'd better stay there. You're wasting your time coming here.'

'I'm not here on my own account – I have instructions to seek someone out.'

'Well, go to his house, then; but leave us in peace; we're afraid of folk who call themselves elders and go around dressed in goatskins: you yourselves may be all very holy, but each of you has seven devils tagging along behind him.'

'Goodness!' thought Hermius. 'How time has changed men's habits. The old custom of welcoming strangers seems to have passed out of use altogether. Everyone's familiar with the desert legend that an ascetic has more devils in tow than a plain ordinary sinner, and because of that things have got worse, not better. And here I am – a desert anchorite who has stood in the same place for thirty years: in the shadow of my pillar men have been cured of their illnesses, yet no one will allow me to come in under their roof, and not only may I be murdered by evil-doers – I may be insulted and dishonoured by men without shame who have perverted the course of nature. No, I now see clearly that I have been subjected to the mockery of Satan, that I have been sent here not for the good of my soul, but in order to bring about my total perdition, as unto Sodom and Gomorrah.'

At this very moment, however, Hermius noticed someone quickly crossing the street in the darkness. Laughing, this person said:

'I say, you've really given me a laugh, old man!'

'In what way?' Hermius inquired.

'Well, I mean, you're so stupid that you go asking men who are rich and of noble birth to let you spend the night in their homes! It's easy to see that you've no understanding of life.'

The stylite thought: 'This is doubtless a thief or a prodigal, but he's a talkative fellow: I shall ask him what I must do, and where I may find shelter.'

'Stay for a moment, whoever you are,' he said. 'Tell me, are there any men in this city who are known as philanthropists?'

'Of course,' the man replied. 'There are men like that here.'

'Where are they?'

'You've just been knocking at their doors and talking to them.'

'Their philanthropy's not up to much in that case, then.'

'That's what all sham philanthropists are like.'

'What about men who are God-fearing, do you know any of those?'

'Yes, I know some of those, too.'

'Where are they?'

'It's after sunset now; they'll all be at prayer.'

'I'll go to them.'

'Well, I don't advise it. God help you if you disturb them with your knocking while they're standing at prayer; their servants will throw you to the ground and inflict injuries on you.'

The elder threw up his hands:

'What sort of a state of affairs is this?' he said. 'One can't convince the philanthropists of one's need, and one can't call the devout away from their prayers, your night is dark, and your customs are dreadful. Oh misery me! Alack and alas!'

'I'll tell you what to do: instead of standing here feeling sorry for yourself and looking for people who are God-fearing – *go and see Pamphalon.*'

'What did you say?' the anchorite asked, and again received the same answer:

'*Go and see Pamphalon.*'

8

The anchorite was glad to hear this mention of the name Pamphalon. It meant that his journey had not been in vain. But who, he wondered, was this talking to him in the dark? If it was a guiding angel, that was good – but what if it were the Devil?

'I do want to see someone called Pamphalon,' Hermius said. 'In fact, I've been sent to find him; but I'm not sure whether he's the Pamphalon you're talking about.'

'What were you told about your Pamphalon?'

'Much that I wouldn't relate to just anyone; but I was informed that everyone knows him here.'

'Well, if that's the case, then we're talking about the same Pamphalon. He's the only Pamphalon whom everyone knows.'

'Why is he so well known?'

'Oh, because he's an agreeable man who cheers people up wherever he goes. No festive gathering or entertainment is complete without him, and he has a friendly word for everyone. As soon as people hear the bells on the collar of his long-muzzled dog, they say, cheerfully: "There's Pamphalon's Acra. That means Pamphalon himself will be along in a moment or two, and then we shall all have a merry time."'

'Why does he go around with a dog?'

'To add to the amusement. That Acra of his is a wonderful, intelligent and faithful dog, it helps him to cheer people up. And he also has a bird of bright plumage which he carries about inside a hoop on the end of a long pole. It, too, is a rare asset: it whistles like a pipe and hisses like a snake.'

'But why does Pamphalon need all this – a dog and a bird of bright plumage?'

'Why, he wouldn't be Pamphalon if he didn't have things with which to amuse people.'

'And who is he, this Pamphalon of yours?'

'Do you really mean you don't know?'

'Yes. All I know about him is what I heard in the desert.'

The man looked surprised.

'There's a remarkable thing!' he exclaimed. 'That means our Pamphalon's known not only in Damascus and the other cities, but also in remote parts of the desert. Well, that's as it should be, for there's not another soul on earth as cheerful as our Pamphalon; no one can help laughing as they watch him playing his merry pranks, winking, waggling his ears, moving his legs up and down, whistling, clicking his tongue and twisting his curly head.'

'He moves his legs up and down and twists his head,' the anchorite repeated. 'He makes faces, moves his body and jumps . . . What is he, then?'

'An entertainer.'

'What? This Pamphalon? The one I'm looking for? He's an *entertainer*?'

'That's right. Pamphalon's an entertainer; he's so universally well-known because he goes capering through the streets, spinning around like a wheel on the square, winking, moving his legs up and down and twisting his head.'

Hermius nearly dropped his anchorite's staff and said:

'Be gone! Be gone, devil: you have mocked at me long enough!'

But the man who had spoken in the darkness did not seem to hear this curse, and added:

'Pamphalon is at present living just round the corner from here, and I expect the light will still be shining in his window, because in the evening he gets his entertainer's contrivances ready before he goes off to give performances in the houses of the *hetaerae*. But if there's no light in his window, then you should count along in the dark until you come to the third small house on the right, go inside and spend the night there. Pamphalon's doors are always open.'

And with this, the speaker in the dark vanished off somewhere, as though he had never existed.

9

Struck by what he had heard about Pamphalon, Hermius remained in the darkness, thinking:

'What shall I do now? Surely it's impossible that the man for whose sake I was brought down from my rock and led out of the desert in order to meet should be a common entertainer? What virtues, worthy of eternal life, can be imitated from a mountebank, an actor, a conjuror who spins around on the squares and provides entertainment for revellers in houses where wine is drunk and dissolute behaviour indulged in?'

It all seemed quite incomprehensible. But the night was dark, and there was nothing for it but for Hermius to go to the house of the entertainer.

The anchorite needed shelter for the night, for even though he was accustomed to all the inclemency of the elements, to stay out on the streets at night was in those days far more dangerous than it is now. At that time thieves went plundering and desperate people roamed about, the like of whom was seen only in the days before the burning of Sodom and Gomorrah. They were worse than animals; they spared no one, and a man could expect to encounter the most infamous molestation at their hands.

Hermius remembered all this and was accordingly very relieved when no sooner had he turned the corner than he saw a welcoming light. The light was coming from one of the small houses, and in the darkness it burned as brightly as a star. This must be where the entertainer lived.

Hermius walked into the light and saw that here indeed was a very small, low house, the door of which was standing wide open; the doorway's rush curtain was raised, so that everything inside was visible.

The dwelling was not a large one – it contained only one room which, although it was not very lofty, was none the less fairly spacious. This room was entirely exposed to view, revealing the householder, his household, and all his trade. And from all that was visible it was not difficult to guess that it was not a respectable person who lived here, but a professional entertainer.

On the grey wall immediately opposite the open door hung an earthenware lamp with a long spout, at the end of which a wick soaked in fat burned with a red flame. This wick was giving off a great deal of black smoke, and fiery drops of boiling fat kept falling from it. Along the entire length of the wall hung various strange objects which it would really have been more accurate to describe as junk. Here were Saracen, Greek and Egyptian costumes; here too were multicoloured feathers, bells, rattles, tambourines, red poles and gilded hoops. In one corner a hook had been fixed to the ceiling; to this a thin pole, like a long fishing-rod, had been attached by means of a piece of rope, and on the end of this pole, affixed by another piece of rope, there was a wooden hoop, inside which a bird of bright plumage perched asleep, its head tucked under its wing. One of its legs bore a slender chain, by which it was fettered to the hoop. In another corner there were some boards which had been bent into a semi-circle, and behind it lay tambourines, drums, wooden pipes and even stranger items, the names of which the anchorite, who had not been exposed to the frivolity of city life for a long time, could not even remember.

On the floor in one corner there was a bed of rush matting, and in another stood a trunk; on this trunk, in front of a bench which served as a table, the master of the house sat immersed in some aspect of his craft.

His outward appearance was strange: he was a man no longer young, and was indeed on the elderly side; he had a swarthy face which was cheerful and good-natured, with a constant, even expression; his eyes bore a light gleam; but his face was painted, and the half-grey head was garlanded all over with little curls, on top of which sat a thin copper fillet from which jangling, glittering circlets and stars were suspended. Such was Pamphalon. He sat huddled over a bench on which various entertainer's costumes lay strewn about, and in front of his face there were a little earthenware brazier and a soldering pipe. He was blowing through the soldering pipe on to the hot coals, fastening some small rings together, one after the other, and did not notice the stern anchorite who had now been standing for a long time staring fixedly in at him.

At that moment, however, the long-muzzled dog which had been lying in the shadow at Pamphalon's feet sensed the presence of a trespasser, raised its head and got to its feet, uttering a growl; as it did so, the bells on its brass collar began to jangle, and at this sound the bird of bright plumage woke up, bringing its head out from under its wing. It gave a start and produced a noise which was a blend of a whistle and a sharp clacking of its beak. Pamphalon straightened up, removed his lips from the soldering pipe for a moment, and shouted:

'Be quiet, Acra! And you too, Zoia! Don't frighten this man of leisure who has come to summon us to entertain the bored and rich. And you, light emissary,' he added, raising his voice – 'whoever has sent you here, come closer now and tell me without delay: what do you require?'

Hermius responded to this question with a sigh:

'Oh, Pamphalon!'

'Yes, yes, yes; I'm the same old Pamphalon – dancer, entertainer, singer, fortune-teller and anything else you please – which of my gifts do you wish to avail yourself of?'

'You are mistaken, Pamphalon.'

'In what am I mistaken, friend?'

'The man who is standing outside your house has no need of those gifts of yours whatsoever. I haven't come to summon you to perform your entertainer's tricks.'

'Oh well, it doesn't matter. The night is young – someone else will come and summon us to perform, and I'll earn some money for tomorrow, both for myself and for my dog. But what can I do for you, then?'

'Please let me have shelter for the night; I would also like to talk with you.'

When he heard these words, the entertainer looked round, put his wire rings and soldering pipe back in the trunk and, using one hand to shield his eyes, said:

'I can't see you properly, I don't know who you are, and your voice doesn't sound familiar to me . . . But please by all means make yourself at home, and as for the talk . . . You must be making fun of me.'

'No, I am not,' Hermius replied. 'I'm a complete stranger here, and have come from a long way off in order to have a talk with you. The light of your lamp drew me to your door, and I've come to ask you for shelter.'

'Well, I'm glad that the light of my lamp doesn't shine only for revellers. Whoever you are – don't stand out there. If you really can't find a better place in all Damascus in which to spend the night, then I beg you, step inside so that I may put you at your ease.'

'Thank you,' Hermius replied. 'May God bless you for your hospitality, even as he blessed the welcoming roof of Abraham.'

'Oh I say, please stop making speeches! What I'm offering you is absolutely nothing, yet there you go bringing Abraham into it. Take a simpler view of the matter, old man. It will mean a great deal to me if you'll bless me when you leave my house again after you've rested from your journey and have taken your ease, but for now just come quickly inside: while I'm here, I'll help you to get washed – but it may be that someone will summon me out to provide a nocturnal entertainment, and then I shan't have any time to attend to you. Business is not very good here at the moment: entertainers from Syracuse have begun visiting Damascus. So sweetly do they sing and play their harps that they've taken all the best work from us. We can't afford to let a single opportunity pass: we have to go running off at the double to wherever we're summoned, and just now is the very hour when rich and well-born guests come to feast with the gay *hetaerae*.'

'An accursed hour,' thought Hermius.

But Pamphalon went on:

'Well, come in, then, please, and don't pay any attention to my dog: that's Acra, my faithful hound, my companion. Acra isn't there to frighten people, but to do the same job I do – to entertain them. Enter my house, traveller.'

So saying, Pamphalon stretched out both arms towards his guest and, leading him up the steps out of the darkness of the street into the illuminated room, momentarily recoiled from him in horror.

So wild and terrible did the anchorite who entered seem to him!

The former nobleman, who had stood for thirty years exposed to the wind and the fiery sun, had practically ceased to possess a human appearance. His eyes had grown completely colourless, his sun-scorched flesh had gone black and withered, and clung to his bones, his arms and legs had dried up, and his overgrown fingernails had turned inwards and were growing into the palms of his hands; on his head there remained only a single tuft of hair, and the colour of this hair was neither white, nor yellow, nor even green, but bluish, like a duck's egg, and this tuft stuck up in the very centre of his head like the crest of a drake.

These two quite disparate individuals stood facing each other in bewilderment: the entertainer, who had hidden the natural aspect of his features beneath a layer of paint, and the sun-bleached anchorite. They were observed by the long-muzzled dog and the bird of bright plumage. All were silent. But Hermius had not come to see Pamphalon in order to be silent, but in order to have a talk with him – a profoundly significant talk.

Pamphalon was the first to recover his composure.

Noticing that Hermius was carrying nothing with him, Pamphalon asked him in bewilderment:

'Where are your basket and gourd?'

'I've nothing with me,' the anchorite replied.

'Well, thank God that today I have something to offer you in the way of hospitality.'

'I don't need anything,' the elder said, interrupting him. 'I didn't come here for your hospitality. What I want to know is how you manage to please God.'

'What?'

'How do you manage to please God?'

'What are you talking about, Elder? How could *I* ever please God? It's out of the question for me even to think of such a thing.'

'Why? Everyone must think about his own salvation. Nothing is more dear to a man than his own salvation. But salvation is impossible without pleasing God.'

Pamphalon heard him out, smiled, and replied:

'Oh, Father, Father! If only you knew how funny what you're saying sounds to me. You've obviously been out of the world for a long time.'

'Yes, I have: it's thirty years since I've been down among men; yet what I say, I say in all sincerity and in accordance with my faith.'

'Oh,' replied Pamphalon, 'I won't argue with you. All I'll tell you is that I'm a man who leads a very irregular life – I'm an entertainer by profession and I don't have much time for thinking about piety – I hop, spin around, play musical instruments, clap my hands, wink, twist my legs and shake my head so that people will give me something for the amusement I give them. What kind of God-pleasing could I ever think about living a life like that?'

'Why don't you give up that way of life and start leading a better one?'

'Ah, my dear friend, I've already tried that.'

'With what results?'

'It didn't work out.'

'Then try again.'

'No, there's no use trying now.'

'Why not?'

'Because the other day I let slip an opportunity of improving my way of life such as it would be impossible to better.'

'How do you know? You may think it's impossible, but with God all things are possible.'

'No, please don't talk to me about that, as I really don't want to tempt God any further, if I can't hope to enjoy his mercy. I've left myself without salvation, and that's that.'

'So you've despaired, have you?'

'No, I haven't despaired. I'm just a merry, carefree fellow, and to talk to me about questions of faith is simply – out of place.'

Hermius shook his head, and said:

'But what does your faith consist in, merry, carefree fellow?'

'I have faith that I myself, on my own, am incapable of making anything good out of myself, and if in time my Creator manages to make something better out of me, then that's his affair. He's capable of surprising everyone.'

'But why don't you care about yourself?'

'I've no time to.'

'What do you mean, no time?'

'Well, I live a frivolous life, you see, and whenever I make an effort to save myself, I fall into a state of melancholy, and instead of anything good coming of it, things work out even worse than before.'

'You're talking nonsense.'

'No, it's true. When I start to meditate, my weak character makes me anxious and I end up undoing all my good work and returning to my profession of entertainer.'

'Well, that means you're a lost soul, then.'

'That may well be.'

'And I really don't think that you can possibly be the Pamphalon I need to see.'

'I can't answer that,' the entertainer replied. 'Only it seems to me that at this moment when I'm so fortunate as to be able to attend to your pilgrim's requirements, I'm just the Pamphalon you do need to see; as for the other things you may require, we'll find out about those tomorrow. Now I shall wash your feet and you will eat of what I have and go to bed, and I will go out entertaining.'

'I need to hear your wise words.'

'My wise words?' Pamphalon exclaimed again.

'Yes, I need to hear your wise words, that's why I've come to see you, and I shan't leave your side until I've heard them.'

Pamphalon looked at the elder, touched him by his blue top-knot, and then suddenly burst out laughing.

'What do you find so amusing in my words, my merry fellow?' Hermius inquired.

And Pamphalon answered:

'Forgive me my foolishness. I burst out laughing because I'm in the habit of playing the jester. You say you won't leave my side, and I thought that perhaps it might be a good idea if I were to take you with me around the town. It would be good for business if I could show you off around Damascus. Everyone would come out to see you, but I'm ashamed to think of you like that, even though you ought to be ashamed of laughing at me.'

'I'm not laughing at anyone, Pamphalon.'

'Then why did you tell me that you wanted to hear my wise words, as though you hoped to receive instruction from them? What instruction can I, a good-for-nothing entertainer, give you, a man who has the power to meditate on God and man in the holy silence of the desert? The Lord has not entirely deprived me of His most holy gift – reason, and I know what a difference

there is between you and myself. Don't offend me, old man –
allow me to wash your feet and offer you my bed to rest on.'

'Very well,' said Hermius. 'You are the master in your own
house, and you must do as you wish.'

Pamphalon fetched a tub of fresh water and washed the feet
of his guest. When he had finished, he offered him some food,
and then showed him to his own bed, saying:

'Tomorrow we shall talk. But now I ask you only one thing:
don't be alarmed if some revellers should come knocking at my
door or throw something at the wall. All that means is that some
devotees of idleness have come to summon me to entertain them.'

'And you'll get up and go out?'

'Yes, I go out at any time of the night or day.'

'And do you really go anywhere in the town?'

'Of course: after all, I'm only a lowly entertainer, and I can't
choose the places I perform in.'

'Poor Pamphalon!'

'What's to be done, Father? It isn't sages and philosophers
who ask for my services, but devotees of idleness. I go on to the
squares, stand outside the arenas, spin myself around at ban-
quets, frequent the suburban groves where the rich young men
go carousing and, most often of all, pass the nights in the
houses of the gay *hetaerae* . . .'

At these last words Hermius almost burst out weeping and,
in a most piteous voice, exclaimed:

'Poor Pamphalon!'

'What am I to do?' the entertainer replied. 'I really am very
poor. After all, I'm a child of sin, and since I was conceived in
sin, I grew up with sinners. I know no other skill besides entertaining, and I had to live in the world because it was here that
my mother, who conceived me in sin and gave birth to me,
lived. I should not have been able to bear it if my mother had
had to stretch out her hand for bread to strangers, and I supported her by means of my entertaining.'

'But where is your mother now?'

'I have faith that she is with God. She died in the very same
bed on which you are lying now.'

'Are you well-loved in Damascus?'

'I don't know the meaning of the word "love", but I suppose I am – at least, people throw me money for the amusement I provide, and they invite me to sit at their tables. I drink costly wine at others' expense and pay for it with my jokes.'

'You drink wine?'

'Oh yes – I like it, there's no question about that. And anyway, it's impossible for a man who keeps lively company not to drink wine.'

'Who was it who introduced you to that kind of company?'

'Chance – or perhaps it would be truer to say . . . but I can't explain that to a pious man like yourself. In her girlhood my mother was gay and pretty. My father was a nobleman. He abandoned me, and none of the other respectable citizens would take me in – I was taken in hand by another such as myself, an entertainer who beat me and knocked me about a great deal, but to whom I am none the less grateful – he taught me his craft, and now there is no one who can juggle with rings better than I, no one who is so good at clicking his tongue, making faces, clapping his hands, moving his legs up and down and twisting his head.'

'And this craft hasn't yet grown loathsome to you?'

'No. I often don't like it, especially when I see the nobles, who ought to be giving thought to the happiness of the common people, passing their time with the *hetaerae* instead and bringing the flower of youth into the houses of pleasure, but this is the career I was brought up in, and this is the only way I know of earning my daily bread.'

'Poor, poor Pamphalon! Look, your hair has already begun to turn white, and yet here you are still clapping your hands, mincing your legs and twisting your head in the company of prostitutes who have lost their souls. You will lose yours, too.'

But Pamphalon replied:

'Don't feel sorry for me because I twist my legs and hang around in the company of the *hetaerae*. The *hetaerae* may be sinners, but they are compassionate towards us weak ones. When their guests get drunk, they themselves go and collect money from the revellers, and sometimes they even use their caresses to wheedle a little extra for us.'

And, noticing that Hermius had turned away, Pamphalon touched him gently on the shoulder and said in a tone of admonishment:

'Believe me, esteemed old man: where there's life there's hope – in those *hetaerae* there often beat hearts of gold. But it saddens us to be present at the feasts of the rich masters. One meets unpleasant people there; they are proud and arrogant, and they want enjoyment – yet they won't tolerate levity or uninhibited laughter. There they demand what human nature is ashamed of, there they threaten us with blows and injuries, there they tweak the feathers of my bird of bright plumage, there they blow and spit in the face of my dog Acra. There they make light of all the insults they inflict on the lower orders and next morning . . . they go to church simply for appearances' sake.'

'O woe, woe!' Hermius whispered to himself. 'I see that he is still very far from realizing the degree to which he has become ensnared – but his nature and intelligence may be good . . . That is doubtless why I have been sent to him – in order to set his gifted soul on a different path.'

And to Pamphalon he said, in a tone of exhortation:

'Give up your loathsome craft.'

But Pamphalon replied:

'I'd very much like to, but I can't.'

'Say a prayer to God, and He will help you.'

Pamphalon trembled, and said in a lowered voice:

'A prayer! . . . How is it that you are able to read in my soul the very thing I want to forget?'

'Aha! I expect you've taken a vow and broken it again?'

'Yes, you've guessed it. I did that evil thing: took a vow.'

'Why do you call a vow an evil thing?'

'Because Christians are forbidden to swear oaths and make promises, and I, in spite of everything, am still a Christian. I took a vow and broke it. But now I know that it isn't possible for a weak person to take a vow before the Almighty, who has pre-ordained what he is to be and who moulds him as the potter moulds the clay on his wheel. Old man, I must tell you that I had the chance of giving up my entertaining, but didn't take it.'

'Why didn't you?'

'I couldn't.'

'I've heard that reply of yours before: you "couldn't"! Why could you, and yet couldn't?'

'Yes, that's it: I could and yet couldn't – because I'm – careless. I couldn't spend time thinking about my soul when there was someone who needed my help.'

The elder raised himself on his bed and, fixing his eyes on the entertainer, exclaimed:

'What did you say? You think nothing of ruining your soul for all eternity, merely in order to help someone during this brief life? Have you any idea of what the furious flames of hell are like, the depths of the eternal night?'

The entertainer smiled, and said:

'No, I know nothing about that. And anyway, how could I know anything about the lives of those who are dead, when I don't even know everything about the living? Do you have knowledge of Tartarus, old man?'

'Of course!'

'Yet I see that there is much upon earth that you don't have knowledge of. I find that strange. When I tell you that I'm a ne'er-do-well, you don't believe me. And I don't believe that you have knowledge concerning the dead.'

'Unhappy man! Have you even the slightest conception of God?'

'I do – only a very slight conception, it's true – but I don't expect to be greatly condemned on that account, because, after all, I didn't grow up in a noble family and haven't attended lessons with the scholastics in Byzantium.'

'It is possible to know God and serve Him without knowing the teachings of the scholastics.'

'I agree with you; that's the way I've always addressed God in my mind: "You are the Creator and I am Your creation – it's not for me to understand You, or why You have stuffed me into this chasuble of skin and thrown me down on to the earth in order to labour. All I do is drag myself about the earth and labour. I should like to know why everything has been created so ingeniously – but I don't want to be like a lazy slave, gossiping about You with all and sundry. I shall simply be obedient to You and not attempt to discover what You are thinking – I shall simply take and fulfil that which Your finger has traced in my soul. And if I do evil, forgive me, because after all it was You who created me with a compassionate heart. It is by it that I live." '

'And in this fashion you hope to justify yourself?'

'Oh, I don't hope for anything – I'm simply not afraid of anything.'

'What? Aren't you even afraid of God?'

Pamphalon shrugged his shoulders, and replied:

'No, not really. I love Him.'

'You'd do better to tremble!'

'Why? Are you afraid?'

'I used to be.'

'But now you've grown out of it?'

'I'm no longer the man I once was.'

'I suppose you're better than you were?'

'I don't know.'

'Well said. The man who knows is merely a looker-on, not a doer. He who acts is invisible to himself.'

'And have you ever felt that you were good?'

Pamphalon was silent.

'I entreat you,' Hermius repeated. 'Tell me, have you ever felt that you were good?'

'Yes,' said the entertainer. 'I have . . .'

'When was that?'

'Can you imagine? It was at the very moment at which I distanced myself from Him . . .'

'Lord! What is this madman saying?'

'I am telling you the whole truth.'

'But how did you distance yourself from God?'

'I did it in a single breath.'

'But tell me, what did you do?'

Pamphalon was about to describe what had happened to him, but at that very moment the rush curtain that hung over the door was thrown back by two swarthy, braceleted female arms, and two resonant female voices said, vying with each other in chorus:

'Pamphalon, ridiculous Pamphalon! Get up and come with us. We've run all the way to your house in the dark to fetch you, our *hetaera* sent us . . . Hurry, be quick now, our grotto and alleys are full of rich guests from Corinth. Bring your rings, and your harp, and Acra and your bird. Tonight you'll be able to earn something by your ridiculous antics, and even make up for your lost trade a little.'

Hermius surveyed these women with their warm, glistening skins, their half-open mouths and their sultry eyes whose gaze was directed into space; he was struck by the complete absence of thought in their faces, and by the scent of their voluptuous bodies. It seemed to the anchorite that he could hear the dark mutter of the blood in their veins, and in the distance he sensed the trampling of hooves, the sound of panting and the odour of Silenus's acrid sweat.

Hermius shook with fear, turned to the wall and covered his head with a bast mat.

Leaning over towards him, Pamphalon said quietly:

'You see how much time I have for thinking of lofty matters!' – and, at once exchanging his tone for one that was loud and cheerful, he replied to the women:

'I'll be with you this very moment, my serpents of the Nile.'

Pamphalon whistled to Acra, took the pole on which his bird of bright plumage sat inside its hoop and, snatching up his other entertainer's paraphernalia, snuffed out the lamps and went off.

Hermius was left alone in the empty dwelling.

Hermius did not quickly find oblivion in sleep. For a long time he meditated on how he was to match his conception of why he had come here with what he had actually found. It was, of course, easy to see at once that the entertainer was a good-hearted fellow, but all the same he *was* rather frivolous: he increased the sum of pleasure by clapping his hands, kicking his legs in the air and twisting his head, and he was unwilling to renounce these devilish amusements. Would he indeed be capable of such a thing, so deeply was he immersed in this debauched existence? Consider, for example, his present whereabouts, after he had gone off with these shameless women who had left behind them in the air the mutter of their blood and the odour of Silenus's acrid sweat.

If such were the emissaries, what must she be like whom they served in her house of depravity? . . .

The anchorite trembled.

Why, after thirty years of standing in the wilderness, had he been required to come down from his rock and walk for days and days to the point of terrible exhaustion merely in order to come to Damascus and see . . . the same loathsome spectacle of sin he had left behind in Byzantium? No, it could assuredly not have been an angel of God who had sent him here – it must have been some tempter-demon! There was no point in giving further thought to the matter – he must get up forthwith, and leave.

It was hard for the elder to get up – his legs were tired, the way was long, the desert was hot and filled with terrors; but he did not spare his body . . . he rose and wandered through the streets and squares of Damascus in the dark. He ran past it all:

the singing, the drunken chime of goblets from the houses, the ardent sighs of the nymphs, and Silenus himself – all of it rose against him like a tidal wave; but his legs seemed endowed with an untold strength and vigour. He ran and ran, at last caught sight of his rock, found himself clutching at its flinty sides, and was about to crawl into his hidey-hole when someone's horribly powerful arm yanked him downwards by the legs and placed him fairly and squarely on the ground, and an invisible voice boomed at him:

'Stay with Pamphalon, ask him to tell you how he completed the work of his salvation.'

And together with these words Hermius received such a hefty gust of air in his face that he almost choked; he saw that it was daylight, and that he was back in Pamphalon's dwelling once more – there was the entertainer himself lying asleep on the bare floor, and his dog and his bird of bright plumage were dozing too . . .

By the head of Hermius's bed stood two clay vessels, one containing water, and the other milk; on fresh green leaves lay soft goat's cheese and luscious fruits.

None of these things had been here the night before . . .

The anchorite reflected that this must mean he had slept soundly; when his weary host had returned home he had not lain down to sleep straight away, but had first attended to the needs of his guest.

The entertainer had put out for his guest all the things he had obtained somewhere, so that in the morning the guest might refresh himself upon rising . . .

There had been neither cheese nor fruit in Pamphalon's house – he had evidently been given all these things at the place where he had performed his antics, entertaining the revellers at the house of the *hetaera*.

He had received a gift from the *hetaera* and had brought it home for the pilgrim.

'My host is a very strange man,' Hermius thought; getting up from the bed, he went over to Pamphalon, looked into his face and studied it. The evening before he had seen Pamphalon by lamplight, ready to go out entertaining, with his head

swathed in a turban and his face painted, but now the entertainer was asleep; he had washed the greasepaint from his
features, and his face was calm and beautiful. It seemed to Hermius that this was not a human being at all, but an angel.

'Well I never!' thought Hermius. 'Perhaps I'm not mistaken
after all, perhaps I haven't been tempted, and this really is the
same Pamphalon who is more perfect than I am and from
whom I must learn something. Lord! How am I to find out
what it is? How am I to resolve this doubt?'

And the old man began to weep, got down on his knees
before the entertainer and, embracing him around the neck,
began to call his name through his tears.

Pamphalon woke up and asked:

'What do you want of me, my father?'

But seeing that the elder was weeping, Pamphalon gave a
start, quickly got up and began to speak.

'Why do I see tears on your aged countenance? Has someone offended you?'

But Hermius replied to him:

'No one has offended me; no one, that is, except you. I came
from my desert in order to learn from you things that would be
advantageous to me, but you won't tell me how it is that you
have managed to please God; please don't conceal it from me,
don't torment me: I can see that you live in frivolous surroundings, but it has been revealed to me that you are beloved of
God.'

Pamphalon thought for a moment or two, and then said:

'Believe me, old man: there is nothing in my life that could
be made the object of praise. On the contrary, everything in it
is bad.'

'But it may be that you yourself aren't aware of it.'

'No, how could that be? I'm aware that I live – as you've
seen – a frivolous life, and what's more I have such a wretched,
feeble heart that it won't even allow me to take up a better trade.'

'Well, tell me about that, then. What harm has your heart
done you, and why will it not allow you to take up a better
trade? How was it that you felt you were good, when you had
done evil?'

'Aha! Very well,' Pamphalon replied. 'If you really want me to. I'll tell you about that incident – but I don't think you'd feel like coming back to my home again after I've told you the story. We had better go out of town, into the fields; there in the wide open spaces I shall tell you about the event which completely robbed me of all hopes of salvation.'

'Let's be off, for God's sake, as soon as possible,' Hermius replied, covering himself with his rags.

Together they left the city, and sat down on the edge of its wild, precipitous moat. Acra lay at their feet, and Pamphalon began to tell his story.

'Not for anything in the world would I tell you what you ask me to relate,' Pamphalon began. 'But since you insist on regarding me as a good man, and since that makes me feel ashamed, because I'm not worthy to be considered such, but merit only contempt – I shall tell you. I am a great sinner and drunkard, but – what is worse – I am a trickster, and not a simple trickster: I tricked God with regard to the vow I took before him at the very moment I was granted the opportunity of fulfilling it. Listen to me, please; and judge me sternly. In your judgement I wish to receive the healing wound I have deserved in punishment from you.

'You have seen the impurity of my entertainer's life and so you will be able to understand everything that I am about to tell you. I live surrounded by filth and depravity. I was telling you the truth when I said that I'm not qualified to judge about divine matters, and because of the kind of life I lead they seldom enter my thoughts, but you are perceptive – there have been times when I have thought about my soul. You spend the night spinning round in front of carousers to amuse them, but when you return home towards dawn, you think: is it really worth living like this? You sin in order to earn your bread, and you eat your bread in order to be able to sin. It's all a kind of circle. But you know, Father, man is a sly creature and in every situation he seeks fig leaves with which to conceal his nakedness. That's what I'm like, too, and on several occasions I've thought to myself: "I have become mired in sin out of necessity, and what I earn I can hardly live on; now if I were suddenly to receive the kind of windfall that would make it possible for me to buy just a very small plot of land and work it, then I would immediately give up my entertaining and live like other respectable people." Yet I couldn't attain to this, and it wasn't because no money ever came my way – no, I had money, but it always seemed to happen that no sooner had I saved up what I needed than I would instantly spend it; someone would be in trouble, I would feel sorry for him, and would give him all my money. If at any one time a large sum had come into my hands I would probably have abandoned my entertaining and taken up a proper trade, even though I'm all thumbs. Why did God make me this way? But if one day in his generosity he helps me – then I shall take myself in hand and begin to live well, like other decent folk who are revered by monks and clerics and who all expect to see the Kingdom of God.

'And what do you suppose? It was as if fate had been listening to my words: I suddenly had the kind of stroke of fortune I had not dared to hope for. Listen to me carefully, and be my stern judge.

'This is what happened to me on one occasion in my life.

'I was once summoned to entertain the guests at the house of one of the *hetaerae* here in Damascus, a woman named Azella. She is no longer young, but her beauty is long-lasting, and she is more beautiful, voluptuous and intelligent than any of the other women in Damascus. There were a great many guests, and they were all either foreigners from Rome or boastful magnates from Corinth. They were all getting drunk on wine, and they kept making me sing and perform for them. Some of them wanted me to make them laugh, and I served them all as they desired. But when I grew tired they didn't want to know, and they laughed at me insultingly, pushed me and forced me to drink wine which they had doctored with an unpleasant additive; they poured cold water over me and tormented my poor Acra, pulling her by the haunches and spitting into her muzzle – when she growled they beat her and even threatened to kill her. I put up with all this merely in order to earn some of their money, because, I will confess to you, I wanted to help a crippled soldier get back to his home country. But Azella, the clever *hetaera*, observing how I was being insulted, turned everything in my favour: she opened her tunic and made all the guests throw her some money for me; the drunken guests threw her a lot, especially one, a haughty and obese Corinthian named Or, who had a bloated belly and no neck. Or said in a loud voice:

' "Azella, show me how much gold the others have thrown into your tunic."

'She showed him.

'Or looked, and squinting at the Romans with a haughty smile, added:

' "Listen to what I have to say, Azella: tell all these guests of yours to go away, and take from my servant here ten times the amount they have given for your entertainer."

'Azella said to her guests:

' "Wise men: it is not often that fortune descends among mortals, but to Pamphalon it has never before descended – not once in his life. Make way for it now, and yourselves depart in peace and go to sleep."

'Reluctantly the guests departed. Azella ushered me out last and handed me so much money that I was unable to count it all. In the morning, when I did manage to count it, I found that it added up to two hundred and thirty *litrae* of gold. I was delighted, and at the same time scared.

' "After this," I thought, "I really can't go on being an entertainer. It's as though God had heard my vow. I've never before managed to earn so much money in one go. It's time everyone stopped insulting me and making fun of me. I'm not a pauper now. I put up with grave insults in order to obtain this money, but from now on there's going to be no more of that. I'm through with entertaining! I shall find myself a small plot of land with a spring of pure water and a leafy palm tree. I shall buy that plot of land and begin to live decently, as do all men with whom neither clerics nor monks are ashamed to associate."

'And I gave myself up to various forms of day-dreaming. I began to indulge in self-admiration as I summoned up thoughts of the worthy life I would lead: I would get up early in the mornings – not, as I did at present, go to bed at dawn; I wouldn't whistle, but sing psalms instead; during the daytime I would sit by *my* spring, under *my* palm tree, think about *my* soul and keep an eye open for a passing traveller. And were such a traveller to appear, I would get up and go to meet him, invite him into my home, put him at his ease, give him food and drink, and then in the quietness hold a conversation with him about God beneath the starry sky. My life would change entirely for the better, and when in my old age I should lose my strength, I would no longer be an entertainer. In order to fortify my resolve even more, and so that infirmity should not creep up on me from the side, I fettered my hands with an unbreakable chain . . . I did the thing you described: I took a vow that I would become a completely different person from that moment on. But listen to what happened then, and what it was that shook the resolution of my oath and promise.'

'So as not to spend any of my earnings, I did not send my impoverished soldier home, but instead buried all my money under the floor below the head of my bed, and in the morning kept my rush curtain lowered. I pretended to be ill, as I had no intention of going out carousing with the revellers. To anyone who came to summon me, I replied that I was ill and was going out of town into the mountains in order to breathe fresh air and look for medicinal herbs with which to cure myself. Then, on the sly, I went to see a procurer, a Jew named Capiton who knows all about what is for sale anywhere, and asked him to find me a good plot of land with water and the shade of a palm tree. Capiton the procurer satisfied my wish at once.

' "I can think of the very spot for you," he said.

'And he described to me a piece of land that was for sale; the description was so marvellous that I scarcely dared to hope. There was a spring and a palm tree, and even a shrub of balsam which shed its fragrance for more than a whole mile around.

' "Go," I said, "and buy that piece of land for me as soon as possible."

'The Jew promised to arrange everything.

' "There," I thought. "Now my disorderly existence is well and truly coming to an end; now I shall say goodbye to all my shouting and whistling, I shall cast off my ridiculous costumes and put on the respectable *leviton*,[1] I shall cover my head with a head-dress and work on my plot of land during the day, and in the evenings I shall sit by my humble cottage and emulate the hospitality of Abraham."

'I will not, however, conceal from you that during all this time I felt uneasy. I kept thinking that none of what I had undertaken would ever come to anything.

'On my way back from Capiton's I was seized with terror: what if someone should have discovered that I had received money from the proud Corinthian, come to my house in my absence and stolen my money from the place under the bed where I had buried it? . . . I ran home at the double, in a state of anxiety such as I had never known before; when I reached there, I immediately got down on the floor, dug up my cache and counted the money: all the two hundred and thirty *litrae* of gold which Or, the proud Corinthian, had given Azella for me, were safe, and I picked them up again and reburied them; when I had finished, I lay down on the spot, guarding them like a dog.

'Do you know who I was afraid of? I wasn't merely afraid of those thieves who go around pilfering – I was also afraid of the thief who lived eternally with me in my heart. I didn't want to know about anyone else's misfortune, in case it deprived me of the steadfastness that is necessary to a man who desires to amend his way of life, and who pays no attention to what happens to others. I was not to blame for their misfortunes.

'And since my visit to Capiton and my journey back again had made me pretty tired, I was overcome by sleep; but my sleep, too, was filled with anxiety: I dreamed that I had long ago bought the plot of land Capiton had told me about, that I was living in a light and spacious house, with the spring of fresh water bubbling not far away from me, the balsam shrub exuding its scent for me, and the luxuriant palm tree casting its shade on me; but then I dreamed that something kept spoiling this beauty: in the spring I saw a vast number of leeches, enormous toads were hopping around the palm tree, and a viper was coiling itself at the foot of the balsam shrub. When I caught sight of the viper, I was so frightened that I actually woke up, and at once thought: is my money safe? It was – I was lying on top of it, and no one could have taken it from me without a struggle. It then suddenly occurred to me as being probable that it was no longer a secret in Damascus that Or had given me a fortune at the house of Azella. Or, the proud Corinthian, had not showered me with money at the feast of a *hetaera* in order for it to remain a secret. He had naturally only done it so that everyone should envy him his wealth and put into circulation a piece of gossip which would be flattering to his pride. Now people would discover that I had money; they would come to my house at night and rob me and beat me, and if I were to offer any resistance they would kill me.

'Now since my rush curtain was lowered, the room had become intolerably stuffy, and I went to raise it. As I did so, I saw two young boys walking along the street carrying baskets full of bread; before them went a donkey which was loaded with more, similar baskets. The boys were driving the donkey along and talking to each other ... about me!

' "Look," one of them was saying. "Our Pamphalon hasn't raised his curtain today."

' "Why should he?" the other replied. "He doesn't need to give himself airs any longer: he's a rich man – he can sleep as much as he wants to. I mean, you must have heard the things the people who came to our bakery for bread today were saying about him."

' "Yes, yes, I know. I was so keen to eavesdrop that the master gave me a nasty cuff on the ear. Some haughty fellow from Corinth who wanted to show up our Damascus magnates in a poor light threw Pamphalon ten thousand *litrae* of gold at the house of Azella the *hetaera*. Now he's buying a house, and orchards and female slaves, and he's going to spend his time lying beside a fountain."

' "It wasn't ten thousand *litrae* of gold, it was twenty thousand," said the other boy, correcting him. "And what's more, the money was in a casket that had been sprinkled with pearls. He'll probably buy a piece of land that has a church on it, surround himself with some good-looking boys with fans, gather various scholars together and make them discuss the Holy Spirit in various languages."

'From the conversation of these boys, who were delivering bread from a bakery, I discovered that my sudden acquisition of wealth was already known to the whole of Damascus, and that, moreover, the sum which had fallen into my hands as a result of the haughty Or's caprice had been more than ten times exaggerated.

'But who could know that the sum I had been given by the haughty Or was less than three hundred *litrae* of gold – far less than the twenty thousand I was supposed to have received? Of course, only I myself could know that, because even Or had doubtless not counted what he had given me.

'But even this was of little importance compared to the manner in which the passing boys had ended their conversation. One of them had gone on to say something which suggested that everyone was very interested in where I had hidden such a large sum as twenty thousand *litrae* of gold. It was a matter which would be of especial interest to the flute-player Ammun, a desperate ruffian who had served as a soldier in two armies that were at war with each other, had then become a bandit and had murdered pilgrims, had subsequently become a monk in the Nitrian, and had finally appeared among us here in Damascus with a flute and a negress whore attired in the sheepskin coat of a Nitrian brother. He had probably murdered the brother, and had sold the whore naked to a house of pleasure; but for a long time he used the sheepskin coat to wipe the dust and dirt from the feet of the revellers who in the evenings approached the dwellings of the *hetaerae*. He also frequently played his flute at my performances, but on most occasions the *hetaerae* would drive him away. For this Ammun himself was to blame, as he began to shamelessly rouge his cheeks and train his eyebrows as if he were a member of the opposite sex. Because of this the women began to regard him with loathing, as their rival. Ammun had a terrible hatred of me. I knew that he had even tried several times to get men who were drunk to attack me by night and do me harm.

'This desire to inflict harm on me must now, of course, have intensified, and his old brigand's habits would help him to put his evil intentions into execution. He had gold, and he took men into bondage and made them do his bidding.'

'The thought of the danger Ammun presented to me flashed into my brain like lightning, and took such a hold of me that it even prevented me from drawing the bast curtain over my window and calling back the boys who had passed me, and from whom I had wanted to buy myself some fresh loaves.

'In the days when I had capered and spun around for what people would throw me, I had always had enough to eat and had even fortified myself not infrequently by drinking my fill of wine; now that I had gold, however, I would pass the entire day without a bite of food or a sip of wine, beset, what is more, by a state of anxiety that was growing in me with the speed at which our dusk passes into dark night.

'I had no thought of food: I was afraid for my fortune and my life. Ammun the flute-player and his bondsmen stood perpetually before the frightened eyes of my imagination. I fancied that the situation must be thus: during the daytime Ammun would have gone to see all those who were like him and who would agree to take part in the evil deed, and now, under the cover of the approaching darkness, they would all be gathering in some cave or catacomb; when darkness finally fell, they would come here in order to take my twenty thousand *litrae* of gold from me. But when they found I had less gold than they thought I had, they would not believe that Or the Corinthian had given me such a meagre sum, and would put me to the stake and torture me.

'Then suddenly to my horror I remembered that I had never taken proper care to see that the locks on my poor dwelling were secure ... During my absences I had left it merely looking as though it were locked up, and at night had often slept without even sliding the bolts into place on my doors and windows.

'Now this would not do, and since nightfall was now very close, I would have to hurry to inspect everything and arrange things as best I could so that it would not be so easy to break into my home.

'Just as I was deliberating how I could bar my door from the inside, and had begun to take the necessary steps to do so, my rush curtain was thrown open right before my very eyes, and a muffled-up person entered my room less by his own effort than as if some alien hand had flung him. He fell upon me, embraced me round the neck and then froze, groaning in a voice of despair:

' "Save me, Pamphalon!" '

'Still taken up with the thoughts that filled my head at that moment, and fearing Ammun, I at first suspected that this was the beginning of his attack, conducted with the kind of subterfuge at which his brigand's mind was very skilled.

'I was already waiting for the pain I would be bound to feel when the sharp knife in the hand of the visitor who had fallen upon me plunged into my breast; in my desire to preserve my life, I pushed the stranger away from me with such force that he went flying against the wall and, stumbling on a log, collapsed in a corner. At once surmising that it would be easier for me to deal with one person – who, moreover, did not appear to be very strong – than with the several who might be following him, I lost no time in closing the door and securing it with a heavy bolt; then I took a pole-axe in my hands, and began to listen. I firmly resolved to bring the pole-axe down on anyone who might appear in my dwelling, and at the same time kept a watchful eye on the newcomer whom I had flung into the corner.

'I began to find it strange that he continued to lie motionless in the corner where he had fallen, and where he occupied no more space than a child, displaying not the slightest shiftiness towards me but, on the contrary, seeming to be entirely at one with me. He was alertly following my every movement and, breathing quickly, kept whispering:

' "Lock up your house! ... Hurry and lock up! ... Hurry and lock up your house, Pamphalon!"

'This surprised me, and I said sternly:

' "Very well, I will lock up, but what do you want of me?"

' "Hurry and give me your hand, let me have water to drink and sit me down by your lamp. Then I will tell you what I want."

' "Very well," I replied. "Whatever your intentions may have been, here is my hand, and here is a cup of water and a place by my lamp."

'So saying, I stretched out my hand to the guest, and a light, childlike body took wing before me.

' "You're not a man, you're a woman!" I shouted.

'And my guest, who up until now had spoken in a whisper, replied to me in a female voice:

' "Yes, Pamphalon, I'm a woman." And with that she threw open the long, dark cloak in which she was wrapped, and I saw a young, beautiful woman whose face was familiar to me. Together with its beauty, it expressed a terrible grief. The woman's head was covered by a fine braiding of hair, and her body gave off a strong odour of amber, but she was not immodest, though she spoke dreadful things.

' "Look, am I not pretty?" she asked, shielding herself from the lamp with one hand.

' "Yes," I replied. "You're unquestionably beautiful, and you'd do best not to waste your time on me. What do you want?"

'She said:

' "I see you haven't recognized me. I'm Magna, the daughter of Ptolemy and Albina. Buy me, Pamphalon, buy Ptolemy's daughter – you've a lot of money now, and Magna needs gold to save her husband and deliver her children from captivity."

'And, the tears watering her cheeks, Magna began hastily to undo the belt of her tunic.'

16

'Old man! I had seen a great many people before in my life, but never had I had a guest such as this one . . . She was attempting to sell herself, she was suffering, and this combination seemed to squeeze at my heart.

'The name Magna belonged to the most beautiful, distinguished and unhappy woman in Damascus. I had known her in her childhood, but had not seen her since the time that she had left us in the company of Rufinus the Byzantine, whom she had married at the behest of her father, and of her mother, the proud Albina.

' "Stop!" I cried. "I know you, you are indeed the virtuous Magna, the daughter of Ptolemy, in whose orchards and with whose permission on several occasions I entertained you with my performances when you were a child; from your tender hands I received coins and wheaten bread, raisins and pomegranates! Tell me at once: what has happened to you? Where is your husband, the splendid Byzantine magnate Rufinus, whom you loved so greatly? Have the waves swallowed him up, or has his young life been cut short by the sword of the barbarian Scythian who has crossed the Black Sea? Where is your family, where are your children?"

'Magna, lowering her gaze, was silent.

' "At least tell me when you appeared in Damascus and why you're not with your kinsfolk here or with your former rich friends – the clever Photina, the learned Taora or the wise maiden Sylvia? Why have your swift feet brought you to the poor dwelling of an inglorious entertainer whom you mocked so cruelly just now when you jokingly made me such an improbable suggestion!"

'But Magna sadly shook her head and replied:

'"Oh, Pamphalon, you don't know all the terrible misfortunes that have befallen me! I wasn't mocking you: I've come to sell myself in earnest. My husband and children! . . . My husband and my children are all in captivity. My grief is terrible!"

'"Well, tell me then at once the reason for your grief, and if I can do anything to help you, I will do it instantly, with joy."

'"Very well, I will tell you everything," Magna replied.

'And at that very moment, anchorite, I was assailed by the temptation which caused me to forget my vow, my oath and eternal life itself.'

17

'I had known Magna since the early days of her girlhood. I had never been in her father's house, but only in its orchard as an entertainer, when I had been summoned there in order to amuse the child. They received few visitors, as the magnificent Ptolemy was a proud man and did not associate with people of easy morals. In his house there were none of the sort of gatherings which required the presence of an entertainer; the people who assembled there were learned theologians who talked solemnly about various lofty subjects and about the Holy Spirit. Ptolemy's wife, Albina, the mother of the beautiful Magna, was a fitting match for her husband. The worldly women of Damascus viewed Albina with distaste, but they all acknowledged her purity. Albina's fidelity could stand as a lesson for all. The excellent Magna took after her mother, whose attractive features she had inherited; but her youthfulness inclined her to be soft-hearted. The magnificent orchard of Ptolemy, her father, adjoined a large ravine, on the other side of which a wide field began. I often crossed this field in order to avoid having to go the long way round to the suburban house of the *hetaera* Azella. I would always be carrying my entertainer's bundle and would be walking in the company of this same dog that you see here. Acra was young in those days and didn't know all the things that an entertainer's dog is supposed to know.

'In my progress across the field I would stop halfway, directly opposite Ptolemy's orchards, in order to take a rest, eat my barley cake and train my Acra. I usually sat down on the brow of the ravine, to eat and make Acra repeat out there in the wide-open spaces the lessons I had given her at home, in my narrow dwelling. Once, while I was engaged in these pursuits, I caught sight of the beautiful face of the adolescent Magna. She had concealed herself behind the branches of some trees, and from the verdure was watching with curiosity the lively tricks my Acra was performing. I observed this and, without letting Magna know that I had seen her, conceived a desire to provide her with more and better entertainment than Acra could afford her at that stage of her training. In order to impel the dog to greater agility, I gave it a few lashes of my belt; but at the very moment the dog yelped, I noticed the verdure that concealed Magna stir and move, and the girl's beautiful face disappeared . . .

'This made me so annoyed that I dealt Acra another couple of blows, and when she started to raise a piteous howl, I heard a voice say from the other side of the orchard fence:

' "Cruel man! Why are you tormenting that poor animal? Why are you compelling a dog to do things that are not in its nature?"

'I turned round and saw Magna emerging from her arboreal hiding-place; she was visible from chest-height above the leaf-grown fence, and as she addressed me her face blazed with anger.

' "Don't be too hard on me, young mistress," I replied. "I'm not a cruel man, and the training of this dog is a part of my trade, which provides us both with a living."

' "Your trade is a contemptible one, which is needed only by contemptible idlers," Magna retorted.

"Oh, mistress!" I said. "Every man lives by doing what he can to earn bread for himself, and it is good if he does not live at the expense of others or cause unhappiness to his fellow human beings."

' "That doesn't apply to you," Magna replied. "You corrupt your fellow human beings." In her eyes I could perceive the same severity that always distinguished the gaze of her mother.

' "No, young mistress," I said. "You judge me so severely and talk in that fashion because you have little experience. I'm just a simple chap – I could never corrupt people of higher rank."

'And I turned on my heel and was about to go away when she stopped me by calling my name, and said:

' "It doesn't become you to make judgements concerning people of higher rank. You'd do better to . . . here, catch my purse: I'm giving it to you so you can let your poor dog have enough food."

'So saying, she threw me her silk purse; it failed to reach my side and, as I stretched over in order to pick it up, I lost my grip and fell to the bottom of the ravine.

'As a result of this fall I sustained the most terrible injuries.'

18

'My consolation in the disaster which had befallen me was that on each of the ten days I spent in the little cave at the foot of the ravine the virtuous Magna came down to see me. So much sumptuous food did she bring me that there was more than enough for both myself and Acra; she herself soaked cloths in the spring with her maidenly hands, and put them against my injured shoulder, trying thus to lessen the intolerable burning caused by the bruise. As she did so, we had conversations that delighted me, and I took pleasure in both the purity of her heart and in the clear light of her intelligence. The only thing I found annoying in her was her unwillingness to make allowances for anyone else's weakness and her excessive tendency to see everything in terms of herself.

' "Why doesn't everyone live as my mother and my friends Taora, Photina and Sylvia do?" she would say. "Their lives are as pure as crystal."

'And I saw that she deeply revered them and wished to emulate them in every respect. In spite of her youth, she wanted to reform me and make me renounce my way of life, and when I refused to do this she grew angry.

'Then I told her how things really were.

' "Are you really unaware," I said, "that one vessel is required for honour, but another for abuse? You live for honour, but I live for abuse, and, like the clay, I don't argue with the potter who has fashioned me. Life has compelled me to be an entertainer, and I shall go my way like a horse with a bridle."

'Magna was unable to comprehend my simple words and put it all down to habit.

' "There is a wise saying," she replied, "that habit arrives like a wanderer, remains like a guest and then itself becomes the master. The tar which has been in a clean barrel makes it unfit to contain anything but more tar."

'It wasn't hard for me to detect that she was growing impatient, and that in her eyes there was now little to distinguish me from a barrel of tar, and I fell silent and regretted that I could not get out of the ravine more quickly. I began to find her self-conceit annoying, and she herself began to concern herself with the question of how I was to be brought out of the ravine and returned to my dwelling.

'To do this would not be easy, as I could not walk unaided, and the girl was not strong enough to offer me any assistance. At home she did not dare to tell her proud parents that she was talking to a man of my contemptible profession.

'And just as one action often leads a person to take another, so it was in this instance with the virtuous Magna. In order to help me, the contemptible entertainer, who because of his unworthiness was undeserving of her attention, she found herself compelled to confide in a certain youth by the name of Magistrian.

'Magistrian was a young artist who decorated the interior walls of luxurious houses with beautiful murals. One day he took his brushes to the house of the same *hetaera* Azella whom I have already told you about; she wanted him to paint a scene depicting a feast of nymphs and satyrs on the walls of the new pavilion in her orchard, and as he was crossing the field near the spot where I lay in the ravine, my Acra recognized him and began to set up a piteous howling.

'Magistrian halted but, thinking it was probably a corpse that lay at the bottom of the ravine, he began to continue quickly on his way. He would doubtless have left the scene had it not been for Magna who, observing him, managed to stop him.

'Magna, carried away by her feelings of compassion for me, threw apart the dense green foliage and said:

' "Passer-by! Please don't go away without helping a fellow human being in distress. At the foot of the ravine here lies a man who has fallen and hurt himself. I myself am unable to get him out of there, but you are a strong man, and can afford him the assistance he needs."

'Magistrian immediately went down into the ravine, examined me, and then ran off into the town for stretcher-bearers to carry me back to my dwelling.

'All this he did with dispatch and, when he was left alone with me, he began to ask me how it had happened that I had fallen into the ravine and hurt myself, and how had I been able to survive for two weeks without food?

'And since Magistrian and I had long known each other and been friends, I made no attempt to fob him off with any concocted story, but told him the truth, as it had happened.

'And hardly had I reached the point of telling him how Magna had fed me and how she had soaked cloths in the water with her own hands and had placed them against my injured shoulder, when young Magistrian's face lit up and he exclaimed in delight:

' "Oh, Pamphalon! How lucky you are, and how I envy you your lot! I would willingly let you break my arms and legs, if only I could see that nymph, the generous Magna."

'I at once realized that the heart of the artist had been stricken by the powerful emotion that is called love, and I hastened to bring him to reason.

' "You are poor of spirit," I said. "Ptolemy's daughter is beautiful, there can be no arguing about that, but a man's health is what matters to him most, and in any case Ptolemy is so stern, and Magna's mother, Albina, is so haughty, that if your soul feels the flame of this girl's charms, nothing good can come of it for you."

'Magistrian turned pale, and replied:

' "What needs to come of it? Do you really think it isn't enough for me that she inspires me?"

'And he continued to be inspired by her.'

19

'When I had recovered, and arrived for my first evening at Azella's house, Magistrian led me into the *hetaera*'s pavilion and showed me the murals he had painted on its walls. The pavilion was a large and spacious building, and it was divided into the "hours" of which each day of a person's life is composed. Each division had been dedicated to the joys of life of the hour it represented. The entire building was dedicated to Saturn, a portrait of whom gleamed beneath the cupola. Near the main rotunda there were two wings in honour of the Horae, the daughters of Jupiter and Themis, and these divisions had subdivisions: here were chambers dedicated to Auge, from which the dawn was visible, Anatole, from which the sunrise could be seen, Musaea, where one could occupy oneself with study, Nymphaea, where baths were taken, Spondaea, where one could sponge oneself down, Aphrodite, where enjoyments were partaken of, and Eileithyia, where prayers were offered . . . And it was here, in a remote corner which had been set aside for solitary reveries, that the artist had with a light brush depicted a pious dream . . . The mural showed a feast, attended by well-dressed and voluptuous women, each of whom I could identify by name. They were all Damascan *hetaerae*. They were reclining with their guests amidst flowers, at a sumptuous table, and a young man lay asleep with his head in one of the flower-baskets. His face could not be seen, but I could tell from his toga that this was the artist, Magistrian. Above him was a scene of persecution: the lions in a circus were attacking a young girl . . . but she was standing resolutely, whispering prayers. She was Magna.

'I patted Magistrian on the shoulder and said:

' "Well done! ... You've painted a very good likeness of her – but why do you assume that she wouldn't be afraid of wild animals? I know her family: Ptolemy and Albina are renowned for their nobility and pride, but fate has been merciful to them, after all, and their daughters, too, have not so far had to face any ordeals."

' "So what?"

' "Well, the beautiful Magna doesn't know anything of life's misfortunes, and so I don't understand why you have discerned in her the characteristic of fearlessness and resoluteness in the face of a wild beast. If it's meant to be an allegory, life is always far more terrible than any wild beast and is capable of intimidating each and every one of us."

' "All except Magna!"

' "Alas, I would say: *even* Magna!"

'I spoke in this fashion so that he should not become too captivated by Magna; but he interrupted me, whispering:

' "I was asked to design the screens for her bedroom, and while I was drawing with my stick of charcoal, I talked with her ... She inquired about you ..."

'The artist paused.

' "She finds it a pity that you occupy yourself with a trade such as entertaining. I said to her: 'Mistress! Not every man is so fortunate as to be able to lead his life in the fashion he chooses. Fate is inexorable: it can compel a mortal to drink from the muddiest spring, at the bottom of which there are leeches and vipers.' At that she gave me a scornful smile."

' "A smile?" I asked. "In that I recognize the daughter of Ptolemy and the proud Albina. You know, I ... I should like it better if she had made no response at all, or – given a quiet sigh of compassion."

' "Yes," said Magistrian. "But she also said: 'It is better to die than to live in dishonour', and I believe that she is capable of that."

' "You are hasty with your judgements," I replied. "It may be better to die than to live in dishonour, no one is arguing with that; but could it be said by a mother who has children?"

' "Why not? Remember what the mother of the Maccabees did!"

' "Yes. The Maccabees were killed. But if their mother had been threatened with having her children made into entertainers such as myself, and say she had been Magna – God knows which she would have preferred: shame or death in exchange for their deliverance?"

' "Why do you say that?" Magistrian exclaimed.'

20

'Rufinus the Byzantine was of noble birth and very elegant in appearance; he was, however, the most dreadful hypocrite, and was such a skilful dissembler that even in Byzantium it was considered he went too far. The vain Corinthian Or and all the others who squandered their money and their energies at the feasts of Azella the *hetaera* were, in my opinion, better men than Rufinus. He had arrived in Damascus with an open letter of introduction, and had been received by Ptolemy in royal fashion. Rufinus, like the dissembler he was, would spend the entire daytime at home, asleep, but told everyone he was reading books on theology; in the evenings he would go out of town, ostensibly for edifying consultations with an aged anchorite who at that time lived near Damascus, standing on a rock during the day and moaning in an open grave by night. Rufinus would go to him in order to pray, standing in his shadow at sunset; but from thence winged Aeolus would invariably lead him under the roof of Azella, where he always appeared with a facial disguise, thanks to Magistrian's art. It was for this reason that we were well acquainted with him, since, being my friend, Magistrian made no secret to me of the fact that he was the author of Rufinus's disguise, and on several occasions we had a good laugh together on the subject of this Byzantine duplicity. Azella also knew about it, since when they had seen their clients off at the end of the night, they would often chat with us, and they took a liking to us, finding that we simple folk possessed both heart and intelligence, qualities they did not always encounter in their rich and noble clients.

'It should be said that Azella was in love with my artist; it was a hopeless love, as Magistrian only had thoughts for Magna, whose pure image he carried inseparably with him. The sensitive Azella had guessed this secret, and it made her behaviour with him all the more tender and graceful. On those occasions when Magistrian and I stayed in Azella's house, she would often, at sunrise, as she was seeing off her clients, tell us what she thought of each of them, and she never concealed from us her especial distaste for Rufinus, calling him an infamous dissembler, capable of deceiving anyone and of committing the very basest acts. But she understood the others, too. Once, after Or the Corinthian had been senselessly throwing his money away, she said to us:

' "He's a poor peacock . . . Everyone has a tweak at his feathers, and when he comes here with Rufinus the Byzantine, you might do worse than give Rufinus's cloak a shake."

'This meant that Rufinus could be a thief . . . Azella was never mistaken, and both Magistrian and I knew it.

'But Ptolemy and Albina had their own opinion of the Byzantine, their good-hearted daughter was obedient to her parents' wishes, and her destiny was sealed. Magna became the wife of Rufinus, who took her, together with a rich dowry provided by Ptolemy, and carried her off to Byzantium.'

21

'Ptolemy and Albina were soon punished by fate. The disembling Rufinus turned out not to have much money, and to be less famous than he had given himself out to be in Damascus. Worst of all, however, he proved to be dishonest, and was so heavily in debt that Magna's rich dowry all went on settlements with the creditors who were pressing him. Magna soon found herself in poverty, and there were rumours that she was receiving cruel treatment at the hands of her husband. Rufinus made her ask for more silver and gold from her parents, and when she was unwilling to do this, he dealt roughly with her. Rufinus spent all the money that Magna's parents sent her in an ignominious fashion, forgetting all about the debts he had to pay and about the two children Magna had borne him. Like many other Byzantine nobles, he was having an affair with another woman in Byzantium, and in order to keep her happy robbed and humiliated his wife.

'The proud Ptolemy was so grieved by this that he became subject to frequent illnesses, and soon died, leaving his widow only the most meagre of incomes. Albina gave it all to her daughter, hoping to save her, and spent all her own money on gifts to the retainer of the exarch Valentus, who was himself a greedy voluptuary and was looking for a chance to possess the lovely Magna. Rufinus had apparently given his consent to this. It was even said that he had forced his wife to comply with this suit of Valentus's, adjuring her to agree to it for the family's sake, as Valentus was threatening to abandon Rufinus and all his dependants to the mercies of his creditors.

'Albina was unable to cope with this experience and soon passed away into eternity, leaving Magna and her children in the most wretched poverty. Yet still Magna did not yield to the depraved pursuit of Valentus, who thereupon, in a fit of rage, carried out his threat.

'Rufinus's creditors had him sent to gaol, and took poor Magna and her children into slavery. In order to make this experience of slavery even more bitter, the creditors separated Magna from her children; they sent the infants away to a village to be looked after by a eunuch, and gave Magna into the charge of a brothel-keeper, who in exchange for her pledged himself to pay them three *litrae* of gold a day.

'In vain did poor Magna cry and wail and seek protection. She was told: "There is one law above us all. Our law protects the wealthy. They are the strongest in the land. If our former ruler Hermius were still in office there might have been a chance that he, being a just and merciful man, would have intervened and not allowed this to happen; but he has gone strange in the head: he has renounced the world in order to devote his entire attention to his soul. Cruel old man! May heaven pardon him his anchorite's vanity."

As he spoke these words, the entertainer noticed that the anchorite who was sitting beside him trembled and clutched him by the hand. Pamphalon asked him:

'What is it, are you sorry for them?'

'Yes, I'm sorry . . . sorry . . . Both for them and for myself,' Hermius replied. 'Continue your story.'

And Pamphalon went on.

'In order to avoid unpleasant gossip in the capital and be more confident of obtaining his money, the brothel-keeper did not allow Magna to remain in Byzantium, but sent her to Damascus, where everyone knew her as a virtuous and inaccessible woman and where men would therefore doubtless now be eager to possess her.

'Magna, being a slave, was kept under careful observation, and all the means of escape were removed from her. She was unable even to take her own life – but she had no thoughts of suicide, because she was a mother and was desperate to find her children and rescue them from the eunuch who held them in captivity.

'So she was brought to Damascus under guard and in secret, and on the following day – the very same day on which I shut myself up in my house and lay in bed on top of my gold – it became known that Magna's keeper was charging five *litrae* of gold a night to any man who wished to possess her.'

'The man who had undertaken to make money out of Magna naturally lost no time in seeing to it that his venture was as profitable as possible, and to this end he sent a female courier out to the houses of all the rich men in Damascus, who informed them of the exquisite goods he had to offer.

'The dissolute men went flocking to the brothel-keeper's house, and throughout the day it was only by means of her tears that Magna could protect herself. When evening came, however, the brothel-keeper threatened to have a word with the eunuch who had taken her children into custody and instruct him to castrate them, and she decided to comply . . . After that, her strength left her; she fell into a deep sleep and dreamed that someone came quietly to her side and said: "Rejoice, Magna! You have this day acquired the one thing all your life you have been lacking. You have stayed pure, but have taken pride in your virtue, like your mother; you have condemned fallen women without perceiving what it was that brought them to their fall. That was a grievous fault. But now, when you yourself are ready to fall and know what a horrible experience that is, now your pride, which was offensive to God, has been shattered, and now God will keep you pure."

'Just then, a timid client knocked at the door of the house where Magna was being held; concealing his face in the folds of his simple cloak, he quietly summoned the brothel-keeper, whispering:

"Oh, I'm a shy man, but I'm dying of desire. Take me to Magna at once – I'll give you ten *litrae* of gold."

'The brothel-keeper was pleased, but before he took the stranger to Magna, he said to him:

' "I feel bound to tell you, sir, that this woman is of noble birth, and keeping her in bondage is costing me a lot of money which I'm not getting back from her, since she has succeeded in moving to pity all the men I have taken in to her. I cannot be held to blame if you listen to what she says to you and her words soften your heart. I must have my gold, as I'm a poor man and paid a high price for her."

' "Don't worry about that," the stranger replied, still keeping his face hidden. "Here, take your ten *litrae* of gold. I'm not that sort of fellow: I know what women's tears signify."

'As the brothel-keeper took the ten *litrae* of gold he pulled a cord which overturned a brass cup containing a brass ball. The ball rolled along a canvas duct to the canopied partition where Magna was kept, and fell with a loud clang into a basin, also of brass, which stood by the head of her bed. After this, the brothel-keeper immediately led his client in to her.'

24

'The stranger entered the remote apartment, which reeked of spikenard and amber, and there by the light of a flower-shaped lamp he saw Magna lying asleep. She had not been woken by the sound of the ball falling into the basin, because just at that time she was having the dream in which she saw her high-minded fortitude vanishing into thin air and in which she was now saved because of her recognition of her own weakness.

'The brothel-keeper reproached Magna for not having heard the signal and, pointing to the stranger, said to her coarsely:

' "Don't pretend you didn't hear the ball! Here's someone to whom I've given up all authority over you until tomorrow. If you're sensible you'll do as he wants you to. And if I lose any more money because of your behaviour I'll take you to a place where your clients will be grim soldiers, and you won't get any mercy from them."

'So saying, the brothel-keeper picked up the brass ball and went out. The client shut the door behind him and, turning round, said to Magna quietly:

' "Don't be afraid, ill-fated Magna. I have come to rescue you." And he threw off his cloak.

'Magna recognized Magistrian, and burst into sobs.

' "There's no need for tears, lovely Magna. Now is not the time for weeping and despair. Be calm, and have faith that if Heaven has preserved you for this hour, your salvation must now be assured, if only you will agree to help me so that I can get you out of captivity and return you to your children and husband."

' "Agree?" Magna exclaimed. "Why, kind youth, how could I possibly fail to?"

' "Then hurry and do as I tell you. I shall now turn away so I can't see you – let us exchange costumes as quickly as possible."

'And so Magna put on Magistrian's cloak and tunic, and all the rest of his male apparel, and he said to her:

' "Be quick now, make yourself scarce! Hide your face in the folds of my cloak, just as I did when I came in, and walk boldly out of this house. Your despicable master will himself show you out through his accursed doorway."

'Magna followed his instructions and left the house without incident. No sooner was she outside, however, than she began to quake inwardly: where was she to run to, where was she to conceal herself, and what would happen to the poor youth when on the morrow their deception was uncovered? Magistrian would be put to the rack for infringing the rights of creditors; he would not, of course, have enough money to pay off the whole of the debt for the sake of which Magna had been given into bondage, and he would be thrown into gaol for life and be tortured, while she herself would still not be able to see her children, as she would not have the means to buy them out of captivity.

'It was then that this woman conceived the idea that was to deprive me forever of the chance to mend my ways and lead a respectable life.'

25

'When Magna revealed to me the disasters which had befallen her, and told me about the risk Magistrian was exposing himself to for her sake, an abyss seemed to open up before me. I knew that Magistrian could never from his own meagre resources have found the ten *litrae* of gold which he had paid for Magna and which still would not rescue her from her degrading situation, as they represented only a fraction of the price of her bondage, and yet left nothing over with which to buy the freedom of her children from the eunuch in Byzantium. But where could Magistrian have obtained these *litrae* of gold? He worked in Azella's house; there the *hetaera*, who was in love with him, always kept a chest full of her treasures . . . My soul was gripped by a sense of horror . . . I thought: what if his love for poor Magna had driven him mad and he had stolen the treasure-chest? From this day on the name of Magistrian would be without honour: *he was a thief!*

'Meanwhile, poor Magna, who was continuing to make the air resound with her sighs and moans, once more repeated the words with which she had begun when she had so unexpectedly entered my dwelling.

' "Pamphalon!" she wailed. "I have heard that you have become a wealthy man, that some proud Corinthian has given you incalculable riches. I have come to sell myself to you: take me as your slave, but give me money so that I may buy my children out of captivity and save Magistrian, who is going to perdition because of me."

'Anchorite! You have lived your life in the desert and so will perhaps not understand the sense of sorrow I experienced at hearing despair speak through the lips of this woman, whom I had known as a pure creature, proud of her virtue! You have risen above all human passions, and they have no power to shake you, but I have always been soft-hearted, and at the sight of such terrible calamities experienced by a fellow human being I ruined myself . . . and once again light-mindedly forgot about the salvation of my soul.

'I began to sob, and through my sobs, I said:

' "As God is merciful, unhappy Magna, desist! My heart will not bear this! I may be a simple man, an entertainer – it's true that I pass my life in the company of *hetaerae*, idlers and prodigals, that I'm a barrel of tar, but I won't buy what madness and sorrow have driven you to offer me."

'But Magna was suffering so dreadfully that she did not take in what I was saying.

' "You are refusing me!" she exclaimed in horror. "Oh, how wretched I am! Where am I to obtain the gold I need to prevent the mutilation of my children?" And she wrung her hands above her head and fell to the ground.

'This filled me with even greater horror . . . I trembled as I saw how misery had degraded her to the point where she sought to sell men her caresses as if this would bring her happiness.'

26

'I hastened to console her.

' "No!" I cried. "I'm not refusing you at all! I am your friend and I will prove it to you by helping you in your misery. Only never mention again the reason why you came here. Get rid of that braiding of your hair, which makes you look like a *hetaera*; wash from your shoulders with clean water that aroma of sweet-smelling nard, with which people who desire your disgrace have covered them, and then tell me: how much does your husband owe?"

'She sighed and said quietly:

' "Ten thousand *litrae* of gold."

'I saw that she had been deceived: the riches the extravagant Or had given me were a paltry amount compared with the sum required to pay her debt and redeem her children.

'Magna got up without saying anything, picked up the cloak which Magistrian had taken off, and once more began to hide her head in its folds.

'I guessed that she was about to leave me with some bad aim in view, and exclaimed:

' "Are you going, Mistress Magna?"

' "Yes, I'm going back where I came from."

' "You're going to try to set Magistrian free, aren't you?"

'She merely nodded silently to demonstrate that this was so.

' "Don't do it," I said. "It won't be any good. Magistrian is so noble-spirited and devoted to you that he won't come out of there, and by going back you'll merely make things more confused. All I have is two hundred and thirty *litrae* of gold . . . That's the amount I received from Or the Corinthian. If people think I have more than that, it's either as the result of a rumour, or because that braggart Or has been boasting. But you must look on these two hundred and thirty *litrae* of gold as your own. Don't raise any objections, Mistress Magna, don't raise a single word in objection! This gold is yours, but you will have to find a lot more in order to pay your husband's debt. I don't know where to get any more, but the night has only just begun . . . Magistrian will be safe until tomorrow. Your keeper firmly believes that the two of you are locked in each other's embrace. Stay here with me and put your mind at rest. My Acra won't let anyone near you in my absence, and I will go right now and tell of your misfortune to your highly placed friends Taora, Photina and Maid Sylvia, whose virtue is renowned in all Damascus . . . Their servants all know me and will, in exchange for gifts, allow me to visit their mistresses. They are rich and chaste, and they will be generous with their gold. You will be able to buy your children out of captivity."

'But Magna quickly interrupted me:

"Pamphalon, don't go troubling Taora, or Photina, or the maiden Sylvia – none of them will do anything to meet your request."

' "You are wrong," I retorted. "Taora, Sylvia and Photina are virtuous women, they are quick to apprehend all forms of depravity, and many are the *hetaerae* who have been expelled from Damascus on their say-so."

' "That doesn't mean anything," Magna replied. She revealed to me that before the calamity which had befallen her family had reached its present degree of misery, she had gone to ask for help from the highly placed ladies I had mentioned, but they had left all her pleas unanswered.

' "And since now," she added, "to all that has been added the disgrace into which I have fallen, any request I make of them will seem to them like an insult to their honour. I was once as they are, and I know that it is not from them that a fallen woman may expect deliverance."

' "Well, even so, wait here with me for what merciful Heaven may send us," I said and, putting out the lamp, locked up the entrance to my dwelling, in which Magna remained under the protection of Acra, and then dashed off along the dark alley-ways of Damascus as fast as my legs would carry me.'

27

'I did not heed Magna's warning and with the help of servants managed to obtain entry to the house of Taora, Sylvia and Photina ... It embarrasses me now to recall what I heard from their lips ... Magna was right in everything she had told me about those women. My words merely provoked them to fiery anger, and I was thrown out of their house for having dared to enter it with such a plea ... Two of them, Taora and Photina, ordered me to be thrown out with the mere mention that I deserved a good hiding; but the maid Sylvia ordered me to be flogged in her presence, and her servants beat me with a copper switch – I emerged from her chamber bleeding all over and my throat parched. Thus, tormented by thirst, I stumbled into Azella's kitchen, in order to ask for a little wine and water, so that I could continue my journey. I had no idea where I would go.

'No sooner had I appeared in the covered passage, however, than I was met by Azella's confidante, the blonde Ada. She was carrying a pitcher of some cooling drink as if it were specially intended for me, and I said to her:

' "Be merciful, fair Ada: refresh my lips – I am dying of thirst."

'She smiled and said, in jest:

' "What sort of dying will you be doing now, *Sir* Pamphalon? You aren't poor any more and you can afford slaves who will cool your water for you."

'But I replied to her:

' "No, Ada, I'm rich no longer, thank God – now I'm as poor as I was before, and what's more ... I have to admit – I'm badly injured."

'She tilted the jug for me to drink – as I drank, Ada stood bending towards me; she had observed on my shoulders the blood which was oozing from the cuts inflicted by the copper switch I had been beaten with in the presence of the maiden Sylvia. The blood was seeping through my thin tunic, and Ada cried in alarm:

' "O unhappy man! Indeed, you are covered in blood! You must have been set upon by nocturnal thieves! . . . O luckless man! It's a good thing you came in under our roof to escape from them. Stay here and wait for a little until I return: as soon as I have taken this cooled drink to the guests I shall come back and wash your wounds . . ."

' "Very well," I said. "I'll wait for you."

'And she added:

' "Perhaps you would like me to whisper a word about this in Azella's ear? She's at present feasting with some friends of the governor of Damascus: perhaps he will send some men out to find those who did this to you?"

' "No," I replied. "That isn't necessary. Just bring me some water and a clean tunic."

'Once I had put on a clean tunic, I intended to go and see Ammun, the former monk, who involved himself in all kinds of business, and offer to place myself in bondage to him for my entire lifetime, if only he would give me money enough to free Magna's children from the captivity in which they were being held by the eunuch.

'Ada soon returned, bringing with her the things I needed.

'But she had also told her mistress about me, and no sooner had she finished wiping my wounds clean with a cool sponge and covering my shoulders with the linen tunic she had brought than, in the portico where I lay leaning sideways against a tree, appeared Azella, dressed in extravagant attire.'

28

'Azella was covered in gold and pearls, one of which was of enormous value. This rare pearl had been given to her by a great magnate from Egypt.

'Azella approached me with concern and made me tell her everything that had happened to me. I proceeded to give her a brief account, and when I reached the subject of Magna's misfortunes, I noticed that Azella's gaze grew serious; Ada, too, began to look into the distance and I saw the tears stream down her face.

'Then I thought: "Now is the time to reveal the secret of Magistrian," and I suddenly said, without warning:

' "Azella, are these all the treasures you possess?"

' "No, I have more," Azella replied. "But what business is it of yours?"

' "It's very much my business, and I beseech you: tell me where you keep them, and are they all intact?"

' "I keep them in my treasure-chest, and they are all intact."

' "O, joy!" I shouted, all my pain forgotten. "It's all intact! But then where did Magistrian get hold of ten *litrae* of gold?"

' "Magistrian?"

' "Yes."

'When I told her what Magistrian had done, Azella began to whisper:

' "There's a man who truly loves! My Ada saw him leaving Ammun's house ... I understand it all now: he sold himself into bondage with Ammun in order to set Magna free!"

'And Azella the *hetaera* began quietly to sob, and to remove her gold bracelets and necklaces and her enormous Egyptian pearl, and said:

' "Take all this, take it and hurry, rescue poor Magna's children from the eunuch before he mutilates them!"

'I did as she urged: I took her treasures, added to them the money I had been given by Or the Corinthian and sent Magna off with it all to buy back her husband and her two sons from captivity. And it all worked out successfully, except that I had to say goodbye forever to any prospect of improving my way of life and thus to any hope of eternal blessedness. So I am still even now an entertainer – I'm a comedian, a dissolute fellow – I caper, I play, I beat my tambourine, I whistle, I move my legs up and down and shake my head. In short, I'm a barrel, a tar-barrel, I'm a good-for-nothing who's beyond redemption. That's my story, anchorite, the story of how I lost the chance of improving my way of life and how I broke the vow I made to God.'

29

Hermius rose, reached for his goatskin, and said to the entertainer:

'You have put my mind at rest.'

'You're joking!'

'You have made me happy.'

'In what way?'

'You have shown me that eternity will not be empty.'

'Of course it won't!'

'Why won't it?'

'I don't know.'

'Because by the path of mercy will enter many of those whom the world despises and whom even I, a proud anchorite, forgot in my self-admiration. Go home, Pamphalon, and carry on doing what you have been doing, and I shall move on.'

They bowed to each other and went their separate ways. Arriving back in his desert, Hermius was surprised to see a nest of crows in the cleft where he had formerly stood. The inhabitants of the village told him that they had tried to frighten these birds off, but that they would not leave the rock.

'That's as it should be,' Hermius replied to them. 'Don't stop them building their nests. Rocks are places for birds to live in – human beings must serve other human beings. You have many cares – I want to help you. I am infirm, but I will do what I can. Entrust your goats to me, I will drive them out and graze them, and when I return with the herd, give me bread and cheese.'

The villagers agreed, and Hermius began to drive the herd of goats and instruct the local children out in the open air.

And when all the village had fallen asleep, he would come out, sit down on the hillside and turn his eyes towards Damascus, where he had got to know Pamphalon. Now the elder liked to think about the good Pamphalon, and each time he cast his mind back to Damascus he seemed to see the entertainer running through its streets with his dog Acra. On his forehead there was a copper wreath, and it was an extraordinary thing: from day to day this wreath grew brighter and brighter, and finally one evening it shone so brilliantly that Hermius was unable to look at it. In amazement the old man shielded his eyes with his hand, but the radiance penetrated from all sides. And through his closed eyelids, Hermius saw that not only was the entertainer glowing with radiant light – he was rising higher and higher into the sky, leaving the earth behind and soaring straight towards the incandescent, scarlet sun.

What was he doing? He would be burned to a frazzle, there would be nothing left of him! Hermius rushed after Pamphalon, in order to hold him back or at least not be parted from him; but suddenly, in the hot light of the setting sun, a barrier arose between them . . . It was a paling or lattice, in which each bar was different. Hermius saw that these bars were some kind of symbols – smudged across the whole of the sky as if in charcoal and soot stood the word 'self-conceit', written in large, Hebrew letters.

'This is as far as I go!' thought Hermius, and he stopped. But Pamphalon took his entertainer's cloak, waved it about and in a trice wiped the word from the entire, vast space, and Hermius saw himself in a fabled world and felt himself flying at a great height, holding on to Pamphalon's hand, and they were both talking to each other.

'How were you able to wipe out the sin of my life?' Hermius asked Pamphalon as they flew.

Pamphalon replied:

'I don't know how I managed to do it: I just saw that you were in difficulty, and I wanted to help you as best I could. That's the way I always did everything when I was on earth, and that's the way I'm going now to the other abode.'

No more of their words were heard by the chronicler of this legend. A cool veil of cloud covered the trail of their passage from earth in dense shadow, and in the rubicund glow of the sunset their departed souls fused together.

A WINTER'S DAY

(*Landscape and Genre-Painting*)

'They meet with darkness in the daytime, and
grope in the noonday as in the night.'

Job, 5:14

'At St Saviour's the clock strikes, at St Nicholas's
it tolls, at old Yegor's it talks.'

V. Dahl[1] (proverb)

I

A northern winter's day with a slight thaw. Two o'clock. Dawn has hardly had a chance to get a look in, yet once again twilight has fallen.

At the table of a second-rate drawing-room sits the lady of the house and a female visitor. The lady of the house is old, and it might even be possible to call her appearance venerable were it not for the fact that her face bears the marks of excessive worldly anxiety and favour-seeking. She has seen better days, and has not yet given up hope of resuscitating them, but does not know what she should do in order to bring this about. In order not to let any chance slip, she is prepared to be anything under the sun: she is a 'vessel' once cast 'in honour', but nowadays serving as a 'vessel of dishonour'. The female visitor whom we find at the lady's home is also getting on somewhat in years. At any rate, she has reached an age at which it is possible to renounce the game of the emotions, but this, it would appear, she has not yet done. This woman was doubtless once very attractive, but now that she has shed her blossoms, there remain of her previous charms only the '*beaux restes*'; her figure is, however, still lissom, and the features of her face have preserved their regularity; but her expression is dominated by a remarkable show of mixed feelings: at one moment she gazes around her like a gentle doe, while at the next this doe will prance up like a kicking nanny-goat.

It would be impossible for one to fall for this lady now unless one had some ulterior motive, but perhaps something of this kind might still be possible were she to pose the question differently. In her attitude towards the sedate lady of the house the female visitor displays a demeanour that is especially warm and deferential, even, one might say, daughterly – but these ladies are certainly not relatives. What unites them is a friendship that is founded, not on some mere concurrence of tastes alone, but also on a concurrence of aims: they are united by their *métier*.

Now they are drinking tea, which has been served in a Harrach teapot covered by a knitted cosy, and the female visitor is telling the lady of the house the events of note that have recently taken place, and what people are 'talking about'. What people are talking about is the rivalry of two would-be thaumaturgists, and what has taken place is even more interesting and worthy of attention: yesterday, quite unexpectedly, Cousin Olympia[1] arrived home from abroad. She is a well-known public figure, who has devoted herself to 'issues' for as long as anyone can remember and who spends all her time living in other people's countries; when she comes back to Russia, however, she always brings a whole host of news with her and 'livens things up'. The life she leads is quite astonishing: she is not rich – oh, not at all rich! In fact, she doesn't really have any means at all, yet even so she never borrows from anyone and never complains about her situation, but instead brings all sorts of benefits to her country.

There are, thank goodness, a number of such ladies nowadays – but among them it is Olympia who occupies the most prominent position. She has a large and excellent family. She is even related to the two ladies who are talking about her here. In everyone's eyes Olympia is a very considerable woman, and everyone has faith in her, in spite of the caution with which Dickens advises us to treat all those who live on uncertain means.

Olympia invariably returns home, to the land of her birth, suddenly and only for short periods of time. She arrives, takes a quick look round, meets this person or that, 'replenishes her resources', and once again departs. Many say that she is very talented – but, even more importantly, she is entirely indispensable.

The lady of the house is slightly annoyed with her, and makes a remark about the draught that is blowing in through the windows. Moreover, she says that Viktor Gustavych still regrets that Olympia doesn't want to 'be on good terms'. If only she would change her mind, she would without any question be *thoroughly* indispensable.

'At any rate, it doesn't seem to prevent Olympia from conducting herself admirably,' the lady of the house says in conclusion, 'since even Viktor Gustavych himself isn't certain of anything any more. That says a great deal.'

The female visitor gives one of her doe's-eye looks, signifying agreement; as she does so, she makes one of her nanny-goat movements – just a small one – and casts a glance at the *chaise-longue* that is situated in front of the hearth between the lattice and the screen.

To one side of the ladies, in a very deep armchair behind the lattice, a pretty girl of twenty-three or twenty-four is reclining with her eyes closed and her arms folded. She is evidently not at all interested in what the ladies are talking about: she is tired and having a rest – she may even be asleep. This girl is the lady of the house's niece; to members of the family she is known simply as Lydia, to others as Lydia Pavlovna. She is not popular with her family, as she does not do as her mother and brothers would like her to. Her brothers are dashing officers – one of them has already fought his first duel. Lydia is also out of favour with her aunt, whom she is now visiting for the first time in an age, but then she has been making no secret of the fact that she feels out of place here.

The lady of the house gazed at Lydia, and said:

'She's asleep. Anyway,' she added, 'even if she isn't, it wouldn't make any difference to her: she couldn't care less about social issues. Anything that doesn't have to do with those courses of hers, she doesn't want to know about. But to get back to Olympia: she has intelligence and connections, I grant you, but she's fairly come down in the world since the time on her last visit when she tried to make a fuss about those Bulgarians who were publicly flogged. Do you remember the nonsense that nearly got started over that? They found out she was coming and arrived here in their hordes saying that where they came from everyone was flogged and that they'd even been flogged themselves, every one of them. Olympia wanted to put them to some use, but she got carried away, and when people tried to argue with her that these men were simply showing off, she insisted that they'd been examined in the editorial offices of some newspaper here, and then, in order to try to give them a little more importance, she conceived the idea of having them open a ball; but then everyone started saying that no European ladies would go to it, because, well, picture it for yourself, there are those who don't want to dance with men who've been flogged.'

'Yes, I remember. And, as you say, the idea of dancing with men who've been flogged . . . It . . . It *is* rather strange!'

'That's right,' the lady of the house went on. 'And then afterwards someone discovered that the whole thing was pointless anyway, since these men had apparently been flogging one another in some back lane or other, having acquired the notion that they could get more attention that way . . . It was said at the time that Olympia was apparently in on the whole conspiracy . . . Heaven knows what all that was about! . . . And then later on that proved to be untrue, as well, because although they had indeed been flogged in a back lane, it had absolutely nothing to do with all the rest of the business – what had actually happened was that some fellow-countryman of theirs had been flogging them as part of some medical treatment or other, a kind of massage . . . Lord knows what one's supposed to make of it all, or where the truth really lies.'

'Yes, it was all such a muddle that the only thing that seemed certain was that they'd been flogged in their own country and that they'd been flogged over here.'

'Precisely so – the impertinence of it! And it led to a great loss, too, because brother Luka got angry and not only stopped contributing money to Slavdom, but wouldn't let anyone try to explain. He's as stubborn as a mule, you know, and he just said straight out: "It's all a hoax!" – and it wasn't just the Slavs he banned from the doorstep, but Olympia herself – he even sent her a feather as a gibe.'

'What sort of feather?'

'I don't know – they said it was a magpie's feather, the kind one puts in one's hat.'

'Really?'

'I tell you, it's so! As if he were saying: "Here you are, magpie, now fly away!" And now he won't have anyone in the house.'

'What reason does Luka Semyonych have for supposing that anyone wants to visit his house all that badly?'

'He's rich and he isn't trying to get anything out of anyone – so he doesn't have to receive visits from anyone he doesn't want to see.'

'But has he no influence apart from that?'

'None. But everyone's afraid he won't invite them.'

Lowering her voice, the female visitor asked:

'Have you been *chez lui* this winter?'

The lady of the house made a negative signal, and said:

'He's far too prickly.'

'Arkady doesn't go calling on him either, does he?'

'Neither Arkady nor Valery have anything to do with him: he detests both of my sons.'

'Quarrelsome old man! Who *does* he invite, then?'

'Of all the members of my family there are only two who ever go there: brother Zakhar and – Lydia over there.'

The female visitor nodded at the lattice, and smiled.

'That he receives Lydia Pavlovna – that I can understand. Refusing to receive people of weight and substance, yet lavishing affection upon a niece who's a trainee surgeon's assistant and flouts all the established social conventions – that's his style. I suppose it must be Luka Semyonych's own special way of showing his disdain for those who would like to be invited to his house. But why, out of all the members of his family, should he make a second such exception for Zakhar Semyonych? Our dear general is just a poor sinner like all the rest of us.'

'The old man has a soft spot for Zakhar: "Our brother Zakhar has been punished enough for rubbing shoulders with the wrong sort of people," he says. "Let God forgive him for all the harm he's done to himself."'

'Ah, so that's it!'

The girl behind the lattice began to show some signs of life. The ladies observed this, and the female visitor said quietly, with a smile:

'Do you think she'll go back to sleep?'

'I expect so,' the lady of the house replied. 'She's the same wherever she is: she arrives, takes a nap and then runs off to that stinking lair of hers to do her duty – cutting up some dead body or other.[2] I must say, though, that Bertenson[3] has been keeping them well in hand, particularly since that time when they gave him all that trouble.'

'But that taught them a lesson, didn't it?'

'Yes, but even so they do put up with a lot from that man.'

'Why can't she sleep in her own home?'

'Oh, there's chaos in that family – not one of them gets along with the other, she doesn't like having to listen to her brothers talking about racing at the Hippodrome and duels, and they don't like having to listen to how she spends her time, and the entire household is like that: everyone pulling in opposite directions ... It must be said, though, that brother Luka does lavish a great deal of affection on her and even sends her flowers in that stinking lair of hers.'

The female visitor nodded in the direction of the sleeping girl, and quietly inquired:

'She'll have finished her studies and be a surgeon's assistant soon, won't she?'

'Yes, that's right, she will.'

'I seem to remember some time ago that she was learning how to do bandages, if I'm not mistaken?'

'Oh, there's no end to her studying: she has the gymnasium, the pedagogical institute, the women's courses – she's been through them all, and she's removed her earrings, and doesn't wear a corset any more, and goes around like a plain simple Susan.'

'Like one of Tolstoy's followers, you mean?'

'M-m ... Well, nowadays, you know ... the young folk have no time for him any more. I always said that would happen eventually, and I needn't have worried: "The Devil's never as bad as his urchins".[4]

The female visitor smiled and observed:

'That's true: people are fed up with his moralizing – but you know there was a time when you wouldn't have quoted that proverb – you used to be quite partial to him.'

'Me? Yes, I've changed, why should I conceal it? I've always loved reading, and in those days I was right behind Tolstoy in all things. His Natasha, for example! Isn't she lovely? She used to be my idol and my goddess! She's so captivating that I never noticed all that ultra-realism of his flying out at me – all that stuff about swaddling clothes with baby stains.[5] What of it? Babies do get dirty. They wouldn't be babies, otherwise, and that didn't put me off the way it did a lot of other women. And do you remember later on in that book, the way he describes our Alexander I?'[6]

'What, you mean the bit where he's getting dressed?'

'That's right. Do you remember the part where he's fastening his braces?'

'Oh, that's simply heavenly!'

'Yes, and you don't just see his braces, either. I mean, the whole man rises up before us as though he were there in the flesh! ... When I read that part I can see him, I can feel him!'

'Napoleon's awfully good too, with those dark eyes of his.'

'Napoleon had grey eyes, actually.'

'But they looked dark.'

'Well, I won't argue with you; in that, as in everything else, Tolstoy is beyond comparison. There can be no argument about that; but when he started to get those abstruse ideas, gave up his true task and began writing stupid articles forbidding people to eat meat, saying that no man should ever take a wife, and telling girls to sew their dresses up to the neck and not to marry, then I for one said: "That's a load of rubbish. You might as well take all our menfolk to the Skoptsy[7] and have done with it." But, as an Orthodox believer, I can't go along with him on that.'

Here the female visitor quietly observed that Tolstoy nowhere actually *forbids* anyone to eat meat and even apparently suggests that some men should get married.

'Yes, I know he never *actually* forbids it, *but* – why does he write about it all in such a powerful, booming voice?'

'Yes, well, of course, he writes very boldly – but in our country he hasn't yet acquired the right to forbid anything.'

'No, indeed, thank God! But why does he keep going on and on about those things, and nothing but them? Why? He tries to persuade us that one shouldn't offend evil-doers, or tries to prove that without faith it's impossible to work, and that's all very fine, but then he suddenly breaks off and starts writing stupid things again – "Why use soap?", for example. Well, tell me honestly: doesn't he know what soap's for? I mean, what would life be like if nobody used soap? How would we ever wash our hands and faces, how would we get our linen clean? What does he want us to do with it – rub it in ashes? Even so, I could still forgive him that, because of his earlier writings. To tell you the truth, all men are stupid when they venture into areas where they're out of their depth. But I don't need to tell you that. An inch breaks no square; freedom for the free and may the Lord save the rest of us.[8] It's the same where meat's concerned. Let those who prefer fish or starch be the ones to abstain from meat. Whatever government's in power, people should never be constrained in such matters, no matter where they are . . . If you please! Then, perhaps, the price of fillet steak might come down a little for the rest of us. Don't you agree?'

'Naturally.'

'Yes, that's how it should be. And as for those people who don't want to get married, let them stay as they are. You know what the Good Book says about that, don't you? "And there be eunuchs . . ." They're off their heads, of course.'

The female visitor nodded her agreement.

'When my sons were still just boys,' the lady of the house went on, 'they had a tutor who was a seminarist – very ambitious, but a bit of a giggle, really. He was always preparing to go off to a monastery and become a monk, and when we'd say to him: "You'd do better getting married, monsieur!" he'd reply straight out: "Why should I need to?"'

The lady turned slightly in the direction of the lattice and said:

'Lydia, are you awake now or are you still asleep?'

'Yes, *ma tante*,' a drowsy contralto voice replied.

'What's that supposed to mean – are you awake or aren't you?'

'What is it, *ma tante*? Are you talking about something that's not for my ears? Do you want me to get out of the room?'

'I want you to get married, finally, that's what I want.'

'Well, all I can say is what your seminarist used to say: Why should I need to?'

'So that people may talk while you're in the room without being embarrassed by your presence.'

'Oh come off it, you're not in the slightest embarrassed.'

'On the contrary: we are.'

'I suppose you think I'm still an innocent. Why can't you just pretend that I'm married and that I know everything you do?'

'Just listen to the things she says about herself! But there was something I wanted to say to you ... Ah, yes! ... I expect you've heard everyone talking about that hussar who claimed to be related to Count Tolstoy[9] and went to call on him wearing his parade uniform – the close-fitting kind. The Count went and found a nanny's apron and tied it round him, and wouldn't let him into the drawing-room unless he kept it on.'

'Yes, I've heard that story ... It's supposed to be true, too.'

'I expect so. And if you want my opinion, I think those hussars' uniforms are – a little immodest.'

'Yes, but they're awfully attractive!'

'Attractive – yes. But that apron! I mean, that was a piece of insolence, too. A hussar wearing an apron! That's exactly the sort of thing I can't forgive him – his insufferable shrewdness. It causes harm to society.'

'That's it – we can't be having that, can we? Go on, I'm listening: where do you see the nub of the affair?'

'Well, the nub of it is: what right does the Count have to go interfering with our servants? If he's learned how to do his own tidying up, that's fine for him – but the rest of us haven't set our sights that high yet. Have we?'

'Of course not.'

'So why does he go trying to force on us this impossible business of being on familiar terms with servants who are coarse and depraved?'

'It's stupid of him.'

'Of course it is! I told Arkady he ought to write some humorous verses about it and read them aloud in public. A lot of society people think very highly of his talent, you know.'

'Yes, so everyone says, and he's such a charmer, too . . . Oh, he'll get on in the world all right!'

'Possibly – I daresay even probably; but one can't predict the future: the future is, as they say, "in the hands of the Almighty Lord". However, there's no doubt that his appealing talent will help him in his career. My other son, Valery, is quite different: he's the practical sort!'

'Oh, I'm sure he is,' the female visitor replied, slightly embarrassed. Adroitly, she changed the subject. 'But tell me, in what way does Tolstoy spoil our servants?' she asked.

'Very well,' the lady of the house replied. 'Let us discuss servants, like real government officials' wives. But it isn't a trivial matter: Schopenhauer writes about servants. Servants can either set one's mind at rest or they can put one to a dreadful lot of trouble. I shan't quote all those lengthy precepts of Tolstoy's concerning servants at you; instead, I'll give you a direct illustration from my own experience of the effect they can have. I had a dreadful lot of trouble with my housemaid ... I can't tell you the *whole* story, since Lydia's present, but I simply can't resist telling you some of it.'

'For heaven's sake, *ma tante*, tell her anything you want!' the girl said in response to this. 'I'm just going to have the last part of my nap, and then I shall be off.'

'To put it in a nutshell,' the lady of the house continued, 'I had to give the wretched hussy her notice just before the holiday. Well, you know what those Russian peasants of ours are like before a holiday, and how difficult it is to find a decent replacement. They're all so greedy, they all expect to be given presents, and they have absolutely no love for their masters. The Russian people are best seen from a distance, especially when they're at prayer and look as though they've got some religious belief in them. Take that painting by Repin, for example – "The Cross and Banners".[1] You remember, the one where he shows all those master sergeants of the various guilds ...'

'Yes, or that watercolour by Pyotr Sokolov ...'[2]

'Oh, that one. But there's a little too much blue in it.'

'That's true: he put too much blue in.'

'None of our Russian artists really have any sense of moderation.'

'No. But what really matters is the impression a painting makes ... You know, I have a friend – you know her: we all call her "the female apostle". I'm sure you know her!'

'Of course I do. You mean Marie, don't you?'

'That's her. There are quite a number of poor souls like her these days, but I wouldn't compare her with any of the others. She's not like other people, and anyway she's quite prehistoric, from the days when everyone still spoke French, and neither Zasetskaya nor Peiker were in vogue, and even Radstock himself hadn't yet arrived ... Lord, I mean the real mists of antiquity! The days when Vasily Pashkov was still in the army, and Modest Korf was crossing himself with both hands and holding public prayer meetings wearing a gentleman-in-waiting's full-dress coat. And as for Aleksei Pavlovich Bobrinsky,[3] he was still a Galician diehard in those days, and shouted in such a loud voice that he made the ministry windows rattle. Seryozha Kushelyov actually went to the length of drawing caricatures of them all, and he used to take them around and show them to everyone, and we all laughed.'

'I remember.'

'Yes, and you know it isn't fair when people say Tolstoy was the one who started the craze for going about barefoot and doing manual labour – Marie was there first, long before anyone else. She used to scrub her own floors, and she would take out the chamber-pots from the rooms of the sick, even the most revolting messes! She even went around the beer-halls a few times with Nikolai Andreyevich with the idea of rescuing some wretched girl or other who merely laughed them off the premises ... It wouldn't have done to rescue them all, of course – that would have been a silly thing to do: those girls are necessary; but even so, Marie did show her good intentions ... And since Annenkov[4] was with the police in those days, he took care of the whole business and there wasn't any scandal.'

'I remember. People used to tell it as an amusing story.'

'Oh, it was fascinating. But Marie's still the same, you know: "Mother Mary grieving for all." She was never jealous of Radstock and Pashkov concerning God, and she isn't jealous of Tolstoy now: it's as if she thinks of them all as being somehow related to one another, and even with regard to herself one can't really say other than that although she's a sectarian and a black sheep, she nevertheless has a lot of kindness and compassion for other people. That's of more value than all her religion.'

'Yes, I suppose it is.'

'Of course it is! What sort of religion do they have, anyway? I mean, a lot of those girls are utterly pitiable: men seduce them and then throw them on the scrapheap ... Berton[5] used to do that, don't you remember? He'd abduct you, throw you on the scrapheap and then leave you to get on with it. But Marie devotes her entire life to taking care of others. If you're looking for a warm, loving person, go to her: she always has a ready supply of "the insulted and the injured". I went to see her to ask her to recommend a modest, truthful girl to me, so that there shouldn't be any hypocrisy or bad examples in the house.

And Marie was so delighted! "Oh, how pleasant it is for me to hear you talk like this," she said. "Lying is the sin with which Satan began his undoing of mankind. After all, he deliberately *deceived* Eve, didn't he?" Yes, yes, yes, I thought; you've read a lot, but you're overdoing things a bit with all this stuff about our ancestors and Satan – all I've come to see you for is to ask you about a chambermaid.

'"Oh yes, I know the very one!" Marie replied. "I have exactly the right sort of first-rate girl staying with me in my home just now – she's just dying to find a position."

'"Not a malingerer, or a butterfly?"

'"Oh, how could she be? She's a Christian!"

'"Well, you know, everyone in Russia's baptized, they're even Orthodox believers, but they've all got rotten morals and absolutely no sense of right and wrong."

'"Oh, how can you say that? Christians have an excellent sense of right and wrong. And anyway this is a girl who's always occupied with something, she works and reads those 'Intermediary'[6] books."

'"Aha, so she's a follower of Tolstoy! Oh well, it doesn't matter: I detest all forms of utopianism, but to have one's servants fix their sights on non-resistance to evil sounds rather a good idea to my ears. Give me your non-resister! Of course, I shall let her have time off to go to prayers. Where do they gather in order to do their praying? Or don't they pray at all?"

'"I don't know," she said. "It's a matter of conscience, one's not supposed to talk about it."

'"Oh well, of course, that's none of my concern, it's her business. But what's her name?"

'"Fedorushka."

'"My, what an ugly name!"

'"Why do you say that? Very well, then, just call her Feodora, or even Theodora. What could be better?"

'"No, they both sound too much like something from the theatre, I think I shall just call her Katya."

'"But why?"

'"Oh, it's just my way of doing these things."

'Marie made no attempt at any retort to this remark, and sent me her non-resister – and, just fancy, I found the girl thoroughly to my liking, and I took her on.'

'On what sort of pay?'

'Seven roubles a month.'

'How very inexpensive!'

'Yes. But she didn't ask for any more than that. In fact, she didn't ask for anything at all, but simply said: "Just pay me what you think I'm worth." So I fixed a sum. But I'm sorry, that's not really what we were talking about. Anyway, I took quite a liking to her, because she looked so neat and modest. Though I must confess that when I heard she was a non-resister, I was a bit apprehensive about whether she'd be clean enough, because there are all those tirades against soap in their books, and I remembered my nurse once having read me a story when I was small about a shameless blackamoor who set upon a certain lady saint, but who, since the lady saint never used soap, fairly leapt away from her again.'

'How dreadful!'

'Yes, all the other saints had to submit to the fellow, but not her; though I must say I really don't know if that's the reason why Tolstoy is against soap.'

'Oh, but you've missed the point. Don't tell me you've forgotten what soap's made from?'

'Meat juice.'

'Well, there's your answer for you.'

'Aunt!' came the voice of the girl behind the lattice. 'Aren't you ashamed to talk such rubbish?'

'What do you mean, rubbish?'

'Soap isn't made from meat, and what's more, a great deal of soap isn't made from animal, but vegetable fat. And then there's soap that's made from eggs, which you yourself buy.'

'Ah yes, true, true! You're quite correct, there *is* soap made from eggs. It's made in Kazan, where Skaryatin[7] was governor; but I don't buy it nowadays. I used to buy it for ages and used it a great deal to wash myself with, but ever since the Shah of Persia[8] was here and I found out that he uses that soap for washing his feet, I've taken a dislike to it, and I don't buy it any more.'

'Whatever made you go and find out a thing like that?'

'Well, why not? They didn't teach us grand behaviour like that in the institute courses we went to. And, if you ask me, I think it's more profitable to take an interest in personages like that than in people who don't wash. You know, I remember when Arkady was in his final year at university, all sorts of characters used to drop in on him; those non-resisters used to go and see him, too, and they all wore that uniform of theirs, dreary-looking, all of them, and their boots were never clean.'

'Dreadful "urchins"!' the female visitor said.

'Yes, that's what they are . . . with their little fat rumps and sheep's tails. They put on their belts, and it always makes a little sheep's tail at the back. They never wear galoshes – and they leave dirty footmarks everywhere. That's uncleanliness for you! But this non-resister girl came to me looking thoroughly clean and tidy, and she was a splendid worker; but she turned out to be completely hopeless as far as practical matters were concerned.'

'Why so?'

'Ah yes, there are many sides to practical matters, and she turned out to be worse than all the rest of the non-resister girls put together!'

'Did a non-resister boy put in an appearance, then?'

'Oh no! Nothing like that. You'll simply never guess!'

3

'I may as well start from the beginning: as I was flicking through her passport, I once again ran up against the fact that her name's Fedora. "My dear," I said to her, "I don't like your first name, I'm going to call you Katya." Immediately, she replied: "If you want a servant in your house to bear a name that is not her own, that is all the same to me: these are *human customs*!"'

'How amusing!'

'Frightfully amusing! "Human customs!" . . . And then there are their "direct obligations to God". But I was brought up in the country, and I like to chat with the servants from time to time, so I said: "I'm going to call you Katya, and that's the name you'll answer to." "Yes, ma'am," she replied. "And there's something else, something I forgot to tell you," I said; "your duties also include helping our cook to clear up the crockery and wiping down the lavatory floors." But just imagine, she wiped the floors and answered to "Katya", but if any of my friends asked her what her name was, she always stubbornly replied: "Fedora". I told her, I said: "Listen, my dear! You were told that your name is Katya – please try to remember that! Why are you so contrary?" And she began to argue: "I answer according to your instructions," she said, "as you told me that was the way things were done in your house, and it doesn't prejudice my interests: but I myself *cannot tell a lie* . . ." "What nonsense!" I said. "No," she said, "I can't tell a lie – that would harm me."'

'There's a fine to-do!' the female visitor exclaimed. 'Madame doesn't wish to be harmed!'

'Oh, certainly not! There was something punctilious about her, you know, something narrow and obstinate, like Martyn

Ivanych Luther himself. Oh, how I detest that cold Lutheran-
ism! What a good thing it is that those Lutherans have been
held well in check in our country. I asked her:

' "What sort of harm would it do you? Would it make your
head ache, or your stomach?"

' "No," she said. "It might not make my stomach ache, but
there are things that are of more consequence than one's head
or stomach."

' "And what might they be?" I asked.

' "The human soul," says she. "I want my conscience to be
clear at all times." '

'That was a poisonous remark, wasn't it?'

'It was plain insolence!'

'Yes; but, as brother Zakhar says, "It may not be to one's
liking, but after that auspicious nineteenth of February[1] – it's
inevitable." '

'Yes, ever since that February we've been in their hands.'

'Especially just before a holiday. I mean, we can't go to the
door ourselves and tell our visitors that we're not at home, can
we? Things haven't yet come to such a pass on the whole, but
that's exactly what that non-resister urchin of a girl caused to
happen in my home.'

'What on earth?'

'It's a fact!'

'Really, you know, our only hope is the governor now.'

'Yes, he'll sort them out – "hands behind your backs!" At
the holiday I had it out with her. "Katya," I said, "there are
visitors coming. You must tell them that I'm at home and ask
them to come in." And she did. But then Viktor Gustavych
turned up. You know, a man of his position and authority, and
I with my two sons, both so different in temperament: Arkady's
a terrible dawdler, while Valery – you know him – is rather a
lively spirit. You'll understand that I do get concerned about
them, and I wanted to have a few words with him about Valery,
who didn't do as Arkady did, but ended up in that . . . university,
which he'll finish next year, with no connections, or anything at
all . . .'

The female visitor made a scarcely perceptible movement.

'So I made Viktor Gustavych sit down, then ran off to her and said: "Now, Katya, if anyone comes to the door you must tell them that I've *gone out* and that I'm *not at home*." You'd think even the most brainless hussy could understand an instruction like that and carry it out!'

'How could she fail to?'

'Precisely, the most ordinary sort of request. But, just imagine, she started telling *everyone* that I'd *told her to say* I'd gone out and wasn't at home!'

'Oh, good heavens!' the female visitor exclaimed, and burst out laughing.

'But imagine, everyone merely laughed when she did it, just as you're doing, and not one of them took offence, because they all knew perfectly well that everyone tells lies in that sort of situation . . . It's the accepted thing to do . . . But the young folk started saying to me: "*Ma tante*, your non-resister girl seems to be a shallow-brained halfwit." However, I surmised – correctly – that it was just her religious faith coming out, and I explained to them that this was just Count Tolstoy popping out of her, pulling that enormous nose of his at all educated people in that high-and-mighty way of his: "Social visiting's quite unnecessary! It's all a lot of tomfoolery, making the horses swish their tails about for no reason: if it's exercise you want, go and scrub the floors."

'Without soap?'

'That's right, just use plain water.'

'So what did you do with your non-resister after that?'

'I gave her a good talking-to. "Just reflect," I told her, "that you were recommended to me as a very good girl and a Christian, too; yet you're sly and stubborn. What sort of a trick is that on your part, trying to make out I'm a liar?" But she just made excuses in a naive sort of way:

' "I couldn't say any different."

' "Why couldn't you? You poor benighted numbskull! Why couldn't you say any different?"

' "Because you were at home."

' "Well, and what was wrong with that?"

' "I'd have been telling a lie."

' "Well, what if you had been telling an ever-so-tiny lie?"'

' "I can't tell lies of any kind."'

' "None at all?"'

' "No."'

' "But you're a *servant*! You applied for a position, you're being paid a salary! . . . Why did you ever apply for the post if you have ideas like that in your head?"'

' "I applied to do a job of work, not to tell lies, I can't tell lies."'

'And no matter which angle I tried to approach her from, she would keep harping on with her "I can't tell lies!" and refuse to budge.'

'Such narrowness, narrowness!'

'Unspeakable! "I mean," I said to her, "you must be able to distinguish between the kind of lies that are acceptable and the kind that aren't. Ask any priest."'

' "No, no, no," she replied. "I don't want to make such distinctions. You must forget about them, I don't even want to know of their existence. There's nothing in the Gospels about making distinctions like that. What isn't true is a lie – and Christians must never tell lies."'

'And then I remembered that when I'd taken her on, I was of the opinion that among servants and the lower orders of society in general a bit of non-resistance might not go amiss, and might even be good for them – but that turned out to be far from being the case! It turned out to be a disaster there, too, and so we must now resist it wherever it rears its ugly head!'

The lady of the house earnestly knit her brows and said she had discussed this 'insolence' with the priest, who had explained to her that it was 'the outcome of a free, *personal* interpretation of the Gospels'.

'Yes, but what sort of freedom is it when it's so horribly narrow?' the female visitor interjected with a learned air.

'I agree with you – and besides, one man's meat is another man's poison.'

The lady of the house gave the table a menacing slap with one hand with a rattle of turquoise finger-rings, and continued:

'You know, I very well remember the heyday of Evropeus and Unkovsky.[1] Things weren't at all then as they are today, and it once happened that we were dining together at a certain house, and someone had brought Shevchenko[2] along ... you remember, that Ukrainian fellow ... he was a bit naughty and paid dearly for it; anyway, he suddenly took a drink of vodka and right in the middle of the meal delivered himself of an impromptu remark which was so embarrassing that none of us knew where to look. One of us somehow managed to recover enough equilibrium to say: "Believe you me, what's all right for the few is quite emphatically not all right for the many." And that saved us all, even though we later found out that it had been said first by Pushkin, on whom Shevchenko's not a patch.'

'Just imagine if Pushkin had used language like that! . . .'

'Oh, he never would have, of course,' the lady of the house said, interrupting. 'He lived in society, and even the Decembrists knew they couldn't measure swords with him. But Shevchenko

rubbed shoulders with every Tom, Dick and Harry, and heaven
only knows whether there's any truth in the story that Perovsky
himself gave the order for him to be flogged in military fashion.
That was the sort of time it was: he was a soldier and they
flogged him, as was right and proper. Pushkin pointed that up
when he said: "What's all very well for London won't do for
Moscow."[3] And that's the way it's remained: "It may be all very
well in London, but it won't do in Moscow."'

'There's no one left in Moscow now . . . Katkov[4] is dead.'

The sound of restrained laughter was heard from behind the
lattice.

'What's so comical, Lydia?'

'Katkov's dead. The way you said it, it sounded as though
you meant to say: "The great god Pan is dead."'

'And your eyes "flashed" when I said it, like Diana's.'[5]

'I don't remember Diana's eyes flashing.'

'But it's so beautiful!'

'All beauty makes me sick. What I do remember, though, is
that Diana was the patron of the plebs and the slaves, that her
priest was a runaway slave, who had once himself killed a
priest, and that although she herself was a virgin, she helped
other women in childbirth. *That's* beautiful!'

'Beautiful?'

The lady of the house shook her head, and observed:

'You're completely without shame.'

'No, I'm not, *ma tante*.'

'Well, what are you trying to say, then? What is it you want?'

'I want girls not to find being girls a tedious bore, because
they've nothing to do: I want them to be able to give help to
other women who're in distress.'

'But why does it have to be women in childbirth?'

'Because it's such a dreadful experience. A lot of women suffer agonies without any help at all, while young upper-class
girls spend all their time making eyes at men. They ought to
help others; then they'd see what awaits them, when they stop
staring at themselves in the mirror, as Dianas.'

'Oh, but wait,' said the female guest, 'I wasn't talking about
that Diana: I meant the one whose eyes flash in an island forest,

when the news comes from a ship that "the great god Pan is dead". That's how it goes in Turgenev, isn't it?'

'I've forgotten how it goes in Turgenev.'

The lady of the house continued:

'People have no time for literature nowadays, all they do is repeat what they read in those "Intermediary" books.'

'Have you ever drawn Viktor Gustavych's attention to those books?' the female visitor inquired.

'Oh, he despises them – but then, he's a Lutheran, you know, and in his view, if goodness is the subject under discussion, then it's all right by him.'

'But your non-resister girl wasn't exactly good, was she?'

'Well, I wouldn't go so far as to say that. She was never actually unpleasant to anyone, but when I'd been arguing with her for a while I used to notice something flashing in her eyes, too.'

'Never!'

'I assure you it was so. You know that way, if one tried to pull her leg in a gentle sort of manner, her eyes would light up . . . with a kind of fire in them.'

'Good heavens! But why did you keep her on?'

'Yes, yes, there was one occasion on which I thought to myself: "Aha! You've got a dangerous spark in you!" – and eventually I gave her her notice. But of course before I did that I wanted to find out what one can expect from people like that, and I probed her.'

'How interesting!'

'I once asked her: "What would you do, my dear, if you were working in a house and something happened which had to be kept secret and concealed from everyone? Wouldn't you consent to cover up the shame or sin of whoever it was?" She grew flustered, and began to babble: "I haven't got round to thinking about that yet . . . I don't know!" I took advantage of that, and said: "Say you were summoned to give evidence in court, and you were questioned about your employers, well, I mean, you'd have to . . . What good, loyal servants there were in the old days; yet when it came to the crunch they'd say whatever was required of them." Imagine what she said in reply to that! "Whoever made them do that was guilty of a sin."'

'"What, even though they did it as part of an instruction?"'

'"That doesn't make any difference."'

'Never!'

'Yes. I said: "You could suffer for this, you know." And she replied: "I'd rather suffer than go astray from the path I've chosen in life."'

'There's non-resistance for you!'

'Well, you can see what I was up against!'

'Actually, you know, if you look at it from their point of view and adhere to what the Gospels tell us, then she's not entirely in the wrong . . .'

'No, she may even be very much in the right, but, I mean to say, society isn't run according to the Gospels, and we can't be expected to change just like that, all of a sudden.'

'No, more's the pity. But if you break all that down and trample it underfoot, what are you going to put in its place?'

'The nihilists used to say: *nothing*!'

The lady of the house twisted a piece of paper in her fingers for a while, as though she were turning over in her mind something that had happened long ago, and then said:

'Yes, *nothing*: all they knew was how to set women in a tizzy and teach them how to have tea *à trois* without being embarrassed.'

'And how did that non-resister girl behave in that kind of situation?'

'You mean the kind of situation one can't talk about in front of Lydia?'

This time Lydia, who had now apparently had all the sleep she wanted, and was feeling thoroughly refreshed, intervened in the conversation with a voice that was no longer drowsy.

'About a woman like Fedorushka you can say anything in front of anyone,' Lydia said. 'And anyway, *ma tante*, when are you going to get used to the fact that I'm not a child any more and have a better notion than you have not only of what soap is made from but of how babies are born?'

'Lydia!' the lady of the house said, reprovingly.

'Yes, really, *ma tante*, I know about that.'

'Good Lord! . . . How can you know about it?'

'Surprise, surprise! I'm nearly twenty-five, you know. I live, I read, and I'll be a surgeon's assistant soon. So do you really think I'm going to pretend to be a stupid little girl who tells lies to make people think she believes storks deliver babies in their beaks?'

The lady of the house turned to the female guest and said, imposingly:

'Here you have Jonah the cynic[1] in female form. And what's more, she's a Diana, she's a Puritan, a Quaker, she reads and admires Tolstoy, but she doesn't even share a large number of his opinions, and she's at loggerheads with the whole world.'

'I don't think I'm all that quarrelsome, actually.'

'Well, you haven't made any close friends, have you?'

'You're wrong there, *ma tante*. I have friends.'

'But you've given them up. I mean, there was a time when the non-resister boys enjoyed your favour, but now you've gone off them completely.'

'They're hopeless.'

'But you used to like listening to them.'

'Yes, I listened to them.'

'And you got sick of listening to them, didn't you?'

'No, why do you say that? I'm prepared even now to listen to what they have to say, as long as it's well thought out.'

'In the old days you used to take their side to the point of tears.'

'I used to take their side because your sons – my cousins – would send them on their way making ridicule of them. I can't stand it when people are jeered at.'

The lady of the house laughed, and said:

'There's no sin in laughing at what's funny.'[2]

'No, *ma tante*, it's wrong, and I always felt terribly sorry for them . . . They're good people, and they want what's good, and I used to cry just thinking about them . . .'

'And then you yourself lost your temper with them.'

'No, I didn't. I just saw that they spent all their time talking and talking and talking, and never lifted a finger. They were so incredibly dull. If you thought that lot who were forever getting ready to "work on Buckle"[3] were a pain in the neck, you should have seen these boys: all they could do was poke about in the straw with sticks. Both the one and the other do a disservice to the very things they want to teach people to treat with respect.'

'Oh, you were simply annoyed because they argue against science!'

'Yes, and I still find it annoying!'

'But on that point I agree with them! Really, why have you gone on studying for so many years and holding your own opinions when it's obvious that all your learning will merely end by you becoming assistant to some disreputable doctor who'll put you away in some corner somewhere.'

'*Ma tante*, that's just more of your nonsense, you know it perfectly well.'

'Yes, he'll make you sit out in some ante-room or other, while he himself will go into the best bit of the house and eat fruit tart, but to you he'll say: "Stay out in the ante-room, my dear." '

'That's not going to happen.'

'But what if it does, what will you do then?'

'I'll feel sorry for a man who is treating me in such a cruel fashion just because I haven't any more rights than that, and for the simple reason that I haven't been granted them.'

'And won't you feel you've been slighted?'

'Because of someone else's stupidity? Of course I won't.'

'But wouldn't you do better to go and get married, like everyone else?'

'Not I.'

'But why not?'

'I don't want to get married.'

'You really do have a strange way of expressing yourself. It's a law of nature, you know.'

'Well, perhaps it just hasn't reached me yet.'

'And religion demands the same thing.'

'My religion doesn't demand it.'

'But Christ was in favour of marriage.'

'I don't remember reading about that.'

'Why do you think he blessed the bride and the bridegroom?'

'When was that?'

'You'll find out if you read the New Testament.'

'That's not in it.'

'What do you mean, not in it?'

'It just isn't, that's all.'

'Good heavens! What are you saying? ... I suppose that means you've crossed out all those bits.'

The girl laughed quietly.

'There's no reason to snigger: I know there used to be something about that, and if it wasn't in the Gospels, then it was in the Epistles of St Paul. Anyway, he was in Cana of Galilee.'

'Well, and so what?'

'That means he approved of marriage.'

'And didn't he also visit the publican?'

'Yes.'

'And talk with the woman of Samaria? Does that mean he approved of what they did, too?'

'What a dreadful arguer you are.'

'I'm merely replying to the points you raised.'

'But what about Peter's mother-in-law? Christ healed her, didn't he?'

'I suppose you think he wouldn't have healed her if she hadn't been someone's mother-in-law?'

'You really do have a most unpleasant mind.'

'Yes, a lot of people say that, *ma tante*, and all it does is make me even more certain that I shouldn't get married!'

'I mean, there you are, you see: you're just like a snake, writhing and twisting this way and that so that no one can get hold of you to crush you.'

'*Ma tante*: why should it be necessary to *crush* me?'

'I should jolly well like to . . .'

'I'm sorry, *mon amie*; we can't arrange the world to be just as we'd like it.'

'Oh, I don't mean that; what I'd like to know is what sort of a scripture teacher you have, and how it is he can't see that you're all a lot of pagans.'

'We all get A pluses from him.'

'You don't say? What is he doing giving you A pluses?'

'He can't very well not give us them: we're all such first-rate students.'

'And just look at what characters you've developed!'

'Oh do stop it, *ma tante*; what's all this about characters? Characters emerge, characters mature – they're somewhere ahead of us, and we're not fit to hold a candle to them. But they'll come, sure enough. "The rustle of spring will come, the merry rustle!"[4] Soundness of mind will come, *ma tante*! It will! We live in that faith! If you lived in it, too, then . . . things would go well with you, always – no matter what people did to you!'

'Thank you, my dear – but no.'

'Don't be cross, *ma tante*.' And Lydia Pavlovna suddenly turned to her aunt's female visitor, and said to her: 'I believe you wanted to know if Fedora had any love affairs. I can tell you about that. She had a fiancé who was a watchmaker, but Fedorushka rejected him because she had a sister who had "reconciled herself to life". The sister had hoop petticoats, a brooch and earrings, and two children. She cherished the brooch and earrings, but wanted to have the children carted off to the foundling hospital. But Fedora took compassion on them and paid for their keep to the tune of almost all that she earned.'

'But she didn't have a proper love affair?'

'Yes, but she'll never be able to find enough money: with her sort of character and principles she'll never stay long enough in one place.'

'Other people will help her.'

'You see? ... They're real sectarians, they do everything *communally*,' the lady of the house said, in response to this. 'Persecute them and they don't mind – in fact, they love it!'

'That's as it should be,' the girl said, in confirmation.

'A lot of flim-flam!'

'But it's what the Gospels tell us: we must rejoice when we suffer persecution for the sake of the truth; actually, this greatly helps the dissemination of our ideas. We are persecuted, driven away, but we just go on to the next place and keep telling more and more people the good news . . .'

'That's all very well, but tell me: what *is* your faith, really, eh?'

'It's such a delicate question, *ma tante*, that I won't let anyone touch upon it.'

'So that's the way they answer questions about their faith nowadays! That's not the way we were taught.'

'No, it's not the way you were taught,' Lydia replied, laughing. 'The way you were taught was "for it is seemly to ask him that entereth: speak, child, what is thy faith?"'

The lady of the house rapped the table with her fan and said to her niece in a threatening voice:

'Lydia! On this occasion I shall ignore what you have said here. We will let it pass – but in future remember that you have a mother and that you mustn't stand in the way of your brothers and their careers!'

'That isn't easy to forget, *ma tante*!'

'Well, and stop playing the liberal.'

'Is that what you call liberalism? "What is thy faith, my child?"'

'For one thing, it's out of season just now.'

'Well, *ma tante*, I'm sorry, but life is only given to us once, you know, and it's very wasteful to try to adapt it to any sort of season . . . Things will all soon change.'

Having said this, the girl got up from behind the lattice and came out into the middle of the room. It was now possible to see that she was extremely pretty. She had a shapely figure of astonishing resilience and agility, which really did call to mind the little statue of Diana at Tanagra, and her face, with its bold and intelligent eyes, had a charmingly pure expression.

6

The aunt surveyed her niece, and her face expressed a sense of artistic satisfaction; she brightened up and quietly observed:

'What I'd like to know is where the eyes of the people are who dare to say anything against our class. Lydia, are you really not wearing a corset?'

'I always go around like this.'

'And as shapely as a goddess, too. But Valery was telling me that you have a lot of depraved girls among you, and that they've *all* taken off their rings and have decided not to wear earrings or any other kind of ornament.'

'What business is it of his?'

'It's his business to the extent that he takes an interest in everything. But tell me – is that really true?'

'Yes, it is.'

'Well, I warrant you you'll see that a lot of them won't be able to hold out.'

'Very possibly.'

'If earrings suit a girl she won't hold out, she'll wear them.'

'So what? If she doesn't hold out, she'll at least have had a few lessons in holding out, and that's better than nothing. Farewell, *ma tante*!'

'And if a girl has a terrible figure she'll do better to wear a corset.'

'Really, *ma tante*, how can such nonsense possibly interest us? Goodbye.'

'Goodbye, my pretty Lydia, such a pretty girl you are! The only thing that worries me is that you'll end up going to live with one of those non-resisters.'

Lydia smiled a cool but affectionate smile and said:

'*Ma tante*, how can one tell what may happen to one? Well, at least I won't run off with an opera singer.'

'No! For the love of God, no! Anyone you like, but not one of those non-resister boys. Those "urchins" with their little rumps and tails . . . there's nothing more repugnant than them!'

'Oh, *ma tante*: perhaps I've simply lost my sense of what's repugnant.'

'Well, better let everything be repugnant than be like those people whose teaching consists in trying to forbid us to marry and have our children baptized. Marry, and then may God preserve you as it pleases Him.'

At this point the girl's aunt stood up and proceeded to make the sign of the cross over her; then she accompanied her into the vestibule and there whispered to her:

'Don't think badly of me for being sharp with you just now. I had to do it, with that woman there, and I'd advise you to be careful, too, in her presence.'

'Oh, fiddlesticks, *ma tante*! I'm not afraid of anyone.'

'Not afraid? . . . Don't talk of things you know nothing about.'

'Oh, *ma tante*, I don't even want to know about them: there's *nothing for me to be afraid of*.'

Having said this, the girl began to fuss and flutter, looking for the door-handle, and emerged on to the staircase in a state of some confusion, her face aflame, exhibiting a mixture of embarrassment, anger and regret, all at the same time.

As she passed the hall porter she lowered her veil, but the porter, with his keen, observant gaze, saw that she was crying.

'That girl's forever being told off,' he remarked to the yard-keeper, who was standing by the gate.

'Yes, she's caught it for something, by the looks of her,' the yard-keeper replied, being no less observant.

Meanwhile the lady of the house returned to her 'salon' and asked:

'How do you like that little specimen?'

The female visitor merely lowered her eyes like a gentle doe and replied:

'It's hard to know what's going on inside her, but there's a common strand running through it all.'

'Oh, she was relatively quiet today, but last time it almost developed into a scandal. Someone had begun to reminisce about the good old days, when no one ever dared to say "no" to the prospective son-in-law's father. And she just said straight out: "What a good thing we're at least spared that nowadays." '

'They leave those gymnasia so practical-minded that the warmth and affection of life in the women's institutes are quite simply beyond their comprehension.'

'Quite so. On that occasion I asked her straight out: "Wouldn't you find it touching if you were presented with a fiancé?" And would you believe it, she flared up and said: "I'm not one of your serf-girls!" '

'It's as I say – there's a common strand running through it all. And the arrogance with which she talks so confidently about the personal affairs of that Fedora's wretched sister!'

'She has a lot of feeling for children.'

'But what's a woman to do with the rest of her life? Children can't fill it indefinitely.'

'Oh, children mean a dreadful amount of trouble!'

'Yes, even the simplest, most unrefined people seek oblivion in love affairs if they have children. I have an excellent woman who lives here and works as a laundress; she's forever having to struggle with herself, and the result is that every year she sends a new inmate to the foundling hospital. And her anonymous author keeps on writing her letters, never signing them, and won't listen to a word of reason: he turns up on her doorstep, gives her a good hiding and then helps himself. And that's what all our women are like. There's a kind of "Monsieur Alphonse"[1] mentality in our way of life. And when I said to her: "Give them all up, or else turn to religion: that will help you," she took my advice and went off to Kronstadt,[2] but on her way back she bought some Viborg krendels[3] and dropped in on the villain to have tea with him, and now she's carrying another burden around and is as pleased as can be. What's to be done about it? "I can't help it," she says. "The Devil's stronger than me." When a woman admits her own weakness, one must simply accept it.'

'Yes, one accepts it because that's our simple, native Russian way.'

'Just so, just so. There it is, our poor Russian female flesh, not like those, what are they? – English oilcloth dolls. Pure, but cold.'

'Oh, how cold! I mean, she's all for children, but mark my word – she doesn't like them.'

'Never!'

'I tell you, she cares about children in general, but she never makes a fuss of them, and doesn't even kiss them.'

'That's actually not such a bad thing – that she doesn't kiss them, I mean.'

'Oh, it's supposed to be unhygienic, of course, I'll admit that – but she doesn't even enjoy it!'

'Really? But surely it's an instinct that's inborn in women – to cuddle children.'

'Cuddling, no! All she'll permit is caring about them. She says one must only love those who themselves have love for other human beings. And she says infants are incapable of that.'

'But does anyone really know what a little one will grow into later on?'

'That's exactly what she says: "I don't like *unknown* quantities, I like what I know and understand." '

'Such casuistry!'

'That's what I say, too: it doesn't sound as though it comes from the heart, it sounds like mathematics. She doesn't even believe that other people really like children, either . . . "Otherwise," she says, "there wouldn't be those wicked people who've brought the Russian Christian name into contempt among the educated." I mean, they don't put a very high price on our upper classes. And, just fancy, they quote Maikov[4] to support this attitude:

> The greatness of a people lies
> In what it bears within its heart.'

The lady of the house and the female visitor both exchanged glances and both immediately sank into reflection; as they did so, their faces assumed an unfeminine, official expression. The female visitor was the first to emerge from this state, and she remarked:

'At the same time as we Russian women sign Madame Adam's[5] salutatory address, we could do worse than to protest against those institutions which fail to instil respect for our Russian origins.'

The lady of the house began nervously to twist the piece of paper in her fingers again. Knitting her brows, she whispered reflectively:

'But who will take the first step?'

'Does it really matter who takes it?'

'But, however . . . In the old days my brother Luka . . . He's a man of independent means and has never been a liberal, and he has no reason to fear for himself . . . In the old days he would strike up a conversation about anything under the sun, but nowadays he won't do it, not for the world! He has given us the cold shoulder in no uncertain manner, and has taken Lydia under his wing instead, and that's terrible, because his entire fortune is an acquired one, and he can give it away to anyone he pleases.'

'Do you mean that Lydia Pavlovna could get her hands on it all?'

'Nothing would be simpler! My sons aren't in Luka's good books, and brother Zakhar he considers a spendthrift and a "cesspool". He'll support Zakhar's family, but he won't leave Zakhar himself anything.'

The female visitor rose to her feet and walked over to the open upright piano. A moment later she asked:

'And where are Zakhar Semyonych's wife and daughters just now?'

'His wife . . . I don't exactly know . . . she's in Italy or France.'

'Something delayed her in Vienna.'

'Oh, but that was ages ago! If you were to count all the times she's been delayed, we'd be here all evening. But she only has three of her daughters with her just now. Nina, the youngest, was married to Count Z. last year, you know. He's awfully rich.'

'And awfully old?'

'Oh yes, he's at least seventy – some people say he's more than that – and she's only twenty. There are a lot of them, you know: four girls. And the old man, the Count, married to spite his relatives. He still hopes to have children. We offered up prayers in church for him.'

'May God help him!'

Just then the door opened wide and in walked a cheerful, rotund, grey-haired general with a scholar's badge on his lapel. His eyes were lively and penetrating, and were set in a large face which was capable of assuming the most diverse expressions.

This was brother Zakhar.

The lady of the house extended her hand in greeting to him, and said:

'Speak of the devil; we were just talking about you.'

'Why, precisely?' the general inquired, sitting down and acknowledging, rather stiffly, the presence of the female visitor.

'What do you mean, why? We were just talking about you, that's all.'

'In our country no one ever talks about others without saying nasty things about them behind their backs.'

'But there are exceptions.'

'Only two: they're *père* Jean and *père* Onthon.'[1]

'You insist that his name should be pronounced Onthon, and not Antoine?'

'That's how it's pronounced by people who know a lot more about these things than I do, and whose religious faith is a lot stronger than mine. I'm not much of a believer myself.'

'You ought to be ashamed of yourself.'

'But what can one do if one doesn't believe in anything?'

'That used to cause our mother no end of suffering.'

'I remember, and I used to try to obey her, but I couldn't keep up the pretence. She would say: "May your guardian angel go with you" – and I went everywhere with my guardian angel, and that was as far as it went!'

'Olympia's in town.'

'I always think her name's "Olympiada". Not that I find her especially interesting.'

'She has a lot of news, and some of it concerns you. Your daughter, Countess Nina, is pregnant.'

'Really? I expect the little slut is acting out that story of Boccaccio's, *The Magic Tree*. All the same, I'll drink a bottle of champagne today and send a telegram of congratulation to the Count. Incidentally, the other day I ran into a friend of my son-in-law and discovered that the fellow's only fourteen years older than me.'

'Does anyone know anything about how they're getting on together?'

'I've no idea.'

'But haven't you been to see Olympia?'

'I? No, my guardian angel hasn't taken me there. It's true that I did see some woman rattling along in a carriage, whose driver had a clock on his back, facing her. "Who's that vulgar woman who's suddenly appeared from nowhere?" I thought. Then suddenly I realized it was her. And immediately she made life lose its savour for me. Then, in my effort to escape from her, I ran smack into a Jew to whom I owe a very large sum of money.'

'Poor little Zakhar!'

'But, thank God, my guardian angel was watching over me, and our meeting happened outside a church. I immediately rushed inside and walked up to the pulpit, but the Jew took fright and hung back in the doorway. The only thing was – there are such extraordinarily inconvenient arrangements in churches nowadays! Imagine, they only keep one door open – all the others are locked. Why do they do that? In Paris all the churches are open all day.'

'In our country, my dear, people often steal things . . . There have been several thefts.'

'The mischief-makers! And just imagine – because of that I ended up having to stand through several services in succession. But in the end I managed to give the Jew the slip. He was waiting for me outside the main door, but I managed to nip out through the door at the back of the altar with the help of a priest I know, and then – quite by chance – I bumped into Lydia. She was feeling a bit depressed, and in order to cheer her up I told her all about how first I had nearly fallen into the clutches of Olympia and then of the Jew, and had finally escaped through the sanctuary. Hearing about it brightened her up, and she came along with me to have a cup of hot chocolate.'

'And you consoled her? What a kind uncle!'

'Yes, but I had another motive, too. At the place where I went to there was a . . . ballerina, who'll certainly never succeed in portraying a goddess . . . I showed Lida to her and said: "Look, you silly woman, that's what a goddess looks like!" But who's been upsetting Lida, and where did it happen?'

'I haven't a clue. I expect she met her match, that's all; though she herself said in this very house that it was impossible for *anyone* to offend her.'

'Oh, that's just more of those dreadful Tolstoyan *bêtises*! I swear to you that it's Leo Tolstoy who gets them into such a tizzy and makes them say such stupid things. *Da ist der Hund begraben.* I really don't understand what that old man is after. It all comes of everyone shouting from every corner of the globe that he's the wisest man that ever lived – the whole thing has simply turned his head. And I can't for the life of me understand what they see in him that's so wise.'

'Neither can I.'

'No, and neither can anyone. He gets it all from abroad. I once actually lived on the same street as him, and I must say I never noticed there was anything particularly wise about him. I remember, too, once seeing him at the theatre, and afterwards at the house of a mutual acquaintance; when everyone had been served with tea he said to the manservant: "Bring me a glass of vodka, Brother."'

'And he drank it?'

'Yes, he drank it and took a snack – Oh, I don't remember, a roll or a slice of bread, perhaps. At any rate, it was all perfectly ordinary – and yet now he's taken to behaving strangely and has ended up among the wise men! . . A fluke, if you ask me! But even though I can't go along with his brand of

Christianity, which would mean the end of all decent behaviour, I do have a certain respect for him.'

'Why?'

'Not because of his great wisdom, of course! That's a lot of nonsense. No, it's those non-resisters of his I like – one can really have a good chat with them over a cup of coffee.'

'I must say I haven't noticed it.'

'Oh, but you're mistaken! ... They have a most original view of a great many things. I wouldn't go so far as to say that it would ever be possible for any of their fantasies to be realized, of course. The times aren't right for that sort of thing. But where's the harm in talking about it? I mean, after all, even Bismarck used to enjoy talking with the socialists. But these "urchins" are on an opposite tack to the socialists.'

'How do you mean, on an opposite tack?'

'It's like this: these non-resister fellows, you know, always renounce their inheritances in favour of other members of their family. That's exactly what Peter the Great tried to achieve by means of the right of primogeniture ... It ought to be encouraged, so that estates don't get broken up. All that's wrong with Tolstoy is that he's devilishly vain; on the other hand, he does have a lot of character. That's something rare in our country. You won't bend *him* into the shape of a ram's horn or make him bleat, ram-like, for some civil decoration: "ba – a – ah!" '

The general prodded his throat with his fingers and produced some sounds which much amused the lady of the house and her female visitor.

'But why does he have that intolerable shrewdness, and why does he keep going on about doing without everything?'

'Oh, that's just the bad side of him. But I usually put my mind at rest with that Russian proverb of ours: "The Devil's not as bad as his urchins." '

'That's just what I always say, too: he sits tucked away out there, heaven knows where, but these "Figaro here's" and "Figaro there's" multiply like chickens.'

'Chickens is the right word ... Why do they go around puffing themselves up as though they were growing their tail-feathers?'

'They ought to be made the subject of an inquiry, so we can find out.'

'Well, that *might* upset them, I suppose.'

'They don't have any qualms about upsetting religion.'

'My religion can't be upset: where religion's concerned, I'm a follower of Byron: I eat my oysters and drink my wine, and I don't give a damn about who created them – Jupiter, Pan or Neptune, it's all the same to me. I mean, I don't intend this as blasphemy, but his intolerable shrewdness with regard to our affairs is positively loathsome. And why does he have to keep telling us that the saying "Neither cast ye your pearls before swine" has got nothing to do with warning people not to go blabbing their heads off about anything and everything to the first sordid brute who comes along? Everybody knows that some people are angels, and others are pigs.'

'Except that I hope those charming creatures stay in their proper places.'

'Yes, they all need to be kept in their sties, but sometimes things are different – sometimes the pigs sit themselves down in drawing-rooms.'

'Good Lord! What abominations!'

'Oh yes, there are a lot of abominations around.'

'But, on the other hand – are there any angels anywhere?'

'Yes, there are . . . There are even angels such as our Lydia!'

'I disagree. Girls who don't really know what an angel is.'

'You ladies torment them in the most godless fashion; one might even go so far as to say that you torture them.'

'In what way?'

'You keep carping on at them and teasing them, and when the poor girls are unable to endure any more and blurt out something to you in confidence, you tell it to all and sundry and thereby cause them immense hurt. Quite frankly, I think that's rather mean!'

'I've never heard of anything of the sort.'

'Well, believe me, I have. They say that when Lydia came to one of your balls wearing a high-necked dress you made a stinging remark about it to her.'

'I never did!'

'You made fun of her in an offensive manner: you said that when she became a lady she would probably appear before her future Adam dressed as a Carmelite nun, in a double hood, and she apparently replied that she might very possibly go to her Adam dressed as Eve, but that she didn't feel like displaying her shoulders to strangers at a ball.'

'Do you know, it's true – she really did say that!'

'She said it because you kept on at her as you did, and you shouldn't have. Byron made the splendid observation that "Even a broken-down nag will kick if the harness cuts her flesh," and, I mean to say, Lydia isn't a nag, she's a bold and attractive young girl. Blow me if it wouldn't be worth giving up all one's privileges and going back to being a student again.'

'Are you courting her, is that it?'

'Oh, not really – but you should hear what my elder brother Luka has to say about her! He says he spent the happiest summer of his life with her. I mean to say, he'll soon be getting on for eighty! And the fact is that she did indeed work the most remarkable wonders over there on his estate last year. He has a muzhik called Simka, the fellow used to round up the bears whenever there was a bear-hunt on. He was a man of about forty-eight, and he'd contracted sciatica. He'd been sweating a lot, and had sat down on a frozen stone – that's how he got sciatica . . . It's a disease of the sciatic nerve . . . I expect you're aware of which part of the body it affects?'

'Please spare us the details.'

'Well, for the past three years the doctors had been giving him various forms of treatment without much result, and the poor fellow had gone on coughing up the necessary cash; faith healers had had a go at trying to cure various parts of his anatomy, but they hadn't much success either – just took the prayer-money. And the whole enormous family of this Hercules had arrived at the point of ruin. But Lydia came to her uncle's for a visit, and said: "This man can be helped; only we must work on him patiently."'

'I say, she really had no business taking on something like that,' the lady of the house observed with restrained sarcasm.

'Yes, she proceeded to lay out that big hulk of a muzhik on his belly twice a day and massage him below the waist. Can you imagine? With those wonderful, classical hands of hers, on that area of a muzhik's body? I just took one look and said: "How will any man ever be able to kiss your hand again after this?" And she said: "Our hands weren't given us in order to be kissed, but in order to be of use and service to other people!" When brother Luka saw it – he's really turned into a nervous wreck of an old man, you know – he fairly burst out sobbing . . . The priest came to the house to ask him for some firewood, and Luka took hold of the muzhik, dragged him outside and exhibited him to the caller: "Look!" he said. "Do you see this?" And the priest replied: "Yes, I do, your excellency."

' "And do you grasp its significance?"

' "Yes, I grasp it, your excellency," he said. "Those of little faith are only lazy about going to church; they're not so slow when it comes to practical matters."

' "You bet they're not slow! Now you go and offer up a few prayers for them in church. That's your job. And if you do that, I'll see you get some firewood."

' "Certainly, your excellency," said the priest. "I shall make the greatest of efforts."

'And he didn't make any efforts at all, I suppose?'

'Well, what would you expect? He'd be a fool to go and exert himself when the firewood was already as good as his. The only thing is that now Simka's on his feet again and earning a living for his family, whenever he sets eyes on Lydia he immediately starts weeping and squawking "Don't ever die, miss! Let me go to the grave in your stead . . . You're like a mother to us!" Oh, say what you like, but those girls are wonderful.'

'Except that they'll bring the human race to an end.'

'How so?'

'They'll never marry.'

'Nonsense! If the right man comes along, they'll marry him. But the other way might be better, anyway, because to tell the truth, we men have turned into such villains that no girl with any sense ought ever to consider marrying us.'

'Even though they end up old maids.'

'And what's wrong if they do?'

'Women who end up old maids always develop sour characters.'

'Only the ones who desperately wanted to get married and whom their temperament makes that way.'

'It has absolutely nothing to do with temperament; it's rather that old maids are looked upon as rejects.'

'That's how idiots view them; those with a bit of sense, however, look with a certain amount of respect on a mature woman who simply didn't care to get married. I mean, even the Church approves of celibacy and spinsterhood. Or am I mistaken? Perhaps that isn't so?'

The lady of the house smiled, and replied:

'No, you're right: but I must say I find it interesting to see *you* stepping in on the side of celibacy, my unconscionable little Zakhar.'

'What else can I do, my dear? I'm not the man I once was, either, and now that I'm sixty-five, instead of some vivacious grisette it's the thought of death that visits me, and compels me to reflect. Now don't you go laughing at that. When the Devil himself starts getting old, he'll become a hermit. Just go and take a look at our Old Believers, not here but out in the back-woods. I mean, they all live it up and sin away like mad, but they do have one excellent custom: when a man's gone sixty, he moves out of the *chulan*,[1] leaving the woman with whom he has cohabited there, and often moves out of the house altogether. In the kitchen garden he builds himself a shack – it looks like a small bath-house – and there he settles down with a spe-cially chosen lad, a sort of "Gehazi"[2], and lives out the rest of his days in the reading of the Evangelist or *The Source of Enlightenment*,[3] ceasing to have anything to do with money or practical affairs, and in general keeps out of the way of the young, whose turn it now is. I really commend that. Let them say what they like about the old hermits dropping in on their old women in the *chulan* once a week, on Saturday nights, for old times' sake – I personally am convinced they only go there in order to pick up their clean underwear ... Dear old men and women! What a good time they'll have in eternity after all that!'

'Poor little Zakhar! You sound as though you'd like to be one of them, too!'

'Oh, without question! But what chance of that have we unbelievers? By the way, do my eyes deceive me, or has your Arkady acquired another boy?'

The lady of the house knitted her brows and replied:

'I can't think why that should interest you.'

'Oh, it doesn't, it was simply the mention of Gehazi that put it into my head, but if it's not all right to talk about it, let's change the subject. How's Valery, getting his university course into the bag all right, is he?'

'Why does it have to be "getting it into the bag"?'

'Oh all right, "finishing", then. It's the same thing, isn't it? He hasn't been bitten by the Jacobin bug, I hope?'

'My son was brought up on a healthy diet, and he need fear no bugs.'

'Don't be too hopeful: an upbringing at home is equivalent to the temperature at home. The warmer it is in the room, the greater the danger that the children will catch cold when the bacillus strikes.'

'A plague on your wicked tongue! But I have no fears for Valery: God takes care of him.'

'Oh yes, I had forgotten: he's a "warm believer", isn't he?'

'You shouldn't make jokes about such things. We Russians are all warm believers.'

'Yes, we're a jolly fervent lot! But wait, ladies – I've just seen one of Ge's[4] new paintings.'

'Another of his omelettes?'

'No. This one is positively an *atrocity*! It's the most dreadful sight!'

'I'm very glad they're turning him out of all the exhibitions. He was pointed out to me once . . . Lord! Those trousers and that coat!'

'It's a coat that has swallowed a lot of solar radiation, but that's not the serious part.'

'But is his daubing serious, in your opinion?'

'I'm not talking about his daubing – I'm talking about his coat.'

'What nonsense!'

'It isn't nonsense. He was to have been presented at court, but he couldn't go because he'd given his coat away to a flunkey of his acquaintance.'

'But how did people ever come to hear about it?'

'He told everyone himself.'

'How stupid of him!'

'And insolent!' said the female visitor, backing her hostess up. But the general concluded:

'It's wonderful, because these – whatever it is you call them – "non-resister fellows", or "urchins", are all fighting something; whereas we who suppose we're "*resisters*", and therefore grown-up, aren't really fit for a damn thing except licking up the slops on our plates.'

'Just listen to him!' the lady of the house said, jokingly. 'He won't stop talking until he's planted a thorn in someone's side.'

And, having delivered herself of this remark, she gave a condescending sigh and went out of the room with the air of being about to attend to some household task.

The general and the female visitor were left alone in the drawing-room, and the tone of their conversation altered at once.

The general knitted his brows and began to address the female visitor in a somewhat peremptory fashion:

'I thought I would rather talk to you here, as your sick husband came to see me yesterday and was extremely persistent. If you will permit me to say so, it was very cruel of you to send a sick old man on an errand of that kind.'

'What errand of what kind?'

'The sort of errand that has no name in the language of decent people.'

'I don't know what you're talking about; what I do know is that I sent you a letter, and that you, being a careless person, failed to answer it.'

'Allow me to point out that in order to have sent you a satisfactory reply to that letter I should have had to send you a thousand roubles.'

'Yes.'

'Well, that's just it! I'm not the Shah of Persia, who simply has to pick up a handful of diamonds in order to settle a matter.'

The lady turned pale; her eyes flashing with anger, she asked:

'What does this mean? That's the second time someone has mentioned the Shah of Persia in my presence today.'

'How should I know why people keep mentioning him in your presence? All I can tell you is that there are people for whom I have long ago done all that I could and even that which I could not, and which I would not have done for anything in the world, had it only been myself who had been threatened with unpleasantness, and not others as well.'

The general was plainly angry, and in vehement tones he said:

'Twenty years have passed since your husband so astonishingly discovered that I had been at your house and . . . I rescued myself and I rescued you, but I didn't rescue my diary, and so here I am taking care of people . . .'

'Oh, you're not still harping on about that old tale of woe, are you?'

'With your permission, madam: I am! I'm not a cad, and so I'm harping on about it and performing base actions for your sake – anything, just as long as I take all the blame upon myself. I go to intercede on your behalf among persons with whom I should much prefer to have no dealings at all, but that's still *not enough* for you. Tell me, when will you finally be satisfied?'

'Other women get more.'

'Now why do you say that? Look, you really must forgive me! I don't know anything about all that, about how much you get, how much you've been awarded. It may be that some women are cleverer than you . . . or that they put more effort into it and perform a greater number of favours . . .'

'Nonsense! None of us are capable of performing favours. You can't make fish soup without fish . . .'

'Well, I give up . . . "Without fish", you say? Good Lord! Are there really no fish left?'

'Just imagine, there aren't any! We're fishless!'

'Well, I don't know what you can do then . . . I've told you that I really have no idea about these affairs of yours. I may be guilty of anything and everything, but that is one kind of abomination I have never been involved in.'

The general raised one arm high in the air and fervently crossed himself.

'Here,' he said nervously, taking an envelope out of his pocket and handing it to the lady. 'Here, madam! Please take it, and quickly. It contains exactly one thousand roubles. I'm a poor, bankrupt fellow, but I never steal other people's money. A thousand roubles. That's the allowance I've managed to wheedle for you, the second time this year. Only please, please don't thank me! I'm doing this with the greatest of loathing, and I beg you . . .'

The lady was about to say something, but he got in before her:

'No, no! I beg you, don't send that wretched husband of yours to me again! I beseech you, for I have nerves and at least the remnants of a conscience. You and I once basely deceived him, but that was a long time ago, and in those days I was able to do it because back then he was deceiving others in his turn. But now? . . . That palsied look of his, those shaking knees . . . Oh, Lord deliver me! For God's sake, spare me that! Otherwise one of these days I shall throw myself on my knees before him and confess everything to him.'

The lady burst out laughing and said:

'I'm sure you'd never do anything so stupid.'

'I would, you know.'

'Well, somehow it doesn't greatly scare me.'

For a moment, a fleeting smile traversed the general's features – it was, however, a smile which he suppressed. Then he said:

'Aha! You mean it wouldn't be anything new for him! O Lord! Please strike me down, so that there may be an end to our accursed liaison!'

'You really are an old windbag, you know.'

The smile reappeared on the general's face; rising to his feet, he replied:

'Yes, yes, I'm an old windbag – how "wonderfully" you put it.'

And, making no attempt to conceal his disdain for the female visitor, he put on his peaked cap right there and then, in the drawing-room, and went out, barely deigning to confer the merest of nods on his interlocutress.

In the vestibule a housemaid with a Chinese slant to her eyes and the figure of a porcelain doll came out to attend to him. She gave him a quiet nod and helped him on with his coat.

'*Merci*, my dear,' the general said to her. 'Please tell my sister that I couldn't wait for her today, because . . . I took some medicine today. And here,' he added in a whisper, 'take this as a keepsake.'

And he lowered a rolled-up ten-rouble note into the neck of the girl's dress; when she bent forward in order to keep the note in place, he kissed her on the neck and said, quietly:

'I'm an old man and I don't permit myself to kiss women on the lips.'

With that, he pressed her hand, and she pressed his.

Downstairs, by the front door, he put on his galoshes and, after digging in his pocket for a moment, produced two copeck pieces from it and gave them to the hall porter.

'There you are, my good fellow.'

'Thank you very much, your excellency,' the hall porter said, keeping his hand near the peak of his cap in military fashion.

'They're real, my good fellow . . . Those ones weren't made in Peski[1] . . . You can confidently take them down to the corner shop and exchange them for a pound of ground coffee. But be careful – it spoils the gastric juices!'

'Oh, I'll be careful, your excellency!' the hall porter replied, as he buttoned the general into the rug of the hired sleigh. But all the while the general kept up this cheerful banter, he made an 'indiscriminate search' about his person with both hands, and when he was at last satisfied that he had not a single copper left on him, he quickly told the driver to halt, hopped out of the sleigh and set off on foot.

'I'm going to take a stroll instead,' he said to the hall porter. 'It's a fine day now.'

'Very good, your excellency.'

'That's it, my fellow, "very good"! Consider me in your debt to the tune of one rouble for that witty remark.'

The general muffled himself up in his moth-eaten beaver coat and turned the corner of the street on his tired, worn-out legs.

When he had disappeared from view, the hall porter shook his head and said to the yard-keeper:

'It's over two months now since he borrowed two roubles from me to pay the cabby, and he forgets that every time!'

'Must be frustrating,' the yard-keeper replied, as he scratched his back.

'Oh well, what of it . . . When he does have money, he stuffs it into everybody's pockets.'

'Wait till he's flush, then!'

'I will, don't worry.'

No sooner was the female visitor alone than she immediately opened her velvet purse and, hurriedly pulling out the money she had stuffed into it, began to count it. The full sum of one thousand roubles was there. The lady folded the notes in a more orderly fashion, and was about to close her purse again, when someone seized her by the hand.

She had not observed the well-fed, pink-complexioned young man, with a mobile Adam's apple and a candid smile on his lips, who had soundlessly entered the room. He placed an agile hand on the bronze lock of the velvet purse, and said:

'Confiscated!'

The female visitor's initial reaction was to give a start, but her momentary sense of fright vanished almost at once, and was replaced by a different emotion. She brightened with happiness, and quietly said:

'*Valerian*! Where have you been? Goodness me!'

'Where have I been? Where I always am: everywhere and nowhere. Actually, I've just come down from heaven in order to reclaim this little bag of earthly impurity.'

The lady was about to say something to him, but he pointed with one finger towards the closed door of the adjacent room, took the purse from her hands, took all the banknotes out of it and put them in his pocket.

None of this appeared to make the slightest impression on the female visitor. Looking at her, one might have supposed that she had long been accustomed to being treated in this fashion, and that she actually enjoyed it. With both hands she held on to Valery's free arm and, looking him in the face, said quietly:

'Oh, if only you knew! . . . If only you knew how dreadfully worried I've been! I haven't seen you for three whole days! . . . They've seemed like an eternity!'

'Ah yes. But what can one do? I shan't forget these past few days myself in a hurry. Where haven't I gone dashing in order to get that idiotic thousand roubles? No, I'm now convinced that the surest means of getting money out of people is to devote one-self to the welfare of the poor! It's also one of the Lord's blessings that there are on the earth fools such as *oncle Zacharie*.'

'Don't say wicked things about him!'

'Oh, but I'm grateful to him: this is the second time he's given us a break.'

'Well, don't land yourself in this situation a third time, my dear.'

'If I lose as stupidly as that again, I'll hang myself.'

'What nonsense you talk!'

'No, seriously! They say it's a very pleasant form of death. Something like a kind of . . . Look, I even carry a length of string about in my pocket, just in case. I've tested it. It'll hold.'

'Oh good heavens, what are you saying?' the female visitor expostulated. Then, lowering her voice, she whispered: '*Avancez une chaise!*'

The young man made a comical face and again pointed in the direction of the curtained door.

The lady wrinkled her brow and, in a whisper, inquired:

'What is it?'

The young man put the palms of both hands to his mouth, and replied through the funnel thus formed:

'Maman is eavesdropping out there!'

'And that's not true, either! You're forever saying nasty things about your mother.'

Valery crossed himself and quietly assured her:

'It's all too true, alas; she's forever eavesdropping.'

'You ought to be ashamed of yourself!'

'No, on the contrary, I'm thoroughly ashamed of her; but I never condemn her, I simply warn others. I know she does it from the very best of motives . . . A mother's sacred emotions . . . '

'*Approchez-vous de moi*, my dear.'

'You mean you don't believe she's eavesdropping? . . . Very well, then I'll call her in.'

'I think we can do without those sort of experiments, thank you very much!'

'The best thing you could do is go home right away, and in twenty minutes . . .'

'You'll be there?'

He nodded, to indicate that he would.

She pressed his hand, and asked:

'You really mean it?'

'Of course I do – and you don't have to scratch my hand with your fingernails.'

'Sometimes I just can't help it.'

'Rubbish!'

'Just give me one kiss!'

'Whatever next?'

'Why not?'

'Oh, all right, then!'

The young man gave her a kiss and rose from his place beside her: he would very much have liked his lady to get up and leave right there and then, but she did not; instead, she kept whispering something. Her continuing presence here was a source of torment to him, and this was expressed in his features, which were distorted with rage. At the same time, however, he took her hand and, pressing it to his lips, said:

'*Lilas de Perse* – that's nice: I love that scent!'

The lady jumped to her feet and, clutching her forehead with one hand, teetered slightly off balance.

'What's wrong with you?' Valery asked her. 'Quick, you must get out into the fresh air!'

She gave him a sullen look, and hissed:

'That's despicable! . . . mean! . . . dishonourable! . . . After I went to the length of explaining it to you frankly . . . You have no right . . . You have no – right, no – right . . .'

'Oh for God's sake don't let's have you with hysterics! . . . The sooner you get out into the fresh air the better.'

'Fresh air ... nonsense ... I had to put on that performance ...'

'Yes ... and so you did ... Now go home at once and everything will be fine.'

'By all means! Please stay: Maman will be here in a moment.'

He rose to go, but she restrained him.

'I think I am going mad,' she said, putting the insides of her
fingers, which were growing cold, to her throbbing temples,
and again said: 'Help! I think I'm going mad!'

Valery was alarmed by the martyred look on her face, and he
began to make the sign of the cross over her. She pushed him
away indignantly, and whispered:

'Baptist!'

'What is it you want?'

'I? Humiliation and never-ending insults! I want you to be
with me!'

'But I *am* with you!'

'Oh, I don't mean here!'

'Well, go home quickly, then, I'll join you there in a moment,
and then you can die to your heart's content.'

'Oh how much I want that – I deserve to die.'

She was about to add something further, but instead she
kissed his hand and he, in his turn, bent over her and touched
with his lips the tress of hair that flowed down the back of her
neck.

The woman's distorted features were lit by a flash of sensual
ecstasy, and she hastily covered her hair with her veil and went
out of the room. Large, hysterical tears rolled down her cheeks,
her eyes grew cloudy, her lips and nose red and prominent, and
her entire face began to resemble the protruding muzzle of a
bitch on heat.

She realized that she looked a mess, and drew her veil
completely.

As she was walking past the hall porter he silently handed
her a letter which he had been keeping under the cuff of his liv-
ery jacket, and which was marked with the address of the
'lively spirit'; she threw him a three-rouble note and got into

the sleigh, tapping the driver on the back without saying anything to him.

'She can't see a thing for her tears!' the hall porter observed to his colleague. 'And what does he care?'

'Yes, members of the male sex don't lose their heads easily nowadays.'

When the lady had gone, young Valery himself closed the door after her and, returning to the drawing-room, took the crumpled banknotes out of his trouser-pocket and began to count them.

From behind the door which Valery had pointed out to the female visitor, his mother's voice did indeed make itself heard.

'Are you engaged on business?' she inquired.

'I've finished now.'

'Why don't you buy some "industrials"? Everyone says they'll have doubled in value by spring.'

'I know of things that are a little more profitable, Maman.'

'And what might they be, may I ask?'

'Oh, all sorts of things! I mean, nowadays they're packing the moneylenders away in mothballs, and even our "mutual acquaintance" Michel has thrown in the towel ... We need something new in their place.'

'Quite so, we do. But what?'

'Ah, Maman! Something that is only possible for someone like myself, someone whom people consider a careless spendthrift with not a copeck to his name.'

From behind the door came a sound of scissors cutting something, and then being put down.

'Are you sewing, Maman?'

'Yes, my son, I'm patching my holes, I'm mending things, sewing up the rags I don't want my housemaid to see ...'

'How very sensible and noble, Maman.'

'And unpleasant.'

The young man was about to say something in reply to this, but he remained silent, his Adam's apple working furiously up and down.

Once again from behind the door there was a sound of a strip of material being cut with scissors, and of the scissors being put down. As this happened, the lady of the house said:

'I think you'd stand to gain far more if you were to help Uncle Zakhar set right the ruinous follies of his youth. Luka would probably appreciate that, and might start inviting us to his home.'

'That may very well be so, Maman, but you know I'm not vain and am not given to boasting about the houses I'm invited to.'

'But the plain fact is that he'd give you lots of money.'

'Well, that would be very nice, but how would I go about it?'

'You'd have to buy the securities Zakhar is afraid of buying.'

'What you mean, dear mama, is that I should have to *steal* them!'

'You have such a vulgar way of talking that it's impossible to hold a conversation with you.'

'I'm not being vulgar, Maman; just making clear what would have to be done.'

'It isn't true. Anyway, that woman will do it all for you.'

'Aha! That's where you're mistaken! That woman may be an excellent agent and an excellent mathematician – but you won't pull the wool over her eyes.'

'But she thinks you're a gambler and a spendthrift.'

'Yes, Maman, but I'm making a very great effort to build that kind of reputation for myself, solely because it will stand me in good stead in the new conditions of the market.'

'To tell you the truth, I don't really see the necessity for it.'

'But it's so simple! Don't you see that everyone has tried the "goody-goody" sort of life and has had enough of it? . . . What's to be done? The human race is vicious and ungrateful. *Felicitas temporum* is taking its leave . . . We need a reaction . . . A reaction is required.'

'And what will happen in the reaction?'

'That isn't yet clear, Maman, but everyone knows that nothing happens the same way twice, and that sunshine follows after rain; and so to have a reputation as a spendthrift and a libertine carries with it a certain amount of advantage nowadays – it means to discover within oneself a certain trustworthiness, which very soon comes in handy.'

'Oh, you young people are prepared to do anything!'

'What else do you expect? After all, that's the way we're brought up: prepared to do anything.'

'But, my dear! How easily won your wisdom is.'

'Oh, Maman, what's wisdom to us? Even the satirists who write in the newspapers have read somewhere that "wisdom is a blessed inheritance", and they keep repeating it over and over again – yet there you and Papa went and failed to provide us with one.'

'Christian parents are not obliged to provide their children with an inheritance.'

'Oh, but I'm sorry – they are.'

'Where does it say so?'

'Oh, in the epistles of St Paul, which people are so fond of quoting. He says there, somewhere: "For the children ought not to lay up for the parents, but the parents for the children."'

'That's something out of Tolstoy's version, it's not in the regular one.'

'Not so! Why don't you take a look at Chapter Twelve of the Second Epistle to the Corinthians in the regular version?'

'How do you know all this – which epistle, and which chapter?'

'Ha! It's something that interests me. I'm out to nobble Tolstoy with it.'

'So nobble him! That'll put you ahead if nothing else will.'

'With your permission. The time will come.'

'Why should time come into it? Everyone's had enough of him.'

'Indeed so, but one shouldn't do anything gratis. You can't make a fur coat out of kind praise. Ever since the days when paper money was first invented people have had to pay for the services they receive: if I provide a service with this hand, you must place a banknote in it.'

'But you may still receive an inheritance.'

'Oh, you still haven't stopped thinking about Uncle Luka, have you?'

'That's right, I haven't.'

'Well, I'll set your mind at rest: that inheritance has had it. "Abandon hope for ever!"'

'You can't know that for certain.'

'Oh yes, I can. My dear mother, I bought the knowledge from a notary's clerk. All the money's been given away to "nutritional establishments" and "public education".

'You're not serious?'

'Perfectly.'

'And what about Lydia?'

'She doesn't need it; she doesn't want to stir up envy and quarrelling, and so she's renounced it.'

'The silly idiot!'

'A pernicious one, too. She gave it to someone outside her own family.'

'But that can't be allowed!'

'It shouldn't be, I agree!'

'So what are you going to do?'

'Save my skin by whatever means are available, even if it's by a miracle.'

'So you believe in miracles nowadays, do you?'

'Oh, Maman! I believe in what I please. I want to live:

> "And I feel that I shall live, e'en though it be
> By miracle – oh, in miracles I do believe!"

'There's also something else I'd like to tell you – but let this be between ourselves.'

'Naturally.'

'We shall have to produce a new miracle-worker!'

'Such nonsense you talk!'

'No, I'm serious: it must be done. And I know where to find just the man.'

'But what can he do?'

'Oh, don't worry about that! ... He's already doing small items of work, and not at all badly, but we shall have to bring him out into society and promote his cause in the right quarters. Oh, I know what's needed in life!'

Mother and son stopped talking. Both appeared suddenly wearied by all the things they had been talking about, and by the difficulty of coming to this kind of decision. Having taken it, each felt the need of some kind of external stimulus or diversion; its arrival was not long delayed. During the very minutes when mother and son were brooding in silent horror on the course of action they had determined for themselves, there began to encroach from outside in the street a steadily accumulating noise, which suddenly became a violent roar, dispelling all the torments of their conscious minds. Valery was still sunk in silent meditation, but the lady of the house took alarm and started up in animation. Running out into the drawing-room, dressed only in her négligée, she rushed to the window and cried:

'Look, what a crowd of people!'

Valery stretched lazily, as though he were still half asleep, and, hardly opening his mouth, replied:

'That's no sort of a crowd, Maman. It's not even worth looking at.'

'Yes, but, I mean, it's so touching!'

'If you ask me – it isn't, not at all.'

'Well, yes, I know what you mean – but it's faith in action, you know.'

'To tell you the truth, I don't know.'

'But just think: our hall porter – he must be a complete nihilist.'

'Apparently he used to have a different sort of reputation.'

'What was that?'

'He was one of the lot that helped to round up the nihilists. Your general knows about him.'

'But wait a minute – I asked him: "What's the meaning of all this?" And he replied: "They're just a crowd of flibberty-gibbets rushing around without knowing why or wherefore."'

'Actually, that wasn't a bad reply.'

'Oh, that will do from you! But what a stupid lot they are, really. And why do they want everything at once?'

'Probably what they really want is to be flogged and sent into exile.'

'And what a nasty-looking lot they are: all haggard and wearing those tattered clothes!'

'Well, yes. They're "those who labour and are heavy-laden". I expect Jean and Onthon are down there somewhere.'

'Oh, do come and look! There's that pushy woman, the one everybody complains about. Really, will you look at how she's scratching them!'

At last Valery came to life and rose to his feet.

'Aha!' he said, smiling. 'Now her I do care about. She's got character, they call her Yelizavet Sparrow,[1] or some such name; she creates celebrities and then scratches and lambastes the very same public that has made them famous. If you want my opinion, she and Meshchersky[2] are the only two people who've understood the needs of those who don't know what they want. I'm going out to watch her crack those nuts!'

Valerian walked out into the vestibule, which was in darkness. Near the lamp, however, fussing about with matches, was the same attractive, slant-eyed housemaid who a little earlier had affectionately permitted the general to kiss her on the neck. When he caught sight of her, Valerian frowned and began to put on his gloves.

The maid threw the matches down and was on the point of leaving, but stopped again. She was uneasy, and her face grew flushed and took on a brazen expression.

Noticing this, the young man tossed his peaked cap on to his head and began to put on his coat unassisted.

The maid watched him briefly out of the corner of her eye, and then decided to help him. She held the coat for him, but hardly had he begun to put his arms into its sleeves than she threw it to the floor and disappeared behind the little cubby-hole that served as her living quarters. From this cubby-hole a small window, curtained round with blue taffeta, looked on to the front steps.

'Bitch!' Valery whispered after her and, retrieving his coat from the floor, he shook it out and put it on without help from anyone else. Then he went out on to the front steps and hastily descended them. His speed was to no avail, however, and as he ran a resonant voice from the window shouted:

'Look at him, with his hunched-up guilty back! He thinks I don't know where he's running off to! Damn you and your old women!'

But Valery kept running and tried not to hear the words one must suppose he had deserved.

At the foot of the steps the two brothers ran into each other – Arkady and Valery, the 'dawdler' and the 'lively spirit'. Arkady (the dawdler) was six years older than Valery (the lively spirit), and far more dependable than him. He was also a high-class 'half-breed': pudgy and with a prominent Adam's apple, like Valery's, but looking as though he were sitting up on his hind legs. His facial features at once resembled those of a puffy child and the muzzle of a circus wolf. There was always an unusual scent from him, which recalled the odour of apple seeds.

The dawdler found the door to his mother's flat open. It had remained so ever since Valery's recent emergence from it. Arkady drew his mother's attention to this fact in a disdainful voice. She shrugged her shoulders, and said:

'What am I to do? I mean, we're not even at liberty to have the servants we would like. Engaging and dismissing a servant is a most involved procedure, and the servants know it and aren't afraid – instead they do as they please.'

Arkady interrupted her:

'What's required is for Valery not to put himself in a position where he's dependent on a woman!'

His mother gestured with one arm and said:

'Oh, stop saying nasty things about women!'

As if in response to this, from the small room behind the coat-rack there came the sound of quiet, hysterical sobbing.

The lady of the house got up, closed the door and once again sat down.

'I shall never grow tired of saying that female servants are no good,' Arkady said quietly.

'They're less expensive and they're more useful,' his mother replied.

'Yes, but on the other hand you have to put up with all her escapades.'

'Oh, I don't know whose escapades are the worst! I think all this is the sort of thing that can drive a person mad.'

'You're forever saying that these days, Maman . . . But why did you send for me?'

'Brother Zakhar was here with me . . . When will all this come to an end?'

'Really, what *has* got into you? Uncle is always talking rubbish . . . he's famous for it.'

'Well, perhaps he does talk rubbish, but don't you go ruining your career. I really tremble for you!'

'There's no need for you to tremble, Maman. The days when blackmail was considered a cultured activity are over. Nowadays all the boys in the lowest form at school know that blackmail carries a penalty, and what's more, I don't much feel like staying here when that *fabulator elegantissimus* is making up heaven knows what sort of stories about us all. Aunt Olympia herself promised me she would settle this matter with Gustavych. His son-in-law is being transferred to the West, and I'll be given an independent appointment out East.'

'Oh, if only it were as easy as that for her to make up for her sin against me.'

'What sin is that?'

'What sin? The bane of my entire life.'

'Oh, I expect this is one of those things we children are not supposed to know about.'

'You don't know anything other than what concerns yourselves. Anyway, when is she going to arrange it all for you?'

'Today . . . perhaps at this very moment! If I have got the appointment, Aunt Olympia will look in here . . . I say, there she is,' he added, looking out of the window down at the street. 'I can see her carriage outside the front door and the driver with the clock on his back.'

The dawdler went into the vestibule and opened the door on to the front steps, up which an elderly, extremely massive lady was making her way; she was wearing a *talma* of the type worn by ladies of the diplomatic corps – a style much favoured by our Russian cooks. Beneath her fur *talma*, which she wore as though it were some kind of knightly cloak, a beaded cuirass glittered on her mighty bosom. The lady was breathing a little heavily, but was climbing the steps briskly enough. To the dawdler she said, with a smile:

'Look, I shall soon be sixty-five, yet my heart's forging away like a trusty blacksmith.'

As she said this, she took her nephew's hand and placed it against her cuirass. Then, entering the vestibule, she proffered her cheek to the lady of the house for a kiss, and went on:

'Do forgive me, I've just popped in to see you for a minute. I shan't take my cape off, I've merely come to tell you the good news: Arkady, you've got the appointment! Go, go to him at once and thank him. That will bind him, and cut off his path of retreat.'

'I shall go this very minute, *ma tante*,' Arkady replied, and began to look for his coat.

From behind the coat-rack the housemaid appeared, but Arkady quickly dodged away from her and left the house at the double.

Observing this, Olympia said with a smile, as she went into the drawing-room:

'He's still the same as ever . . . the same clown . . . afraid of women.'

'Alas!'

The lady of the house made a despairing gesture with one arm.

'There, there, my dear, it isn't worth a second thought! . . . They're not at all so unusual nowadays! Though I must say it's a relief that *il ne met plus de manchettes*.[1] Now he looks just like any other man. Well, *adieu*! Perhaps sometime I shall drop in and have a heart-to-heart talk with you, but just at the moment there are a thousand things I must attend to. Goodness, you've all gone to sleep in here! It won't do, you know! You're simply *frowsting*, as they say – chewing the cud . . . You need waking up! Wherever one looks these days one sees people who need waking up. Your slumber is holding back the whole of Slavdom. Holy Russia is the strength of the world – *sila mira* – and that will one day be its name: *Silamira*! But it is a strength that sleeps as yet! In time it will be otherwise. Then I shall no longer need to return from the West in order to give you a shove, as now, when you start grunting and snoring in such a thoroughly scandalous manner . . .'

'Yes, but in Russia we're all believers nowadays.'

'You're even poor in the matter of your faith, in my opinion: yours is a sleepy sort of faith . . . it's as if you were dreaming . . . as if you were only barely managing to keep yourselves afloat and only barely managing to believe, and as if at any moment you were going to sink and drown in oblivion . . . Farewell! . . . Until we meet again . . . I suppose you must have heard what Zakhar's daughter Nina has gone and done?'

'They say she's . . . going to be a mother.'

'Forget about what "they say". It's a fact! Of course she's going to be a mother . . . But how did it happen? . . . I mean, the Count's so old and stupid that he only got married in order to spite his daughters Goneril and Regan . . .'

'Such immoral behaviour!'

'Yes, but I bet you don't know the whole story, do you? *C'est un inceste!* She was given the task of driving a nephew to the station – he's still a cadet or something of that sort, even now . . .'

'Oh Lord! Lord!'

'Yes, it's a real "criminal *conversation de Byzance*"!'

Olympia began to make agitated movements with her head and arms, and walked towards the door, but the lady of the house detained her on the threshold and said:

'You've worked wonders in getting Arkady fixed up with a position again, but I'm so afraid – what if he really is mad?'

'Oh, leave off worrying and set your mind at rest,' Olympia replied. 'Remember what Oxenstjerna[2] used to say: "The exercise of politics requires a minimum of intellect."'

Olympia clasped the palms of her hands against her cuirass, and added:

'It's not up to us to supply the whole world with intellects – our *métier* is quite different, and it consists solely of putting salt on the tails of all who are striving forwards.'

Having thus explained her vocation, the lady gave her cuirass another slap and, shaking hands with the lady of the house in the English manner, went downstairs, got into her carriage and sat down at an oblique angle to the clock which jutted out from the small of the driver's back, and whirled off in order to *jouer un tour de son métier*.

The lady of the house, being left alone, lost no time in asking for her coat and galoshes to be brought for her; putting a bottle of smelling salts in her pocket, she left the house, saying she wanted to buy something at the 'bric-à-brac boutique'.

She was now experiencing that terrible fatigue that can only be imagined by an actress who is playing a role which means she must spend the entire act of a play on the stage.

She was very tired, almost exhausted, but there was still a great deal of strength left in her for the kind of struggles that faced her. Soon she would set herself to rights again out in the fresh air, and be in a position to give the very best account of herself in the place to which she had been appointed.

But while the cat was away, the mice of the house began to play . . .

Upon the lady of the house's departure, the housemaid with the slanting eyes and the figure of a porcelain doll walked through all the rooms and opened the casement windows in each of them. She then tugged back the curtain from the door and opened the door from the drawing-room into the boudoir, which also served the lady of the house as a study and a hiding-place. Here the maid cleared up all the mess, then took out a specially designed key, used it to open the desk and, having taken from it a scented sheet of ivory paper, lit a candle and, in a painstaking hand, wrote:

'If your proposals are reliable, then even though our ages are not similar, for the sake of politeness I agree to have complete sentiments for you, only on no account in your own home or in the presence of your servants.'

She read over what she had written, and then at the bottom, underneath her signature, added the following postscript:

'But please reply through the mail.'

Having finished her letter, the maid took an envelope from her mistress's blotting pad and began laboriously to write out the address, character by character. Just then the curtain over the door on the other side of the boudoir opened and into the room, her goitrous neck protruding like that of a goose, came a strapping, fair-complexioned woman of about forty-five, with a large mouth and a double chin. This was the cook.

'Give me a couple of her cigarettes,' she said to the housemaid.

'Take them yourself,' the maid replied, and resumed the addressing of her envelope.

The cook took one or two cigarettes out of the cornelian box, lit one of them and, sitting down on the silk pouffe in front of the mirror, began to squeeze a pimple on her chin with her fingernails, powdered the spot with her mistress's powder-puff, and said:

'I can't stand these pimples!'

'Don't slurp so much of that black beer, then.'

'I don't drink it any more.'

'Well, then stop cuddling those boys who bring the groceries.'

'What, seen me at it, have you?'

'You bet I have! I saw you tickling the boy from Zelenschikov's half to death yesterday. A proper old witch, you are.'

'He's just a baby, he hasn't any idea of what I'm up to.'

'Well then, you ought to wait until he does have an idea!'

'For heaven's sake, all I do is pet them and rumple their hair, the pretty boys. My godson was all of sixteen years old, and then he had to go and die – leaving me to pine for him. Anyway, what about you? Who are you leading into temptation now? Who are you writing to?'

The maid did not reply.

'Do you think I don't know? Oh, I know, all right!'

The Chinese maid still said nothing.

'Do you want me to tell you who it is?'

'All right, go on, tell me!'

'It's the general you're leading astray, that's who it is.'

'Yes, I admit it – it's him!'

She put the stamp on the envelope.

'There you go, laughing at me for giving the boys a fondle, when you're involved in something much worse.'

'I'm not involved in anything.'

'Then why are you shouting and looking such a sight?'

'I'm shouting because I've been a fool – I thought I was going to live in faithfulness.'

'There you are, you see! And now you look pregnant.'

'No, I don't. It doesn't show yet.'

'Then why was it that when the priest last called he blessed me and let me drink tea out of his saucer, but not you?'

'My hair was a mess: he doesn't like that. Anyway, what of it? Not all the things he says come true.'

The cook shook her head; then, sighing, she said in an instructive tone:

'Yes, to be sure, it's a mystery how he manages to get so much for the merchantry by his prayers, yet can't do it for the other professions.'

'He doesn't deliver.'

'You shouldn't say things like that, my dear, because even though he doesn't deliver and not all of what he says comes true, well, we've all got to have faith in the Lord's message, even though I personally . . . would like to tear all the tresses off that termagant, the way she scratches!'

'They'd have the law on you,' said the maid, who was of a mischievous but timid disposition. But the cook, who had more experience, retorted boldly:

'That's nothing: "disorderly behaviour likely to cause a breach of the peace" – eight days in nick. By God, I'll give her a hiding, you bet I will!'

Just then there was a sudden ring at the doorbell. The cook and the housemaid both leapt to their feet like lightning. The maid dextrously lowered the letter into her pocket and ran off to open the front door, while the cook went along the corridor that connected the vestibule with the kitchen, and hid herself near the door.

Valery entered and asked in a quiet voice:

'Who's at home?'

'Nobody,' the maid replied.

'What about Mama?'

'She's gone out.'

'And what about that idiotic carrying-on of yours – has it gone out too?'

'It's not idiotic! Anyway, tell me if you think I haven't got good reason for carrying on?'

The maid had assumed her most argumentative tone of voice.

'Please take these and stop sulking like a lady.'

'What are they?'

'Earrings.'

'I don't need earrings – get me some stuff to stop me being pregnant.'

'I'll get it for you later.'

'No, you're trying to pull the wool over my eyes. I'm not one of your idiots!'

'Take these for just now.'

'I don't want them.'

'You're so silly! Who shall I give them to, then?'

'What's that to do with me? I don't want them! I don't want anything from you, because you're not a gentleman, nor a scholar, but the very lowest of the low!'

Valery was about to interrupt her with a piece of crude behaviour, but she gave a convulsive shudder, said: 'Don't you dare!' and ran away to her cubby-hole.

The young man whisked off after her and said, affectionately:

'Listen . . . After all, you did want them . . . You asked for earrings . . . You might as well take them, now that I've gone and bought them!'

'Bought them? Where? In which store? Or did you pull them off some prostitute for a lark?'

'Why do you say such vulgar things?'

'I have to ask, don't I? I mean, what if I can't wear them?'

'What sort of a silly remark is that?'

'What I mean is, what if that honeysuckle rose of yours sees them and tears them off my ears?'

The young man flared up in anger.

'What "honeysuckle rose"?' he shouted.

'That old woman . . . your Kamchatka[1] . . . Well, she's sort of . . . honeysuckle-like . . .'

'What Kamchatka?'

'You mean you don't know?'

'Of course I don't know!'

'You've played the fool with me enough!'

'I tell you, I don't know who this Kamchatka is, or why you're going on about her.'

'Well, you go and ask her whether her real name's Kamchatka or whether she's just called that because other people get sent to Kamchatka because of her. All I know is that I'm not afraid of her, and I say she's a vicious old cow who ought to have died long ago instead of taking on little boys who're worse than the most blabber-mouthed girl.'

'I say, you really are forgetting yourself quite intolerably.'

'So what? I'm still able to. But I won't when I'm an old woman.'

Valery threw his gift on to the maid's chest of drawers and, taking her hand, said:

'I hate you!'

'What could be more noble than to hate me?'

'You've taken things to the point where you disgust me!'

'If I disgust you, why did you come here?'

'I only wanted to tell you that you're vile!'

'Very well! Please go right ahead! ... That's it, I'm vile! You've got it! ... To some people I'm not vile, but you've said it, and now you can leave. Your pulse throbs entirely in vain!'

'You're wrong, my pulse isn't throbbing!'

'It is! I can see it!'

'Well, I'll explain to you in a moment why it's throbbing.'

'Oh no, you won't, dear boy, no, no! I've grown so depraved by all these explanations of yours that people are beginning to notice it.'

He said something, but she replied: 'No!' Then again she said: 'No!' And then again:

'No, no, no! Wha-a-t? ... Aha! ... No! The present you gave me is no part of it. No, you're to blame and you must ask my forgiveness.

'And now ask it again.

'And again!

'Right, that's it! And now go ... Boys like you need to be scolded!'

At these words the eavesdropping cook went into raptures; beaming a merry smile, she spat and whispered:

'Ah, the rogue! She's not long out of her village, yet she knows the way to do it! She's got him on his knees again! Pah! Confound me if the Devil doesn't put honey in her mouth.'

And the cook held her breath even harder in an attempt to hear what would happen next, but there was no sound of any further scolding, because the door into the little cubby-hole swung to; meanwhile, from the other end of the corridor, where all concern was focused on the preparation of food, there crept a choking cloud of fumes.

The cook rushed to her seething altar and discovered the kitchen range in a state of utter chaos: the contents of one pan had boiled over and spilled, those of another had charred black, and the whole room was filled from ceiling to floor with a dreadful stench of burned food.

The cook lost her temper, and shouted:

'Ah, the Devil take you with your pulses and your scolding! You fallen angels will have to go without anything to guzzle today!'

So saying, full of wrath, she leapt up on to the table, opened the casement window and swung open the door that gave on to the back stairs; but no sooner had she done this than she beamed all over; fortune had smiled her way, too! Right there in the doorway stood a ruddy-faced grocery boy with a basket on his head, unable to bring himself to go inside.

'Ah!' the fair-complexioned woman cried gaily, greeting him. 'I *thought* I heard something! I wondered who it was creeping and crawling along, and it was you – hush, hush, shopmouse in a rush! Hullo, Petrushka!'

The boy sulked and was silent, and the curly-haired matron burst out laughing. Then, pulling him by his apron into the kitchen, she said briskly:

'That's enough of your sulking! . . . You silly boy! You're still alive, after all!'

'Only just,' the rosy boy replied tearfully. Immediately, however, he assumed a different tone of voice, and shouted: 'Come on then, take the basket, what are you waiting for? I haven't got all day!'

'What business is that of mine? Don't put it down here! . . . Can't you see this room is full of smoke? Take it in there, into my room.'

The boy set off with the basket and then stopped once again in indecision, but the cook pushed him into her room, and from it a pathetic whining at once became audible.

The evening settled down. All was quiet.

Clearer air had re-entered the kitchen; the smoke had drifted outside. Looking around him, the grocery boy timidly emerged from the cook's room; on his head he bore the empty basket, upside down. It covered his face entirely, a fact in which there was evidently some convenience for him. The cook saw him to the door and detained him a moment longer on the threshold; silently, she made him a threatening motion with one finger, then poured out for him a handful of her mistress's dried fruit. Lastly, she lifted the basket off his head, took his scarlet cheeks in her hands and kissed him on the lips. Both partners to the kiss laughed as she implanted it.

The boy had now shed his childish timidity, and she whispered to him:

'Let's go to the fête together. You wait and see what fun it is! . . . I'll make you a blue shirt for the occasion. Only you'll have to come back here tomorrow so I can measure you.'

'I'll come,' the boy replied.

She gave him another hug and, pressing his head against her bosom, said to him with maternal tenderness:

'And when they send you to the washerwoman at the laundry, don't you go talking to those girls of hers who do the ironing . . . do you hear? . . . They're flighty little things, they might lead you astray . . . '

'No-o-o! I wouldn't!' the boy replied. 'They make me feel too bashful.'

'So that's how it is, is it? Well, anyway, dearie, it doesn't matter. I'll bribe all the yard-keepers, and they'll report anything to me at once.'

The boy began to whistle, and as he walked down the front steps he really did display a "magnificent pride".

The yard-keeper came to greet him and gave him a bundle of firewood, saying:

'How old are you, Pyotr?'

'Thirteen.'

'My, my – an old man! And how is life treating you?'

'Oh, all right.'

'That means the best is yet to come!'

Pyotr thanked the old man and went off in expectation of the best that was yet to come, thinking: 'I'll go to the fête, she'll give me a shirt. Eventually I'll ask her to buy me a watch. And if she doesn't, she can go to the Devil!'

In the vestibule and the kitchen the well-polished lamps had begun to burn. The contents of the saucepans on the kitchen range had been added to and touched up, the storm had raged past and died away, and once again order and cleanliness reigned, as was proper. Now it was time for people to get their uniforms on and start working.

The cook turned on the tap and let the water splash into the sink until it formed a cold jet. She filled a tin ladle with this water and drank it all. She drank with avidity, like an overheated horse, her ears moving up and down with each gulp she took. While she was still washing herself, the housemaid also came into the kitchen, and she too silently took the ladle, filled it with water, and drank with avidity, her red ears quivering with every swallow.

Then she, too, washed herself in cold water over the same sink, drying her wet hands on her hair, as she had forgotten to bring a towel with her.

She was not in the mood for talking.

The cook understood this, threw her the clean end of her towel and, bowing to her in a feigned curtsey, said:

'I wish you a pleasant *bonjour*!'

The housemaid made a jocular face, and replied:

'And the same to you, on those affairs of *yours*!'

It appeared that they recognized as genuine 'affairs' only the affairs of nature, which multiplies life without worrying about its purpose or significance.

Notes

MUSK-OX

Chapter 1

1   *Yulian Simashko*: Yulian Ivanovich Simashko (1821–1893), the author of a number of works on zoology, including the book: *A Russian Fauna, Being a Description and Depiction of the Animals to be Found in Russia* (St Petersburg, 1856–1861).

2   *When Vasily Petrovich was out of boots,* etc.: these details are taken from Leskov's own reminiscences of the radical P. I. Yakushkin.

3   *the banks of the Tuskar or the Seym*: the Seym is a tributary of the River Desna.

4   *doobek*: Chelnovsky's jocular version of the word *chubuk* (= 'chibouk').

5   *makhorka*: a kind of shag.

Chapter 2

1   *a party of young recruits*: it was the policy of the Russian government to forcibly induct young Jewish boys into the army; there they were given a Russian identity and were converted to Orthodoxy.

Chapter 3

1   *'dilettantism in science'*: the title of a work by Herzen which appeared in the journal *Fatherland Notes* during 1843.

2   *Stand alone before the storm,* etc.: a quotation from Pushkin's poem *Poltava*.

Chapter 4

1   *the hospices of the hermitages at P— and L—* : the reference is
    to the 'hermitages' of Ploshchansk and Livny, towns in the prov-
    ince of Oryol.

2   *the River Orlik*: the Orlik is a tributary of the River Oka.

Chapter 5

1   *when 'all the impressions of existence were still new to me'*: a
    quotation from Pushkin's poem *Demon*.

2   *like a painting by Teniers*: David Teniers the Younger, a Flemish
    painter (1610–1694), famed for his depictions of rural life.

Chapter 8

1   *'szlachecki', and not 'pański'*: szlachecki is Polish for 'aristo-
    cratic', *pański*, in the same language, means 'landowning'.

Chapter 9

1   *odnodvortsy*: peasants from the lowest military ranks in ancient
    Russia.

2   *zhiristy*: A corruption of 'Girondistes'. *Zhir* in Russian means
    'fat, grease'. 'Fat-ists'.

3   *'off to a shady nook'*: words spoken by Khlestakov in Gogol's
    The Inspector-General (Act 4, scene 13).

LADY MACBETH OF MTSENSK

Chapter 2

1   *eight puds*: a *pud* was equivalent to 36 lbs (16.38 kg).

Chapter 9

1   *Livny*: see Musk-Ox, chapter 4, note 1 above.

Chapter 10

1   *to have a particle taken out for him*: in the worship of the East-
    ern Orthodox Church, a particle is 'a portion taken from an
    oblation, but not consecrated, in commemoration of particular
    persons or classes of people, living or departed'. *The Orthodox
    Liturgy* (SPCK, 1982), p. 109.

Chapter 15

1   *At the window in the shadow,* etc.: a Russian romance; the
     words are by Ya. P. Polonsky (his poem *The Call*).

THE SEALED ANGEL

In the original Russian this story contains a great many ecclesiastical and specialist terms relating to the art of icon-painting. Some
of these are not directly transferable into English, since there exist
no equivalents for them in that language, and the translator has
in such cases had to provide an approximate rendering which at
least gives the sense. The notes which follow attempt to elucidate
as many of the more obscure references as possible.

Chapter 1

1   *on the eve of the Feast of St Basil*: i.e. on 31 December; the Feast
     of St Basil falls on 1 January.
2   *cross himself broadly with two fingers*: i.e. in the style favoured
     by Old Believers.

Chapter 2

1   *by the earliest Novgorod or Stroganov isographers*: The Novgorod
     school of icon-painting ('isography') dates from the fourteenth to
     the sixteenth centuries; the Stroganov school derived from the
     Novgorod school after a number of Novgorod icon-painters
     (among them the Stroganovs, who were rich merchants) moved
     from there to Solvychevodsk and Veliky Ustyug. The icon which
     Leskov's Master Sevastyan paints is executed in the 'fine style' of
     the Stroganov school.
2   *Deises:* a *Deisis* (Gr. δέησις) is a three-figured icon depicting, in
     the centre, Christ, with the Virgin Mary and John the Baptist at
     either side.
3   *an image of the Saviour with wet hair*: on certain icons the hair
     and beard of Christ were painted straight, without curls, 'look-
     ing as though they had been wetted (an expression of Russian
     connoisseurs)'. I. P. Sakharov, *Studies in Russian Icon-Painting,*
     Part 2 (St Petersburg, 1849), p. 32.
4   *the 'Indict'*: with this icon began the enumeration of the icono-
     graphic subjects in the 'Iconographic Annals' – a handwritten

guide for 'isographers', which contained directions as to themes, composition, and which saints were to be depicted: the saints were ordered according to the Church calendar, which began on 1 September.

5   *the 'Saints'*: a multi-figured icon with a depiction of the saints according to the days of the month.

6   *the 'Heavenly Host'*: the Russian name is 'Sobor'. Icons with this name depict the archangels Michael or Gabriel holding a round icon of the boy Emmanuel (Christ), surrounded by a host of angels.

7   *the 'God the Father'*: an icon which depicts God the Father with the Christ-child in His arms, holding a dove.

8   *the 'Week'*: an icon divided into six parts according to the days of the week.

9   *the 'Benefice'*: an extremely rare type of icon, which appeared at the end of the eighteenth century. It depicted saints, with indications as to which illness each could cure.

10   *the 'Septenary'*: an icon depicting the seven gifts of the Holy Ghost.

11   *Palikhov*: more commonly known as Palekh, a village in the Ivanovsk region of Russia. Palekh was, from the sixteenth century onwards, a centre of icon-painting; it made its most important contribution during the eighteenth century.

12   *executed on the Greek model by the old Muscovite masters of the Tsar*: the reference is to the icon-painters who worked on state commissions in Moscow during the seventeenth century.

13   *depicting Our Lady,* etc.: Icons of this type date exclusively from the eighteenth century.

14   *thongs*: the Russian term is *torotsy* (more correctly, *toroki*), derived from the Mongolian word for a saddle-tie – 'Angels have thongs above their ears; these are the abode of the Holy Spirit, which exercises its influence upon them.' F. Buslayev, *A Historical Outline of Russian Folk Literature and Art*, (St Petersburg), vol. II, p. 297.

15   *proper*: i.e. not canvas (or *demicoton*) like the lining.

Chapter 3

1   *a large stone bridge*: the first chain suspension bridge across the Dnieper, constructed at Kiev during the years 1849–1853.

2   *the Byzantine 'hook' method*: prior to the early eighteenth century the Russian Orthodox Church used its own special system of musical notation, consisting of a series of 'hooks' placed above

the texts of the prayers and liturgies. The system has still not been adequately deciphered.

3   *an ant-lion*: a mythical creature. According to the Old Russian symposium *Fiziolog*, 'its front part is that of a lion, while its rear part is that of an ant'.

Chapter 4

1   *each one the thickness of a grown man's arm*: the bolts were, in fact, 12.5 centimetres in diameter.

Chapter 9

1   *the bishop . . . himself was said to have disapproved of such barbarity*: the 'bishop' is evidently Filaret Amfiteatrov (1779–1857), the Metropolitan of Kiev and Galicia.

2   *the Euchologion of Metropolitan Peter*: the reference is to the liturgical guide published in 1646 by Pyotr Mogila (1596–1647), the Metropolitan of Kiev.

3   *Mstyora*: a settlement in the Ivanovsk region of Russia, which developed into a centre of icon-painting during the eighteenth and nineteenth centuries.

4   *Ushakov*: Simon (Pimen) Fyodorovich Ushakov (1626–1686), a Russian painter and art theoretician, one of the most important artists of the second half of the seventeenth century. He introduced a marked element of realistic portrayal into his work.

5   *Rublyov*: Andrei Rublyov (c. 1360–1430), a great Russian painter who created the Moscow school of icon-painting. Rublyov was extremely popular in Muscovite Russia, but later his work fell into neglect, and was only rediscovered in the twentieth century.

6   *Paramshin*: Paramsha, or Paramshin. All that is known about him is that in 1356 he made an 'icon and cross, forged in gold'.

7   *a folding tripartite icon,* etc.: in fact, the icon was painted no earlier than the second half of the seventeenth century. It is known as the Caponi Icon, or Caponi Screen, after the Italian archaeologist and bibliographer A.-C. Caponi (1683–1746), who bought it from one of the relatives of Gerasim Fok, confessor to Peter the Great, who had made him a gift of it.

8   *they've even gone so far as to depict Christ the Saviour as a Jew*: Leskov may have in mind the painting by the Russian artist A. Ivanov 'The Appearance of Christ to the People' (1832–1856), but it is more probable that he is thinking of the arguments

that surrounded Kramskoy's painting 'Christ in the Wilderness' (1872).

9   *the way the starry heavens are painted in Novgorod*: 'the icon named "Sofia, the Wisdom of God" in the Church of St Sofia at Novgorod shows the sky depicted as a long, dark-blue cloth, scattered with stars and supported by angels'. D. A. Rovinsky, *A History of the Russian Schools of Icon-Painting Up To The End of the Seventeenth Century* (St Petersburg, 1856), p. 62.

Chapter 10

1   *reft'*: a medium produced by mixing blue and black paints.
2   *white oil*: this was used for dissolving gold.
3   *the lamentation of Joseph*: a Russian liturgical song.
4   *The Gates of Aristotle*: the title of a symposium, no copies of which are now extant, which circulated in Russia until the eighteenth century. It was banned as heretical in 1551.

Chapter 12

1   *Solomia*: the midwife who, according to apocryphal legend, is supposed to have been present at the birth of Christ.
2   *'For whosoever shall be considered worthy'*, etc.: this is a near-quotation from the text of the patriarchal law included in Buslayev's article *General Principles of Icon-Painting* (Moscow, 1868).

Chapter 14

1   *'Sing a catabasis!'*: a catabasis is the last part of each of the ten songs of the Orthodox canon (a series of hymns, based on the nine Scriptural canticles, sung at Lauds), which in monasteries are supposed to be sung in the centre of the church by the choirs which move there from both sides.

PAMPHALON THE ENTERTAINER

Chapter 4

1   *the remote town of Edessa*: the capital of one of the Roman provinces in Northern Mesopotamia, where there were three hundred monasteries, and where in the fourth century A.D. lived one of the Fathers of the Christian Church, Ephraim of Syria.

Chapter 13

1   *leviton*: a tunic worn by peasants in the early Christian era.

A WINTER'S DAY

1   *V. Dahl*: V. I. Dahl (1801–1872), the distinguished Russian lin-
     guist and writer. He compiled the famous *Tolkovy slovar' zhivogo
     velikorusskogo yazyka* (Defining Dictionary of the Living Great
     Russian Language), which at times almost reads like a source-
     book for Leskov's own Russian, containing as it does myriad
     colloquial popular Russian sayings and turns of speech.

Chapter 1

1   *Cousin Olympia*: according to Leskov's son Andrei, 'Cousin
     Olympia' is a portrait of 'a certain Olga Novikova'. O. A. Novikova
     was a writer, the widow of General-Lieutenant I. P. Novikov, a
     former trustee of the Kiev, and subsequently the St Petersburg
     educational authorities. Novikova began her literary career in the
     second half of the 1870s. She took up residence in London and
     published a number of works on Anglo-Russian relations.

2   *cutting up some dead body or other*: in the original Russian this
     comes over as an inexact quotation from a heroic poem by A. K.
     Tolstoy.

3   *Bertenson*: L. B. Bertenson (1850–1929), a St Petersburg balne-
     ologist, hygienist and public figure.

4   *'The Devil's never as bad as his urchins'*: this is a distortion of an
     old Russian saying, *'ne tak strashen chort, kak ego malyuyut'*
     ('the Devil's seldom as black as he's painted'); what the lady of
     the house says is: *'ne tak strashen chort, kak ego malyutki'* (*maly-
     utki*: little ones, offspring, 'urchins'). The effect is obviously
     impossible to translate.

5   *all that stuff about swaddling clothes with baby stains*: the refer-
     ence is to *War and Peace*, vol. 4, Epilogue, part II.

6   *the way he describes our Alexander I*: see *War and Peace*, vol. 2,
     Part II, Chapter XX.

7   *the Skoptsy*: a sect of Russian religious dissenters who practised
     voluntary castration.

8   *freedom for the free and may the Lord save the rest of us*: another
     distortion of a Russian saying: 'freedom for the free, and Para-
     dise for the saved.'

9   *that hussar who claimed to be related to Count Tolstoy*: accord-
    ing to Andrei Leskov, this incident is based on a story his father
    heard during the three or four days he spent as a guest in the
    Tolstoy household.

Chapter 2

1   *'The Cross and Banners'*: the reference is to the painting by I. E.
    Repin (1844–1930) which bears the title 'Cross and Banners in
    the Province of Kursk'.

2   *Sokolov*: P. P. Sokolov (1821–1899), a Russian watercolourist
    who painted subjects from the life of the common people and the
    military. He was awarded the St George Cross in the Russo–
    Turkish war of 1877–1888.

3   *and neither Zasetskaya nor Peiker, etc.*: Yu. D. Zasetskaya, M.
    G. Peiker, V. A. Pashkov, M. Korf and A. P. Bobrinsky were all
    members of a religious sect called the 'Pashkovites' (*pashkovtsy*),
    who were followers of the English Protestant missionary Lord
    Radstock, who from 1874 onwards visited St Petersburg each
    winter to conduct prayer meetings among the Russian aristoc-
    racy. Leskov wrote a book about Radstock, entitled *The Society
    Schism* (*Velikosvetsky raskol*), which was published in 1887. In
    1944 the Pashkovites, who had renamed themselves 'Evangelical
    Christians', merged with the Baptists, forming the third largest
    religious grouping in the Soviet Union after the Russian Ortho-
    dox and the Old Believers.

4   *Annenkov*: General I. V. Annenkov (1814–1887), who from
    1862 until 1867 was the chief of the St Petersburg police, and
    subsequently became Commandant of the city.

5   *Berton*: the reference is probably to the French actor Charles-
    François Berton (1820–1874), who acted on the St Petersburg
    stage.

6   *'Intermediary'*: the reference is to the Tolstoyan publishing house
    and journal *Posrednik*, founded in 1884.

7   *Skaryatin*: N. Ya. Skaryatin was governor of Kazan from 1867
    until 1880.

8   *the Shah of Persia*: Shah Nasreddin (1831–1896), who visited
    Russia in 1889.

Chapter 3

1   *that auspicious nineteenth of February*: 19 February 1861, the
    date of Alexander II's proclamation announcing the emancipa-
    tion of Russia's serfs.

Chapter 4

1　*Evropeus and Unkovsky*: A. I. Evropeus (1826–1885) was a member of the Petrashevists, and was sentenced to death along with F. M. Dostoevsky, but saved by amnesty. A. M. Unkovsky (1828–1892) was a marshal of the nobility in the Province of Tver, where he took part in the preparations for peasant reform, but fell foul of the law for his leading role in the Tver opposition movement, and was exiled to Vyatka in 1859.

2　*Shevchenko*: Taras Shevchenko (1814–1861), the Ukrainian national poet.

3　*'What's all very well for London won't do for Moscow'*: a distorted quotation from Pushkin's *An Epistle to the Censor*: 'What London needs, for Moscow is too soon.'

4　*Katkov*: M. N. Katkov (see introduction), who died in 1887.

5　*like Diana's*: the reference is to one of I. S. Turgenev's prose poems, *The Nymphs*.

Chapter 5

1　*Jonah the cynic*: a character from A. F. Pisemsky's novel *Troubled Seas* (1863).

2　*'There's no sin in laughing at what's funny'*: a distorted quotation from N. M. Karmazin's poem *An Epistle to Aleksandr Alekseyevich Pleschcheyev*.

3　*Buckle*: Henry Thomas Buckle (1821–1862), an English empirical historian, the author of *A History of Civilization in England* (1857–1861), which was extremely popular among young Russian radicals of the 1860s.

4　*'The rustle of spring'*, etc.: a paraphrase of a line from N. A. Nekrasov's poem *The Rustle of Spring* (*Zelyony shum*).

Chapter 6

1　*'Monsieur Alphonse'*: a reference to A. Dumas's play – here 'pimpishness'.

2　*Kronstadt*: a reference to John of Kronstadt, bishop of the Andreyevsky Sobor. Leskov wrote about him in his tale *Midnight Folk*.

3　*Viborg krendels*: rolls made in the form of the letter 'B'.

4　*Maikov*: The Russian romantic poet A. N. Maikov, from whose poem *Three Deaths* (*Tri smerti*) the lines that follow are quoted.

5   *Madame Adam*: Juliette Lambert Adam (1836–1936), a French
     woman political writer who worked for an alliance between
     France and Russia.

Chapter 7

1   père *Jean and* père *Onthon*: '*père* Jean' is John of Kronstadt.
     '*père* Onthon' is probably Father Antony (A. V. Vadkovsky,
     1846–1912), a Church leader and religious writer, who in 1887
     was nominated rector of the St Petersburg Spiritual Academy,
     and in 1892 became Archbishop of Finland.

Chapter 8

1   *chulan*: a storeroom in a peasant's house.
2   '*Gehazi*': see II Kings 4.
3   *The Source of Enlightenment*: *Klyuch razumeniya*, a collection
     of sermons by Ioaniky Galyatovsky (d. 1688), which was pub-
     lished between 1633 and 1659.
4   *Ge*: N. N. Ge (1831–1894), a noted Russian painter of religious
     subjects who was a friend of Leskov and Tolstoy.

Chapter 9

1   *Peski*: a village in the Province of Moscow.

Chapter 12

1   *Yelizavet Sparrow*: Yelizavet Vorobey, the dead serf woman
     whose name Sobakevich changed to a masculine form and whom
     he sold to Chichikov along with the male serfs (Gogol's *Dead
     Souls*, Chapter 8).
2   *Meshchersky*: Prince V. P. Meshchersky (1839–1914), editor of
     the journal *The Citizen*.

Chapter 13

1   *il ne met plus de manchettes*: a reference to Valery's pederasty.
2   *Oxenstjerna*: a reference to Baron Axel Oxenstjerna (1583–1654),
     the great Swedish diplomat and chancellor. Oxenstjerna's maxim
     actually reads: 'With how little wisdom the world is governed.'

Chapter 15

1   *Kamchatka*: a region in Eastern Siberia to which persons considered
     dangerous criminals were exiled by the Russian government. The
     maid is alluding to the fact that the female guest probably has links
     with the secret police.

PENGUIN CLASSICS

THE HOUSE OF THE DEAD
FYODOR DOSTOYEVSKY

'Here was the house of the living dead, a life like none other upon earth'

In January 1850 Dostoyevsky was sent to a remote Siberian prison camp for his part in a political conspiracy. The four years he spent there, startlingly re-created in *The House of the Dead*, were the most agonizing of his life. In this fictionalized account he recounts his soul-destroying incarceration through the cool, detached tones of his narrator, Aleksandr Petrovich Goryanchikov: the daily battle for survival, the wooden plank beds, the cabbage soup swimming with cockroaches, his strange 'family' of boastful, ugly, cruel convicts. Yet *The House of the Dead* is far more than a work of documentary realism: it is also a powerful novel of redemption, describing one man's spiritual and moral death and the miracle of his gradual reawakening.

This edition includes an introduction and notes by David McDuff discussing the circumstances of Dostoyevsky's imprisonment, the origins of the novel in his prison writings and the character of Aleksandr Petrovich.

Translated with an introduction and notes by David McDuff

PENGUIN CLASSICS

THE IDIOT   FYODOR DOSTOYEVSKY

'He's simple-minded, but he has all his wits about him, in the most noble sense of the word, of course'

Returning to St Petersburg from a Swiss sanatorium, the gentle and naive Prince Myshkin – known as 'the idiot' – pays a visit to his distant relative General Yepanchin and proceeds to charm the General, his wife and his three daughters. But his life is thrown into turmoil when he chances on a photograph of the beautiful Nastasya Filippovna. Utterly infatuated with her, he soon finds himself caught up in a love triangle and drawn into a web of blackmail, betrayal and, finally, murder. In Prince Myshkin, Dosteyevsky set out to portray the purity of 'a truly beautiful soul' and to explore the perils that innocence and goodness face in a corrupt world.

David McDuff's major new translation brilliantly captures the novel's idiosyncratic and dream-like language and the nervous, elliptic flow of the narrative. This edition also includes an introduction by William Mills Todd III, further reading, a chronology of Dostoyevsky's life and work, a note on the translation and explanatory notes.

Translated by David McDuff with an introduction by William Mills Todd III

PENGUIN CLASSICS

NOTES FROM UNDERGROUND *AND* THE DOUBLE
FYODOR DOSTOYEVSKY

'It is best to do nothing! The best thing is conscious inertia! So long live the underground!'

Alienated from society and paralysed by a sense of his own insignificance, the anonymous narrator of Dostoyevsky's groundbreaking *Notes from Underground* tells the story of his tortured life. With bitter sarcasm, he describes his refusal to become a worker in the 'ant-hill' of society and his gradual withdrawal to an existence 'underground'. The seemingly ordinary world of St Petersburg takes on a nightmarish quality in *The Double* when a government clerk encounters a man who exactly resembles him – his double perhaps, or possibly the darker side of his own personality. Like *Notes from Underground*, this is a masterly study of human consciousness.

Jessie Coulson's introduction discusses the stories' critical reception and the themes they share with Dostoyevksy's great novels.

'*Notes from Underground*, with its mood of intellectual irony and alienation, can be seen as the first modern novel ... That sense of the meaningless of existence that runs through much of twentieth-century writing – from Conrad and Kafka, to Beckett and beyond – starts in Dostoyevsky's work' Malcolm Bradbury

Translated with an introduction by Jessie Coulson

PENGUIN CLASSICS

DEAD SOULS   NIKOLAI GOGOL

'It's not a question of the living. I've nothing to do with them. I'm asking for the dead'

Chichikov, a mysterious stranger, arrives in the provincial town of 'N', visiting a succession of landowners and making each a strange offer. He proposes to buy the names of dead serfs still registered on the census, saving their owners from paying tax on them, and to use these 'souls' as collateral to re-invent himself as a gentleman. In this ebullient masterpiece, Gogol created a grotesque gallery of human types, from the bear-like Sobakevich to the insubstantial fool Manilov, and, above all, the devilish conman Chichikov. *Dead Souls*, Russia's first major novel, is one of the most unusual works of nineteenth-century fiction and a devastating satire on social hypocrisy.

David Magarshack's introduction discusses Gogol's plan for a novel in three parts, tracing Chichikov's progress from sin to redemption, and tells how Gogol destroyed part of the manuscript in the grip of madness. The surviving sections, volume one and a fragment of volume two, are translated here.

'Gogol was a strange creature, but then genius is always strange'
Vladimir Nabokov

Translated with an introduction by David Magarshack

PENGUIN CLASSICS

A HERO OF OUR TIME   MIKHAIL LERMONTOV

'I'm still in love with her ... I'd give my life for her. But she bores me'

Proud, wilful and intensely charismatic, Pechorin is bored by the stifling world that envelops him. With a predatory energy for any activity that will relieve his ennui, he embarks on a series of adventures – encountering smugglers, brigands, soldiers, lovers and rivals – and leaves a trail of broken hearts behind him. With its cynical, immoral hero, Lermontov's novel outraged many critics when it was published in 1840. Yet it was also a literary landmark: an acutely observed psychological novel, narrated from a number of different perspectives, through which the true and complex nature of Pechorin slowly emerges.

Paul Foote's fine translation is accompanied by an introduction discussing the figure of Pechorin within the literary tradition of 'superfluous men' and the novel's influence on Tolstoy, Dostoyevsky and Chekhov. The edition also includes a chronology, explanatory notes and a historical note on the Caucasus.

'Vigorous and audacious ... it retains its power as a psychological study'
Julian Barnes

Translated with an introduction by Paul Foote

PENGUIN CLASSICS

THE DEATH OF IVAN ILYICH AND OTHER STORIES
LEO TOLSTOY

'Every moment he felt that ... he was drawing nearer and nearer to what terrified him'

Three of Tolstoy's most powerful and moving shorter works are brought together in this volume. *The Death of Ivan Ilyich* is a masterly meditation on life and death, recounting the physical decline and spiritual awakening of a worldly, successful man who is faced with his own mortality. Only in his last agonizing moments does Ivan Ilyich finally confront his true nature, and gain the forgiveness of his wife and son for his cruelty towards them. *Happy Ever After*, inspired by one of Tolstoy's own romantic entanglements, tells the story of a seventeen-year-old girl who marries her guardian twice her age. And *The Cossacks*, the tale of a disenchanted young nobleman who seeks fulfilment amid the wild beauty of the Caucasus, was hailed by Turgenev as the 'finest and most perfect production of Russian literature'.

Rosemary Edmonds's classic translation fully captures the subtle nuances of Tolstoy's writing, and includes an introduction discussing the stories' influences and contemporary reactions towards them.

Translated with an introduction by Rosemary Edmonds

PENGUIN CLASSICS

THE KREUTZER SONATA AND OTHER STORIES
LEO TOLSTOY

'We were like two prisoners in the stocks, hating one another yet fettered to one another by the same chain'

'The Kreutzer Sonata' is the self-lacerating confession of a man consumed by sexual jealousy and eaten up by shame and eventually driven to murder his wife. The story caused a sensation when it first appeared and Tolstoy's wife was appalled that he had drawn on their own experiences together to create a scathing indictment of marriage. 'The Devil', centring on a young man torn between his passion for a peasant girl and his respectable life with his loving wife, also illustrates the impossibility of pure love. 'The Forged Coupon' shows how an act of corruption can spiral out of control, and 'After the Ball' examines the abuse of power. Written during a time of spiritual crisis in Tolstoy's life, these late stories reflect a world of moral uncertainties.

This lucid translation is accompanied by an introduction in which David McDuff examines Tolstoy's state of mind as he produced these last great works, and discusses their public reception. This edition also contains notes and appendices.

Translated with an introduction by David McDuff

PENGUIN CLASSICS

RESURRECTION LEO TOLSTOY

'In the very depths of his heart, he knew that he had behaved so meanly, so contemptibly, so cruelly'

Serving on a jury at the trial of a prostitute arrested for murder, Prince Nekhlyudov is horrified to discover that the accused is a woman he had once loved, seduced and then abandoned when she was a young servant girl. Racked with guilt at realizing he was the cause of her ruin, he determines to appeal for her release or give up his own way of life and follow her. Conceived on an epic scale, *Resurrection* portrays a vast panorama of Russian life, taking us from the underworld of prison cells and warders to the palaces of countesses. It is also an angry denunciation of government, the upper classes, the judicial system and the Church, and a highly personal statement of Tolstoy's belief in human redemption.

Rosemary Edmonds's fine translation is accompanied by an introduction discussing how *Resurrection* relates to Tolstoy's own spiritual development and how the scope and depth of the book are even more ambitious than his other works.

Translated with an introduction by Rosemary Edmonds